'If poetry was the supreme literary form of the First World War then, as if in riposte, in the Second World War, the English novel came of age. This wonderful series is an exemplary reminder of that fact. Great novels were written about the Second World War and we should not forget them.'

WILLIAM BOYD

'It's wonderful to see these four books given a new lease of life because all of them are classic novels from the Second World War written by those who were there, experienced the fear, anguish, pain and excitement first-hand and whose writings really do shine an incredibly vivid light onto what it was like to live and fight through that terrible conflict.'

JAMES HOLLAND, Historian, author and TV presenter

'The Imperial War Museum has performed a valuable public service by reissuing these four absolutely superb novels covering four very different aspects of the Second World War. I defy you to choose which is best: I keep changing my mind!'

ANDREW ROBERTS, author of *Churchill: Walking with Destiny*

'With a dead body on the first page and a debonair RAF pilot as the sleuth, this stylish whodunit takes you straight back to Blitzed London and murder most foul. Several plausible suspects, a femme fatale, witty dialogue, memorable scenes and unexpected twists – it boasts everything a great whodunit should have, and more.'

ANDREW ROBERTS, author of *Churchill: Walking with Destiny*

PLENTY UNDER THE COUNTER

Kathleen Hewitt

IMPERIAL WAR MUSEUMS

First published in Great Britain
by Jarrolds Publishers Ltd 1943.

First published in this format in 2019 by
IWM, Lambeth Road, London SE1 6HZ
iwm.org.uk

Text © The Estate of Kathleen Hewitt, 2019

About the Author and Introduction
© The Trustees of the Imperial War Museum, 2019

ISBN 978-1-912423-09-5

A catalogue record for this book is available from the
British Library.

Printed and bound by CPI Group (UK) Ltd, Croydon CR0 4YY

Every effort has been made to contact all copyright holders.
The publishers will be glad to make good in future editions
any error or omissions brought to their attention.

Cover illustration by Bill Bragg
Design and art direction by Clare Skeats

FSC
www.fsc.org
MIX
Paper from
responsible sources
FSC® C020471

About the Author

Kathleen Hewitt (1893–1980)

The daughter of a country parson, KATHLEEN HEWITT left home at 18 with only £1 and 5 pennies to her name. Having attended drawing classes in her youth she was determined to win an independent livelihood as an artist. She rented a room, the first of many, in Earls Court and her 1945 autobiography *The Only Paradise* relates how she struggled to earn a living with her fashion drawings and became in turn an artist's model, film extra and chorus girl. Following the break-up of her marriage to marine artist Neville Pitcher, Hewitt took the bold step of sailing to South Africa where she lived on a farm for several years. She returned to England and opened a hat shop in Reading.

During these years she was constantly writing, but it was not until 1932 at the age of 39 that her first novel was published. Twenty-two more books followed which included best-selling thrillers and murder mysteries.

In the Second World War Hewitt lived in a flat in Marylebone next to the Mason's Arms pub. She belonged to the The Olde Ham Bone, a bohemian club in Soho (later destroyed by a bomb), as well as frequenting the Ivy, The Cafe Royal and the Pen Club. She enjoyed friendships with many literary and artistic figures of the day, including Olga Lehman, Nina Hamnett and the poet Roy Campbell. The title of her 1943 whodunit *Plenty Under the Counter* refers to the illicit wartime black market; its milieu is London bedsitter-land, which together with its denizens was well known to the author.

Introduction

War novels are often associated with the First World War, with an explosion of the genre in the late 1920s. Erich Maria Remarque's *All Quiet on the Western Front* was a bestseller and was made into a Hollywood film in 1930. In the same year, Siegfried Sassoon's *Memoirs of an Infantry Officer* sold 24,000 copies. Generations of school children have grown up on a diet of the poetry of Wilfred Owen and novels of Sassoon. Yet the novels of the Second World War are often forgotten, and the aim of this series is to bring some classic war novels of that later war back into print. Moreover, many of the novels of the Second World War which *are* celebrated were written by men, who had served on the front line and drew directly from this experience in their writing. In the case of *Plenty Under the Counter* (though the protagonist is still male), the female author and the novel's focus on life on the home front make this a particularly interesting candidate.

The most celebrated manifestation of the British home front (and indeed the home front which children still learn about today), was the eight months of 1940-41, during which Britain was bombed relentlessly from the air and the war was brought to the very homes of civilian men, women and children, who paid the price in their thousands. For a while, this 'Blitz' *was* the front line as British soldiers, sailors and airmen were dying in far fewer numbers than civilians were at home.

Throughout the summer of 1940, the German Luftwaffe attacked shipping in the English Channel and mounted an all-out assault on the RAF's fighter bases in the great and sustained aerial conflict known as the Battle of Britain. Almost daily between July and September 1940 fleets of Luftwaffe bombers, protected by fighter planes, took off from airstrips in Occupied Europe in search of targets. In response, the Royal Air Force's thinly stretched squadrons of Fighter Command did everything they could to stop the bombers getting through. In the first few pages of *Plenty Under the Counter*, we learn that the protagonist Flight Lieutenant David Heron is back in London on convalescent leave, having bailed out of an aircraft (presumably during the Battle of Britain), to be found on a dinghy in the English Channel. He has taken four months to recover from his ordeal, and has also been awarded the Distinguished Flying Cross. David is suitably modest (he is the novel's hero, after all), commenting that it was 'sheer fluke', but 'then he felt embarrassed, for the phrase sounded like mock-modesty, though the exploit that had earned his decoration had, in sober truth, been the result of a series of chances in which he himself had had the opportunity of being somewhat original'.

***

Partly in retaliation to the Allied bombing of Berlin in August, Luftwaffe bombers attacked London. This city was not only the capital of a country, but of an Empire and Commonwealth. It came to stand as a defiant symbol of resistance against Hitler's conquest of most of Europe. On 7 September 1940, around 1,000 German aircraft targeted England and London in particular. Reichsmarschall Herman Goering, head of the Luftwaffe, was exultant at the result, proclaiming to the German nation that it represented an 'historic' moment. He had good reason – only a small percentage of his armada of aircraft, around 40, had been shot down. Though RAF losses were under 30, they were relatively more damaging. Parts of the East End were ravaged, and more than 4,000 Londoners were dead, with four times that number injured. This signalled the start of the Blitz. For the next eight months, London, as well as other British towns and cities, was continually bombed. The dropping of nearly 19,000 tons of bombs on London alone during the Blitz aptly reflects the incessant nature and magnitude of this bombardment.

In this new battle, civilians were to be the front line. And every major raid would leave its trail of ruin and misery. There were the dead to be buried, the injured to be cared for and the trapped to be dug out. People who had lost their homes had to be fed, clothed and rehoused. Water, gas and electricity breakdowns had to be repaired, the streets cleared of unexploded bombs, and road, rail and telephone communications maintained; this all had a huge impact, and for Londoners, sleep became a precious commodity, and lack of it caused nerves to fray. However the resilience of Londoners also became apparent. Mrs Hilda Neal, who lived in Kennington, South London, and ran a typist agency on the Strand, wrote in her diary (held in IWM archives) in September 1940:

> Burton Street, Bond Street and Park Lane all bombed yesterday; much damage to the two former, but people are carrying on as usual. Milkman delivers slowly, pushing his trycicle during raid; the paper comes and so on and so forth. Wonderful stoicism.
>
> Three women Legion officers have been killed in East End; Mrs Noel and Misses Cooper; yesterday while running a mobile canteen. Several fireman too; and two were blown over a building on an escape ladder, which was broken in half. One is just stunned to read of these happenings which often are beyond belief. Such heroism everywhere in all classes.

The Blitz continued for 72 nights (excluding two nights of bad weather in November). Overall there were 354 attacks on London, with a corresponding casualty count of almost 20,000 civilians. But morale had not been destroyed – Londoners learned how to adapt and endure.

It is against this backdrop that novelist Kathleen Hewitt set *Plenty Under the Counter*. The main location is a London boarding house: a living arrangement where a landlady, in this case Mrs Meake (known as Meakie) or landlord rented out rooms, often in their own house, to lodgers. These houses were common during the period and will be familiar to readers of other wartime novels such as Patrick Hamilton's *The Slaves of Solitude*, and *London Belongs to Me* by Norman Collins. Heron's girlfriend, Tess Carmichael, is a nurse working with children at St Margaret's Day Nursery which, because of the evacuation of children from London, serves as a transit depot for those children who had not been evacuated, and also as a temporary refuge due to families being bombed out of their homes. Indeed childcare increased dramatically during the war as mothers were expected to contribute to the war effort. In the opening chapters of the novel, David jokes to Inspector Gracewell that Tess has 'eight babies, and adores them all'.

Yet if the Blitz in some ways brought out the best in thousands of Londoners, it also had an under-appreciated dark undertone, and it is this which drives the plot in Hewitt's novel – it is ultimately a detective story, featuring murder, a 'Fancy Goods Emporium', gangsters and more. For a minority of Londoners, wartime, the black out and the Blitz presented opportunities to continue, or even begin, a life of crime. For many more people, the advent of so many new rules and regulations governing everyday life made it so much more tempting to cheat the system, and claw back some sense of pre-war normality. Looting during the Blitz was a major problem. By the end of 1940, more than 4,500 cases of looting had occurred in London. Mrs Mary May, who lived in Sandgate Street, Camberwell, was just one of the unfortunate victims of looters. After having to evacuate her bombed-out home in 1940, she stayed with friends; on returning to her house, however, she found it had been robbed by her neighbour, who had gone off with her piano, armchairs and sewing machine, among other items. Accounts of similar experiences proliferate.

A pervasive entity in a time of shortages and rations was the black market – if you knew who to ask and could afford the prices charged. Most of London's black market was centred in Soho, where servicemen on leave and deserters congregated. The soldiers, and particularly the US troops when they arrived, had plenty to sell, including cigarettes, surplus rations and nylon stockings. Deserters had services in kind to offer, such as selling on these desirable goods. The biggest trade was in selling and buying coupons for petrol or clothing, but pretty much anything was available on the black market for a price, from fur coats to underwear.

This is the world in which Thelma Meake becomes embroiled, and the world which David Heron must attempt to navigate in order to solve the mystery. Notable are the scenes in the Fancy Goods Emporium (which sells black market goods) – and the novel makes it clear that it is not only 'gangsters' who shop there – Tess confesses to David, 'One day, when the smokes famine was at its height, I got a tin of a hundred cigarettes there, and then I had to put ten shillings in a Red Cross box, to try to make myself feel better again'. Shopkeepers did indeed sometimes keep special supplies 'Under the Counter' as in the book's title, and there are numerous accounts of this in the letters and diaries of the time. Vere Hodgson, who kept a diary throughout the war (also in the IWM archives) – later published as *Few Eggs and No Oranges* – relished her own 'Under the Counter' experience on 22 February 1941: 'had some luck over cheese. Went for my bacon ration and while he was cutting it had a word with the man about the Cubic Inch of Cheese. He got rid of the other customers and then whispered, "Wait a mo". I found half a pound of cheese being thrust into my bag with great secrecy and speed!'

More sinister is the threat of violence to David on one of his later trips to the shop, and his commandeering of a stolen army truck, not to mention the physical assault he is subjected to as he edges closer to the truth. Indeed, major gang crimes were often helped by wartime conditions. Billy Hill and his gang were suspected of a number of West End smash-and-grab raids on jewellers in the first year of the war, both during the day and in the blackout. He was eventually caught but after two years in gaol, he turned to black market racketeering, dealing in anything from army bedding to whiskey; it was a less dangerous occupation than smash-and-grab raids, and it proved rather more profitable.

***

This murder mystery was written in 1943 by the prolific Kathleen Hewitt, against the backdrop of the Blitz and wartime London, once the bombing had almost ceased. During the war years Hewitt lived in a flat in Marylebone next to the Mason's Arms pub. She belonged to the The Olde Ham Bone, a bohemian club in Soho (later destroyed by a bomb) and for a time served on its committee, as well as frequenting the Ivy, The Cafe Royal and the Pen Club. The novel's milieu is West London bedsitter-land, which together with its denizens was well known to the author (prior to the war she had also rented a room in Earl's Court, a location which was immortalised in another London classic, Patrick Hamilton's *Hangover Square*). *Plenty Under the Counter* challenges the stereotype of the 'Blitz spirit', showing the violence and the prevalence of the black market – indeed for much of what happens in the story, war is the essential catalyst. The book is also very evocative of everyday life in the city, and incorporates landmarks that are still familiar today. Even though it is light-hearted and slightly tongue-in-cheek in tone, this enjoyable novel underlines the irrefutable significance of home front London in the wider story of the Second World War.

Alan Jeffreys
2019

ONE

WHEN DAVID HERON WOKE in the dark he felt the high waves tossing his rubber dinghy. He was bobbing about like a cork in mid-channel. Then, as he twisted his head on a downy pillow, he realised that it was four months since the dinghy incident. He had been in hospital, he had met Tess Carmichael, and here he was snugly in bed at Mrs. Meake's. His Flight-Lieutenant's uniform was on a hanger hooked on to the outside of the wardrobe.

One week more and he'd be flying again.

In the meantime, where the devil was his morning cup of tea? The clock on the bedside table indicated that it was eight-thirty. There was an ornamental lamp beside the clock, and a telephone. Both were innovations. This room hadn't sported either of these amenities when he'd lodged with Mrs. Meake in the intervals between theatrical tours.

Good old Meakie! She would give you credit and would bolster up your vanity when you felt down-hearted. She would let you wander about in her kitchen and nibble at this and that during cooking processes. This was more of a home than an ordinary apartment house or hotel could ever be. Anyone, reflected David Heron, could have the Savoy and the Dorchester for all he cared. Yes, and the Ritz, the Berkeley, and Uncle Tom's Cabin and all. If he were a millionaire he'd still have to come back to 15 Terrapin Road, just for the friendly feeling of the house.

There was a tap at the door and Mrs. Meake herself came in with the tea-tray.

'Ever so sorry I'm late, ducks,' she said, 'but there's been a bit of bother.'

'Don't tell me we've got the brokers in.'

'Nothing so low class,' said Mrs. Meake.

'My respected father used to play rummy with ours, in the ancestral mansion. At least, the mansion that was ancestral till the moneylenders got really impatient.'

Mrs. Meake moved a volume of Shelley and a packet of cigarettes and set down the tray. 'They've found a body in the bit of garden at the back,' she said.

'A – did you say a body?'

'Yes.' Mrs. Meake spoke calmly. 'A dead one.'

'Good heavens, whose is it?'

'I don't know and I'm sure I don't care. There's police all over the place, getting in Annie's way and making the breakfasts late. I just left the Inspector with Miss Trindle in the hall floor front.' Mrs. Meake moved to the window and drew the curtain. Her short, plump figure became a silhouette. The morning sun struck across her henna'd and frizzed hair. She had been in musical comedy an unspecified number of years ago, and her make-up box had not been allowed to fall into disuse. She never appeared till rouge and mascara had been applied almost as lavishly as if she still had to face the footlights. She had bright blue eyes and a round amiable face – plump, double-chinned, but pleasant.

'They've put a bit of sacking over him.' Mrs. Meake turned and poured out a cup of tea as David bounded to the window, knotting the cord of his pyjama trousers on the way. His room was the first floor back, a perfect observation post for the scene below. In the small patch of ground there were three policemen and four men in plain clothes who stood talking in a group. Two of the men in uniform were near the wooden gate in the wall, the third stood guard over a sinister oblong of sacking. There was one wintry leafless tree in the garden, a broken glass forcing-frame accentuated the impression of neglect and decay.

David exclaimed: 'Is it murder – or suicide?'

'There was a knife in his back,' Mrs. Meake said, as casually as she would have commented upon a rasher of bacon.

'Gosh! – "Murder though it hath no tongue will speak, with most miraculous organ." *Hamlet*, act two, scene two.'

'I'll give you *Hamlet*.'

'I wish you could. I never got nearer than being a gravedigger. Now I view the spectacle my theatrical quotation seems extremely apt. Look, it's like a scene in a melodrama rehearsal, when someone's

2

forgotten his lines and everything's come to a standstill. We're in the front row of the dress circle.'

In his excitement David turned and drank his cup of tea without realising that he had omitted to sugar it. 'They'll be asking you questions,' he told Mrs. Meake.

'They've been asking them for the last forty minutes. A fat lot of good that's done them. The tall one in the soft hat is the pathologist.'

'What sort of a knife was it?'

'Knife?'

'The one you said was in his back.'

'How should I know? They just said a knife. A blessing for me I only had to take a quick look at his face.'

David stared inquiringly. Mrs. Meake added: 'They wanted to know if I'd recognised him. They asked me if I'd mind and of course I minded, no one wants to look at a dead face at eight o'clock in the morning, it's not what you'd choose for entertainment. But the Inspector kept on and on and in the end I obliged.'

'And you didn't know the man?'

'People I know don't get murdered.'

'A Jerry tried to murder me when I was in my jolly little dinghy praying for a lifeboat.'

'That was in the English Channel. This is London.'

'Proving what? That the Channel's safer? You ought to be in the Brains Trust with your genius for logic.'

'Go on, don't be aggravating, as if I haven't got enough, with the laundry list to make out – '

The door opened abruptly. Annie, the new maid, was indifferent to such formalities as knocking. 'Please'm,' she said, 'There's that Inspector, 'e 's finished off Miss Trindle an' says where are you, if it's convenient.'

'Anyone would think I was a Cook's conducted tour,' snapped Mrs. Meake. 'What's he want now?'

'It's about a ladder,' Annie said.

David exclaimed: 'I've just spotted it. A rope ladder, it's slung over the wall all tangled up with the dead creeper.'

'That's 'ow IT got into the garden,' Annie opined.

3

Mrs. Meake went out, saying over her shoulder: 'Come on, Annie.'

Annie did not move. She was a colourless scraggy girl of twenty or so, remarkably tall. Half an inch more or less than six feet, David guessed. She had small eyes and a receding chin, her hair was scraped to the top of her head with a formidable collection of metal grips and fancy combs. David warned her, as he slipped into his dressing gown: 'Don't be too ready with theories, or they'll think you did the knifing act.'

Annie grinned amiably, revealing two patchy rows of teeth. 'I wouldn't mind. It would be exciting to be in the dock and sentenced to death and then proved innocent, with your picture in all the papers.'

'But not so exciting if they just sentenced you to death and left it at that.' David snapped up the lid of the enclosed wash-basin and began scrubbing his teeth.

'Oo-er,' Annie exclaimed. As David turned her teeth again jumped into view with her sudden smile. 'My picture would be in the papers, just the same.'

'You'd better buy a press cutting book and be prepared,' David said, his mouth foaming with tooth-paste. 'But take my advice and get a small one, you feel such a fool when you've only got a couple of pages of clippings and a hundred blanks. I ought to know.'

'You!' Annie guffawed. 'I've seen your notices, three 'ole books of them Mrs. Meake showed me.'

'Extracts from the *Wigan Weekly* and the *Brixton Advertiser*. Not quite the Noël Coward touch in publicity.'

'Lovely all the same,' sighed Annie.

'Lovely, my foot. I wish you'd hop it, my gal.'

Annie went on dreamily: 'I'm a good mind to confess, just to see what they'd do to me.'

David threw down his toothbrush, swilled out the glass. 'I say, it wasn't you who knifed the gent, was it?'

Annie guffawed again. 'I wouldn't dare. The sight o' blood turns me funny.'

'But the deed was done in the dark, you wouldn't have seen one scarlet spot.'

'Nor I would. I mean, nor I did.'

David said impatiently: 'Well, just run along and confess. It won't get you far. The police are bored to death with confessions, they get dozens for every murder.' Again he glanced out of the window. The strip of sacking had been removed, no doubt to facilitate the inspection of the corpse by the tall man, who according to Mrs. Meake was the pathologist. The body was lying in a twisted position with the head towards the gate, that led – like the others of neighbouring back gardens – into an alley.

Annie grumbled: 'Oh, well, I s'pose I got to get along. There's Mr. Cumberbatch shoutin' the place down like 'e always does for coal. The scuttles 'e uses, you could run one of your airyplanes on all them scuttles.'

Cumberbatch had the front room on the first floor. David said absently: 'He's lived in the tropics.'

'Tropics or not, 'e's a terror on the coal. An' 'e goes out an' comes in, you'd 'ardly believe it but it's gospel, with sticks an' logs.'

'Oh, buzz off,' said David.

Annie went out. Within half a minute she reappeared. 'The Inspector's comin' up 'ere,' she grinned. 'P'raps 'e 'll make out you done it.'

'He's welcome to.' David hastily swallowed another cup of tea and lit a cigarette. He heard Mrs. Meake's voice.

'That's right, Inspector, straight in front of you. And if you want me for the rest of them just call out.'

'Come in,' said David, to the bulky shadow on the landing.

TWO

DETECTIVE INSPECTOR GRACEWELL was unlike everything that David had ever imagined about such an official. Certainly he was tall and broad, but his manner was diffident, giving almost an impression of shyness, and he moved slowly, as if uncertain of his object. There was none of the traditional pomposity of the law about him, his smile might have been that of a shy boy arriving in a new school. He apologised for his intrusion, refused a cigarette, and took the one armchair only after David had settled on the end of the divan.

'It's no trouble at all,' David assured him. 'After all, the affair happened almost under my nose.'

'Exactly. Now, sir, if I may have your name – ?'

David supplied details. To further questions he explained that he was on a week's leave after several months in hospital, the result of a slight aerial dispute with a Jerry. Inspector Gracewell glanced at the uniform hanging on the wardrobe. 'I see you've got the D.F.C.'

'Sheer fluke,' said David. Then he felt embarrassed, for the phrase sounded like mock-modesty, though the exploit that had earned his decoration had, in sober truth, been the result of a series of chances in which he himself had had the opportunity of being somewhat original.

The Inspector made notes placidly. He glanced up. 'I suppose you occasionally use that back gate?'

'Good heavens, no. Never thought of it. Front doors are good enough for me. Besides, it would mean going via the basement.'

'Did you spend last night in this room?'

David nodded. 'Sleeping like a top.'

'You were in here from – what time?'

'Let me see – my girlfriend had to get back to her kids at ten. And, of course – ' David grinned, 'the pubs shut at ten on a Sunday, so when I left her I came straight back here. Must have been ten-past ten when I got in.'

Inspector Gracewell looked pained. 'Did I understand that your girlfriend has – ahem – children?'

'Eight babies, and adores them all.'

The Inspector pursed his lips. 'I'm afraid I must explain, sir, that we must be serious.'

'I realise that. Tess – my friend, Miss Carmichael, works at a kind of crèche. She's got a whole sheaf of certificates for child welfare stuff.'

'Oh – quite. I see. I'm afraid I misunderstood. Now I'd like to know whether you heard anything in the night. Any unusual sounds?'

'I'm no good to you there. I sleep too well. Didn't so much as blink between eleven and eight-thirty.'

'You say you arrived here yesterday. Is this your first stay in the house?'

'Lord, no. It must be eight years since I arrived with a cardboard suitcase and a swelled head. Country lad, stage-struck, seeks fame and fortune in the big city. That's how it goes. I believed I'd show the world just what Shakespeare really had in mind when he wrote his tragedies.'

'But, of course, your residence hasn't been continuous.'

'I've been in the Air Force since the war started. Even before that I was only here on and off, when I was out of a job and haunting Charing Cross Road in search of one. I never got a chance in London, except for being a flunkey in musical comedy and a duke in a farce that ran for three nights.'

'So you've known Mrs. Meake for eight years?'

'Yes, bless her. She's a darling.'

'Ahem.' The Inspector coughed delicately. 'Apart from that – ?'

'Apart from that she'll press your pants and lend you a bus fare – and she loves a bunch of flowers by way of interest. She understands the business – the stage, I mean – so she's ideal to grumble to. She was in the front row at the Gaiety years ago, and played leads in touring revues.'

'I understand she's a widow.'

'I suppose she is. Funny, I never even wondered about that, and naturally I wouldn't ask.'

'You know her daughter, of course?'

'Thelma. Lord, yes.' David made no attempt to keep the scorn out of his voice. Thelma was a perfect pain in the neck. She'd been a conceited spoilt brat of fourteen when first she came here. Now she was imitation Hollywood of the most blatant kind. She had brassy red hair – and though she had her mother's blue eyes, no glint of her mother's genial character ever shone through them. Her features were a mask, with all expression painted out. She read film magazines and dreamed of owning a Rolls Royce and several mink coats. Thelma. Plastic-unbreakable. A bunch of affectations. She had spasms of copying Garbo, Dietrich, Hepburn, without the capacity for hard work of any of them.

David had been silent. He added lamely: 'Sorry, but I'm afraid I'm a bit warped about Thelma.'

'I'm told she wasn't in this house last night,' Inspector Gracewell pursued.

'Wasn't she?' David didn't give a rap where the girl was. The further away the better.

'Now about the other tenants of rooms here – '

'Just a minute. I'd like to know, first, whether you definitely connect this man's death with someone now on the premises.'

'At the moment I'm just making a few general inquiries. And naturally I like to begin on the spot. The rope ladder over the back wall suggests that the deceased may have been on his way to see someone here. Or he may have been leaving after a visit.'

'Obviously wasn't paying an ordinary call. And coming via the garden he'd have to get in the back door, that opens into the basement passage alongside the kitchen. I believe it's kept locked as a rule. And Mrs. Meake and Annie – the maid, you know – are for ever popping about in that passage.'

'Not throughout the night,' the Inspector remarked.

'Of course not. But they'd be sure to lock the back door when they turned in.'

'So I have been assured.'

'At what time – I mean, when do you think the deed was done?'

'The Divisional Surgeon made only a preliminary examination. He places it at about three a.m. That estimate, of course, is subject to revision after further examination.'

'Nasty business altogether.' David shuddered. He was beginning to feel that he needed his bath. The sun was breaking through the early morning grey and he felt frousty in his present state.

'I wonder if you'd mind coming down with me? You might recognise the victim.'

'What, look at a corpse before I've shaved?'

'It won't take more than a minute or so.'

'If Mrs. Meake didn't know him I'm not likely to. What's his name?'

'That's what we still have to discover.'

David kicked off his slippers and shuffled into a pair of thick shoes. 'Hasn't he got any papers on him? Identity card or something?'

'Not a shred.'

'Robbery the motive? I mean, if his wallet's gone – '

The Inspector said heavily: 'The motive will be a matter for inquiry.' He rose and moved to the window. 'Oh, by the way, now I can get more of a bird's eye view of the surroundings, perhaps you can give me information that may prove helpful. That street over on the right is Cannock Road, isn't it?'

Only the backs of the houses were visible from this point.

'Yes.'

'And that building at the end of the alley running from Cannock Road?'

'It's a garage. Ramshackle sort of place, all falling to bits, as you can see.'

'Know who owns it?'

'Haven't any idea. I used to see cars and lorries going in and out.'

Beyond the garage were more small gardens and the backs of the houses in the next parallel road. Away to the left were the backs of houses in another street at a right angle. The back wall enclosing all the gardens was broken by more or less derelict wooden gates into the alley that looked as if they were rarely opened. The wall continued right round the oblong yard in which the garage stood; the alley was about thirty yards long, of a width to take a single vehicle running to or from Cannock Road. Anyone wishing to approach any of the houses from the rear would have to be familiar with the lay-out of the alleyway and gardens. It was probable that most of the gates were kept bolted for safety, in which case a visitor would have to be admitted – or be ingenious enough to find a way over the seven-foot wall.

Why the unfortunate unknown should have chosen to enter Mrs. Meake's garden was certainly a mystery. Tradesmen always used the front area door.

David followed the inspector downstairs. They had to descend to the basement to gain access to the garden, and as they passed the open kitchen door David heard voices raised in argument. Miss Trindle, who occupied the front room on the hall floor, was protesting to Mrs. Meake.

'I'm leaving today. I can't be dragged into this sort of thing… Proper disgrace… police. A lot of questions, it isn't reasonable.'

'Reasonable or not,' rapped Mrs. Meake, 'it's not the first time you've been mixed up in a scandal.'

'You're a nice one to dare to say that!'

Again Mrs. Meake began to speak explosively, but fell silent as a warning 'S-ssh!' came from Miss Trindle.

David and the Inspector stepped up to the garden. The latter remarked: 'I'm afraid I upset Miss Trindle. Pity. Got to question everyone within hearing distance, matter of routine.'

'Of course.'

Inspector Gracewell said musingly: 'Not the first time she's been mixed up in a scandal, eh? D'you happen to know what that means?'

David hesitated. He knew the story well enough. He knew what had happened on the sunny Sunday morning of the outbreak of war, when the papers were too packed out with real news to have more than a line or so for the sudden death of the old Marquis of Leafe, in a flat in Jermyn Street. He knew that Miss Trindle had been the book-keeper at that shady block of flats, and that she had arrived in Terrapin Road within two hours of the Marquis's death. But he was reluctant to betray what Mrs. Meake had told him in confidence. He said: 'No. It's difficult to associate Miss Trindle with scandal, she's so stiff and starchy. Whenever I speak to her she souses me in vinegar.'

'Vitriol was my pickle,' the Inspector chuckled.

'Those blameless women always seem to get their accumulators full of acid. This one thinks she's running the war.'

'By the way, what's her job?'

'She works in an office where they check food coupons and points and such-like.'

'Enough to make her a bit snappy out of office hours.'

'It would make me completely murderous,' David said – and then realised that he had used what was, in the circumstances, a particularly slanderous word. They moved on, picking their way over the rough ground, towards the humped oblong of sacking.

THREE

BOB CARTER'S VOICE came over the telephone: 'That you, David? I got your note. How long will you be in town?'

'A week. They let me out of hospital yesterday.'

'I'm spitting mad, wild as a coot, crazy as hell. They've turned me down for the Navy again. This idiotic heart of mine, it ticks like the time-signal on the B.B.C. – not the pathetic little two-note tune, it's the old ghost in goloshes, *glog-glog-glog*.'

'I say, Bob – '

But Bob continued explosively: 'These doctors don't know anything, I'm going to write to *The Times* and have the medical service voted obsolete and I'll do it all in blankety blank verse – '

'This isn't the time for verbal embroideries. I'm sorry about the Navy, old chap, but there are lots of other ways you can give a hand.'

'I know, I know. I've got a spanking good idea already, it's sizzling in a special section of my brain just above the right ear.'

'Well keep it sizzling, I can't listen, I'm in the thick of a murder.'

'Murder? Serious?'

'It's down the garden path, right Beverley-Nichols-well under my window. A sequence of the most sinister-looking and important gents keep inspecting same, hoping to be trusted with further orders and assuring everyone of the best attention. Ten minutes ago a Superintendent completed the picture. It's quite put me off my toast and marmalade.'

'Who is it?'

'Nobody can ever guess. You'd better come round if you've got nothing better to do, and wear rubber gloves so you won't leave finger-prints and fix up a lot of false alibis to make the whole thing more complicated.'

'Gosh, you flying chaps are cold-blooded. A poor devil gets done in and you think it's a big laugh.'

'My dear Bob, if you'd inspected the victim as I had to, you wouldn't think death was a tragedy. *De mortuis nil nisi bonum* and all that, but this chap's uglier than Cinderella's sisters. Quite terror-striking, even in eternal repose.'

'Tell me the rest when I arrive. I'll be along right away, and I *still* think doctors suffer from delusional fixations, the whole bagload of them.'

Bob Carter was a journalist by profession. Before the war he had written a society gossip page for a fashionable weekly. He knew by sight everyone who mattered and never felt that they mattered very much. The main advantage of his job had been that he could entertain his friends at the expense of theatrical managers, film magnates and social climbers. For two years now he had been making attempts to get into one of the services. The *Social Mirror* had expired, he had written a book on working conditions in factories – a subject on which he was surprisingly well informed – and the typescript of it was destroyed in an air raid. It was the best part of a year's work and the disaster depressed Bob for quite twenty-four hours – a record, for normally he had the buoyancy of a barrage balloon. He was twenty-eight, two years older than David.

As David waited for his ebullient friend he paced up and down his first floor back. He had bathed, shaved, and breakfasted and now felt capable of facing the day. He had partly dressed and now was wearing a dressing gown over shirt and grey flannel trousers. He intended to wear mufti while he was at large. In appearance he was just over medium height, brown-haired, thin, with a fresh complexion and hazel eyes; when seeking stage engagements he had often lamented the fact that he was too ordinary looking to inspire managers to reach for contract forms. But even in his dressing gown he had a well-groomed air; he had acquired the habit of holding himself well through seeing himself in films, when he had been horrified by his earlier youthful slouch. He had, though he was not aware of it, a sensitive and humorous mouth. He had experienced enough of life, had suffered enough disappointments, to appreciate the ironies of human existence, to be aware of the contrast between the sentimental dramas in which he had appeared and the sharpness of reality.

And at least he had learned that one had to be a realist before the full flavour and fun of life could be savoured.

He mooched about the room and inspected Tess Carmichael's photograph, framed in leather and cellophane. For a moment he wished that she were one of those idle glamour girls who stayed in bed till midday, so that he could phone her and go round and mix her a drink while she lay languidly against frilly pillows. Then he remembered how slick and cute she looked in her grey nurse's uniform and recalled the wish. A glance out of the window informed him that the body of the murdered man had been removed. A police van stood in the alley at the back. And now, as Bob Carter still failed to appear, David trotted downstairs to get the latest bulletin from Mrs. Meake.

She was clearing breakfast trays in the kitchen. David asked: 'Where's Thelma?'

'You know you can't stand the sight of her.'

'She's all right,' David said insincerely.

'Why the sudden interest?' Mrs. Meake scraped out a marmalade jar.

'I just wondered where she was.'

'In bed, of course. You know she's never up early.'

'That's the best of doing essential work in a theatre manager's office.' To avoid the call-up, Thelma had discovered a sudden enthusiasm for typing. David had seen samples of her impressionistic spelling. But perhaps spelling didn't matter so much when civilisation was staggering. He went on: 'But I thought she was away.'

'What put that idea into your head?'

'Inspector Gracewell said she wasn't in the house last night.'

Mrs. Meake put down the marmalade jar so forcibly that its impact against the enamel table sounded like a revolver shot. 'You seem to have had a nice gossip,' she said sharply. 'Well, if you're so eager to know just where Thelma is, she stayed last night at my sister Millie's.'

'What, not at Mrs. Higgins?'

'Millie hasn't been so well, she gets nervous, she felt ever so queer yesterday. I let Thelma go to keep her company.'

'But listen, Meakie. Thelma sends her aunt screaming mad.'

'Oh, don't come bothering me, as if a murder isn't enough without you nagging about Thelma and Millie. They're my relations, not yours, and I'll thank you to mind your own business.'

'Sorry.' David was silent for a minute or so, thinking that he had never before known Mrs. Meake to be so touchy. 'I see they've shifted the body.'

'And let's hope that'll be the end of it.'

'I'm afraid it won't. We're in the party, in a way.'

'We're nothing to do with it. He got over the wall for some reason of his own and I ought to get damages for the disturbance. It's upsetting, that's what it is. But I know how to keep my head, I've toured in too many continents to let little things upset me. Why, I remember when I was in South Africa we did *She Stoops to Conquer* with a native rebellion going on all round the theatre, that was the week before we played Johannesburg and a fellow who'd found an outsize diamond bought me a couple of race-horses that would have made a lot of money if the trainer hadn't been a crook.'

This was more like Mrs. Meake, with her endless reminiscences about her past. 'You've been a bit of a card in your day,' David remarked, wondering if she was deliberately trying to fog the point under discussion. He added: 'Miss Trindle seemed a bit upset, earlier on.'

'Well, you don't expect any woman to be pleased at what you might call a nasty affair.'

'You might have given her a lesson or so in coolness under stress.'

'She isn't worth it. Good riddance, that's what I say. She's packing now, she phoned the food office that she'd be late.'

'So you'll have the ground floor front to let.'

'Lord there's the doorbell again and Annie's out shopping.'

'I'll go. I expect it's Bob Carter for me. So long – and don't keep on scraping inside that marmalade pot, it's been empty for the last five minutes. You're a calm one, Meakie, but you're not always as calm as you pretend to be.'

'If you think you can tell me what to do with marmalade pots – '

'There, there, don't get all het up.' David moved to the table and slipped an arm round Mrs. Meake's ample waist. 'It's a damn shame, all this business. I'm sorry, and if you want a second line of defence, just call on little David. Always your faithful servant and defender.'

'Oh, hop it and answer that somethinged bell before I slap your face for you,' was Mrs. Meake's unromantic rejoinder.

FOUR

BOB CARTER LOLLED on the unmade divan bed with one elbow on the oak headboard. His hat was on the standard lamp, he had not taken off his overcoat. He was a man of rather less than medium height, with light brown tousled hair, and an unhealthily pale skin. Even in repose he gave an impression of restlessness, almost of suppressed excitement. By nature he was optimistic, volatile, impatient.

David was saying: 'As I was telling you, the first I heard of it was when Mrs. Meake came in, and I must say she seemed as unconcerned as a potato.'

Bob was not attending. 'I had three tries to get into the army, and now this to cap the lot – '

'You'd have thought any ordinary woman would have had hysterics or something.'

'Of course, some days the old heart is almost normal. I swear it is. They keep telling me about the left and right valves, as if they think I'm some kind of a ruddy wireless set – I say, I wish you'd listen instead of butting in with your murder. What I've got to say affects the whole course of the war. It's a plan for stabilisation of national morale, etcetera etcetera. But, of course, if you think a cheap sensation is more important, I can't hope to impress you.'

'You always impress me. Have a gasper.'

Bob sighed. 'All right. Spill your story. But once upon a time I used to get paid for listening to drivel.'

'All there is to it is that a bloke was found with a knife in his back at seven-thirty this morning in the patch of garden at the back. He might have remained undiscovered for heaven knows how long if a copper prowling down Cannock Alley – that's the bottle-neck that leads to the yard where the garage stands – hadn't spotted a rope ladder over the wall. And I've since gathered that the one thing that gets a copper on the tip of his big toe is any sort of a ladder over a wall. It stirs up all his speculative faculties, if you follow me.'

'To the last centimetre,' said Bob. 'So the copper climbed the ladder and saw the corpse.'

'Not quite. He tried the door in the back wall. And, lo and behold, it opened, though Mrs. Meake is certain she unbolted it for the dustman two days ago and rebolted it firmly at six-fifteen on the same day. No one admits to unbolting it since.'

'Go on,' snorted Bob Carter, 'go on. With your passion for trivialities you'll be telling me the dustman's life story.'

'Think nought a trifle, though it small appear – '

'Just the time of day for poetical quotations. Have you got any beer?'

'Have a heart. I only arrived yesterday and straightway I went walking out and courting. Still, "The Volunteer" round in Cannock Road is due to open in eight and a half minutes.'

'We'll set off in six and a half.' Bob yawned. 'You may as well complete your absorbing narrative.'

'Where was I?'

'The dustman's life story, bin by bin.'

'No. Bobby finds body. Before you could say knife he'd found one between the shoulder-blades of Mr. X. Identity hasn't yet been established. The bobby made for the house, and failing to get any reply to his ringing at the back-door bell, for the simple reason that it hasn't been used for years and is out of order, he thumped on the kitchen window. The beauteous Annie was just astir. She's the new serving wench, and she was just about to light the fire that brews the morning tea. She saw the copper and ran to Mrs. Meake, who sleeps on the hall floor, screaming that there'd been a burglary. Robert phoned the station and along came a natty little carload of more Roberts and a detective sergeant. Then a pleasant-mannered detective inspector joined the circle, and a superintendent popped along for a short while to add tone to the affair. Everyone in the house was questioned, but there doesn't seem to have been any useful reaction from any of them. We're a peaceable lot at fifteen Terrapin Road.'

'Murders seem awfully dull these days,' Bob remarked.

'This one is. No clues, except a nasty sharp knife that will almost certainly bear no finger-prints. Just a rope ladder and an ugly corpse in what looked like a continental overcoat, worth nobody's good coupons. Dark grey gabardine with wide lapels. The chap looked like a southern European. Italian, maybe. His hat was quite revolting, even off the head.'

'Italians are listed pretty thoroughly these days.'

'Oh, they'll find out who he is,' David retorted with airy assurance. 'But with a face like that he must have had a thousand enemies, so I doubt if they'll spot the villain. I'd have liked snow on the ground, and melting traces of queer-shaped boots, and a scream in the night, and someone fainting at seeing the Inspector.'

'Sickening for you to be disappointed. But after this week you'll get all the thrills you want.'

'Flying isn't thrilling. It's just work and when it's done one's tired, that's all.'

'Lovely exhibition of *sang-froid* on your part. I could almost wish the *Social Mirror* hadn't perished.'

Bob Carter spoke quite sourly. David was smitten with compunction, remembering that Bob was feeling sore at his last rejection by some conscientious doctor. 'To hell with flying, too much fuss is made about it. Lots of people are doing jobs far more useful without a lot of drum-banging and postscripts to the news. Look at Mrs. Meake, sorting out the rations and producing the breakfast rasher like a Maskelyne and Devant rolled into one.'

Bob said suddenly and brightly: 'I was going to tell you about my plans. I've got a pretty snappy idea. Twenty-six allied nations, we've got thousands of their men in this country, and every one has got some sort of club or meeting place in which he can hobnob with his own countrymen and sing his own anthem. But I'm going to start a club for the whole blazing lot, so they can work up a sort of *entente cordiale* before the real fight over peace negotiations.'

'Just a moment. Did you say the real fight?'

'Yes. When peace is signed the big scrap will start in earnest. Can you imagine twenty-six nations agreeing to the same conclusions at the same moment, even when Hitler and the Japs and the Wops are in the soup?'

'They'll have to.'

'Of course they will, in the end. But how much easier it'll be if the nations have mixed good and plenty and have a chance to understand each other's points of view. A club called the Twenty-Six Nations, or Just the Twenty-Six, that's my idea. Frenchmen will meet Czechs and pal up with Greeks and Chinese, and they'll all get a flavouring of each other's angles, then when the tough argument starts they'll already be infected with each other's views and won't be so pigheaded.'

'It's an idea,' David grinned. 'Arise, ye starvelings of slumber – '

'You're off the mark. I'm planning something international without the 'E' on the end of the word. Come on, "The Volunteer" must be opening.'

David moved to get another glimpse of the garden. The oblong of sacking had disappeared and the rope ladder no longer trailed over the dead creeper on the wall. The men in plain clothes had gone, but the two policemen still stood just within the gate. Except for them the scene was normal.

'I wonder if he shouted,' David mused. 'Or perhaps it happened too suddenly and he expired without a whimper. If you like I'll point out just where the deed was done.'

'I'm not particularly interested.'

'A half-hearted fish, that's what you are.'

'I'm whole-hearted in one direction,' Bob retorted. 'And that's beer. Let's go.'

FIVE

DAVID LED THE WAY downstairs. The hall door was open, and as they reached the front steps they were cautioned to pass warily. Indeed there was only just room to pass, because one side of the steps was roped off, and within the temporary enclosure a man in plain clothes was scraping at the concrete with a small glinting instrument.

Bob exclaimed 'What's the game?'

A man lounging against the railings of the area supplied the answer. 'It's blood. Nasty splash o' blood was there. Gentleman's collectin' it to put in the Chamber of 'Orrors.'

Two uniformed policemen stood on the pavement, and a shifting group of inquisitive idlers straggled along the street, exchanging speculations and pointing out irrelevant features of the house's exterior as they chattered. Most of them were women with shopping baskets.

'Blood!' David exclaimed, as he and Bob hastened on. 'It's a funny place to find it, when the deed was done in the garden.'

'Deed may have been done on the front steps and the gent dragged to the garden.'

'That would mean he was carted right through the house. Not likely.'

'Or round the corner and down Cannock Alley and over the wall.'

'Which is even more unlikely. Can you imagine a murderer supplying himself with a rope ladder, slinging it over a wall, and using it to dump his victim in a spot that's rather less secluded than the alley, seeing that the garden's easily visible from every window at the back of the house, and the alley is usually deserted? No, it doesn't make sense.'

'Few murders do,' was Bob's dry comment.

'Blood may have been there by chance. As likely as not some drunk slipped and damaged himself. Anyway they'll find out if it's the human variety, and what category it belongs to, which'll give a line on whether it could have oozed from the veins of the body

21

they're interested in.'

David and Bob turned sharply left at the corner of Cannock Road, a shopping thoroughfare dominated by the Athenaeum Cinema, an impressive structure of concrete trimmed with gilt pillars. "The Volunteer" crouched humbly beside the picture palace, and in the same block there were shops and a restaurant, the "Blue Lantern", which was exactly opposite the alley that led to the yard and garage behind Mrs. Meake's. Glancing down the alley as they passed the end of it, David saw quite a crowd assembled at one spot – just outside the back entrance to Number 15, he guessed, though he had never investigated the approach to the house from that direction. A car drove in, scattering the curious loiterers. Detective Inspector Gracewell was beside the driver; in the back there were two men in plain clothes. More onlookers trotted into the alley, and among them David noticed old Cumberbatch, the surly tenant of the first floor front at Mrs. Meake's.

Bob had caught David's glance. 'Seen someone you know?' He queried.

'Cumberbatch. My next-room neighbour. Queer old chap.'

'Fellow with white hair?'

'That's him. Gives me the creeps. When you're speaking to him, he seems to be looking at something about two miles away.'

'What's he laughing at now?'

'Oh that's just his usual sickly smile. He communes with dead souls or something. I expect he has happy half hours with Cleopatra when he's sitting in the "Blue Lantern" eating beans on toast.'

As they crossed the road Bob glanced back again. 'Hell of a lot of morbid curiosity,' he commented. 'Wonder how long they'll hang round gaping at nothing.'

'Locally, it's a sensation. As far as the general public is concerned it'll probably be one of those mysteries that fizzle out in a few lines at the bottom of the page. A verdict of murder by some person or persons unknown.'

'And as the victim's unknown, I can't see that it's worth even a few lines,' Bob said.

'Where's your news sense? There's quite a lot of scope for theories.'

'Why not invent a few?'

'Come to that, I might,' David laughed.

They crossed the road to "The Volunteer". The saloon was dimly lit, behind the long curved bar Mrs. Newland, the proprietress, was exhorting Rita the barmaid to bestir herself. Rita merely moved from her lethargic position on one stool to an even more somnolent pose on another, and continued to study her manicure.

'Good morning, good morning.' Mrs. Newland's greeting was brisk enough.

'Morning, ma 'am. Two bitters, please.' Bob slapped down a coin.

'You've had a bit of excitement, I hear,' Mrs. Newland remarked. She had angular features and silver-grey hair that contrasted with her thick dark brows. A faint scar ran from her right cheek to the corner of her mouth. She always wore black and a profusion of imitation diamond jewellery. Her eyes were dark, hard, and she had a way of staring without blinking – like a snake, as a malicious customer had once remarked.

'Just a trifle of murder,' David said. 'Sorry to see you've lost the top button of your cardigan.'

'Fancy you noticing! The trouble is I can't match the other five, and I'll have to get a new half-dozen.'

'Would you be surprised to hear they'd found the missing one under the body?'

'What!' Mrs. Newland stifled a gasp with her hand.

'Because – Here, I say! I was only joking. I was going to say because it would surprise *me*.'

Mrs. Newland had fallen back against the row of bottles on the shelf behind her, her face was ashen, her dark eyes staring.

'I'm sorry,' David said. 'It was a rotten joke anyway.'

'It's nothing,' Mrs. Newland made an effort and seemed to recover. 'You startled me. It's my heart. I'm never too steady in the morning.' She poured herself a short stiff drink, swallowed it at a gulp, and laughed shortly. 'A joke, of course anyone's entitled to a joke, and I'm not the one to mind. Besides, I lost that button a month ago.'

Bob said flippantly: 'You leave the Court without a stain on your character.'

'I've never been in a Court, and I never want to be.'

'You're nearly opposite the alley leading to that garden, so you might have been a vital witness, if you'd had sharp eyes.'

'Fine chance to witness anything, with the black-out and all.'

Bob Carter moved to the fire. Mrs. Newland, who now seemed quite composed, leaned across the bar and muttered to David: 'I'm not telling everybody, but I do know one little thing that might have something to do with it.'

'What's that?'

'Can't tell you now. I'm busy. Yes, sir, a double gin. Rita, look after the lady there. Half-a-crown, thank you, sir – '

The bar was filling up and Mrs. Newland's plea of being busy was justified.

David crossed the saloon to Bob and asked: 'Ready for another tankard?'

'I'm all right. I'm having one with Paton.'

David nodded to Paton, the manager of the cinema next door. Bob went on: 'I was telling Paton about this idea of an international club – '

'I've got to go,' Paton said. 'Charles Boyer always gets a queue and I've got to see it doesn't turn into an obstruction.'

Bob hardly noticed Paton's departure as he ran on volubly about his scheme.

'It'll cost a lot of money,' David cautioned him.

'I've got it all worked out, and I've got premises – '

'Already?'

'Signed the lease on Saturday.'

'You must have come into some cash.'

'I came into thirty guineas on Friday. Sold a series of articles on blondes versus brunettes to a slushy monthly. Written from the services efficiency point of view. Are redheads red-hot at riveting? Black-headed beauties battle better with balloons – '

'Enough, enough!' David exclaimed.

'Canary-headed cuties concentrate on cables – '

'I shall be sick any minute.'

'Anyway, the editor liked it, and I had twenty-five quid handy for the first quarter's rent in advance. The house is a bit dilapidated, so I've got it cheap.'

'Whatever it is the doctors find wrong with you it doesn't stop you being a live wire.'

'That's what I tell them, but they've got a special form of deafness. The place I've taken is in Belmont Crescent, third turning down the High Street. Nice and handy. You'll be able to come in and help get it going.'

'Thanks, but aren't you forgetting I've got a job of my own?'

'You've got a week free. Miracles can happen in a week.'

'You'll need them, to get your stunt under way.'

Bob spoke confidently: 'When you expect them they happen.'

'It's all very well to say you've paid a bit of rent. You'll want finance and furniture and – well, the hell of a lot of things.'

'I've achieved miracle number one. When I did my page for the *Social Mirror* I met all sorts of big pots. Yesterday I went through a list of them and decided that Sir Cuthbert Horley was my pigeon.'

'Name's familiar. Can't place him exactly.'

'Homes are Heaven the Horley Pay Way.'

'If that isn't a breath-taking slogan, I don't know what is.'

'That's the idea. Rob the customer of breath and he can't say no. And I'm giving old Horley a basinful of his own medicine.'

'He must have whole warehouses full of furniture, but that doesn't mean you get any.'

'Just a moment. He started as an errand boy, so naturally he wants to be a peer. Every time he gave a four-figure cheque to a hospital I used to shove his picture at the top of my page, and he'd pay off the most restless of my creditors.'

'No wonder you never had any space for a spot of publicity for my unrecognised genius.'

'My dear fellow, the second lead in a show that's touring the provinces isn't news. Money always is. Or was. Of course, at the moment heroism is the most newsy article, and I seem to remember your mug on various front pages when you collected your D.F.C.'

David grunted: 'Actually publicity doesn't seem so awfully

important as it did. To get back to the furniture department – '

'Well, I rang up Sir Cuthbert last night and went along to see him. I put it to him that the Twenty-Six Nations is a wow as a national – or rather, international effort. For the cause of freedom and all that caper. Backs to the wall, fight in the fields, shoulder to shoulder, *ad lib*. I showed him my lease and a rough draft of my proposed plan of action. I asked him if he'd got a good new studio portrait and reminded him that I've still got a pretty good pull with the press boys, in spite of the fact that my old scandal-rag is no more.'

'Any good?'

'I fairly hypnotised the old codger. He's making oodles of money, of course, with furniture the price it is. I told him he'd be wise to give some away before the Government fixes prices at under cost. At one moment I had him saying yes, and was on the point of asking him when the chairs and tables would arrive, so that I could have a few cameramen handy, when his wife came in. He's a bit scared of her, so he had a fit of coughing and told me to ring him at twelve-fifteen this morning.'

'I wish you luck.'

'I'm pretty certain I've hooked him. He fancies himself as the big philanthropist. And you can't take a crack at anything much bigger than a couple of dozen nations with two more thrown in for fun. I'll get some female bodies to run the kitchen and scrub and all that, and voluntary helpers for the rest of the outfit. Membership will be nominal, a shilling a year, and food and drink will be at prices that just cover expenses.'

'And what are you going to live on?'

'Oh, I'll be among the expenses. But actually the scheme's not a profit-making one, it's idealistic.'

'Dreams are but interludes which fancy makes, when monarch reason sleeps – Dryden. At least I think it's Dryden.'

'What a hell of a fellow you are for quotations. By jove, it's just on twelve-fifteen, I think I'll tell Sir Cuthbert I'll have light oak delivered in plain vans. I must remember to touch him for a cheque as well, while I've got him hotted up.'

'What are you doing about lunch?'

'Depends on the light oak.'

'I might be around,' David said. 'It's all a question of whether Tess can get time off or not.'

'I'm keen to meet the lady.'

'You shall, but wear your smoked glasses, she's dazzling. So long, I'm going to have a word with Mrs. Newland.'

'About missing buttons?'

'That button was a brick. I shall go softly-softly.'

SIX

MRS. NEWLAND'S MOOD seemed to have changed. She was affable, almost gushing, when David rejoined her, and to his suggestion that she should have a drink with him she shook her head firmly. 'No, no, Mr. Heron, you must have one with me.'

'Oh, come on – '

'No, I've never stood you a drink since you've been in the Air Force.'

'Oh, well – ' David accepted a beer, raising his mug to her. 'Cheers.'

'You're welcome. I think you flying boys are wonderful. The day you went off I said to Rita, I said, that Mr. Heron will make his mark or I'm a liar.'

'Oi, I can't take it. Let's talk about the weather.'

'And there you were in the *Evening Standard* the week after that Easter, close up against Clark Gable.'

'Revolting for Clark Gable,' David cut in. 'That's enough about the wonderful Air Force. What's the titbit of news you've got for me?'

'Just a moment while I serve those boys. Light ales? Thank you. And you, sir?' Mrs. Newland again seemed somewhat flustered as she attended to the customers. 'You, Rita, you go and fetch those glasses from off the window ledge.'

At last Mrs. Newland returned to the corner where David leaned against the wall. Her voice dropped. 'They tell me it was done with a knife,' she said.

'That's right, it was.'

'Stuck in his back, wasn't it?'

'So I was told.' David stared curiously at Mrs. Newland, whose angular face was taut with controlled excitement. He realised suddenly that she must have been quite handsome before her face was scarred, before her dark wide eyes acquired their hard expression.

'What sort of a knife was it?' she asked.

'I didn't see it. I think they'd removed it by the time I took a peep. And then I only saw the face and shoulders. Not at all a pretty sight.'

'It would be a sharply pointed knife, wouldn't it?'

'If the murderer knew his job it would be.'

Mrs. Newland nodded silently, turned to attend to a newcomer further along the bar, and returned. 'They tell me he was a foreigner.'

'You seem to know more than I do. Yes, I'd guess he wasn't British. But who told you – ?'

'Syd – the postman – told me there was a bit of excitement this morning, and I popped out. Mr. Smedley, who lodges at Mrs. Meake's – well, you should know that better than I do – he happened to pass on his way to the tube, and I asked him what was up and he told me. He'd had a look at the body, for some reason or other.'

Mr. Smedley was a bank clerk who occupied the room over David's the second floor back. 'I believe everyone in the house looked at it. At the police inspector's request. You see there was a good chance that one of us might recognise the victim, as he was more or less on the premises.'

Mrs. Newland spoke as if reaching a definite conclusion. 'A pointed knife – and a Frenchman. I thought as much.'

'Just a moment. Who says he was a Frenchman?' David waited for a reply and as none came he went on: 'I said the man looked like a foreigner, but I'd have placed him as a chap from the south-east of Europe. He was black-haired, swarthy skinned. After all, the French aren't so different from ourselves as to be easily sorted out – at least, not when they're as silent as this poor devil had to be.'

Mrs. Newland frowned, but still was silent. 'What makes you think he might have been a Frenchman?' David insisted.

'The knife.'

'But what's the knife got to do with his nationality?'

'I saw it, and it was just the thing for a nasty crime. Sharp and pointed, more like a dagger. Last night a kind of sailor chap had it in the bar here.'

'What, d'you mean to say a sailor was waving a murderous weapon among all your worthy customers?'

'No, no, of course not. I'll tell you – '

A heavy hand fell on David's shoulder, causing him to start violently. Bob Carter's voice exclaimed exultantly: 'I've done it, old boy. I've got the light oak and the plain vans and I've got to get

Sir Cuthbert several half-columns or I'll be put in choky for false pretences.'

The interruption was unwelcome, just when Mrs Newland promised to be more than entertaining. David said hastily: 'Good work, Bob. Congratulations. Tell me about it later.'

'I'll have to. I'm meeting international benefactor number one at the "Cumberland" as soon as I can get there, and – I hope – launching the furniture afterwards. Leave a message at Mrs. Meake's where you can be found, if you're not in this afternoon.'

Bob Carter disappeared with the speed of a leaf driven by a hurricane. The interlude had removed Mrs. Newland, and it was some minutes before she returned to resume their discussion. David asked her to have another drink.

'No, thanks. But don't let me stop you having one.'

David decided that he had had all he wanted. He was hoping to meet Tess for lunch. He resumed: 'Tell me about the knife you saw.'

'It was like this. An old sailor chap came in and ordered a double rum – '

'He was in uniform, I take it? Regular navy?'

'Exactly what he was I couldn't say, I'm sure. He was tall and thin as a post. And his face, well, he'd been in few storms in his time or I'm blind. He'd got on a kind of yachting cap, old as old, navy blue and all pulled out of shape, and a great big navy blue coat with the lining hanging down under it. I couldn't see what he'd got on underneath, excepting his trousers were rather short. He'd got a muffler almost smothering his chin. Navy blue with yellow spots it was.'

David laughed. 'No sort of a naval chap. They don't go around in yachting caps with spotted scarves and linings hanging down.'

'He was a sailor all right. I heard him saying he'd been on some islands where the turtles were as big as pianos.'

'Sounds like Galapagos.'

'And he had that kind of a walk that sailors get. I don't know what it is about them. You can always tell a sailor.'

'Well, let's take it he was a sailor. What about the knife he'd got?'

'It was in a kind of holdall, that he opened right there where you're standing now. He was trying to sell things out of it. Mrs.

Wicks, who was complaining about her port and lemon – and what does she expect, when you can't get real port and lemonade isn't what it was? – she bought some amber beads, a little bagful of them, just about enough to make a bracelet. Six shillings she paid for them. I took a look and saw the knife, or dagger, or whatever you like to call it, among the bits of junk he'd got.'

'Did he try to sell it?'

'Not here, he didn't. I thought he was annoying the customers, talking so funny, bits of English and bits of the lord only knows what. I told him I didn't have buying and selling in the bar. You know how it is, these days, if you let people use the place for trading you get a lot of black market fellows with stockings and suchlike. So I told him to buzz off.'

'How did he take that?'

'He got wild and called me something that sounded like "vash", and Mrs. Wicks, who picked up a bit of French when she was a lady's maid, and travelled about, she said it meant I was the French for cow. That annoyed me, I can tell you. So I warned the chap if he didn't get out quick he'd be put out. And off he went.'

'Did he explain where he'd got his junk? Or why he was trying to sell it on a Sunday night?'

Mrs. Newland shook her head. 'He didn't say much, all told, but Mrs. Wicks was certain he was French.'

'You'd know him again?'

'Anywhere. Being so tall and kind of hungry looking and – oh, I told you about him being so full of wrinkles. His trousers, they must have been made for a man inches shorter. I suppose he picked them up second hand.'

David considered the information and Mrs. Newland's conjectures. 'H'm, we've got as far as this French seaman with a knife,' he remarked. 'It might be relevant or it mightn't. Was he alone?'

'Yes.'

'There's not a lot to link him with the murder.'

'He'd got the knife and he was French.'

'Hi, that's tough on our allies.'

'There's plenty of Frenchies against us,' Mrs. Newland said stubbornly. 'Laval and his lot. And I bet this was one of the wrong 'uns.'

'That doesn't make him a killer.'

'Well, the dead man was foreign.'

'But when it comes to murdering someone, a man doesn't necessarily choose one of his own nationality,' David smiled. 'And I'd say the victim was Italian. Or Rumanian, or from round about those southern spots.'

'And just as likely to be set on by this Frenchman.'

David had to laugh. 'Just as likely, I agree. But we've got to establish some definite link before we can pin anything on to your uncivil sailor. Would you be able to identify the knife?'

'That's what I wanted to ask you. Of course, I'd know the knife, it had got a special kind of handle, copper or something like it, and a pattern on it – well, like the feathers on a bird's wing, laid flat in long narrow points.'

David lit a cigarette thoughtfully. 'If by chance it was the same knife,' he said, 'the police ought to know at once.'

'And that's where you can help me. You see I want justice done but I don't want to get mixed up in trouble.'

'But you'll have to speak up, if you can provide a useful clue.'

'What I thought was, that you could say you'd seen the knife in here last night. Now you know what it looked like you can tell whether it's the same one or not. It would be as good as me telling the police.'

'Not a bit of it,' David said firmly.

'About twelve inches long, or say fourteen, handle and all. There couldn't be two knives like it, with that copper handle, in Cannock Road in one night.'

'We don't know that the actual knife was ever in this road.'

'Well, the dead man had to pass this way to get into the alley and over the wall, didn't he?'

'Seems probable. But murders aren't solved by probabilities. You'd better get on to the police right away.'

'I won't, that's all. I only want to help, but if you won't do your part and keep me out of it, there's nothing more to be said.'

'But look here – '

Mrs. Newland rapped: 'I'm sorry I mentioned it.'

'You may be, but I can't leave it at that.'

'I can't see any reason why you can't say you had a look at that knife in the holdall.'

'Simply because I'd be tripped up in a second. When I was in here last night there wasn't any sign of a sailor, with or without a yellow spotted scarf. The police would ask your other customers to corroborate my statements and I'd be in the soup. Your regular customers noticed me particularly, as I hadn't been seen for over six months. Why, it would be enough to make me a likely suspect.'

'Anyone would know you'd never do a murder.'

'Anyone with sense would wonder what the blazes I was playing at, identifying a knife I'd never seen.' David was marvelling at Mrs. Newland's persistence and stupidity, and could he be sure it was stupidity and not an attempt to start a false trail? 'What time was this sailor fellow in here?' he asked.

'Half-past eight, or about that.'

'I'd left before eight.' David remembered exactly, because Tess had been free from eight till ten. 'Now look here, Mrs. Newland, I believe the Inspector is over on the scene of the crime at this very moment. He blew up with a carload of his confederates a short while back. Let me go and bring him in here, then you can clear up this knife puzzle.'

'Don't you, dare. Once you start talking to police, you never know when you'll be done, and I can't get away by flying over Germany like you can.'

David concealed his impatience. 'Who else saw the knife?'

'No one. It was wrapped in some bits of silk and I only got a glimpse of it, when the man shoved his rubbish back after he'd called me a French cow. The knife slipped out of its wrapping, when he was just where you are now, with his back to Mrs. Wicks and the rest. I was looking as hard as I could, because I get the habit of seeing what anyone's trying to sell, in case it looks like stolen goods.'

'Then you'll have to step forward and talk.'

'You don't catch me doing that, and don't you dare mention anything or I'll never serve you another drink.'

David smiled. 'You seem very determined.'

'That's exactly what I am.' Mrs. Newland turned away and there seemed little chance of her being disengaged for some time, for she was questioning an account presented to her by a vanman who lolled against the bar with his eyes on the ceiling.

David strolled towards the door, picking up an abandoned midday paper from a table near it. He was revolving in his mind what he should do about the story of the seafaring man and the fancy-handled knife.

SEVEN

OUTSIDE THE PUB David opened the paper and searched for an account of the murder. There was a headline on the back page, and below it a couple of paragraphs to the effect that the body of an unknown man had been found in the back garden of a house in Terrapin Road in circumstances indicating that he had been murdered. Some details of the victim's appearance were given. Anyone recognising the description was asked to communicate with the police. A copper-handled dagger, it was stated, was the only clue to the identity of the assailant. *See photograph, below.*

David studied the photograph, which was somewhat dwarfed by a map of the Pacific. The fact that the dagger handle was of copper certainly tallied with Mrs. Newland's belief that it was the one her strange customer had carried in his bag, and the markings on it suggested feathers. As David stood in the sunshine, marvelling at the brevity with which a foul crime could be summarised, the police car swerved out of the alley nearly opposite. Some of the more ardent sightseers followed it, and now the alley was almost deserted. On an impulse David strolled across and into it.

He heard stray comments. 'An inspector, the big man was.' 'Chap in the grey overcoat had a camera.' 'Can't think what they'll do with that bit of creeper they cut off.' 'Footprints, they've got enough footprints to arrest the whole neighbourhood.'

After a minute or so only a couple of women remained, still gossiping with ample handplay. David studied the front of the old garage at the far end of the alley. The hinges of the door were dusty, but bright streaks on the metal showed that they had functioned recently. Confused tyre marks overlaid each other on the rough ground. On the dilapidated paint was the announcement in dirty white, GARAGE FOR LARGE OR SMALL VEHICLES. REMOVALS. WAREHOUSING. There was no bell, nor was there any indication as to how a prospective customer might establish contact with the management.

As David stood there, some half dozen yards from the building, he had a sudden feeling that he was being observed. It was a kind of almost-animal intuition, and he glanced sharply to right and left. Now there was no one in sight, but he still had a sense of not being alone.

His eyes ranged over the big doors in front of him. There were no windows in the frontage, but there were two oblong slits high up in the doors, possibly for ventilation.

He forced himself to shed his uncanny idea that he was being watched. It was hardly likely that anyone would be peering through either of those apertures.

He walked back to Cannock Road and on for a few paces. Still the notion haunted him that he had not been alone in the alley. Perhaps, he reflected, the presence of the two policemen on the other side of the seven-foot wall had been the cause of his queer uneasiness. They were probably still there.

On an impulse he stopped, thinking that he might try the door into the garden. If it would open he could reach the house by walking across to the back area door.

He swerved sharply round. As he turned the corner and faced the garage he saw that a man was just leaving it. The stranger, who was carrying a large package, stopped sort and doubled back, pulling the door shut – but not before David had received a staggering shock.

For a moment he thought that he was looking at the man who had been concealed beneath a strip of sacking that morning. Almost the same black crinkly hair with side-whiskers, the same broad pulpy-looking features and stubble of dark beard. This man, who could breathe and walk – and could even seem nervous about meeting someone in the alley – was slightly older in appearance than the dead man. He seemed shorter. But the likeness certainly existed. David had had only a glimpse of the upper part of the murdered man's overcoat; it had suggested continental tailoring. The man who had disappeared into the garage wore a dark green gabardine coat that looked un-English. The short arms gripping the cumbersome package were in full-cut sleeves with deep cuffs.

Astounded, David had stopped short, watching the closing

door of the garage. And again he felt that he himself was under observation.

He debated silently what he could do about this odd coincidence. One couldn't very well bang on the garage door and say to the person who opened it: 'Excuse me, but you're awfully like a corpse I've met.'

He decided to wait. He moved again into the road and stood a few paces away with his gaze fixed on the entrance to the alley. For twenty minutes he waited before he decided that his vigil was ridiculous, for he might wait all day without developments, and Tess, who was going to telephone him, might wonder if he had forgotten her.

At the corner of Terrapin Road a chance side-glance again revived his speculations. The man who had been in the garage was sitting back in a passing taxi, apparently lost in thought and oblivious of all pedestrians, including David. David caught sight of the top of the big parcel, which the passenger was steadying with one hand. At the risk of his life David darted across the road, leapt at a taxi that had just set down a passenger, and told the driver to follow the one in which rode the corpse's counterpart.

'I'll make it worth your while,' he shouted, 'your fare plus a quid. Get going.'

They swung forward at a good speed. Through the window behind the driver's head David called out: 'He's still straight ahead, step on it and we'll just beat the red light.'

The driver obligingly stepped on it. There was enough traffic about to make their chase inconspicuous, and they reached the main road, where buses and other vehicles both helped and hindered their pursuit.

'What's up?' the driver asked, in a rapid over-the-shoulder staccato.

'Fellow – er – Case of false pretences,' David improvised, thinking of his quarry's inexplicable resemblance to the dead.

'Cor. Can't stand twisters.' The driver increased his speed – so efficiently that he overshot the mark, for the taxi they were pursuing had crept to the centre of the road, slowing down for a turn to the opposite side. Some yards further along, on the near side, David thumped on the window and said: 'This'll do me.' He leapt out and saw his man, still carrying the parcel, entering a small shop over which was the sign FANCY GOODS EMPORIUM.

And then a frightful misgiving assailed him. He tapped both pockets of his flannel trousers, those in his tweed jacket, and in his raincoat. He hadn't a farthing on him. He hadn't even got his papers. Yesterday he had been in uniform, and the upheavals of the morning had occupied his attention so completely that when he finished dressing – with Bob Carter chattering like a magpie – he had forgotten to transfer possessions from one set of clothes to another. Bob had bought their first drinks in "The Volunteer" and refused a second. Mrs. Newland had provided one drink and refused another. If he had tried to buy a paper, instead of picking up a stray one, he would have discovered the fact that he was penniless earlier.

Feeling that he was making a complete fool of himself he spluttered: 'Well, that's extraordinary – '

The taxi-driver's experienced eyes had not missed the agitated search from one pocket to another. 'Extraordinary, eh? What is, may I ask?'

'I – er – look here, you'll have to drive me back to near where we started.'

'And what good will that do me?' There was a nasty gleam in the other's scrutiny as he issued the challenge.

'It's awfully careless of me, I changed my clothes and forgot my change, if you gather what I mean.'

'A quid you promised me, on top of the fare.'

'You shall have it.'

'What if I drive you back and at the end of it you've got nothing but a good story?'

David felt exasperated. 'Listen. I only came out of hospital yesterday, and there I got out of the habit of thinking in terms of ready cash. I was there for four months.'

"'Ospital or quod, which?"

'Hospital, you – ' David checked a forcible term. 'I'm in the Air Force, that's how I got bent. I haven't a penny on me, you can take me on and get your fare, or call it a day, or call the police. I don't care.'

Again the worldly-wise eyes of the driver took stock. 'You look all right, young feller-me-lad. I'll take a chance. 'Op in, and 'eaven 'elp you if it's a monkey trick. I s'pose I can go on guessing why you've lost interest in the chap that done you down.'

'Hi – just a moment!' David's glance had been swerving repeatedly from his driver to the open door of the shop over the road, and now the man he was chasing had reappeared, without his parcel. David's breath expired in a long sigh of astonishment and disappointment. Was the man opposite so very much like the corpse, after all? There were so many southern-looking men about that superficial resemblances were bound to occur. Had his own excited imagination conjured up the illusion of a startling likeness?

He might be on a wild goose chase. Or rather a wild alien chase. For still unshaken was his conviction that neither this fellow, who had behaved so furtively at the garage in the alley, nor the murdered man, was British.

Black crinkly hair was common enough. More so than that particular formation of flat pulpy features... Was there a link between the two? Or not? David's decision wavered.

'All right,' he said at last, 'let's get back; 15 Terrapin Road.'

'Cor, that's where the murder was. Now remember what I said. If you're all right then it's all *right*, if you get me.'

'Carry on.' David climbed in. On the way he brooded over Mrs. Newland's story of the seafaring man and the copper-handled dagger. What ought he to do about that? And what about Tess? He had begged her to wangle time off for lunch, and had said that he would be hanging on to his end of the telephone from twelve-thirty onwards in the hope that she would ring up. He didn't know what time it was now, his watch was in his uniform.

They reached Terrapin Road. The driver stared at the policemen as he stopped. 'Cor, don't tell me it's you that done the crime?'

'Not me. I'll pop in and get some cash. If I don't emerge within five minutes you can send part of that squad after me.'

'A taxi fare's not a jokin' matter.'

'I'll be seeing you.' The improvised enclosure had been removed from the front steps, one of which showed a white patch where it had been scraped. David rang the bell, he hadn't even a latchkey. Annie appeared and he bolted upstairs. The phone in his room was ringing and he made straight for it.

'Hullo – Tess! Heaven to hear your voice, darling. Where are you?'

Tess's clear voice came over the line with a touch of asperity in it. 'Actually I'm at the "Ivy" in West Street. It's one of the few places I'm happy about going in when not accompanied by a gent.'

'You won't be unaccompanied for long. I'll be – '

'You said we might lunch here, if you happen to remember, and the waiter's looking at me as if even he is expecting me to eat sooner or later. I don't know a lot about restaurants, but I've got a rough sort of idea that they were invented to supply people with food.'

'It was only a "might happen" date. You were going to let me know.'

'And I rang through half an hour ago and said definitely I'd be here at one.'

'I didn't get the message.'

'Where were you?'

'To start with I was in "The Volunteer".'

'If that's all I matter!'

'I'll come right along now.'

'Don't you dare, I swear I'll make a scene. I believe you're sozzled.'

'No, darling, really, it's just that I got on to a clue – '

'If this is going to be a thriller, I prefer to get mine from a library.'

'I'm sorry you're annoyed – '

'I'm not just annoyed. I'm sizzling. Our lunch is off. I'm going to have it alone, I've only got till two-thirty.'

'I haven't the faintest idea what the time is. I'm terribly sorry. I'll explain, Tess. Start eating and keep on eating, please do, and I'll fairly dash along. I say, you don't mind old flannels, do you, darling?' The door opened, the taxi driver appeared, glowering across the room. 'Oh, lord, *you*. You haven't given me five minutes, you old crook, have a heart, I'm talking to the girl of my dreams. I'd never have got mixed up with you if men didn't go about looking continental.'

Again Tess's voice – and now it was far more gentle. 'I say, David, if you're not feeling fit I'll come right along to you. I think perhaps they let you out of hospital too soon.'

'I'm all right, poppet. Only an awful man is standing over me as if he wants some money and the house is surrounded by police – and oh gosh!' Bob Carter had just come on the scene. 'I simply can't cope with *you*.'

Bob's protests were lost as Tess said: 'Darling, you're raving. Let me phone Dr. Toomb, he knows all about you.'

'Not all, I hope. Just the nice bits. Shut up!' The command was meant for Bob, but it was shouted near enough to the mouthpiece to bring further suggestions of medical aid from Tess.

'No, no,' David protested. 'I'll be there in – let me reckon – fourteen minutes ten seconds, given a fair wind and no fog. I've got a taxi driver right by my side now and he'll deliver me intact. Order lots and lots of something very tasty, it's wonderful how eating passes the time. And have some expensive wine – ' But Tess had rung off.

Bob was saying: 'Look here, old boy, I simply must tell you – '

The taxi-driver's expression had become almost menacing. David said: 'Save it up Bob, can't you see I'm suffering from a crisis?' He rushed to the wardrobe, extracted his wallet and some loose cash from his uniform pockets, and demanded: 'How much do I owe you, driver?'

The man's face cleared at the sight of actual coins after so much verbal complication. 'It's three and threepence on the clock, sir.'

'You're married?'

'Come to that, I am, but it's a matter of the fare and what you promised on the top of it.'

'Here's thirty bob, that's the fare and the extra quid and a bunch of flowers for your missus with my best respects. Now we'll take off for West Street and I'm asking for a world record.'

Bob's voice followed them down the stairs. 'I got old Sir Cuthbert right on the floor inside three minutes and he's furnishing me from top to bottom, and what's more, some of the stuff will be in transit from the warehouse to the "Twenty-Six" this very afternoon.'

'Good. Excellent,' shouted David.

Bob had reached the hall. 'I'm going to recruit lots of voluntary women – '

'Magnificent.' David dashed past Miss Trindle, who was talking to Inspector Gracewell near the front door. She was wearing a brown fur coat that made her look like a weatherbeaten rabbit. David caught the phrases: 'I'm sure there's something funny about Thelma going, her mother never let her – '

The rest was lost as Bob shouted from the front steps: 'I want you to help arrange the stuff.'

'Speed,' said David, as again he dashed into the taxi. 'Speed is all I'm interested in.' So hasty was his movement that an enterprising press photographer – believing in the delusion that the elusive is always worth securing – raced to the edge of the kerb and levelled his camera. David saw to it that he presented a nice view of the top of his felt hat.

EIGHT

TESS CARMICHAEL had completed her training at a London hospital before she decided that she wanted to specialise in children's nursing. The imminence of war had interrupted the special course upon which she embarked and she took a post at St. Margaret's Day Nursery – which ceased to be a day nursery when London children were sent to the country. Since the outbreak of war the institution had served as what Tess described as a transit depot for children who had not been evacuated, who for some reason or another needed temporary refuge. Thus the work kept the staff busy by day and night; the matron, Tess, and two trainees, had an on- and off-duty schedule that they arranged between themselves from week to week.

Tess had met David through her brother Michael. Mike had got entangled in his parachute during a practice operation and Tess had received a characteristic telegram: '*Am slightly dented stop hospital is dry stop prefer gin to flowers.*'

She had taken him some gin – acting against all the ethics of her training – and borrowed a glass from the man in the next bed to enable her brother to imbibe a furtive drop.

The man in the next bed was David Heron. It appeared that he wanted his glass returned. Mike suggested putting some gin in it, by way of interest on the loan.

Mike left the hospital after a fortnight. But Tess had continued to visit it, on every possible occasion, during David's long convalescence after an injury to his spine. And now Tess was sitting at a corner table in the restaurant in West Street, sipping an aperitif and watching the flow of lunch time arrivals. This was a favourite haunt of theatrical stars. Some were not so famous, and inevitably there were those who came simply to enjoy the proximity of the famous.

Tess was brooding over her telephonic conversation. She remembered the introductory gin, and hoped that David – released from the discipline of hospital – was not going to turn out to be a drunkard. He'd been calling someone an old crook and raving about

43

continentals, and police surrounding the house... All rather sinister. She must remember to ask him whether he had cracked his head as well as his spine when he crashed.

As yet Tess knew nothing of the murder. St. Margaret's, as it happened, was not far from Terrapin Road, but little gossip penetrated into the children's home, and Tess had not seen any paper except a morning one.

She took the mirror from her handbag and gave a tweak to her white turban. She had changed hastily from uniform into a green outfit in which she rather fancied herself. After all, it had provoked three proposals of marriage during the time she had been wearing it.

If it hadn't, then something or other had provoked them. She gave her face a quick once-over and decided that it was passable. Blonde curls bobbed under the white turban, her skin was fresh and her grey eyes were clear. She had used a brilliant lipstick and reminded herself that she must wipe it off before she returned, in case she ran into Miss Allardyce, the matron.

Glancing up, she saw that David had arrived. He walked quite steadily between the tables, and though he was smiling delightedly he bore no signs of intoxication. The commissionaire, trotting behind him, was trying to peel off his raincoat – a feat that was an anatomical impossibility while David was extending both hands in greeting.

'Tess darling, you look wonderful. I'm awfully sorry I'm so late, though actually I'm not, as we didn't definitely fix a time, did we? What's that you're drinking? Have another. Oh, here's Mario himself. How are you Mario? Get us a couple of your special what-d 'you call-ems, will you?'

Mario waved an eloquent hand, commanding cocktails.

'And a bottle of Pommard, if it's still on tap.' David ran on enthusiastically: 'I never realised till this moment, Tess, what a smasher you are.'

'Thanks, but there's no need to tell all London.'

'Sorry. Was I shouting?' David sat down, his raincoat having been successfully removed.

'Funny,' said Tess, 'it's quite an effort getting used to you in clothes. Uniform yesterday and now this casual-student effect. But

I did like you in that funny pale blue bed-jacket. It made your eyes look almost blue, which is silly, because actually they're hazel.'

'An appealing shade of hazel, don't you think?'

'What was making you so scatty when I phoned?'

'Oh, this and that. I've had the very hell of a morning. My first day of freedom, and it had to be tinged with crime.'

'What have you been up to?'

'I'm innocent as innocent. What are we going to eat?'

'I've ordered clear soup and chicken done with rice and paprika, and I'll probably top off with a slice of *apfel-strudel*, if that's the right name for oblong apple tart.'

'The same for me,' David told the waiter. And to Tess he added: 'Thank heaven you haven't any anti-eating complexes, like some girls I've met.'

'You've met lots, haven't you?'

'Well, touring with shows isn't anything like living in a monastery.'

'Did you carry on with the girls in the company?'

'Never. I saw them in their true light on railway trains on Sundays.'

'Train lighting isn't what you might call true.'

'I assure you it is. Always take a journey with a man before you marry him. What about a run into the country tomorrow, then we can be married on Wednesday?'

'I'm on duty all day from seven a.m. till four in the afternoon. And we can't be married because we're not even engaged.'

'Of course we're engaged. We'll get a ring this afternoon. My cheque book's awfully healthy because I haven't been using it lately. The hospital bed and the palsied hand and all that.'

'Not this afternoon, David. I told you I've only got till two-thirty and I shall want every minute of the time for eating. What a blighter you are for going off at tangents, you were just going to tell me about tinges of crime when you raced off about food and getting married.'

'It was you who raced off, getting nosey about my past.'

'So you admit you've got a past.'

'If you really want to know, I've dillied and dallied a bit, and once I got as far as being engaged, but that didn't set me back at all, because it turned out the girl was already married to a chap who could bite his own heels while he was walking on a wire. Also he could support two blondes with his teeth while the orchestra played "Rule, Britannia". He used to get terribly red in the face, I'm told, but that didn't make the marriage any less legal. What about your own past, now we're in a morbid, probing mood?'

'Terrible,' Tess sighed, turning her glass in her fingers. 'It would take six months even if I only told you the less scarlet bits.'

'I don't believe you. Mike said you'd had lots of chaps after you and you'd just waved them away.'

'Oh, well, waving keeps the hands supple.'

'You should write a brochure on Arts, Feminine, the Cultivation of.'

'The arts are your cup-o'-tea, not mine. You can do the brochure and be the first actor-author-airman *cum* feminine psychologist.'

'I don't want to do anything except sit here and gaze at you and think how gorgeous it will be to be married on Wednesday.'

'Definitely not Wednesday. Two of my babies are being vaccinated.'

'Bring them to the wedding. As you're so attached to them you could carry them instead of a bouquet.'

'Little human rosebuds,' said Tess, with a deliberately treacly smile.

'Oh, I say, that's rather too much!'

'I'm handing you tit-for-tat for all your lyrical quotations.'

'No need to go completely rose-buddy over it.'

The waiter removed their plates. David said suddenly: 'We had a lovely murder at 15 Terrapin Road last night.'

'Murder!' Tess's eyes widened. 'I'd call that more than a mere tinge of crime. Did you really? Tell me all about it. I'm shuddering already. I say, don't fill my glass again, this wine's pretty heady and I've got to stay clear-minded.'

'Do let me ply you with it. Insidiously. Them's the tactics for any reluctant lady.'

'Insidious, that just describes you,' sighed Tess as she found her glass full. 'I must say that this Pommard is rather heaven. I'm afraid it costs a thousand pounds a bottle.'

'What does mere cash matter?'

'I've got a practical mind.'

'Excellent. You can be a miser and I'll be a spendthrift and we'll be happy ever after.'

'What a hope you've got! I adore expensive hats. And still more expensive shoes. And in a perfume department I'm a positive devil.'

'You can give a diabolical demonstration as soon as we've finished lunch.'

'No time.'

'You ought to have got compassionate leave for the afternoon.'

'Compassion is a word that Sister Allardyce wouldn't understand.'

'She sounds as if she ought to have her heart broken, just once to make her human. It ought to be a compulsory part of every women's education.'

'From which I gather that you think men can be human without being heartbroken?'

'Almost too human, Tess.' He slid a hand across the table and pinched her wrist.

Tess flushed. 'I thought you were going to tell me about a frightful murder.'

'I've gone off the murder. My thoughts are running in very different – and far pleasanter – channels.'

'But please, I'm all agog.'

'Oh, if you're agog I give in. Here I go in an attempt to de-gog you.'

'Full details and no cheating,' said Tess.

NINE

'THE DETAILS,' SAID DAVID 'are rather meagre as far as I can supply them. A copper noticed one rope ladder over one creeper-clad wall – to wit, our back garden wall – this morning. He tried the nearest gate. It was open and lo and behold! There before his startled eyes was an unfortunate gentleman lying huddled up with a knife between his shoulder blades.'

'Gosh, horrible!' was Tess's brief comment.

'No, I'm wrong.'

'Wrong?'

'About the startled eyes. They wouldn't have been startled even by fifty bodies. I ask you, have *you* ever seen a British constable startled?'

'I've never done anything to startle anyone.'

'How dull. You need provocation and guidance.'

'We've got as far as the unstartled bobby.'

'Oh yes. That was at seven-twenty this morning. Annie, Mrs. Meake's new handmaiden, was creeping about the basement. She admitted the copper via the back door. He'd have a job to retain his traditional calm when he confronted *her*. She's six foot and intensely bony and her conversation tends to be erratic. The bobby phoned the police station, and no doubt he jotted down a few well-worn phrases in his little book. I didn't see him because I was snoring.'

'If you snore I shan't marry you.'

'I don't know whether I do or not. You'll have to marry me to find out.'

'The policeman is now writing in his little book.'

'Oh yes. It transpired that the dead man hadn't any papers on him, there didn't seem to be anything to fix his identity. Mrs. Meake, poor dear, was the first to be asked if she recognised the body. She didn't. Nor did Annie. By this time a detective inspector was on the scene making inquiries. He's an amiable slow-motion kind of chap, name of Gracewell. Gives an impression of being casual, but I had a sudden vision and decided that he was – yes, relentless is his adjective, just as insidious is mine.'

'Worse than insidious,' murmured Tess as he refilled her glass. 'I shall be seeing rainbows at any moment.'

'You need a cognac to bring on the rainbows. We'll attend to that in a moment.'

'No cognac,' said Tess.

'Your lightest whim is my command.'

'Then get on with the story.'

'That's a fine way to take my pretty phrases.'

'Pretty phrases would be lovely in a lunchtime as long as eternity. We got as far as the relentless Gracewell.'

'Oh yes. He went right through the house, asking everyone if he or she had heard any queer noises. Nobody had, except of course the plumbing, which we were all too polite to mention. One by one we were led to inspect the horrid corpse. No reactions. The corpse, incidentally, possessed a most unpleasing mug. Why he brought his mug into our garden is a big question mark.'

'Perhaps he was on his way to one of the other houses in your street? There are one or two shady establishments in Terrapin Road.'

'And don't I know it! But in that case why throw a rope over our wall? Much more sensible to throw it over the wall of whichever house he wanted to get at. In any case, the walls dividing the gardens are just as high as the outer one, that is to say about seven feet, so he couldn't have meant to go any further along the street, via our garden, or he'd have trailed his rope ladder along with him, and he'd have been dangling it when he was killed.'

'But didn't you say the policeman came in through the gate? Why didn't the victim use it?'

'It was usually kept bolted, and only unbolted for the dustman. So it looks as if the victim was familiar with the lay-out, and took it for granted that the gate would be bolted as usual, and therefore didn't even try it. Or it may have been the murderer who used the rope ladder to get in, and then he left by unbolting the gate from the inside. But as the rope ladder is a hefty clue, it seems worse than careless to have abandoned it. Of course, someone may have left the house by the back way, done the deed, and departed through the gate, without discovering that the ladder was there.'

'How many doors open from the house into the garden?'

'One in the basement. And there are french windows in the back hall floor room, with about four iron steps leading down to the garden. Shouldn't think those steps are ever used, as that's Thelma Meake's room and she doesn't like fresh air.'

The waiter's attentions again interrupted the discussion. Then Tess asked: 'How many people are there in your house? It's three stories high, isn't it?'

'You get full marks for observation.'

Tess smiled. 'I've taken quite an interest in number fifteen since I met you. I often take the kids from St. Margaret's for walks round that way, *en route* for Belmont Crescent, where they can play in the garden.'

'I'll remember that. A trifle of outdoor play might do me quite a lot of good. Well, let me see, there are about nine people in our house altogether. No, ten counting Annie and when Lipscott's not away at sea. He's the Merchant Navy chap I've mentioned to you at odd times.'

'Is Lipscott there now?'

'No. I suppose he's rolling on some far wide ocean. In the basement there's a kitchen and a large front room that's vacant at present, it was fitted as an air-raid shelter. There's also a small room that's used for storage, mainly of trunks and stuff that people have left behind when they hadn't got anything better than promises by way of rent. Then, taking it bed-sitting-room by bed-sitting-room and starting on the hall floor – Miss Trindle's got the hall floor front. She, by the way, has decamped today. Doesn't like the criminal atmosphere.'

'Isn't her clearing out a bit significant?'

'Might be. But I can't imagine her doing a murder, she's one of those thin thwarted females.'

'I wouldn't do a murder if I were thin, but if I were thwarted I might.'

'I don't think she'd have drawn attention to herself if she's the one. In any case, we must remain impartial till we've got something to bite on. Mrs. Meake sleeps on the hall floor, in the room behind

Miss Trindle's, and I'd guess she goes to bed too tired to wave a dagger in the early hours, when it's estimated the dagger was waved. Then at the back there's a kind of small conservatory converted into a room, which is Thelma's.'

'The ravishing red-head.'

'She never ravished me.'

'But isn't it traditional for young men lodgers to fall in love with the landlady's daughter?'

'I've never been traditional. Look at the way I left the well-bred, if impoverished, family circle to become a vagabond actor. And we've discussed Thelma more than once. She's the one blot on an otherwise ideal household. The only reasonable thing she ever did was to disappear for six months. Just before the war.'

'Where did she go?'

'The answer is the now extinct lemon. We never discovered. She returned, walking in in time for Chamberlain's declaration of war speech. With not a word of explanation, even to poor old Meakie.'

'Inconsiderate, I call that.'

'Oh she's stupid and vain and you never know what colour her hair's going to be, except that it'll be some shade that nature would blink at. She's as lazy as a sloth and she wants to be a film star – a job that needs more energy and determination than any coalheaver ever had. In peace-time she used to drift round the agents offices, and if she could coerce any fellow with a car she'd blow down to the various studios to badger anyone she could get hold of. Or she'd borrow a bus and go on her own.'

'So she can drive?'

'I'm told she's good with cars.'

'What's she doing these days?'

'She's wangled a job as secretary to a theatre manager. He can't be very exacting. Or perhaps there's such a shortage of the genuine thing that he's glad of any substitute. Her stunt is avoiding doing anything useful. Oh, Thelma's one long pain in the neck. But – by gosh, I've just thought of something! The last time I was at Mrs. Meake's, which is over six months ago, Thelma complained that her french windows wouldn't open properly. All that was wrong was that they made a grating sound if you moved them, they'd sunk a little so that they caught on the uneven top step. She got her mother to have it fixed. I'm wondering if she specially wanted to use those windows noiselessly.'

'A girl like that doesn't make plans six months ahead of a murder. And surely killing would be rather too much like hard work for her type.'

'H'mph. There's also the point – or the alleged point – that she wasn't in the house last night.'

'Aha, an alibi, eh? All right, so long as it doesn't come unstuck.'

'Mrs. Meake herself told me, and she ought to know. Then, moving upwards to the first floor, there are two rooms and a bathroom. Mine's at the back, and I'm innocent, unless I acted in a sleep-walking trance caused by wondering how soon you'll marry me. In the front there's an old chap called Cumberbatch who used to plant rubber or some god-darn stuff in Malaya.'

'Likely suspect?'

'He's eccentric. Keeps himself to himself, as the saying goes. Even cleans his own room and won't let anyone in. He must keep the very hell of a fire going, because Annie dumps endless scuttles of coal outside his door, and he dumps the ashes likewise.'

'Queer, but nothing in that to indicate murderous tendencies.'

'I think he's harmless, though I can't say I like him. He's got vacant eyes and spends his time mooching about and being rude to the waitresses in the "Blue Lantern" round the corner. He's got several bees in his bonnet about reincarnation and the transmigration of souls.'

'Where did you eat, when you lived there before the war?'

'Anywhere handy. Mrs. Meake does breakfasts, and she'll do lunch or supper if you make love to her and let her know in time.'

'What about the second floor?'

'Over me there's a bank clerk called Smedley, the last word in quiet respectability. He's exempted from service because he's slightly lame. In the second floor front there's a German doctor with a square black beard.'

'Need we look further? He sounds like a ready-made slayer.'

'Does he? I thought this country was entertaining only the non-killers, but maybe I'm just ignorant.'

'A German with a black beard would be highly proper as a villain. And if he had a guttural voice he would be positively chic.'

'Being only a simple airman I wouldn't know what was chic when it comes to killing. But Hauptmann certainly deserves to swing.'

Tess's eyebrows went up in puzzlement. David explained: 'Because he will use the bathroom on my floor and he leaves a nasty rim round the bath. A crime meriting capital punishment.'

Tess was suddenly serious. 'I say David – all this cracking at Jerry hasn't made you thoroughly callous, has it?'

David considered the idea. 'I suppose it has, in a way. Funny, a pal of mine remarked only this morning that he thought so. But naturally when I'm after a Messerschmitt I'm out to kill. Just that. To crash the swine, kite and all. The more Jerries in it the better. But I wasn't exactly serious about Hauptmann and the rim round the bath, you know.'

Tess's eyes twinkled. 'You take a load off my mind.'

'Actually my angle on this particular murder is that the victim was such an evil-looking object that he simply invited attack.'

'He hadn't much chance to look handsome by the time you took a peek at him.'

'Dead or alive, he'd got black crinkly hair with side whiskers, a low brow, a squashy nose, and a stubble of dark beard. And he'd got great ears that stuck out like the wings of a barrage balloon.'

'Pretty. Well, if the rim is all that is known against him, we can only leave your German doctor with a question mark after his name. Who comes next?'

'The only other room on the second floor is vacant at the moment. Lipscott, the chap in the Merchant Navy, had it, and he's made some arrangement with Mrs. Meake so he can keep it on, for odd leave times. Funny, because it's a rotten room, small and rather dark. His stuff's still there. Lipscott's a straightforward, optimistic sort of chap, crazy about dog racing. He sticks to a system that never works.'

'Then how does his money last out?'

'It never did. In peace-time when he had a job in a house agent's he used to tap an aged aunt. Of course, now he's at sea he comes ashore with plenty of cash and I suppose there's just time to lose it before he's off again. We now move to the top floor. Annie the handmaiden is in the back room. Then there's another bathroom that Hauptmann would use if he had any sense of what was reasonable. I wouldn't mind how many greasy rims he left on the top floor. And in the top front there's Mrs. Poole, she's the manageress of some shop or other. No, she's a dyer's and cleaner's. I've never seen her, she's new since I was last about the place.'

'She may be a *femme fatale*, the sort for whom men do desperate deeds.'

'Then somehow I don't think she'd dye and clean.'

'An irresistible beauty, a woman with a past.'

'That sort of a bird doesn't live in a third floor front. She gets herself a luxury flat or dies in the gutter. Well, Mrs. Poole completes our cast. Now we come to clues – or can't you bear any more of it?'

'Any amount. I shall stop panting with curiosity only when the villain is laid by the heels.'

'Clue number one. The dagger. I didn't see it, but I heard a strange story of a knife or dagger this very morning. Told to me in "The Volunteer", by the lady who owns that house of cheer. Mrs. Newland was insulted only yesterday evening by a seafaring sort of chap who was offering goods for sale – and among the goods was a long sharp knife of strange design. Query, was it the fatal weapon?'

'If it really was of strange design, that can soon be decided.'

'But Mrs. Newland won't step forward and tell the police about her sinister customer.'

'Was he by any chance your Merchant Navy fellow lodger?'

'Can't have been. Lipscott's at sea, and anyway he's fat and round, a tubby friendly kind of chap. The problematical sailor was tall and lean. And hang it all, Mrs. Newland knows Lipscott.'

'Perhaps the problematical one was a friend of Lipscott's, and did the murder to avenge some awful wrong done to his pal.'

'But no one ever did Lipscott an awful wrong, he's not that sort at all.'

'You never can tell,' said Tess.

'As a noted Irishman once declared.'

'Perhaps the killer wasn't a resident, but a visitor calling on someone in the house.'

'That's more than possible. That gets us no nearer to identifying the victim, and it's still hard to see why an encounter should have taken place in the garden.'

'It might go like this. The victim visits a resident furtively, via rope ladder, finds another visitor already on the scene, an argument ensues. Visitor number two is pursued by visitor number one and overtaken in the garden. *Crime passionel*, grade A.'

'But who at number fifteen, could be so awfully *passionel*? Or inspire anyone to be same? Mrs. Meake's a darling, but she's not young and she's too fat anyway. Any woman who knows her onions can remain attractive with a double chin, but Meakie's got a quadruple one. Thelma – there are thousands of Thelmas, and I couldn't imagine anyone risking his neck for her, because the next Thelma would be just as good. Miss Trindle – no. The Annie wench is batty. Mrs. Poole – as yet uninspected. That's the total female element.'

'The female element might not be on the spot. The murderer and his victim could fall out over a woman a thousand miles away,' Tess remarked.

'Exactly. That leads us back to the point that, however and whyever this happened, someone in the house is implicated. And we've got to find out who.'

'Got to find out, David?' Tess looked puzzled.

He hesitated. 'I don't know why, but somehow this thing has got hold of me. I crack merry jests and all that, but actually it's pretty horrible to have someone done in right under the head of your bed. It's sort of put me on my mettle. I feel it's almost a personal grievance that I must set right.'

'You've only got a week.'

'One can do a lot in a week. Which reminds me, you remember I told you about a fellow called Bob Carter?'

'I certainly do. You Bob-Carter'd me at some length.'

'Well, he's tops for quick work. He's starting an international club, and in less than no time he's got premises, and promises of furniture. He was in my room when you phoned, and my attention was also distracted by a suspicious taxi driver, so I couldn't pay proper attention, but through the chaos I gathered, roughly, that it was only a matter of another few seconds or so before Bob would be serving the first rounds of beer in his unique establishment.'

'I don't like clubs. They're full of fruit machines and awful girls and people pretending to be happy.'

'Bob's won't be. He used to be a communist and marched around on Sundays with banners about Russia, but when Russia got really popular he thought up this new stunt. A sort of all-nations meeting place. He always likes difficult enthusiasms. He's mad they won't have him in the Navy.'

'The Navy may be having a lucky escape.'

'Oh, Bob's all right. Just haywire, that's all.'

Tess reverted to the murder. 'Perhaps the villain – or the victim – was a film agent who's been pestered by your landlady's daughter.'

'But I was told that Thelma wasn't there last night.'

'Then where was she?'

'Staying with an aunt.'

'She doesn't sound like the sort of girl that stays with aunts.'

'She isn't. Not with Aunt Millie Higgins, of all aunts. I wonder where she was?'

'You might make it part of your sleuth act to find out. Ask for the bill, there's a sweet. I shall only just about do it and get changed in time.'

David called for the bill. 'Here we've been nattering about murder, wasting time, when I might have been telling you how adorable you are. You looked lovely beside my hospital bed, but I never appreciated you fully till now.'

Tess said musingly: 'I think I liked you best in bed.'

David almost choked. 'Do you realise what you said? And what's more that the – ahem – sitting on your left heard that remark?'

'I don't care. You're almost handsome with your head on a pillow.' Tess rose.

David snatched up some of his change wildly. He was only too conscious of the fact that he could still blush like a schoolboy.

TEN

THE TAXI CUT THROUGH BERKELEY SQUARE. David said: 'It's awful having such a little time with you, and it's all been taken up with this murder palaver.'

'I wish you'd tell me some more.'

'There isn't much.'

'Well whatever there is. I'll be tickled to death to pass it all on to Miss Allardyce, who revels in crimes.'

David was eager to concentrate upon more vital topics, such as the smallness of Tess's hands and the shape of her profile. 'There's really only one more bit. It's that I saw a foreign looking fellow, stout and swarthy and middle-aged, leaving the garage in the alley behind our house, and that's what delayed me so that I wasn't there for your phone call.'

'Was he so entertaining?'

'A hideous fellow. He was carrying a parcel and I followed him in a taxi.'

Tess was bewildered. 'But why?'

'Because for a moment he looked exactly like the chap who'd been murdered. Same crinkly hair, low forehead, pulpy nose. Gave me quite a shock.'

'It couldn't have been the same man.'

'Obviously not, but on the strength of the resemblance I trailed him to a shop in the High Street. And then, when I had a chance to have another square look at him, I wasn't so sure that the resemblance was extraordinary. I mean, the likeness was certainly there, but I began to wonder if there aren't enough men of that type to make it just an odd coincidence that he should have been in Cannock Alley. What was funny, though, was that he was obviously determined to dodge me.'

'Perhaps they were brothers.'

'You wouldn't expect a brother to go calmly delivering a parcel to a shop after such an event.'

'Did you find out what was in the parcel?'

'No sort of chance. He took it into a fancy goods emporium and emerged without cargo.'

'Not the fancy goods emporium next to the space where there used to be a dance hall before it was bombed?'

'That's the one. You know it?'

'I used to get cigarettes there when I couldn't find them anywhere else.'

'I didn't realise it was a tobacconist's as well.'

'You can buy everything there at odd times, from tinned salmon to lipsticks and crepe-de-chine.'

'Sounds like a black market outfit.'

Tess said calmly: 'I'm pretty sure it is, that's why I always feel like a fifth columnist when I go in. One day, when the smokes famine was at its height, I got a tin of a hundred cigarettes there, and then I had to put ten shillings in a Red Cross box, to try to make myself feel better again.'

'Are you just guessing, or do you know something?'

'I suppose I'm guessing. But there's a queer atmosphere in that shop. Sometimes it's stuffed to the ceiling with goods and sometimes it's almost empty. The man behind the counter is large and terribly smooth and furtive. I bet that parcel you saw being taken in contained something utterly illicit and utterly delicious. Eggs. Devonshire cream. Grapefruit.'

'And bananas and opium,' rapped David. But Tess's comments had started a new line of thought about the man who had behaved so strangely at the garage. He added: 'All the same, I might buy an item or so in fancy goods there, just to see if I agree with your views on the shop.'

'If you can get me a pair of silk stockings without coupons you'll admit I'm right?' Tess said.

'And we'll both fall into the clutches of the law,' David reproved her.

'But just as an experiment. In the course of criminal research. The end would justify the means.'

'And you had the neck to call me insidious,' David sighed.

'I'm awfully short of stockings.'

'What have you done with your coupons?'

'Spent them on fluffy white wool to make babies' boots.'

David slipped an arm round Tess and kissed her. She protested: 'Everyone in that bus can see us.'

'Then let's give them something worth looking at.'

The taxi turned a corner. Tess said: 'Don't let's drive right up to St. Margaret's. Nobby and Smithy were awfully nosey about where I was going. They're the two trainees, you know. I told them I was going for a long walk to clear my complexion.'

'With a skin like yours. What an awful little liar you are.' David tapped on the window behind the driver's head and told him to stop.

Tess admitted: 'It wasn't true about the fluffy white wool either. But shockingly true about the stockings.' She got out. 'Good-bye. Thanks awfully for the lunch.'

'Just a moment. When can I see you again?'

'I'll ring you this evening. Will you be in about six-thirty?'

'Sure.'

Tess darted off and David turned back to settle with the taxi driver.

ELEVEN

MRS MEAKE AND ANNIE seemed to be engaged in demolishing the front room on the hall floor. Some of the furniture was in the hall and a glance into the interior revealed a scene of chaos. Now Miss Trindle had left Mrs. Meake was seizing the opportunity to clean the room thoroughly. Annie was on the marble mantelpiece, circling a duster over the tall mirror above it; it was she who caught sight of David's reflection at an angle and said: 'He's come in, m'm.'

Mrs. Meake, on all-fours, peered from behind a dislodged chest of drawers. 'Oh, there you are. The Inspector wants you to telephone and Mr. Carter left a message, would you go round to Belmont Crescent in case he forgot to tell you, he said.'

'What does the Inspector want?'

Mrs. Meake rose, her tone was scornful. 'Now what would he be wanting? D 'you think he's hankering for a nice talk about the weather?'

'Why does he pick on me?'

'You should be the one to know how to answer that,' Mrs. Meake said. She looked hot and flustered, her make-up was smudged, her henna'd hair was hanging in wisps round her ears.

The carpet had been rolled up, and David noticed that a section of board, about fourteen inches long, was loose. He stooped and found that it could be lifted easily. 'This is queer,' he exclaimed.

'What is? Oh – that. I expect a bit was patched in at some time, where the floorboard was rotten.'

'But all the wood's perfectly sound.' David peered into the space beneath the lifted section, and extracted a newspaper. It was the front sheet of the *Daily Telegraph* for September 11th, 1939.

Further exploration brought nothing else to light.

'Fussing about a hole in the floor,' Mrs. Meake said touchily. 'You must be hard up for something to do.'

'But this hole's been cut deliberately. It looks as if someone's used it as a hiding place, especially as it was so carefully lined with paper.'

'Well,' Mrs. Meake remarked. 'A lot of people hide things under floors and there's no harm in it. You put that bit of board back and mind your own business.'

David replaced the wood, reflecting that what Mrs. Meake said was true. People had odd taste in hiding places, and probably the space beneath a floorboard was as popular as any other improvised safe. But any odd detail seemed significant, after the discovery of the morning. He was surprised to hear a sudden outburst from Mrs. Meake.

'It's not enough that I'm worried and tired out, you've got to come nagging at me about the very floor under your feet.'

'I'm sorry. I know all this is pretty rotten for you. The upheaval and inquiries, I mean.'

She said violently: 'It's worse than that. It's unbearable.'

'Come now, no one's going to think any the worse of you for it.'

'Won't they just! It gives the house a bad name. All the morning there were people pointing and saying: "That's where the murder was done, the place is full of criminals".'

David laughed shortly. 'I for one have never been convicted. And I can't see any of the rest of us sewing mailbags. We're a remarkably law-abiding lot.'

Mrs. Meake burst into tears. David took her arm and murmured: 'There, there, never mind, everything's going to be all right,' and other inane phrases designed to comfort.

Annie stepped from the mantelpiece on to a chair and thence to the floor, saying explosively: 'She's never eaten nothing, not a mouthful's passed 'er lips to-day, not even a cup of tea, only a double brandy I fetched from "The Volunteer" in a cough mixture bottle.'

'That's all wrong,' David spoke with avuncular firmness. 'Now then, Meakie, what about coming down to the kitchen and making me a pot of tea? It'll be like old times if I can do a bit of cadging.'

'There's the Inspector waiting.'

'Where?'

'The phone number's written down, it's in your room.'

'Ten minutes this way or that won't hurt him, when I've got nothing to tell him. Come along, I just fancy a cup of tea and a cosy heart-to-heart.'

They went to the basement. The kitchen at the back was large and cheerfully decorated. The red and white check curtains matched the cotton cloth on the centre table; the rather gaudy china on the dresser added a touch of brightness, a row of aluminium saucepans glinted like silver. Outside there was a shallow area, the garden level was at about half the height of the window. The afternoon sun was bright and a shadow was thrown by the iron steps that led from the garden to the room above.

Surely Inspector Gracewell had paid some attention to those possibly relevant steps? If Thelma's room had been vacant – as Mrs. Meake had declared it was – it could have provided a perfect route to the garden for anyone in the house. Or for anyone – for instance a departed lodger who had retained the front door key – who could get into the house.

David perched on a corner of the table and lit a cigarette while Mrs. Meake filled the kettle and laid the tray.

'You sit down,' he said, 'and I'll make the tea. You know I'm a dab hand at it. A spoonful each and one for the pot.'

'And none for the pot, these days.'

David urged her into the wicker chair by the window. He said tentatively: 'Nothing further's happened to upset you, I suppose?'

'It's enough having police in and out and all their questions.'

There were a number of questions that David himself wanted to ask, but he refrained. The kettle was boiling and he made the tea. Then he went to a cupboard, found a cake, and cut a slice for Mrs. Meake. 'No, not for me thanks,' he said. 'I've just eaten an enormous lunch. Fred Emney was at the opposite table, which was an awfully filling experience in itself. There you are, a plate. This takes me back to the days when I was a flunkey in *The Happy Hypocrite*, but then I wasn't allowed to wet my own whistle.'

'Of all the vulgar expressions – ' Mrs. Meake seemed to relax as she sipped her tea. 'Nice,' she murmured. 'This really is like old times, when you used to come back from touring. I thought you might get a bit uppish, now you're an officer.'

'Taking the kite for a ride might be called an uppish job.' David laughed.

'Funny to remember,' Mrs. Meake continued musingly, 'you were only a slip of a lad when first you came. Remember how I told you the top floor front was a pound a week, and you – poor lamb – you thought that meant food and all, and I had to teach you better.'

'You were very kind. There was I, just an ignorant boy from the country, with the Shylocks in the old home hanging their hats on what should have been my pegs. I'd never have got through without you, bless you.'

'More like a son to me, you've been.'

'Remember that time I took you to the opera?' David was encouraging her reminiscent mood, thinking it would ease her nerves.

'It was lovely.'

'And that day at Goodwood?'

'The money you spent!'

'I saved up for it. What's money, after all? "A good servant but a dangerous master," according to the philosopher. You had white flowers in your hat and a gentleman in a grey bowler blew you a kiss.'

'That was Lord Leafe. I was surprised he knew me after so long.'

'Was that who it was? Lordy-lordy! The very marquis who died in his bath on Jermyn Street. I never knew you'd met him.'

'He used to come and see me in *The Parasol Girl* about three times a week. Nearly thirty years ago – and it seems like yesterday.'

'But wait a moment. Miss Trindle was there when he died. No, not in the bathroom, don't be silly, but in the office of that block of flats.'

'What if she was? I suppose that's how she came to lodge here. Lord Leafe must have mentioned me, but I didn't know how he knew I'd taken on an apartment house.'

'Funny,' mused David. 'Especially if you'd quite lost touch with him. How did he know where you were?'

'I don't know, I'm sure. And of course Meake wasn't my stage name.'

'Didn't you ask Miss Trindle how he came to have your address?'

'She used to get touchy if I asked her. And when she first came I was so pleased that Thelma had just come home again, I couldn't bear to quarrel with anyone. And there was all the excitement over the war.'

'Still, it's queer Miss Trindle never explained.'

'It may have been just chance. I'm not surprised she left Boulter's Court. It was a shocking place, a real scandal. There'd been some funny doings there long before the Marquis died.'

'And if Miss Trindle was the book-keeper she must have known all about them.'

Mrs. Meake sighed. 'It's surprising,' she said, 'how blind innocent people can be.'

The reminiscent interlude was interrupted by the ringing of the front door bell. A minute later Annie called down 'It's all right, it's only Mrs. 'Iggins.'

A heavy tread descended the flight of stairs. David wondered why Mrs. Meake looked so flabbergasted at the arrival of her sister Millie Higgins, who no doubt was calling to learn the latest titbits about the murder. Then it flashed into his mind that Millie had been so ill only last night that Thelma had gone to stay with her. This was certainly a quick recovery.

Mrs. Higgins came in. 'Well, well, well,' she exclaimed, 'if it isn't our Mr. Heron back again.'

'Flight-Lieutenant Heron,' Mrs. Meake corrected. She still seemed perturbed.

David moved a chair for Mrs. Higgins and took another cup from the dresser. Mrs. Higgins said again: 'Well, well well,' – and added cryptically; 'Murder, eh?'

Mrs. Meake exploded: 'I can't stand the word. No one says anything else but murder, murder, murder!'

'Now then, dear, don't upset yourself,' Mrs. Higgins said soothingly. She was a large woman with a generally flabby appearance. Her clothes were decorative rather than practical, and she had attached oddments of fur, chiefly the tails of sundry beasts, to various points of her apparel. She had puffy eyes and a habit of blinking rapidly as she talked. 'No need at all, it's likely to happen to anyone, a murder in the back garden. Now don't get excited, but tell me all about it.'

David interrupted: 'I'm sure Mrs. Meake's had enough of it. There's nothing to tell, if you've seen a paper.'

'I bet it's upset Thelma,' said Mrs. Higgins. 'How is she, Daisy?

She never bothers to come and see me, I suppose she's too taken up going to cocktail parties and driving about in motor cars with rich directors, she's always acted the grand.'

David listened in astonishment. If Thelma wasn't staying with Mrs. Higgins, then where was she? And why had Mrs. Meake invented the fiction? Tess had spoken truth when she said that Thelma wasn't the sort to stay with an aunt.

Mrs. Meake, who had looked momentarily dismayed, recovered rapidly. 'You know perfectly well how Thelma is, Millie, seeing that she's staying with you. So why pretend you haven't seen her?'

Mrs. Higgins's mouth sagged open in amazement. David felt that the situation was too embarrassing to be prolonged, and moved to the door, saying lamely: 'Mrs. Higgins was pulling our legs, Meakie. We can take it.' He went out hastily and went up the stairs two at a time, speculating wildly as to where Thelma might be and why Mrs. Meake had improvised her story. And why, in doing so, she had told one thin enough to be exposed by a few casual phrases.

Supposing, he thought, Thelma had used that dagger on the victim? It would be only natural for her mother to wish to prove her innocent, and therefore provide an alibi. But Mrs. Meake was no fool. It was extraordinary that she hadn't made the alibi a convincing one, she might at least have taken care to prime her sister with the story.

It was strange, he reflected, how odd spots of what might be vital information were coming his way. To clear his conscience he would have to pass them on to Inspector Gracewell.

He found the telephone number scrawled on the back of an old envelope. But before he could lift the receiver and ask Mrs. Meake to get him the number – the main telephone was in the basement – there was a light tap on his door, and without waiting for an answer Terry Lipscott came in, tiptoeing as if he feared to be heard.

'Gosh, Lipscott!' David exclaimed. 'When did you get back?'

TWELVE

TERRY LIPSCOTT WAS, as David had described him to Tess, short and broadly built, with a round boyish face. He was, David guessed, about thirty. He had straight brown hair that tended to stick out in spikes, and clear grey eyes.

He was in the uniform of a petty officer in the Merchant Navy. As David sprang up, his hand sliding from the telephone, Lipscott made a warning sound and closed the door.

'I arrived last night. I – er – want to speak to you.'

'So I'm ready to believe, as you've barged in. Last night, eh? I had no idea – cigarette?'

'Thanks.' Lipscott's rather pudgy hand was shaking. 'As a matter of fact, I'm not supposed to be here at all.'

David's smile faded. 'What exactly do you mean by that? Matter of evading duty?'

'No, no. Nothing of that sort. I'll explain. No one will come in, will they?'

'It's not likely.'

'Mind if I turn the key?'

'Look here, Lipscott, what *is* all this?' David rapped as the other locked the door.

'It's devilish awkward, actually.'

David waited grimly. As no further information came he said: 'I suppose you know what happened here last night?'

'That's just what makes things so deuced complicated.'

'Something connected with the murder?'

'In a way, yes,' Lipscott growled.

'Then why come to me? I'm not Scotland Yard or a father confessor.'

'Have a heart, old boy. You've known me for three years.'

'Four, actually.'

'So I thought you'd be able to advise me. I've got myself into a jam.'

'Gambling again?'

'I haven't backed a dog since before the war, and don't care if I never see a tote ticket again.'

'Then what?'

Lipscott took a deep breath and dropped into the armchair. 'I'll have to tell you the whole thing.'

'That's what I'm waiting for, if it's me you must tell.'

'I – I've got a girl in my room.'

David had to smile again. 'That's not what you might call abnormal. Or murderous – I hope!'

'I met her – at least, there was I in the train from never-mind-where to Paddington, all set for eight days' leave and whoopee. I slept for a bit, then some old ladies bothered me telling me how wonderful the Royal Navy is – it's crazy how they never know the difference between the services. Then I noticed that there was a girl in the corner right opposite, she'd got a kind of green knitted thing over her head, so she looked like a pixie.'

'Ah,' David breathed with relief, scenting a romantic solution to Lipscott's dilemma.

'Come to that, she was awfully like a pixie. Very small and quiet, with a little pointed face. She'd got an imitation leather suitcase on the luggage rack.'

'Just like a pixie,' said David.

Lipscott remained serious. 'And she'd got a shabby green handbag that matched her hood, or whatever it might be called. I don't mind admitting it, I tried to catch her eye, but couldn't. Then I asked her if she'd like a look at my *Picture Post*, and she didn't seem to hear and I felt snubbed, so I went to sleep again to prove I didn't mean to be offensive.'

'Well, you'd been no more than tentative,' David said reassuringly.

'And that was all, till we got to Paddington. I was first out of the carriage, being on the platform side, and I knew that the pixie got out next. I lagged behind on purpose, and suddenly she put down her suitcase and turned round, looking absolutely stunned. I wondered what was the matter, and asked her, chancing being ticked off. Well, she'd left her handbag in the carriage.'

'And you streaked back for it.'

'Naturally. But there wasn't a sight of it, and of course there were lots of people about. Anyone might have taken it. The girl began to cry. She'd lost her ticket and identity card and money and everything. We told a porter and he told us where to report it. The ticket collector was a bit awkward, even with me as witness that the girl had actually had a handbag in the train. I paid the fare without her seeing that I did; and shut him up. We went to the lost property office, but there was nothing doing. Then I suggested that we might have a cup of coffee in the refreshment room. Pixie argued a bit, but I practically carried her off by force. You can't leave a penniless kid standing around at Paddington.'

David said dubiously: 'I suppose she was on the level?'

'She'd got eyes like forget-me-nots.'

'Of course, that settles everything.'

'In the refreshment room she told me she'd got to get to a factory at Acton by next morning. That would be this morning. It was a puzzler how she was going to get a night's lodging and her fare on. I offered to lend her a spot of money and she wouldn't hear of it. She said she'd be all right on the station and could walk the rest of the way as soon as it got light.'

'I had no idea pixies were so independent,' David remarked as Lipscott paused.

'She was absolutely stubborn, about taking any money. I told her there must be some kind of hostel where she could get a bed and you'd have thought I was suggesting she should spend the night in jail. Then I wondered if she'd come here. I put it to her that Mrs. Meake was a good sort, and would let her have a room or a shakedown, and again she raised the money argument. Wouldn't even accept my offer to guarantee that she'd pay later. I was fairly stuck.'

Re-living the argument, Lipscott had become quite downcast. For some moments he was silent, before he continued: 'Suddenly I had a brain-wave. I said I'd got an empty room here and made out that I wouldn't be using it anyway, and suggested she should have it. Well, you could have knocked me down, after all the times she'd said no, when she accepted straight off. I smuggled her in, and gave her the tip where the bathroom is, the one on this floor.'

'The one on the floor above you would have been safer. There's only Annie and one other dame up there.'

'But that's where I spent the night.'

David grinned. 'I believe you, millions wouldn't.'

'And I've been there all today, except for when I've tried to get in my own room. The girl won't open the door.'

'Gosh! I suppose she's all right?'

'I can only hope so.'

'Are you sure she's still there?'

'She must be. The door's still locked. Last night I told her to put something against the bottom of it, so the light wouldn't show, then I slid to the top floor. The bathroom door was only tried once last night and twice this morning.'

'That's the devil of it, everyone uses the one on this floor.'

Lipscott went on: 'I was awake bright and early, and after I'd come round from wondering why the ship was so steady, I realised I'd be wise to get out before that door was tried too often and someone started thinking things. Then I heard a cockney voice squealing something outside on the landing, and another voice I didn't know – a woman's – saying: "Murder, I can't believe it," or something to that effect.'

'The cockney must have been Annie, she's the new wench, and the other might have been Mrs. Poole, she's the new tenant in the top front. As for the murder, a man – believed to be a foreigner – was stabbed in our back garden some time during last night.'

'I gathered that something pretty desperate had happened, because I waited till all was quiet, then I tiptoed to have a peep from the landing window. The garden was fairly seething with police. And then I saw the body and a big chap covering it with a bit of sacking. I nipped down at high speed and gave a pre-arranged signal to the pixie, who'd locked the door on the inside. When I'm away, you know, it's kept locked. Mrs. Meake's got one key and I've got the other, so from outside everything seemed normal this morning. Well, the pixie didn't open the door and didn't even answer.'

'May have been still asleep, tired after the journey.'

'I was scared I'd be spotted, so I darted back to my hide-out. And there I've been all day, trying to contact my girlfriend on and off.'

'She can't have been asleep all the time. You're a first-class fool, Lipscott. Why on earth didn't you confide in Mrs. Meake? You know she's a thundering good sport, she'd have helped you to fix the girl up for the night and you wouldn't have had a guilty secret. And lordy, you must be starving.'

'I'm a bit peckish. Luckily I had some biscuits and a ration of chocolate in my suitcase, and I gave half to the kid. I could do with a square meal right now, and I bet she could. I can't think why the devil she won't open the door. I think she's got wind of the murder somehow, and she's nervous.'

'It's devilish queer,' said David. 'You must get in that room even if you have to bust the door in.'

'I don't want to frighten her.'

'Frighten her, my foot! She's up to some hank-panky.'

'You couldn't say that if you'd seen her. She's wonderful, just like – well, it's hard to say what she's like.'

'A pixie,' yawned David.

'During the morning I heard Hauptmann going out, so I slipped into his room to take an eye-full of the road in front and it was full of cops and nosey people. I saw you going down the street, with Bob Carter, that's how I knew you were here. My idea, last night, was that the pixie and I could slip out this morning together and get some breakfast and I'd see her safely to Acton, where some kind of a welfare madam at the factory is going to fix her up with a billet.'

'This house will almost certainly be under observation for days,' David remarked. 'Maybe weeks.'

'When she decides to open the door I might smuggle her out by way of the garden.'

'A first-rate method, if you want publicity,' David retorted.

'You aren't being very helpful.'

'My dear chap, you bring an unknown waif into the house and there's a murder and now you're stumped how to get her out. And I'm supposed to know the answer.' For a moment or so David considered the possibility of Lipscott's protégée having committed the crime; her behaviour was erratic enough to provoke any wild speculation. 'What time did your train arrive?'

'Five-past nine.'

David felt relieved. What was almost certainly the fatal dagger had been on view in "The Volunteer" while Terry was still in the train, trying to scrape the girl's acquaintance. It was highly improbable that she could later have gained possession of the dagger to kill a man in the garden of a house that she had never heard of till that night. There was absolutely nothing to connect her with the affair, except that chance had decreed she should spend the night here. David asked suddenly: 'Do you know a tall thin old sailor who wears a yachting cap and a navy scarf with yellow spots?'

'I should hate to,' said Lipscott. 'Why?' As there was no explanation he went on: 'I'm hanged if I know how to get that girl under way. And it'll be awkward for her if she doesn't turn up at the factory today.'

'She might chance just strolling out. Various people come and go, the police aren't out to interfere with peaceable citizens, and they may not be sure of the appearance of every resident. Inspector Gracewell would be, because he's the chap who combed us through one by one.'

'Lucky, he must have taken Mrs. Meake's word for it that my room was empty. I know she took him over the house I heard them talking as they passed the bathroom.'

'I'm surprised he didn't investigate. But I don't think he was really suspicious about the inhabitants. There wasn't a guilt-provoking feature among us, so far as I know. And no forced locks or broken windows. I believe they photographed the basement doors and windows for fingerprints. As for your pixie – that's all I can suggest. At the worst, if she's stopped, she can tell the truth and she'd have the ticket collector at Paddington to corroborate her story about losing her bag.'

'She'll just say no to everything I suggest.'

'Then she'll die of slow starvation.'

'I wish you'd persuade her, Heron.'

David said: 'Hang it all, she's your baby. And we've got to get in the room first.' Lipscott looked so despondent that he added: 'All right, if you like I'll have a try.'

They went upstairs quietly. Lipscott tapped on his door, there was no reply. He was visibly nervous. He waited, tapped again, and tried the door.

David said: 'Give a good wallop. You can't let this go on.'

Lipscott banged. Still no response.

David said: 'She's not there.'

'She must be.'

'There's a sort of feeling about a room behind a locked door. Kind of deserted and bleak, when no one's inside.'

'You always were a fanciful chap.'

David, bending to try to peer through the keyhole, was conscious of something beneath his foot – a small lump in the mat. He bent down, lifting the corner of the mat, and straightened up, displaying the key he had found.

Lipscott exclaimed: 'Well I'm jiggered!'

David unlocked the door and switched on the light. The room, as he expected, was empty. The curtains were still drawn across the window.

'She's gone,' Lipscott said flatly, as if he could not believe it even now, and was trying to convince himself. 'She locked the door and left the key.'

'Obviously,' David agreed drily.

'She's gone for good, she's taken her suitcase.' Lipscott moved to the divan, on which the blankets were folded neatly. On the top one lay a sheet of mauve note-paper. He read it in silence and held it out for David's inspection.

THANKS EVER SO MUCH was printed in childish capitals. Nothing more.

Lipscott still seemed staggered. He muttered again: 'She's gone,' and dropped on the edge of the divan.

David conjectured thoughtfully: 'I wonder what time she went? It's a fairly sure bet she decamped very early before the coppers took such an interest in the premises.'

THIRTEEN

'IT'S SIMPLE ENOUGH,' David went on rather impatiently, as Lipscott remained sunk in melancholy. 'You can quite see how she felt, imprisoned in a strange room, and knowing how much she'd have to explain if she waited any longer to get to her destination. She summoned up courage and just bolted.'

'She might have left her address. I don't even know her name.'

'The main point is that you're out of what might have been a very awkward situation.'

Lipscott said heatedly: 'I wouldn't care how awkward it was. I'd have seen to it that *she* didn't suffer.'

David regarded him reflectively. 'That pixie seems to have got right under your skin,' he said.

'If you want to know, that's just what she did. She had such a little pointed face. And now I suppose I'll never see her again. Gosh, why didn't I – '

Lipscott broke off as Mrs. Meake appeared in the doorway. The door had been left ajar, David had opened the curtains. 'Well!' she exclaimed. 'If it isn't Mr. Lipscott, I wondered who could be talking in here. When did you get back?'

'Er – about ten minutes ago.'

'Well, I never. You've come on leave, I suppose?'

'That's it.'

'I'll get Annie to make up your bed. Where's your luggage?'

'It's – well as a matter of fact I dodged straight up to the top bathroom and I suppose I left it there.'

'Well, what a queer thing to do.' remarked Mrs. Meake. She did not seem greatly astonished. In fact, David reflected, she had quite a habit of taking unusual incidents calmly – she hadn't seemed greatly surprised at finding one of her floorboards sawn through. Probably keeping an apartment house had inured her to human eccentricities.

She had removed the traces of her recent agitation at Mrs. Higgins's visit, and applied a new layer of make-up. She looked normal, but as her eyes met David's there was a defiant steadiness in her gaze. She asked Lipscott: 'What sort of a voyage did you have?'

'All right.' Lipscott spoke absently, no doubt still mourning the loss of his pixie girl.

David said: 'See you later, Lipscott. I'm rather busy.' As he went out Mrs. Meake followed and on the stairs he asked: 'What's this about Thelma not being where you said she was last night?'

'You leave my girl alone,' Mrs. Meake said aggressively.

To leave Thelma alone had always been David's wish. He said: 'Sorry to seem inquisitive, but I'd better know, in case the Inspector touches on the point. I've got to phone him, you know.'

'Thelma isn't at Millie's.'

'So I gathered.'

'It's a shocking thing when your own sister won't stand by you,' said Mrs. Meake.

'Shocking,' David agreed half-heartedly.

They had reached the first floor landing and were outside his door. He added, provocatively: 'Well?'

'Thelma's gone off again, but I don't want anyone to know.'

The phrase 'gone off', as used by Mrs. Meake, had a definite implication. David said: 'I'm sorry.' He remembered how Thelma had disappeared three years ago. Then she had been only nineteen, and her mother was frantic in her efforts to trace and reclaim the girl.

"I don't want everyone talking about it. She's always been a good girl. Oh, yes, I know she's wilful, and she ran away because she was film-struck. Perhaps she's gone off again on some crazy film idea, I don't know. But no one need know and she'll come home again and it'll be all forgotten.'

'It's unfortunate that she's left in the middle of a kind of crisis.'

'It's enough to break a mother's heart, that's what it is,' Mrs. Meake said in a strangled voice.

Half a dozen questions hesitated on David's lips. It seemed that Thelma was determined to ignore her mother's sensibilities. Where was the girl? And with whom? One of her film associates? Or possibly with the theatre manager for whom, so surprisingly, she played the part of secretary. He could not bring himself to interrogate Mrs.

Meake on that point, but asked instead: 'When did she go, exactly?'

'At six o'clock last night. We had a few words about the – well, about what she was thinking of doing, and then she flounced out and said I needn't expect her back. I never thought she meant it. I sat up till after one hoping she'd come in. Then I was that tired I dropped off as soon as my head was on the pillow.'

David made a mental note of the times. Thelma's departure, six p.m. Mrs. Meake – to bed roughly at one o'clock. An unknown man murdered at three in the morning.

He turned suddenly to confront Mrs. Meake squarely, looking directly down into her lifted eyes. 'Is this true about Thelma? Sorry to query it, but you did pitch me a bit of a yarn this morning, about her being with her aunt.'

'It's true as death,' Mrs. Meake declared. Her gaze was unswerving. 'I didn't want to tell anyone, but I can trust you. I know you never understood Thelma, but I love her, and we – I mean you and me, we've always been good pals. Anything you've been short of, I've always tried to help. Remember how I got your dress suit out of pawn so you could go off with the *Purple Twilight* company?'

'I've been more than appreciative, more than grateful,' David said sincerely.

'I never asked you for anything till now.'

'And now you're asking – ?'

'You won't tell anyone about Thelma?'

David was silent for a full minute before he said: 'It isn't fair to ask me that. But of course I know absolutely nothing about where she is, and why, and anyway probably shan't be asked any questions about her.'

Mrs. Meake's face crumpled. It seemed inevitable that the new layer of make-up would be devastated. But she controlled herself, squeezed David's hand, and ran downstairs.

David returned to Lipscott to say: 'If you take my advice, old man, you'll leave it till after black-out to make your first exit from the house. No one saw you come in, and your failure to announce your arrival may seem a bit eccentric. Someone might start wondering if you didn't spend part of the night in the garden.'

Lipscott was hardly listening. 'If only I'd got hold of her name, then I might have a chance,' he lamented. 'I say, do you think that girls read the "personals" in the daily papers?'

'Oh, go and boil yourself,' said David.

FOURTEEN

'HELLO, HELLO—THIS IS DAVID HERON, 15 Terrapin Road. Inspector Gracewell left this 'phone number and asked me to get in touch with him.'

'Hold the line, please.'

A half-minute later the Inspector's voice came through. David said: 'I've returned and received your message.'

The Inspector's soft chuckle was audible. 'And you've taken your time about acting on it.'

Scotland Yard wasn't so sleepy after all. David said lamely: 'Sorry for the delay. One or two matters held me up.'

'Can you make it convenient to be there in fifteen minutes if I come along?'

'Easily,' said David. 'I'll he here.'

While waiting he revolved in his mind the various incidents of the day. Should he tell the Inspector about Mrs. Newland's sailor salesman? It was obviously his duty to do so; the history of the dagger might solve the whole mystery. Mrs. Newland's attitude was inexplicable; there had been no need for her to mention the seafaring man at all if she wished to keep out of the investigation. And why should she wish to keep out of it? She alone had glimpsed that dagger in the holdall when the alleged sailor had been in "The Volunteer", and she had appreciated that it might provide a vital clue.

As for Thelma – David wondered what that erratic selfish girl might be doing. Not that there seemed any likelihood of her featherbrained indiscretions affecting the chances of the discovery of the killer. The most vivid impression, of the whole complicated day, was the resemblance to the corpse of the man who had emerged from the garage. David wished that it could be possible to see the living man and the dead side by side, just for a few moments, so that he might judge how far the similarity existed in reality.

For the present, he decided, he would withhold any mention of the man with the bulky parcel. Nothing but a swift and possibly mistaken impression connected him with the affair that Gracewell was probing. And for the rest he himself would go cautiously, waiting for cues.

Annie stuck her head round the door. David said: 'I wish you'd learn to knock.'

Annie grinned. 'If you take people by surprise they look guilty and give themselves away.'

'Oh, go and – ' David checked a vulgarly violent phrase.

'It's the Inspector,' Annie said.

Inspector Gracewell was now visible behind her. He came in and closed the door before asking, with a jerk of his thumb: 'Is that maid what you might call a reliable witness?'

'Most unreliable,' David said without hesitation. 'She reads a lot of tosh, so I'm told, and raves about films she sees, identifying herself with the heroines. Personally, I never saw the girl before yesterday, but I've seen enough to believe Mrs. Meake's views upon her. I must confess I was quite scared when she confronted me in the doorway, she must be an inch taller than I am, and all I could see was her teeth.'

'I daresay she's useful, especially now servants are rarer than diamonds. And her height wouldn't be so noticeable if only she weren't so skinny.'

The Inspector himself was so bulky that it seemed expedient to stow him away. David offered him the armchair.

'Thanks. Would you fancy a cigar?'

'I think I'd rather stick to cigarettes.' David took one from the hastily proffered case. So far the atmosphere was pleasantly amicable.

Inspector Gracewell remarked: 'Neat little dump you've got here. Everything very compact.'

'Mrs. Meake understands comfort. That's why I always come back. I've stayed in luxury hotels and haven't been able to keep my toes warm.'

'It's just because you've known the house longer than anyone else here that I'm bothering you. And I want you to regard our talk as confidential. Hope you don't mind?'

'Not at all.'

The Inspector said musingly: 'You're an admirer of Mrs. Meake's, so perhaps you'll be biased. But I'm rather anxious to know what may be her interests, apart from the house.'

'I'd be very surprised to hear she had any. This dump keeps her pretty well occupied. Of course she likes a show when she gets time, which isn't often.'

'I think you said she was on the stage herself?'

'She chucked it over twenty years ago.'

'Does she feed you all right?'

'Oh yes, rather.'

'Unusually well, considering war-time limitations?'

'What on earth – ? I can't say how things have been recently. And all along I've only been here on and off, mostly having meals out.'

The Inspector frowned thoughtfully. David concluded that he was inquiring, obliquely, whether Mrs. Meake exceeded ration restrictions, so he added hastily: 'Mrs. Meake's on the level. She's absolutely pro-British, keen on winning the war, and all that.'

The Inspector made no comment. His appearance indicated that if anyone else went short of food, he certainly didn't. His great bulk was settled comfortably in the armchair, and the ease of his attitude belied the notion that there might be any need for concentration or urgency. Yet he suggested efficiency and power. He was, David decided whimsically, like a vast tidal wave that sweeps forward, noiselessly and without frothing, to engulf a town.

'There's the matter of the weapon,' the Inspector said suddenly. 'It's been tested for fingerprints, of course. But the construction of the handle – expect you saw the photograph in the press – makes it the worst possible surface for dabs.'

'Did the photograph bring in any information?'

The Inspector chuckled. 'Plenty. I left a colleague dealing with the fag-end of it, as it was almost the same recitation from one person after another. Slight variations – a sailor, a seafaring man, an old yachtsman – all of them selling junk. He was a foreigner, a German, a Frenchman, or anyway he had a funny way of speaking. It was the same chap, from slightly different angles. One woman is certain he's a parachutist, selling goods as an excuse to go spying from door to door – though what he's supposed to discover from the front halls of houses round about here I can't imagine. He'd got among other items for sale, a knife, a dagger, or just a nasty pointed weapon – it always had a queer copper handle with a feathery design upon it. That's certainly the dagger we're interested in. Were you asked to buy it, by any chance?'

'I certainly wasn't.'

'Nor was Mrs. Meake, so she assures me. But it was offered from door to door last night, at a dozen houses in Cannock Road, and at several in this road. In fact we have a record of its travels to as near as two houses away, and then no further accounts of it.'

'At what time was all this happening?' David asked.

The Inspector consulted his notebook. He glanced up abruptly and unexpectedly. 'Specially interested in the time?'

'Yes, I am.' Now the knife had been identified as the one that had been in the possession of that questionable sailor, Mrs. Newland would have to tell what she knew.

'Why?'

'Because I've already heard about this nautical gent.'

'The whole neighbourhood seems to be gossiping about him. Do you know anything useful?'

'He was in "The Volunteer" round the corner at half-past eight.'

'Oh, was he? You saw him?'

'No. I was in there, but I left before eight. Mrs. Newland, who keeps the pub, told me. She got annoyed with the chap and told him to buzz off, which he did. She saw the knife in his holdall.'

'He couldn't have sold it there. I've got approximate times at which it was produced later, and one accurate time from a Mrs. Padstow at the corner house. She remembered it was exactly nine-fifteen, because there was a radio postscript to the news that she was waiting for, and just as the speaker was announced she was annoyed by her bell ringing. At the next house they didn't answer the door, but of course everyone who did thought it a precious funny time to be hawking anything.'

So the sailor was still in possession of the dagger after the time of arrival of Lipscott's train. The train had reached Paddington at nine-five. The complication of the pixie and her lost handbag, and having coffee, must have delayed him. But even supposing Lipscott had reached Terrapin Road in time to encounter the pedlar-sailor – No, it didn't make sense. He couldn't have guessed that a weapon would be on sale. And no man intent on a violent crime allows a stray girl to attach herself to him. The girl had existed, there was her note as evidence.

Or even, David's thoughts branched wildly, even if she were a myth, a legend invented by Lipscott, it was fantastic to imagine that a man whom Lipscott wanted to kill, and the implement for killing, should both be waiting conveniently for his arrival. Besides, thinking of Lipscott and his ingenuousness, his one-time enthusiasm for dog-racing, and his present keenness on the sea...

It was beyond the bounds of possibility. Lipscott, so far as David knew, had no enemies.

David's attention returned with a jolt to the Inspector, who was relating how various householders had dealt with the sailor.

'If you've traced that dagger to two doors away,' David said, 'you seem to have a pleasantly restricted area for inquiry, seeing that it was found in our back garden.'

'It may have travelled a long way between nine-fifteen and approximately three this morning.'

'Speaking as an amateur, I'd suggest that isn't likely. X wants to kill Y in Terrapin Road, and X buys a weapon that was in Terrapin Road last night. Surely that makes traveling superfluous – until after the deed was done?'

'We don't know how far that sailor got with his stuff. He may have skipped all the houses in this road, after the first few, for reasons of his own and tried another district, in which his first attempt may have resulted in a sale. And of course the actual purchaser isn't likely to report the transaction,' Gracewell smiled.

'I quite realise that.'

'What about this girl, Thelma Meake?'

The question was fired so curtly that David answered in the same tone: 'Nothing about her, that's all.'

'Eh?'

'I mean, better not ask me. I'm prejudiced. I could never stand her, even when she was a kid. All the years I've been here at odd intervals I've taken care to avoid her as much as possible.'

'She'll be out of a job, now.'

David was startled. So the inspector knew of her indiscretion.

'She never had what might be called a steady job,' he said evasively.

'Till she went to work for Schenk.'

'I didn't even know her employer's name.'

The Inspector produced a morning paper and pointed to a paragraph.

It was headed BLACK MARKET. CANNED GOODS CHARGE. David read that Lazarus Schenk, a theatre manager, had been remanded in custody on Saturday on a charge of being unlawfully in possession of a quantity of rationed foods. A lorry driver, also in custody, had confessed to delivering a number of cases of canned lobster and chests of tea at the theatre.

'No bail,' David commented. 'Looks bad.'

Gracewell shrugged his massive shoulders.

'Still,' David pursued, 'he may have an illegal appetite for lobster and tea, but if he's in clink he certainly wasn't in our back garden last night.'

'Obviously not. But I rather fancy making Thelma Meake's acquaintance.'

'Well, even if the boss is behind bars, she's probably still decorating his office.'

'Could you take me along?'

'You don't need an escort, surely?'

'It would make my call seem less severely official.'

'But I've told you, Thelma and I have never been matey.'

'You know her well enough to ring her up.'

'Yes,' David admitted reluctantly. 'Of course. But I don't know what I'd say.'

'That you hope she'll get home early, as her mother's feeling worried with a crime in the offing.'

'I don't like being a decoy bird,' David protested.

'Then I'll look back later and take my chance of catching her. Though I'd rather have seen her without her mother there.'

This was a problem. If Inspector Gracewell returned this evening Thelma wouldn't be at home. Mrs. Meake might be foolish enough to repeat her yarn about Thelma's staying with her aunt – creating further difficulties for herself. Thelma's sensibilities didn't matter a hoot; David doubted whether she had any. After hasty consideration he said: 'I think I'd better tell you – it's an entirely personal detail about Thelma, and I reckon I must spill it to save her mother from bother. I want it understood that it's confidential.'

'It can be confidential if it *is* merely personal.'

'I think I can assure you that it is. A case of girls will be girls. Poor old Meakie is worried enough without having to put on an act to guard Thelma's precious reputation.'

'You've got me guessing.'

'Thelma's gone off on some silly adventure. An *affaire* of some sort. It's upset her mother a whole heap. To protect Thelma she's likely to invent alibis that wouldn't stand checking, and I'd rather save her the embarrassment of it. That's all. I'm hoping you'll leave Thelma alone.'

'I didn't guarantee that, and I can't. I certainly won't let out what you've told me. But I intended to talk to Thelma, whether or not you provided information. Thanks. You've probably saved Mrs. Meake from doing all sorts of embroidery that would have to be unpicked.'

'That was my idea.'

'Mind if I use your phone?'

'Of course not.' David felt uneasy about Thelma, and angry with her. Why had the little fool got mixed up with black market gangsters?

Gracewell asked for a number and repeated it. David interpolated: 'Mrs. Meake or Annie has to get it for you, I ought to have warned you.'

'It's Annie. Hello!' Again the Inspector repeated the number and after a pause said: 'Mr. Schenk's office? May I speak to Miss Meake?'

David could hear a voice at the far end, but not the words spoken. The Inspector said: 'Can you give me a number where I can ring her? Oh, thanks.' He set down the receiver and swung round to David. 'Miss Meake had a headache this morning and left at midday. They gave me her phone number. *This* number.'

'Oh, lord,' was all David found to say. He was relieved to see that Gracewell was rising, getting into his overcoat. But the Inspector hadn't quite finished.

He asked abruptly, standing in the centre of the room and jerking a thumb: 'D'you know Mr. Cumberbatch? The tenant of the front room?'

'I say hullo to him in passing. I haven't spoken to him since my last leave, though I caught a glimpse of him this morning.'

'Where?'

'Oh, among the crowd who were trying to get an eye-full of the scene of the crime. I suppose you plied him with questions, just as you did me.'

'I plied him. But not in his room. He came out on the landing.'

'Perhaps he hadn't got the place straight. He "does" for himself, you know.'

'So I've been told. I called back later. He was out.'

'Well, it's a fine bright day for a walk. The old boy walks a lot.'

'In Malaya, wasn't he?'

'Some years ago. I hardly know him.'

'Ever been in his room?'

'No.'

'Nor has anyone else. Not even Annie or Mrs. Meake.'

'I suppose he's what you might call a recluse.'

'H'm. Queer.'

David said: 'I wouldn't presume to tell you about human oddities. But when I was touring round the British Isles I used to land in a different digs house every week. And the further I travelled the more amazed I got at the number of eccentric people there are. After I met a man who lived on honey and grass, and a woman who drank kummel through a straw, I stopped being surprised. I'd lost the capacity for it.'

Gracewell said: 'Pity, when you're still young.'

'In this year of grace,' David said portentously, 'no one is young.'

Gracewell laughed heartily. 'You're young enough – or you couldn't spout that bit of bunk.'

'You've asked so many questions, I rather think it's my turn.'

'What's the inquiry.'

'That spot of blood on the front steps – was it the victim's?'

'Too soon to come to any conclusions about that,' Gracewell said. 'Well, so long.'

FIFTEEN

IT WAS REMARKABLE, David reflected, that though his first day of freedom was so packed with incident, it seemed to be passing all too quickly for what he wanted to do. In hospital the days had dragged like weeks.

Now it was late afternoon. He was undecided as to whether to fall in with Bob Carter's suggestion that he should go round to Belmont Crescent. From Bob's disjointed information it seemed that his international club was as good as launched, and David found himself thinking what a live wire his friend would be in some Ministerial capacity. But Bob would have to be top-dog; he had ideas, but no patience with obstruction. He might be the next best thing to Churchill as Prime Minister.

And suddenly David burst out laughing, alone though he was, at the vision of Bob with his quicksilver enthusiasm in charge of the country.

There'd be some trouble with the die-hards and Blimps. And maybe Bob wouldn't be so good. Churchill had the art of confronting a sword in the hands of a critic, taking it gracefully, and making it look like a bouquet as he held it. Bob would seize the sword and make a lunge with it, hitting or missing.

David stopped laughing to consider the question of his next move. His thoughts turned to Tess. She wanted some silk stockings. And he was determined to visit the fancy goods emporium in the High Street, anyway, to find out what sort of an outfit it actually was.

He was trying to convince himself that the cause of criminal investigation justified an attempt to get just one pair of stockings without the tendering of coupons, but inadvertently his eyes fell on the newspaper that Inspector Gracewell had left behind, and at the top of the column he read: DON'T SPEND—LEND.

But if you spent – how much? – say ten bob on stockings and discovered a black market operator who'd committed a murder, then surely the Chancellor of the Exchequer would forgive you? He might even give you a pat on the back.

David tugged on his raincoat and was making for the street when he ran into Annie in the hall. She touched his arm. 'I've done it. I've confessed,' she said.

'Good lord!' For a moment David was taken aback. Then as he studied her face he saw her expression, unnaturally tense with glee. As she drew herself up to her full height her skin was moist, her small eyes glittered. 'Who took your statement?'

'One of the gentlemen from Scotland Yard. He asked me how I did it, and I showed him. Like this – ' Annie lunged about as if she were a toreador dodging a bull.

'Dangerous girl,' said David. 'Had you by any chance got a motive?'

'The motive,' Annie said grimly, 'was revenge.'

'For what?'

'I didn't know it had to be *for* anything.'

'Were you cautioned?'

'Cautioned? No. The gentleman just asked me about Mum and Dad. They're ever so well. Dad gets five pounds a week timbercutting and 'e's only got to pay thirty bob for Mum.'

'What'd you mean? Does he make her an allowance?'

Annie cackled loudly. 'That's good! No, he pays it to the Almoner. Mum's in a Home because she carries on a bit funny at times. She sets fire to 'er own nightdresses.'

'Oh, playful, is she?'

'She gets moods. I told 'er, if she gets in one of 'er funny fits tomorrow, I'll sock 'er.'

'Why tomorrow?'

'I'll be takin' 'er for a walk. They let 'er out once a week.'

'When are they going to hang you, Annie?'

Annie looked vague. 'I s'pose they'll 'ave to 'ave me up to Court first.'

'Well, let me know, I'd hate to miss it.' David made for the street. About eight minutes' walk brought him to the fancy goods shop. It was an ordinary enough sort of place, with a jumble of assorted goods in the window.

Behind the counter there was a tall man with a high bald forehead.

The light was not good, but David noticed the patch of discoloured flesh high on his right cheek and round one eye. It was an irregular circle of bright pink flesh that gave the eye a curious brightness as the man looked up. He was leaning in a lethargic attitude against the shelves behind him, on which were rows of innocent looking tins of carrots.

On the counter there were some faded dolls, a toy tricycle, some tins of ointment, and boxes of soap. The rest of the stock, displayed round the remaining two walls, seemed to be so miscellaneous as to defy classification, but David was sure that it would be all of a kind that might be offered for sale without a qualm to any official posing as a customer – or to an inquisitive airman with an ambition to solve a serious crime.

He said: 'Twenty Players, please.'

'No Players. You can have twenty, loose,' said the bald man.

'Good enough.' David studied the salesman during the counting process. The pink patch of skin round his eye looked like a birthmark. His mouth was thin, colourless, cynical. The dead cigarette dangling from the corner of it looked like a fixture.

'There you are. Twenty.'

'Thanks.' David put coins on the lid of a box of soap. 'Oh, have you got any face creams? For a lady, I mean.'

'No. Sold out.'

'Pity. You know what they are over their make-up.'

The man grinned. It was a truly evil leer. 'I know all right.'

Thinking it wise not to attempt too much progress at the first skirmish, David said amiably: 'Oh well, thanks,' and walked out.

He was satisfied with his brief investigation. Nothing significant had been said, the man had given no hint of illicit stock-in-trade. But in the very atmosphere of the shop, as Tess had said, there was something furtive. For one thing – and it was an important feature – the goods on view were so neglected, so dust-covered, that they did not invite genuine trade. To have inquired for commodities not readily visible would have been a mistake. If the shop was crooked, then Pink-eye would be on the alert for a trap every time a new customer walked in.

It's slow and dogged as does it, thought David, remembering an occasion when he had fairly lazed about in the sky beyond Bremen till the flak over the town dwindled. Then he'd dropped his load, and had a delightful view of blazing hell behind him as he streaked for home.

There's a time for dwindling and a time for speed, he concluded, as he cut through side streets to Belmont Crescent. He had forgotten whether or not Bob had told him the number of the house he had taken for his unique venture, but once in the crescent there could be no doubt about its location.

It was 26 – a number that was a happy coincidence for a club purporting to embrace twenty-six nations. Two cars and a furniture van stood in front of the bleak, uncurtained house. Men were carrying chairs across the pavement. A woman in a mink coat stepped from a saloon car embracing a gilt mirror.

As David approached a girl in the navy blue uniform of the Auxiliary Fire Service emerged from the front door with a length of cardboard, followed by another with a step-ladder. He waited while the A.F.S. girl climbed the ladder. The sign was nailed over the door, the words were painted in black on a white ground and were not yet dry: THE TWENTY-SIX CLUB. MEN OF EVERY ALLIED NATION WELCOME.

'So we're off,' David remarked to a woman who had just left her car and was scanning the house. She was about sixty and colossally fat, but she seemed very nimble. There was little doubt but that her destination was Bob's new club, for her vehicle was stacked with an array of kitchen implements.

'It's thrilling, isn't it?' she said breathlessly.

'I suppose that's the word for it.' David was still puzzled as to how Bob was achieving this miracle. In the days of petrol rationing it was no mean feat to get delivery of furniture and other necessities.

'I wonder if you'll give me a hand?' the woman asked.

'Of course.'

She thrust a bunch of saucepans at him and snatched up some more. 'They really ought to have given us some kind of packing cases. Oh, look!'

She sped away along the pavement and David veered round to discover her objective. A man was fixing a camera on a tripod. The woman struck an attitude with her cargo of saucepans. Bob Carter appeared on the front steps and she cried: 'Come here, Bobbie. I'm sure you ought to be in this.'

Bob obediently ran to her and gripped her free hand. The picture was in the livelier journals next morning over the caption, *Duchess of Spraight on Kitchen Front*, with a boxed paragraph to the effect that a new international club had the patronage of the duchess.

There was a good deal of shouting as willing helpers blundered in with goods, colliding and apologising – or not apologising. David said: 'I'm staggered, Bob. What beats me is how you've got the thing moving like this.'

'Genius, me lad. Like a cup of tea? I've had about enough for the time being.'

'I didn't know you ever drank tea.'

'All this has unhinged me.'

'Where shall we go?'

'Anywhere but the "Twenty-Six". The women down there' – Bob jerked a thumb towards the basement – 'are brewing enough tea for a regiment and vamping an unprotected milkman with a view to supplies.'

'What about the "Blue Lantern"?'

'Sanctuary,' said Bob. A formidable grey-haired Amazon was advancing upon him. He shouted: 'Be back in half an hour. You sign for anything that turns up,' and made off at a smart pace. 'That was the Vicar's wife,' he said. 'She knows where you can still buy unlimited gin.'

At a table in the "Blue Lantern", with a pot of tea between them, Bob explained. 'I returned to the attack on Sir Cuthbert and got him singing over his own port. He guaranteed the goods but couldn't provide immediate transport. I spent an hour phoning all the frightful women who used to want to get their unspeakable faces into the papers. After the first quarter of an hour I had two of them on the spot, and I set them on to touting over a sequence of phones. Of course, they got lots of no replies and wrong numbers, but to make up they hooked some fish I hadn't expected. The allied international effort was the sales-talk.'

A large bite at a doughnut silenced Bob for some seconds, before he resumed: 'I only had to say I wanted cars to collect stuff from the Homes-are-Heaven-the-Horley-Pay-Way warehouse. In the meantime Sir Cuthbert had instructed his head Pooh-bah, in a garbled sort of way, that I was to be given my head up to a certain figure, but don't ask me what the figure actually was, because he had a moment of caution and halved it. Then the Duchess of Spraight got him on the phone, and he became delirious with social ambition and dreams of peerages, and all he would say was: "Good luck my boy, it's a worthy cause," so I took that as instructions to tell the head man to double the number we first thought of.'

'Phew! And I thought I knew something about speed,' David grinned.

'Sir Cuthbert was round in the crescent half an hour ago, in a kind of panic in case he wasn't going to get his moneysworth after all. I threw him to the Honourable Delia Darrington, she'll swallow almost anything. But I do wish he'd spend a little money on his grammar, I don't see how we can push him much further up as he is.'

'What still beats me is how you get these Duchesses and suchlike running errands for you. A good cause-yes, of course, but there are scores of good causes.'

'Camera, camera, camera,' said Bob. 'If you knew their lust for the camera. Maybe it's the universal yearning for some sort of immortality – or anyway, survival after death. Why, it's harder to get photographers than titles, I even had to pay one man to come up from Fleet Street.'

Bob poured himself a third cup of tea and gulped it. 'I suppose I ought to get back. I say, Heron, you haven't got anything that would pass as a camera, have you?'

'Afraid not.'

'Pity. You might have brought it along and pretended to take Sir Cuthbert welcoming the first member.'

'Which reminds me, you can't just fling open a door and call yourself a club. There are all sorts of formalities.'

'I get things done and fix the formalities later, I know I'll have to register and have a committee – you, by the way, are on the committee. I thought it looked well, you being a Flight-Lieutenant and a D.F.C. But I rather think I want some kings as patrons.'

'And I used to think the sky was the limit.'

Bob had risen and was already on his way to the door. The waitress hastily scribbled a bill and David paid Miss McDrew, the proprietress, who was in the cash desk. Miss McDrew had greeted him delightedly, and in the old days she had often given him credit. So now he felt churlish as he hurried out with the brief promise: 'I'll be seeing you again.'

SIXTEEN

OPERATIONS IN BELMONT CRESCENT were terminated by the deepening twilight. The furniture van and the cars had departed. David found himself with Bob and the A.F.S. girl, whose name was Beatrice, and her friend Dot.

Beatrice was dark, slim, and eton-cropped. She had apparently been an interior decorator before the war, and now was waving her arms, describing what she meant to do with the walls of the big front room. Dot was little more than a schoolgirl – about seventeen, David guessed.

Bob said: 'You'll have to tackle one room at a time and let it dry before you start the next, because we're opening on Friday at the latest.'

'Darling, I know where I can get some wizard quick-drying stuff. I'll start on this room tomorrow and work in every spare moment.'

'I thought we'd have the bar over there, and sprinkle those hideous little red tables here and there,' Bob remarked. 'The back room can be my office, complete with the two foul desks.'

'I'm going to run that,' Dot broke in. She was small and as impetuous as a puppy. 'You promised I could, you know. I really can type, I'm getting appallingly quick at it.'

'All right, so long as there's no backing out once the first thrill's worn off.'

Dot exclaimed: 'But, honey, there'll be new thrills all the time, with lots of Australians and Greeks and Russians. The next time my ginger-headed Corporal comes on leave we'll tell him to compose us a club anthem.'

'In what language?' David interpolated.

'No words. Just war cries and national noises, with a lot of cloggy bangs to please the Dutch.'

'Cloggy bangs,' said David, 'would please Dutchmen who wear saxe blue trousers, who nowadays can be counted on the fingers of one hand.'

Bob was ticking off the rooms in his fingers. 'Writing room – we'll get a library going, too – and snack room, first floor. Second and third floors, dormitories for use of members who need a shakedown. We'll need a kind of landlady in charge of sleeping quarters.'

David said: 'It's no good looking at me.'

'But wouldn't your friend Tess take it on? She's a nurse or something, isn't she?'

'Yes, and fully occupied,' David said. 'In any case I wouldn't trust any one of the twenty-six nations with her.'

'Afraid of competition?' Dot asked.

'Desperately.'

Beatrice said: 'We'll never get in drinks and food to open at the end of this week. You have to fill in lots of forms and get permits from Food Offices before you can sell a mouthful to a customer.'

Bob said doggedly: 'I'll get permits, don't you worry. If there's any delay over supplies, I'll get voluntary contributions to start on.'

'People haven't got much to spare these days. The best I could do would be a secret tin of herrings.'

'You'd be surprised what they can spare if they feel like it.'

'You need to be a magician.'

'I *am* a magician,' Bob declared.

'In that case, no further argument.' Beatrice glanced at her watch. 'I've got to get along. Come on, Dot.'

The girls went off. Bob remarked: 'They're good troupers. But I'll have to watch what Beatrice does with the walls. She tends towards palm trees and cactus. I must remember to badger the telephone company again, and to get a quotation for crockery.'

Bob pulled out a notebook and held it near his nose to scribble some notes. The light was almost gone, a suddenly wild wind was rattling the uncurtained, cobwebby windows.

Bob dropped and retrieved some papers. Among them was a cheque. 'That reminds me,' he said, 'I must open a club bank account in the morning. One way and another there are quite a lot of fiddling items to remember.'

'Quite a lot,' David agreed drily.

'I wonder if I could link up with country sports clubs. And youth movements. Nothing like youth.'

'If I were you, I'd get the phone in first,' David suggested.

'It would be a big laugh if the Navy thought better of my heart, and called me up in the middle of all this. I say, let's go and have a drink, I'm parched with all this activity.'

'We might pop in 'The Volunteer', David agreed. 'But I've got to be home by six-thirty, so it'll be a quick one.'

Between them they shut the ground floor windows and locked the doors. The unoccupied house had an eerie atmosphere, and Bob remarked upon it. 'Ideal for a murder,' he said as they walked off. 'Oh, by the way, any developments?'

'Nothing important.'

Bob opined: 'I wouldn't be surprised if that maid at number 15 was responsible.'

'What, Annie? Most unlikely, old boy.'

'She looks weedy, but today I happened to see her carrying a trunk out to a taxi, and she's as strong as a horse.'

'That would be part of the Trindle equipment. Incidentally, Annie has confessed to the crime.'

'What!'

'Not very convincingly, I take it, or she wouldn't still be at large to gloat over the affair. She's a bit unbalanced, her mother's in a mental home.'

'Which makes it all the more likely that she did do it. Guilty men have confessed before now to hasten their trial and acquittal, and be clear of trouble. It's a form of bluff.'

'The police would have run Annie in on the spot if there were any chance of her guilt. As for the physical strength needed by whoever did the dirty work, I touched on that point with the Inspector. Asked him if a powerful thrust had been used. He said no, that anyone of moderate strength could have driven that dagger home, attacking an unsuspecting victim. The blade was as pointed as a needle and razor-sharp.'

'Stabbed in the back, wasn't he?'

'That's right.'

'And which way had he fallen?'

'He'd pitched forward with his head towards the gate, in a kind of twisted position. It's assumed that he was walking away from the house when he was set upon. From my window I had a perfect view of the soles of his boots at one moment, when they whisked away the strip of sacking.'

'Boots – that suggests something. Surely they'll find out who he is from the labels on his clothes?'

'Maybe they will. You can be sure they'll comb every thread for a clue. Pity they can't publish a photograph of him.'

'Why shouldn't they?'

'My dear Bob, his features were distorted and he was stone cold by the time he was found.'

'That's nothing. There's a case on record of a woman who was not only mutilated but mummified. They patched her up and soaked her in some liquid, and more or less inflated her and published a marvellous photograph and caught the murderer.'

'Gosh, how grisly. I didn't know you were such an expert on crime,' David said.

'It's been my hobby for years.'

'That and communism and heraldry and stamp collecting and old pewter.'

'It would be quicker to list the things I'm not interested in,' Bob remarked. 'But crime's high on the list of positives. People laugh at the notion of the perfect crime – that is to say, for instance, a murder without any possible chance of its being detected. But it can be done.'

'If you'd like to indulge your hobby you might aid and abet me. I've set myself the natty little task of solving this back garden mystery. But, of course, you're fully occupied.'

Bob laughed loudly, and without apparent reason. 'I can't work at night at the "Twenty-Six" till they turn on the electric juice and we get some curtains up. By jove, there's Tregunter!'

David was at a loss to know why, having reached the door of "The Volunteer", Bob should dart enthusiastically across the street to greet the little old man who was but dimly visible in the gathering darkness.

'Hi, Mr. Tregunter. Come and have a drink.'

The old man said: 'Well, that's very kind of you, Mr. Carter.'

Bob made a hasty introduction. 'Mr. Tregunter – Flight-Lieutenant Heron.' For David's enlightenment he added: 'Mr. Tregunter has got the best soft-furnishing business in the neighbourhood.'

David was puzzled no longer by Bob's cordiality. The three of them turned into the pub. David noticed that a plain-clothes man who had been sitting behind Inspector Gracewell in his car this morning was at a small table near the door, with a drink in front of him, apparently deep in his own thoughts.

'Evening, Mrs. Newland,' David said brightly.

She stared at him with undisguised and inexplicable hostility as she came forward. It seemed clear that she connected him with the inquiries that Gracewell had almost certainly made about the sailor and the dagger.

David turned to ask the other two what they would have, and caught Bob's words. He was saying: 'Think, Tregunter, what publicity it would be for you. Why, you'd have all Mayfair rushing up to your place and ordering curtains and valances and whatever else they use in Mayfair.'

David asked, 'What will you have, Mr. Tregunter?'

'Thanks, sir. Just a ginger ale.'

'Plain?'

'I never touch strong liquor.'

So Bob wouldn't be able to employ the tactics he had used upon the man who made homes into heaven the Horley-Pay-Way. Sir Cuthbert, from all accounts, flew at a bottle of port in every moment of indecision, and had only to be held close to the bottle while decisions were made for him.

'What's yours, Bob? A ginger ale and two light ales please, Mrs. Newland.'

Mrs. Newland served the drinks, took a note, and slapped down the change. Her face was like stone.

Bob was saying: 'You'd have so much business you wouldn't know which way to turn.'

Mr. Tregunter protested: 'The trouble is, I can't get the material.'

'Instead of doing local trade – why, you might even have royalty in your shop. I'm under royal patronage – or rather, I soon shall be,' Bob said optimistically.

'...can't get the material,' grunted Tregunter.

'We'd put up a notice that you'd done the soft-furnishing. That's another thing I must remember to get, a notice board.'

'...can't get the – Oh, well!' Mr. Tregunter lifted his glass towards David. 'Your health, sir. And good luck. I've got a boy, sixteen last March he was, he's a very good mechanic and he's set on the Air Force – '

Bob interrupted: 'That's settled, then. You do the curtains and my friend here will help your boy in the Service. Hi, Rita, two light ales and a ginger ale and put a tot of brandy in the ginger.' The barmaid moved sluggishly to execute the order. 'That's all right, Mr. Tregunter, you'd better get your strength up, because it's going to be a rush order, and don't say I didn't warn you. I'm not a bit fussy about colour so long as the black-out's all in order. What's your boy's name? – Cecil! Lovely. Why, I can see him as a Commodore already.'

David thought it wise to escape before Bob had made Cecil an Air-Marshal. He made short work of his half-pint and said: 'Sorry, but I've got a date.'

His departure was hardly noticed by Bob, who now had hold of Mr. Tregunter by the lapel of his shabby overcoat. In the old man's face was an expression of bewildered capitulation. There was a certain amount of substance for Bob's claim to be a magician. He obviously had an uncanny gift of persuasion, of infecting others with his own obsessions.

To David's surprise he was overtaken by Mrs. Newland just as he reached the door. She exclaimed: 'There wasn't any need for you to go telling the police how I lost money over that garage.'

This was an unexpected form of attack. At a loss, David said: 'But I didn't know you had.'

'Of course you did. Otherwise how could the police know? You're the only one I ever told, and that was only because I was so upset at the time.'

He shook his head. 'I'm sure you're mistaken. Do you mean the garage at the end of Cannock Alley?'

'You know perfectly well it's that one I mean.'

'How long ago is it since you're supposed to have told me?'

Mrs. Newland looked exasperated. David noticed that the plainclothes officer was leaning forward on his elbows, his hands supporting his head and just behind his ears. Doubtless he was listening intently.

'Why let me see,' Mrs. Newland said, 'it was in the spring of 1939, one evening when there was a lot of news about Czecho-Slovakia or one of those countries, and everyone was arguing about it. And you stood over there, where Mrs. Wicks is standing now, and I told you how I'd paid a good price for that garage, and tried to run it as a business. But one manager after another diddled me till I had to sell it for what I could get. I remember telling you as clear as clear, because I'd just cashed a cheque for you.'

'I remember now! Of course, it was when I got that part in *Fallen Gods*, and had to catch a train at midnight. Why, bless you, I'm afraid I didn't hear a word you said that evening, because a fellow had fallen out of the company and they'd only given me his part that afternoon, and we had to open in Manchester the next night. I was repeating my lines – not aloud – every moment.'

'I remember you looked a bit queer, and it set me wondering if that cheque would be all right.'

'I was fagged out, studying the part. I only came in because I was short of ready cash. And you were a dear, you let me have two quid. I remember that perfectly clearly now. But not about the garage.'

Mrs. Newland's face softened, though her dark eyes still retained their strange intensity, emphasised by the fact that she blinked so rarely. 'So it wasn't you. How did they find out, I wonder?'

'If it isn't being too curious – about what?'

'About me selling the place.'

'Perhaps they traced the cheque.'

'There wasn't a cheque. I took cash. And anyhow, I always thought that bank accounts are confidential.'

'They are.' David hesitated, wondering how far any criminal complication might affect the secrecy of an account. 'Who bought the garage?'

Mrs. Newland looked perturbed. To cover her confusion she dabbed the scar on her cheek with her handkerchief. 'A foreign gentleman. It was for cash, as I told you. And all fixed up quite legal. Mr. Winterborne, who used to come in here, he was a solicitor you know – he drew up the agreement, and I was glad to be rid of a bad bargain.'

'Who, exactly, was the foreign gentleman?'

'To tell you the truth I can't remember. I was so relieved to see some of my money back. I heard he lived on a houseboat at Maidenhead, but it was all arranged through Mr. Winterborne.'

'Where does Mr. Winterborne hang out?'

Mrs. Newland laughed unexpectedly. 'That I couldn't say. Among the angels, it's to be hoped. He got influenza and got in a draught and it turned to pneumonia. After he died they found out his affairs were in a shocking state, a proper muddle. And even his wife wasn't really his wife. You'd never believe it of a solicitor, would you?'

'Solicitors are human,' David observed, 'and likely to make asses of themselves like other men. Well, I'm glad we've cleared up this misunderstanding. I certainly didn't remember that you'd ever owned that garage, and I can't see that it matters, anyway.'

'Nor can I. It's just the police being nosey. They can't do their job, and find out a simple thing like who did the murder, so they've got to come poking their noses into my business.'

'You've heard that your beautiful sailor was trying to sell that dagger he had?'

Mrs. Newland said vaguely: 'Beautiful sailor?' She still seemed to be brooding over the matter of the garage. Then she added: 'He went right up the street and round the corner into your road, ringing everybody's bells, trying to get rid of his rubbish. I knew he was a wrong 'un, I'm glad I sent him packing. Why,' Mrs. Newland's voice dropped, 'they know for certain now that the poor fellow in the garden was killed with that very knife, or dagger, as they're calling it. What's in a name, eh? As soon as a photograph came out in a paper thousands of people went flying to the police.'

The exaggeration made David smile. 'Sorry to rush off,' he said, 'but I'm expecting a phone call, and it's as much as my hope of heaven is worth to miss it.'

He wouldn't miss it. He still had plenty of time. But he made his escape hastily.

SEVENTEEN

WHEN DAVID REACHED number fifteen there was a woman in the hall. She was about thirty, neatly dressed and not unattractive. She was standing beside the hall table, and her glance was mildly speculative.

'Excuse me,' she said. 'You live here, don't you?'

David had used his key for the front door. 'Yes.'

'I'm Mrs. Poole. I've got the top floor front room.'

'Oh, yes. How do you do.'

'I wonder if you'd be so kind – ?' She made a gesture towards the hall table. 'I left my spectacles at the depot and I'm blind without them. Are any of these letters for me?'

David ran through them. The last post had just arrived. 'Dr. Hauptmann. Mrs. Meake. One for me and one for Cumberbatch. No, none for you.'

'Thank you so much. I've only just got in, I suppose there's no more news about this frightful business?'

'None that I know of. The police are working hard, of course.'

'Such an awful thing to happen. Quite frightening.' Mrs. Poole smiled dimly.

'Yes. Pretty awful,' David agreed. 'There's no need to worry, you know. They removed the body quite early.'

To his surprise she laughed gaily. 'Oh, I'm not worrying. Not over the murder, anyhow. It's no business of ours, is it? I'm far too busy at the depot. I run a branch for Perfexo Cleaners, you know. It's enough to turn one grey in these days.'

'Must be quite a tricky job,' David hazarded. He rather liked Mrs. Poole, she seemed at least sensible. He added in a friendly way: 'You haven't been here long, have you?'

'Four months. But I heard all about our Air Force hero as soon as I arrived.'

'Oh, glory. You don't, by that, mean me?'

'Mr. Cumberbatch is a real fan of yours, so I gathered before we had a row.' Mrs. Poole laughed. 'We were great pals, but it was cupboard love on his part, I think. He likes good coffee, and if there's one think I *can* make it's coffee.'

'Stimulating beverage,' said David. 'I suppose it would be awfully impertinent to inquire what you had a row about?'

'Well – I was glad of his company in the evenings. But I got bored when he spun the same old story, over and over again, it seems to be an obsession with him. I suppose there's no secret about it, he never asked me to keep it dark.'

'What?' David was interested. He took a furtive glance at his watch, to make sure that he was running no risk of being late for Tess's call. He still had a few minutes.

'About his wife. She died in Kuala Lumpur ten years ago. Suddenly. There were bruises on her throat and he was tried for murder. He was acquitted – oh, I'm sure he was innocent. But he doesn't seem able to get it out of his mind.'

'Not surprising. Does he offer any explanation of how the bruises were caused?'

'Says a Malay servant with a grudge strangled her. And boasts that he got even with the "boy". He never said how and I certainly didn't ask. I had rather too much of the late lamented Connie Cumberbatch, I can tell you. Mr. C. says she's still with him. He's a bit crackers over reincarnation, but heaven only knows where the soul of his wife is lodged nowadays.'

'So you dropped him?'

Mrs. Poole frowned slightly. 'I had to. He was a little too queer at times. He told me he'd had tropical neurasthenia. He often spoke of Connie as if she was about the place. And really, as I said, the Perfexo depot is enough without being plagued with someone's out-of-date grievances… But heavens, here I am gossiping like an old village mischief! I suppose tragedy makes us talkative.'

David smiled. 'Tragedy starts all sorts of speculations: and talking sometimes clarifies them.'

'Well, you're tactful,' she smiled back. 'Thanks so much for lending me your eyes, I get quite exasperated at being so dependent on spectacles.'

Mrs. Poole went upstairs. David opened his letter. It was from his

Aunt Jane urging him to go to lunch with her in Eaton Square. She wrote:

> *It's awful how you always stay in that dreary apartment house when I've got this big place. I haven't any servants but then no one has in these days. Something that calls herself a cook general has just arrived and of course the faithful Daikin is eternal.*

David was amused at his aunt's aspect of herself as servantless, when she still had a cook and a butler. He'd have to go to lunch with the old girl before the week was up. He ran up to his room and was heartened within a few minutes by his expected phone call from Tess.

She said, however, that she would not be free till eight o'clock and would have to be in by ten. 'I shall have supper here,' she said 'but I think we might be really wild and go to the West End, if there's anywhere we can dance.'

'Not much time for that. But righto, my sweet, I'll be outside St. Margaret's with a taxi on the dot of eight.'

'No, I'll come round to you, by way of a change. I wish you'd wear uniform. Those tweeds of yours are rather vintage.'

'I'll be garbed like a gentleman – but not in uniform, please. I'm going to enjoy myself as a civilian this week. And actually I feel more free to pursue certain inquiries in my pre-war kit.'

'All right, Sherlock. See you at eight.'

It was twenty to seven. David washed and changed hastily. He had just over an hour before Tess would arrive, and decided that by skipping a meal he could carry out his suddenly made plan to inquire for Thelma at the Regalia Theatre.

There was something about Thelma's sudden departure from home that still puzzled him. She and her mother had been on perfectly normal terms on the previous afternoon, when he arrived at the house. By six o'clock they had quarrelled and Thelma – according to her mother – had left for a dubious adventure of her own.

If Thelma had, in fact, embarked upon what was whimsically called a gay life, then the fiction of her staying with Mrs. Higgins might well have been invented to fog the truth. But why had Thelma been her normal lethargic self at four o'clock, and a determined rebel at six? Just over three years ago she had been mysteriously invisible for six months, to reappear – equally mysteriously – on the very day that war broke out. He remembered the pile of luggage stacked in the hall on that momentous Sunday morning; half Thelma's and half Miss Trindle's.

David ran downstairs, and was lucky in picking up a taxi. 'The Regalia Theatre,' he said, 'as quick as you can make it.'

Distances, he reflected, always seemed longer in the dark. How often he'd realised that when streaking back across the Channel! Now drizzling rain began to fall, and he lost all sense of direction as he peered out uselessly and impatiently.

The taxi stopped with a skid. 'Goin' to be a nasty night,' the driver observed.

'Looks like it. Thanks.'

David walked round to the back of the theatre. A large car stood at the kerb. He flashed his torch cautiously – and its rays caught a pair of high heels and silk stockings.

'Thelma?' he said.

She was just getting into the car as he spoke. She swung round. 'Yes?'

'Can I have a word with you?'

'I can't even see who you are.'

'David. David Heron. Don't you know my voice by now?'

'I'm in a hurry.'

'Let me come for part of your way.'

'What is it? What do you want?'

'I can't tell you here. Let's go and have a drink somewhere. Come on, Thelma,' David adopted a persuasive tone, 'be a sport. You can't leave me here getting soaked to the skin.'

'I'm not asking you to stand about.'

'But I should. Hoping you'd come back.'

'Oh, well – ' Thelma sounded nervy, exasperated. 'All right. We can go to the "Mango Grove".'

'By car? Or taxi?'

'It's only a minute. This way.'

David wanted to create an amicable atmosphere. He took Thelma's arm, and as he did so he was struck by the firmness of her forearm as his fingers curved round it. She looked so soft and certainly she had never done any heavy work; she was bored by any mention of sport. But her muscles were well developed and strong; perhaps, he thought, driving had made them so.

He said, with insincere enthusiasm: 'I knew you'd be matey.'

She did not reply, and they reached the entrance to the underground club. The noises common to nearly all such places greeted them as they descended the flight of stairs; the chorus of voices and laughter, the crash of fruit machines, the whine of a gramophone.

David handed his hat and raincoat to a gloomy-looking old man, and they went in.

A crowd surged round the bar, thinning towards a short flight of stairs that led to a floor on a still lower level. David, assuming that club rules would be ignored here, and that guests might pay for drinks, asked: 'What will you have?'

'Champagne cocktail,' Thelma said.

David ordered two. They were given frothy mixtures of wine and ginger-beer. He turned to Thelma: 'Here's fun. Let's shove over in that corner where it's quieter.'

They moved and sat against a curtained window. Thelma, even under the pink-shaded lights, looked haggard and curiously uneasy. She was wearing thick make-up, but it merely made her appear ghastly. In the ordinary way she was pretty enough, though her mask-like standardised prettiness had never appealed to David. A point that struck him now was that her hair lacked its usual careful setting – just when she might be expected to pay some attention to her appearance, if her mother's hints had any foundation. As she slipped off the silk scarf that was over her head, wisps of her hair were sticking to her forehead.

'So you've left our hearth and home,' David said, as an opening gambit.

'Who told you I had?'

'There was a check-up on everyone in the house this morning. But, of course, you know that.'

'Why should I know? As it happens, I don't.'

'Oh, lord, come clean! You've seen the papers, you know what happened in the night.'

Thelma's face was expressionless. Whether she was concealing annoyance or fear, David could only conjecture. 'Yes, I saw a paper. But the murder – it happened in the garden, it's got nothing to do with the house.'

'It was our garden. So it's our murder.'

'You can have it,' Thelma sneered. 'I want another drink.'

She certainly knew how to keep cool. David repeated the order, and as he handed Thelma her glass he asked: 'By the way, what time did you clear out yesterday?'

'I don't know. Eight o'clock. Or half-past.'

Mrs. Meake had said six. David spoke casually: 'Bad luck about your boss being caught on this black market racket.'

'Just too bad,' Thelma agreed coldly. 'It must be breaking your heart.'

'Will you stay on at the "Regalia"?'

'Why not? It's a reserved occupation.'

'I can't see why it should be.'

'My work isn't just in the office. I drive the car, and Mr. Schenk was doing war work in his spare time.'

'He may not have any spare time for quite a while, for war work or any of his other – ahem – numerous activities.'

'Very funny, you are!' Thelma blinked rapidly. He saw that he was getting beneath her armour of affected unconcern. 'What's the idea?' she snapped. 'Have you come round just to make cracks? What have you come for, anyway?'

David put on an innocent expression. 'To ask you to come home. Your mother's worried. All this is pretty rotten for her, you know.'

'I'm not coming home.'

'Where are you living?'

'That's not your business.'

It seemed unlikely that he could make any further progress. One fact had emerged, that it was by no means certain what time Thelma had left Terrapin Road. There was a considerable difference between six o'clock and eight or eight-thirty. Either Mrs. Meake or Thelma was lying. Possibly both of them were.

David glanced at his watch. It was just half-past seven and he had to get home in time for Tess. He asked 'Will you be at the "Regalia" to-morrow?'

'No.'

Thelma was determined to be obstructive. Or perhaps she was merely being antagonistic, which would be no new angle. David rose. 'I've got to get along.'

He expected her to acquiesce in his move to guide her through the mob near the bar. But she turned away. 'I'm staying. I was coming here, anyway.'

'Oh, well – so long. Shall I tell your mother I've seen you?'

'I don't care whether you do or not.'

From the door David glanced back. Thelma was moving towards the room on a lower level. He hesitated at the bottom of the stairs to the street, while the gloomy old man proffered his raincoat. 'Just a moment,' he said, 'I want another word with my friend.'

He elbowed his way through the crush till he was near the top of the shallow stairway. The movements of a group of half a dozen men and girls simplified his chances of observing without being seen. On the lower floor several couples were dancing, round the wall were small tables.

At one of the tables Thelma sat with a short, squat man. Their heads were close together as they talked. David dropped back a step, to make sure of screening himself, and gazed across several shoulders at the couple below.

There could be no mistake about it. Thelma's companion was the man who had emerged from the garage in the alley that morning. And now – David stared in astonishment – he was crying. His mouth sagged to an almost square shape, tears rolled down his pendulous cheeks and dropped from his scrubby dark chin.

Thelma said something sharply and contemptuously. The man made an effort to control himself, failed, and dropped his face in his pudgy hands.

David swung on his heel and again made for the door.

EIGHTEEN

A TELEPHONE MESSAGE awaited David at Mrs. Meake's. He had to ring up Tess, and in a minute or so he heard her voice over the line.

'That you, David? I'm awfully sorry, my dear, but I've had a tough afternoon – several of the nippers have been off-colour – and I don't feel a bit like whoopee or hitting high spots.'

'But I've got to see you, Tess.'

'I'm all washed up.'

'Can't I come round and see you at St. Margaret's?'

'Yes, if you can face Sister Allardyce and Nobby and Smithy in the staff sitting-room.'

A bunch of assorted women was the last thing David wanted. He said desperately: 'Well, can't you come here? I can wangle some coffee or something.'

'Is it all right? I thought you'd only got a bedroom.'

'It's a very sitting-roomy bedroom. Divan, concealed washstand, concealed everything.'

Tess laughed. 'Oh, well – '

It was obvious she was yielding. 'I'm coming round to collect you'.

'Not till after eight. Say half-past, to give me time to get my breath. I'll meet you outside.'

David went down to interview Mrs. Meake. Directly he saw her he felt faint with dismay at the thought of giving extra trouble when she was already tired and worried. She was lying back in the cane armchair by the fire, her make-up was smudged, a crumpled handkerchief had fallen from her hand.

'Sorry to be a bother, Meakie. But I'm having a visitor.'

Mrs. Meake said tersely: 'So what?' She sat up straight and glared, as if to dispel any suggestion that she was not in her normal state. He reflected that Meakie might be enigmatic, but she had plenty of pluck.

'Will you be an angel and make us a pot of coffee.'

'If it's that Inspector, I'll make him a pot of arsenic, and gladly. I'm sick to the teeth of him.'

'Tut-tut! It's not the Inspector and if Annie's not available I'll willingly come down and act as carrier.'

'I've got legs,' Mrs. Meake rapped.

David laughed. 'Bless you, and didn't the gentlemen in the stalls appreciate them?'

'That's a few years ago,' Mrs. Meake sighed, and said wistfully: 'Though it doesn't seem like it. You youngsters can't understand how time passes. Like a flash. One minute you're young and thinking how funny old people are, and the next you're old yourself and everything's a mess.'

'For shame! What's a mess? Here you are with a comfortable house, and a bunch of steady lodgers, and a perfectly lovely young man in your first floor back – and you say we're a mess.'

'It's not you, ducks. It's – just everything.'

'You've had a trying day, with the murder and too many questions to answer. You'd better get to bed early.'

His hand dropped on Mrs. Meake's shoulder. She patted it as if to appreciate his sympathy. Suddenly, on an impulse, he began to tell her about Tess, explaining how he had met her.

'It was a miracle,' he declared fervently.

'My dear boy, it always is.'

'But this is different.' He ignored Meakie's wide, tolerant smile. 'She's the most wonderful person. Truly, Meakie, frighteningly efficient, with strings and strings of certificates. Yet she's remained sweet and human and full of laughter. She's a mixture – well, we all are, of course, and I'm being maudlin. I believe she'd die doing her duty. And still she's been inciting me to get her a pair of silk stockings without coupons. The eternal Eve, I suppose you'd call it.'

'What does she do? Why isn't she called up?'

'She's a nurse. Looks after kids in a home.'

'Children!' Mrs. Meake spoke the word with a strange intensity.

'Yes. Tess is at St. Margaret's, you may know the place.'

'Children,' Mrs. Meake repeated. 'How I love them.'

David said lamely: 'Do you?'

'Why, yes,' Mrs. Meake rose. 'Yes. I ought to have had a large family. I'd have taken such care of them.'

David was thinking that Thelma was not a particularly good specimen of a mother's loving care. But it might have been because Thelma was an only child that she had been spoilt. Mrs. Meake certainly had a maternal nature; and suddenly he realised that she was the only woman from whom he himself had had any mothering.

He glanced at his watch. 'Phew! I'll only just make it.'

He hurried out and ran the quarter of a mile to St. Margaret's, arriving just as Tess emerged. In the dark he could not see how she was looking; she laughed away his apology for not having a taxi handy.

'I'm all right, my poppet,' she assured him. 'Only a bit weary. It'll be lovely just to spend an hour or so quietly. We'll gossip and chew the tasty bits right to the bone.'

Mrs. Meake had evidently heard them come in, for within five minutes she brought up a tray of coffee and biscuits. Under her arm she had something rolled in paper. She said, somewhat abruptly to Tess: 'You look after a lot of little nippers, don't you?'

'Why – yes.'

'I wondered if they could use these.' Mrs. Meake unrolled her package. Several small woollen garments were revealed. 'I used to knit for a day nursery, before it was evacuated.'

'They're lovely,' Tess fingered the woollies. 'Thank you so much. Yes, of course, we can use them, some of our kiddies aren't too well equipped.'

Mrs. Meake hesitated. 'You're from St. Margaret's, I hear.'

'Yes.'

'I wondered – well I don't know if I'm presuming, but could I come and see the kiddies, some time?'

'Of course. We love having visitors.'

'Thank you. It's very kind of you.' Mrs. Meake went out.

David exclaimed: 'Well, you could knock me down! I've often noticed Meakie knitting, but I never wondered what it was she was making. Kids' things! And to think she used to wear pink silk tights and sing naughty songs. What mysteries human beings are.'

'Good and bad, darling. Fat and thin. Now, having reached a new high level in the obvious, let's have a cup of coffee. I'm sure it'll help to settle all the alcohol your poor tummy's trying to absorb.'

'That's a slander. I've had an almost teetotal day, except for a couple of alleged champagne cocktails as a matter of policy. Beer doesn't count as a drink, it's so non-hoppish these days. Have a biscuit?'

'No thanks. I'm full of Spam pie.'

'Then I'll gollop the lot. In my detective ardour I skipped a meal this evening.'

'This is sheer heaven.' Tess leaned back against the cushions on the divan. Very gently, David lifted her feet to make her still more comfortable. And presently, by way of making himself equally so, he dropped beside her and slipped an arm round her shoulders. Thus, completely at their ease, they talked and were silent, and talked again, till it was time for Tess to go.

'It's amazing,' he said as he walked back with her, 'how chewing things over helps to sort out the facts. I've got a feeling I'm on the outskirts of the solution of the back garden crime.'

'You're convinced it's connected with black market gangsters?'

'All I've got as a link-up is the likeness of the man who went into the black market shop with the parcel – I'm going to call him Mr. X till I discover his name – to the victim. Mr. X uses that garage and alley at the back, that's divided by only a wall from the scene of the crime. Mr. X knows Thelma. Thelma's employed by a man who is now under detention for being in possession of black market goods. Mr. X, as I told you, was crying his ugly eyes out this evening. The whole bunch positively reek of conspiracy. And right in the middle of them, as it were, the double of Mr. X gets stabbed – within a few yards of Thelma's room.'

'If we knew *why* he was killed – ' Tess broke off.

'The precise motive means the precise solution,' David opined. 'Have patience, darling, and perhaps you'll live to see me being frightfully clever as a snooper.'

They had reached St. Margaret's, but the house was only vaguely visible. 'Good-night, David. It's been a lovely evening.'

'More than lovely. I can't bear saying good-night. In fact I won't.

"Silence is one of the great arts of conversation," as Cicero said so wisely.'

They remained in each other's arms for a full minute without speaking, under the kindly obscurity of the night. Then Tess ran up the steps and rang the bell.

And David, discovering how little the biscuits had appeased his hunger, and contravening all theories about love annihilating appetite, went to a cafe in the High Street and ate an enormous slice of alleged pork brawn laid upon a hefty wedge of bread.

NINETEEN

THE MORNING WAS BRIGHT, and David woke feeling full of zest. A session with Annie left his spirits undimmed. She was doleful this morning, declaring that she wished she had never made her confession to the police.

'I thought I'd tell 'em and get it over,' she said. 'But if I'd never said anything, as like as not they'd never 'ave rumbled me.'

'Oh, you and your confessions,' David grunted.

'I shall bring shame on me poor old father, and 'im cutting timber to win the war.'

'Throw me that packet of fags and hop it, there's a good girl.'

Surprisingly, Annie sniffed. 'I'm not a good girl, that's why I'm in all this bother.'

'Oh, to be back on my kite and at peace!'

'There's no peace for the wicked, and well I know it.'

David sauntered out before breakfast. There was little chance of seeing Tess before four o'clock, when she expected to have an hour or so free. He noticed that now there was no police guard in front of the house, and from his window he had seen no sign of any officer at the back. He supposed that, having collected all the available evidence, Inspector Gracewell had decided there was no more to be gained from supervision.

But what was that old theory about the criminal being magnetised back to the scene of the crime?

David strolled round into Cannock Road, and glanced down the alley. Instantly his attention was arrested. A girl was looking over the wall into the garden of Mrs. Meake's house. She was standing on several bricks, stacked together, but even so her head barely topped the wall, to which she clung perilously.

She was wearing an odd sort of hood of green wool. And suddenly David remembered Lipscott's story of the pixie girl. She turned as she heard him approaching, and he found himself gazing at a small pointed face with wide, scared eyes.

'Oh!' she exclaimed, and jumped from her perch. She looked as if she wanted to run away, but the garage at the end made the alley a cul-de-sac, and David was between her and escape into Cannock Road.

'Nice view over that wall,' David began conversationally.

'Yes.' The word was a gasp.

'What makes you so interested in it?'

'I just wanted to look at it.'

'Obviously,' David said pleasantly. He found it hard to believe that this quaint girl could be up to any mischief. She might or might not be Lipscott's train acquaintance, but she was certainly like a pixie, with her sharp features and that pointed hood. 'I see you've got your handbag back,' he added. The fact that the bag was green was another corroborative detail.

'I got it at the station. Someone handed it in and didn't steal a thing out of it. That's why they gave me time off, to go and get it.'

So she was the same girl. 'Time off? Oh, from the factory?'

'I don't really start till tomorrow.' Her face clouded with sudden uncertainty. 'How did you know I'd lost my bag?'

'My friend told me. Lipscott. The Merchant Navy chap, you know. He wants to meet you again.'

The girl was obviously terrified. 'No, no, no!' she exclaimed.

'Lipscott's a good sort. You ought to give him a break. I expect he told you, he's only got eight days leave.'

'No,' gasped the girl.

She had quite a habit of saying no. David appreciated now how difficult it must have been to persuade her to accept a night's shelter. 'I say, will you tell me the real reason you were looking over that wall?'

'To see the garden.'

"Heaven give me patience," thought David. "That's more or less why a chicken crosses the road…" 'Of course. But what interests you so much about it?'

'There was a terrible murder there.'

'Yes, that's sadly true. But that's no reason for building yourself a cute little platform and staring at the scene.'

'I've read about murders. I've seen waxworks. But I've never seen a place where one was committed, in real life.'

Could her inquisitiveness be just morbid curiosity? The pixie would not be the first to behave erratically. 'What brought you in this direction? It isn't anywhere near Acton. *Or* Paddington.'

'The murder. I read about it.' She pointed. 'I was in that house once.'

'And don't I know it! You stayed there the night before last, didn't you? Now you come along with me and we'll dig old Lipscott out.'

She shrank back as if in terror. David laughed. 'Good gosh, you can't be frightened? Of me, I mean?'

She nodded her head miserably. 'I am.'

It was a new and unpleasant experience for him. He had provoked irritation and anger. Even derision. But never fear – except when it was his job to put the fear of hell into an enemy. He said awkwardly. 'I can assure you I'm all right.'

'It's easy for you to say so,' she retorted quickly. 'You might be awful.'

He laughed out loud. 'I suppose I am in some ways. But I promise not to gobble you up.' He regretted his facetiousness immediately, for the girl seemed increasingly dismayed. Adopting a hearty, brotherly tone, he added: 'Now then, off we go. Both of us together. We'll dig old Lipscott out, and you can take my word for it he'll be tickled to death.'

The pixie seemed to agree, for she walked obediently beside him to the end of the alley. Then, when he was completely off his guard, she darted impulsively away, running as fast as her legs would carry her down Cannock Road. The pavement was fairly crowded and her flight attracted considerable attention. After a few hasty steps David hadn't the nerve to pursue her. He felt that he, too, would be pursued. He didn't even know the girl's name; he would look something worse than a fool if he had to account for his chase.

Half angry, half amused, he returned to Mrs. Meake's and went straight to the second floor, where he found Lipscott shaving. 'I say, Lipscott,' he said abruptly. 'I've just met your pixie.'

'Where?' Lipscott's swerve round was so violent that his shaving brush slapped a dab of frothy soap against the mirror.

'In Cannock Alley.'

'Where is she now?'

'The lord only knows.'

David gave an account of the incident. It threw Lipscott into a fury of protest: 'And to think that I spent yesterday afternoon and evening walking round Acton!'

'Trying to find her?'

'What else would I walk round Acton for? Didn't you get her name?'

'After all, you didn't when you had a far better chance than I had. I thought she was coming back here with me. She gave me the slip without a hint of warning.'

'You blundering idiot!' Lipscott stormed.

David said patiently: 'You'd better have another shot at Acton.'

The suggestion was made only half-seriously, but Lipscott resuming his shaving, said grimly: 'That's exactly what I intend to do.'

'I can only wish you good hunting,' David retorted as he went out.

TWENTY

THE FANCY GOODS EMPORIUM presented the same scene. Rows of dusty tins and boxes on the shelves, a muddle of tawdry rubbish on the counter. The tall owner, or assistant, or whatever he was, was almost invisible on a low stool behind the cash register, smoking a cigar. Sitting in the shadow as he was, the discolouration of the skin round one eye was hardly visible, but still, as he glowered in an inquiring manner, he looked furtive and ugly.

David bought cigarettes, and some chewing gum that he did not want. He toyed with some pencils and bought one, and then turned his attention to pipe-cleaners. He paid for the items as he slipped them in his pocket; Pink-eye shot the coins in the cash register and slapped down change forcibly, as if to indicate that he hoped their transactions were concluded.

'Handy lot of oddments you've got here,' David remarked.

A grunt acknowledged his comment. He picked up a tablet of pink soap. 'I'll take this too.'

'Got your ration book with you?'

'Er – no.'

'You've got to have a book, before you can get soap.'

'Oh, yes. I'd forgotten it was rationed.' The rationing of soap was a recent innovation. 'Sorry. I've only got a kind of leave card, for sugar and tea and such-like, and my landlady's got that.'

Another grunt. David did not give up. He said: 'It's a handicap, this rationing. I wanted to buy my girlfriend some stockings.' He paused and gave the other a glance that he hoped would be taken as conspiratorial leaning across the counter as if to screen what might pass between them from anyone suddenly entering the shop. 'Of course, I know they might cost quite a bit.'

He felt hot under the collar and had to restrain the impulse to ease his tie.

Pink-eye rolled his cigar from one corner of his mouth to the other. 'I might have a pair,' he ventured. 'I can't remember exactly.

Stock's got in a bit of a muddle.'

'Well, let's see them.' Ostentatiously, David produced his wallet.

'Got to be careful,' said the other.

'Don't I know it?' David gave his voice an inflexion that suggested he spent his time in evading detection. He managed a smile that might imply furtive understanding, and added 'Don't like taking risks myself. But I know I'm all right with you.'

'Just a friendly transaction. All right.' With a movement like that of a conjuror producing a rabbit, the man whisked a pair of stockings from somewhere near his feet.

David fingered them.

'Make up your mind.' The phrase was rapped irritably.

'They'll do.' David pocketed the stockings and held out a pound note.

'Only the one pair?' The salesman seemed astonished.

'Er – yes.'

'Plenty under the counter, you know.'

For a split second David was tempted. If one pair would delight Tess, what might not be the effect of half a dozen pairs? But the whole business was illegal, he was beginning to feel quite degraded by his own mock-affability. He had wanted to discover the character of the shop. Now he'd done so. The sooner he cleared out the better.

'Just the one pair,' he said.

The salesman's mouth curled in a thin, contemptuous line. He took the note and slipped in into a pocket. Apparently the cash register was merely for small amounts. David waited to see if there might be any change. None was proffered.

Suddenly the door between the shop and the back room opened. A youth appeared. Behind him stacks of packing cases were visible. Pink-eye bawled: 'Keep that door shut, can't you?'

The youth slammed the door and slouched forward. He was unhealthy looking, dressed in a flashy blue suit and mustard suede shoes. His hair was greased, his shoulders were widely padded. He looked like a petty crook who had had a streak of good luck.

He said: 'I done the checking up, Mr. Bamberger.'

'Got eyes, haven't you? Can't you see I'm busy? Come yapping round when I'm serving a customer!'

David thought it expedient to retreat. If he heard too much he might not be welcome when he came in again – and he would almost certainly want to return. He said: 'Thanks,' and walked out.

Bamberger. So that was Pink-eye's name. David wondered if Thelma Meake knew him; she knew the man who had delivered the parcel yesterday. Perhaps her employer, Schenk, had supplied Bamberger. Or Thelma might be one of his customers. As he himself was – David smiled ironically. He felt no envy of those who habitually gleaned treasures from under the counter; goods that as often as not were brought by chaps like Lipscott, perilously, from far off ports.

It was midday, and a drink was David's next requirement. He made for "The Volunteer", thinking that Bob Carter might be there.

There was no sign of Bob, but Inspector Gracewell was lounging at the far end of the bar. David joined him and Mrs. Newland served them with two bitters.

The Inspector began to talk of the weather and the war news. David refrained from inquiring what progress the police had made in the murder case, till Mrs. Newland moved off to the public bar, and only the sluggish Rita was left to attend to saloon customers.

Then he asked: 'Any news?'

Gracewell countered with another question. 'Did you have a visitor on Sunday night?'

'I told you I didn't, when you came up yesterday morning. I'd only got back to Mrs. Meake's on Sunday, you'll remember.'

'Did you, by any chance, hear any unfamiliar steps on the stairs between nine-thirty and ten-thirty?'

'I was out with my girlfriend till after ten. And there's quite a thick carpet on those stairs. But why this particular inquiry?'

'Because a taxi driver has come forward.' The Inspector took a long drink from his tankard.

David said: 'It's a fair bet some taxi driver or other will be in the offing in any London mystery.'

'Trouble is they won't always report useful details. Afraid of wasting their time. And getting involved. But this one was the right sort. Blew into a police station this morning and reported that he'd taken a couple to 15 Terrapin Road on Sunday night.'

'I got there – by taxi – at about four.'

'In uniform in daylight, and alone. This other taxi set down its passengers at nine-forty-five or so. Might have been a little later. A man and a girl and some bits of small luggage.'

This sounded like Lipscott and his pixie. David reflected that he himself had probably missed arriving at the house at the same time by only a few minutes, having left Tess at ten.

'Where did the taxi pick them up?'

'Paddington. Driver says he didn't realise they'd got in till the man passenger spoke through the window behind his head. Driver was told to go to 15 Terrapin Road. Then when they got near the girl seemed to be complaining and the man tapped on the window again and asked to be set down. The couple got out at the corner.'

There was a silence. 'Any ideas?' Gracewell asked.

'Was the man – was he a civilian?'

'Driver can't be sure. It was as black as Hitler's heart on Sunday night.'

Sooner or later the time of Lipscott's arrival would come out. The sooner the better, for all concerned. It seemed as if the Inspector were thought-reading, for he asked suddenly: 'When did that Merchant Navy chap, Lipscott, turn up?'

'Better ask him,' David said. 'I'm not his nurse.'

'Funny thing about taxis,' mused Gracewell, 'fares often ask to be set down round odd corners. Well, it may be innocent enough. Chap going home doesn't want his wife to know he's taxi-ing, she might slate him for extravagance. Or wife returning, same tactics. Or a chap smuggling a girl into his place for a bit of whoopsy-daisy.'

David, speculating as to what the Inspector was getting at, said: 'Yes,' non-committally. He took out his cigarettes and as they prompted a train of thought he asked: 'Do you come in contact with the black market racket?'

'I'll say I do. Can't avoid it. It's all over the place, in little bits – and big bits. But it isn't directly my province, I leave it to the experts, tipping them off when I hear anything useful.'

'I remember you asked about meals at Mrs. Meake's, whether

122

they were unusually lavish?'

'It was just a stray query. I wondered if she'd got special sources of supply. If she had, she'd be in touch with some gang or other.'

'I can vouch for Meakie. She's as straightforward as daylight. Anyway, on what we pay her, she couldn't come out square on any under the counter deals.'

'When it comes to making out the accounts, you may be privileged,' Gracewell said. 'You're obviously Mrs. Meake's favourite tenant.'

'Have you found out any more about the gory splash on the front steps?'

'Same blood group as the dead man's, and spilt at approximately the time of his death.'

'Seeing that there are only four groups, that isn't anything like conclusive,' David remarked.

'Odd point is, it was near the centre of the steps, where people would tread. It had dried before anyone walked over that spot.'

'Well, if it was discovered at crack of dawn, and it hadn't been spilt till about three in the morning, that's natural enough.'

'Spilt is the wrong word. It was the merest trace, and would never have been noticed if my men hadn't been called to the house, all alert to notice the smallest detail.'

'Nothing to do with the murder,' David opined with a feeling of certainty.

'We'll see about that.' Gracewell set down his tankard and spoke with an air of finality. 'I must get along. Thanks for your cooperation.'

'It doesn't amount to much, I'm afraid.'

'I still regard you as an ally.'

"Allies can compete", thought David, speculating as to which of them would arrive first at some discovery relevant to the murder. Even an amateur resident had a certain advantage over a professional outsider.

TWENTY-ONE

STROLLING ALONG CANNOCK ROAD, at this time of day crowded with women doing their household shopping, David saw Mrs. Wicks emerging from a greengrocer.

Mrs. Wicks, an ancient and dreary individual with stringy grey hair and scanty teeth, was known as the most garrulous busybody in the neighbourhood. It was she who had bought the amber beads from the strange seafaring man in "The Volunteer" on Sunday night. It was she who, knowing French, had informed Mrs. Newland that to be addressed as 'vache' was no compliment.

David beamed at the ancient crone with assumed geniality. 'Why, Mrs. Wicks, fancy meeting you.'

'Not remarkable if you ask me, considerin' I'm this way every mornin' of my life,' said Mrs. Wicks. She still had a way of mincing her phrases with affected refinement, a habit that possibly had endeared her to the ladies she had attended upon, heaven only knew how many years ago.

'Ah but I'm a stranger in these parts,' David countered.

'These days you are, you bein' in the air corpse. Though no one would take you for an officer, not off-'and they wouldn't.'

Wrinkled eyes made a deprecating survey of David's tweed Jacket and flannel slacks.

David said with careful seriousness: 'A gentleman's a gentleman whatever he's wearing. Just as' – he bowed slightly – 'a lady's a lady.'

'Well yes,' Mrs. Wicks twittered. 'I just popped into this old coat, you know what it is when you're in a 'urry.'

'Precisely.'

'It's terrible about this murder,' Mrs. Wicks went on. 'No one's safe, in bed or out. It's my belief that sailor fellow did it, the one that came in "The Volunteer". Nothink of the gentleman about him, you can mark my word.'

'But he was selling the dagger. Which he wouldn't have been if he'd wanted to use it.'

'Might have changed his mind. He was a foreigner,' Mrs. Wicks said scathingly.

'You've lived in these parts for quite a while, haven't you?'

'Twenty-odd years.'

'Then you know quite a bit about local folk?'

'Everythink,' said Mrs. Wicks.

He suppressed a smile. 'Then perhaps you know who owns that garage down there?' He indicated the alley nearly opposite where they stood.

'Of course I do. It's a Mr. Smith. He had it done up three weeks ago.'

'The place doesn't look like it. By the way,' David made a provocative guess, 'that wouldn't be a Mr. George Smith, would it?'

'How would I know? I only know 'e's called Smith, because of him buying some electric bulbs from the corner shop and they 'ad – had to order them specially. About three weeks ago it was, and Mr. Smith left his name and said 'e'd call back.'

Which, thought David, is poor proof that his name is anything like Smith. 'He's tall, isn't he?'.

Again the guess went wide. ''ardly taller than I am,' Mrs. Wicks rapped. 'A reg'lar little weasel of a man, if you'll excuse strong language. Nothink to look at, for all 'e's got a coat with an astrakhan collar.' She added maliciously: 'It's wonderful what you can pick up in pawnshops. P'raps 'e knows 'e needs a bit of trimming up, with the face 'e's got.'

'Ugly, is he?'

'Looks as if someone dropped 'im – him on his face when 'e was a baby. His nose is flat as flat.'

'Eyes are the most important feature in any face, don't you think?'

The query evoked nothing but the curt remark: 'Quite likely,' from Mrs. Wicks.

David continued on his way, having gained only the meagre information that a flat-nosed, undersized Mr. Smith with an astrakhan collar owned the garage.

He returned to Mrs. Meake's, thinking that Bob Carter might have telephoned. There was no message from Bob. No doubt he was busy uniting the nations round in Belmont Crescent. Annie came up from the basement as he was passing through the hall. She was wearing a ragged scarlet scarf round her head as a turban, and her coat was of an astonishing check pattern; the huge squares of yellow, green and blue exaggerated her gauntness and height.

She was holding a large carrier bag that for no obvious reason she seemed anxious to hide, holding it behind her back.

'Been on the loose?' David inquired amicably.

'On the loose, you might call it. I just been out with my Mum.'

'Enjoy yourself?'

'Like 'ell I 'ave,' said Annie.

'Come, come. That's no way to speak of maternal companionship. A girl's best friend, and all that. Can a mother's tender care – etcetera? Don't you know about the roses round the door, invented simply to make everyone love mother more?'

Annie looked surly. 'You're always a one for a laugh.'

'A laugh a day – Or am I thinking of apples?'

'Mother's that awkward,' Annie said explosively.

'Oh well, maybe we all get awkward as the years roll by.'

'Scares me, she does. I'm glad when I get 'er back where she's safe.'

David spoke more seriously. 'If she's really – well, let's say difficult, you oughtn't to take her out. It's a responsibility. You mightn't be able to manage her.'

'I can't and that's the truth,' Annie admitted.

Looking at her, David speculated again as to why Mrs. Meake had taken on such a human oddity as a general servant. But the labour problem was acute, all the healthy strapping lasses were in the services. He'd worked with some of them as ground staff himself. It was only the specially exempted who were scrubbing floors and dusting furniture in apartment houses.

He found himself wondering where Annie had been on Sunday night, between a quarter past nine and ten o'clock – when Lipscott had smuggled his girl into the house and when, as likely as not, the seafaring man had called trying to sell his wares.

David asked her: 'Why didn't you tell me about the man who called here on Sunday night?'

'Called 'ere?'

'Don't pretend you've for gotten. About twenty-past nine.'

Annie guffawed: 'That's good, me knowing anythink about twenty-past nine. I was in me bed by then. Sunday night's me bath night, and it's no lie to say I was upstairs by nine o'clock.'

So the nautical pedlar might have called – but if so, who had answered the door? David remarked facetiously: 'Weren't you afraid of catching cold, going out to do your murder after you'd had a nice warm bath?'

'Well, I never thought about *that*,' Annie said simply.

There could have been only a short interval between her using the bathroom and Lipscott's taking it over for the night. David asked: 'Who would answer the door after you went to bed?'

'Mrs. Meake, of course. Or anyone who happened to be near and heard the bell. Miss Trindle often used to pop out, just bein' nosey if you ask me.'

Again David pondered upon Miss Trindle's departure. It was not altogether explicable. It was not as if the crime had yet been connected with a resident in the house. Miss Trindle had lived here since the outbreak of war. She must have been firmly entrenched with all her possessions around her. Yet within half an hour of the start of the inquiry she had been packing, and less than two hours later she had decamped.

Was it she who had contrived that secret hiding place under the floorboard? And if so, for what? David stopped when he was on the stairs to ask Annie: 'Where's Miss Trindle gone?'

Again Annie guffawed. 'Don't tell me you're gone on her. That old faggot!'

'I'm wild about her.'

'Well, you better write your passionate letters to the Gen'ral Post Office, 'cause that's the only address she left.' Annie flounced upstairs, still holding the carrier bag so that he should not see it.

TWENTY-TWO

WHEN DAVID CALLED for Tess she said that she would be free till six-thirty, and that she felt like a spot of mild gaiety.

He said: 'Our choice isn't awfully wide. It's a quick tea and the pictures, or a tea dance. Unless you'd like to try some dump that sells drink right round the clock? I daresay we could find one.'

'Not for me, thanks,' Tess said firmly. 'Let's just make it tea somewhere nice. No dancing, I'm breaking in my five coupons worth of crêpe-soled shoes.'

'The best is good enough for us. Call it Claridge's.'

David hailed a taxi. As they drove towards the West End Tess said: 'I've discovered something that may interest you.'

'Anent what?'

'Anent the immediate vicinity of the crime.'

At the moment David was feeling less thrilled by crime and its surroundings than by Tess. She was in grey, her delicate chin was barely visible above soft fur, and a saucer of a hat merely drew attention to the glinting golden hair beneath it. He said: 'You're exquisite, darling. I wish I were Watteau, so I could immortalise you.'

'Watteau be blowed, when I'm simmering with discovery.'

'Of what?'

'Of who owns that garage you're so curious about.'

'Too late, my sweet. I heard about Mr. Smith from an adorable girlfriend of mine.'

'Smith? Then your adorable girlfriend adopts the strangest pronunciation.'

'She certainly said Smith. What's your version?'

Tess put her tip-tilted nose slightly in the air. Her profile was certainly a lovely specimen of nature's draughtsmanship. 'I think I'll keep it for an adorable gent friend of mine.'

'Darling, I'll come clean. My informant was sixty-five or more and she wears a sequin toque with violets on it.'

'I'd like one like that.'

'I'll have it built for you.' David squeezed the hand he was holding. 'Who, according to you, owns the confounded garage?'

'A Mr. Shink.'

'Oh, jehoshophat!' David burst out laughing 'There can't be anyone called Shink.'

'It's comic, isn't it?'

'Who told you, anyway?'

'The mother of one of our kids at St. Margaret's. She – her name's Mrs. Crumping, by the way – '

'We seem to be in for an orgy of this sort of thing. Attractive names, I mean.'

'Mrs. Crumping was telling Sister Allardyce why she couldn't afford to buy her baby girl a spare nightdress. We fixed the kid up of course. But meanwhile we'd heard all about poor papa Crumping and why he was out of work, even in these days. It's his feet, which are said to be so corn-ridden that he has to lie in bed all day smoking cigarettes, and can hardly get to the pub at opening time to rally his failing strength. This Crumping, it seems, labels himself as a handyman, and his wife was complaining that the only job he'd had for months was fixing some shelves three weeks ago in the garage in Cannock Alley. Of course, I pricked up my ears at that, and asked who had given him the job. She said Mr. Shink, who owns the garage.'

'I've got it!' David exclaimed. 'Shink – Schenk. Don't you think she was saying Schenk? If only you'd ask her to spell it.'

'I did, and she just looked dithered. Lots of people never think of a name as it is written down, it's just a sound – and often a vague enough sound, even in the very best circles.'

'Shink and Schenk would be all the same to your Mrs. Crumping. You remember, Tess, I told you about Thelma working for a Mr. Schenk? He's the manager of a theatre when he's not in quod.'

'That doesn't make him the owner of a garage behind Mrs. Meake's.'

'But the garage is connected with a black market shop – Darling, I got those stockings for you, risking my precious freedom in the evil cause.'

'Where are they?'

'I stuffed them in the pocket of my tweed jacket. And then as you see, I changed into this posh lounge suit by way of making myself a worthy escort.'

'Mrs. Meake will pinch them before you get back.'

'My sweet poppet, she's a woman of the highest integrity.'

'Integrity is nothing compared with silk stockings. Oh, well – what else do you know about Shink-Schenk?'

'Schenk's remanded on a black market charge. What would be more likely than that he should own the garage from which emerged one sinister man en route for that fancy goods emporium, where coupons are needed for soap labelled sixpence, but not for a pair of stockings when a full wallet is exposed to view?'

'How much did you have to pay?'

'I tendered a quid, and that seemed to be adequate.'

'I should think so. Absolute robbery! Serve you right for defying the law.'

'Such pretty gratitude! Darling, I did it for two reasons in about fifty-fifty proportions. First to pursue an urgent investigation, and second to win your imperishable love.'

'Your excuses would sound sweet in a court of law.'

'Mrs. Meake had better have those stockings, after all.'

'No – please! I think you're an angel to risk your neck for one. Thanks enormously.'

'I think I've earned a kiss.'

'But not in a taxi. So vulgar.'

'I like kissing vulgarly. There, I didn't even smudge your lipstick.'

Tess became thoughtful. 'I can't help thinking you may be running into danger, mixing with all those crooks.'

'Danger would be such a novelty,' David muttered.

'I'm not joking, darling. Shink or Schenk might be very venomous if cornered.'

'I'm not after him precisely. He was behind bars on Sunday night. It's the murderer I'm out to spot. And if I can learn more about Shink or Schenk I might succeed. Don't you see, my pretty, how it's all linking together? Schenk employs Thelma Meake, and out of Schenk's garage comes the man who's the living image of the corpse? Add that to the location of the crime, committed on a night when

Thelma's whereabouts are a mystery – '

The taxi stopped outside Claridges.

'Let's give over being sordid,' David said.

They went through the hall to the lounge. Not till they were seated at a small table was their conversation resumed, and it was Tess who said: 'Crime detection isn't sordid. It's scientific. I'd like to know for certain if Shink or Schenk are the same person. If only we knew what they look like, separately or singly.'

'We can be fairly sure that Shink and the Smith I heard about are the same man,' David said. 'Shink got your Mr. Crumping to fix shelves. Smith ordered electric bulbs for the garage. Both three weeks ago. I've got a rough description of the alleged Smith. My adorable girl friend of sixty-five gave it to me, under coercion.'

'Then there ought to be a way of checking whether the three names fit one man.'

'We'll think up something to settle that point. In the meantime here's our waiter. Indian or China?'

TWENTY-THREE

THEY WERE SITTING on two stools at the bar of a public house in Soho. Tess said: 'It's what I call a pretty sudden descent from Claridge's to here.'

'I'm used to high dives. And low ones,' David grinned. 'The point is that this pub is bang opposite the stage door of the Regalia, so Schenk is probably quite well known in here. All we've got to do is to get hold of someone who can describe him for us.'

'Someone who can and will,' Tess amended. 'It's not exactly usual to run around with a name asking what its owner looks like.'

'Trust your little David. The ever-bright boy. Character parts played at short notice, satisfaction guaranteed. Or money returned without question.'

'Imbecile,' murmured Tess.

The barmaid was a large woman who looked like a sergeant-major doing an unconvincing female impersonation. Her henna'd hair was like a wig, her pink-and-white make-up was thick upon the front of her face and stopped an inch short of her ears, so that she seemed to be wearing the sort of mask that adds gaiety to children's parties. Her eyes were hard and cynical with experience. David asked her to have a drink.

She said she would have a Guinness. David plunged: 'I bet you miss Mr. Schenk,' he remarked.

The barmaid stared silently, with no expression upon her gargoyle features.

David continued pleasantly: 'He's what I call a Lad, he is.'

'A proper larker, if you ask me.' The barmaid was melting.

'He's been unlucky, that's what he's been.'

''s a shame,' said the barmaid.

David glanced at the walls, which were plastered with glossy photographs of actresses, glamorous and otherwise, actors in dramatic poses, and distorted acrobats. 'You never put his photo up,' he remarked.

The barmaid had a fit of choking. David feared that it might be the prelude to a fit, but was reassured on realising that it was merely a method of expressing amusement. The barmaid, beating her considerable bosom with a large hand, gasped: 'His photo – oh law, *his* photo!'

'It's got as much right to be shown as anyone else's,' said David in the truculent tone of a man defending his closest friend.

'With that face! You'll kill me, you will! Oh, excuse me, I'm sure.' A loud hiccup had escaped. 'Stout always sets me off, it kind of catches me.'

David said encouragingly: 'Come now, he's not that much bad looking.'

'What, with that nose? He had it busted when he was in America or someone's a liar.'

David gave no sign of his elation at confirming one point of resemblance between the Mr. Smith of Mrs. Wicks's recital, and Mr. Schenk of the Regalia Theatre. He racked his brains for ideas that would evoke further confirmation. Tess had become tactfully unobtrusive as she sat twiddling her sherry glass between her fingers. 'I wouldn't say Mr. Schenk was the chap to start a rough house,' David ventured.

'Oh, some of those little 'uns are the most quarrelsome,' the barmaid said.

(What was the phrase Mrs. Wicks had used? 'A regular little weasel of a man...') 'Well, he may be small, but he's smart.'

'Not smart enough to keep out of never-mind-where.'

'I meant in the way he dresses.'

'Overdoes it, to my mind. Did you ever see that light blue check of his?'

'Bit hot, that was,' David hazarded.

'He fancied himself in it, paid twenty guineas for it, he showed me the bill. But that's nothing to his overcoat.' The barmaid leaned closer and said impressively: 'Three hundred and fifty pounds that coat cost, and if you don't want to believe me you needn't. It's lined with mink. I wonder he don't wear it inside out, him being a bit of a swanker. But there, if he did, the astrakhan collar wouldn't set straight.'

(Aha! thought David. The nebulous Mr. Smith and the actual Mr. Schenk had the same taste in fur collars. The two were rapidly being merged into one individual.)

The barmaid was still brooding about the overcoat. 'I told him straight, it's just asking for trouble to walk about in it.'

'He's got plenty of trouble, as it is.'

'Oh, well, we've all got our faults. Human, that's what I say we are.'

'True enough,' sighed David. He turned to Tess, who had kept an admirably straight face during the parley about the incarcerated Mr. Schenk. 'Ready for another sherry, darling?'

'I must go. It's five past six.'

David wished the barmaid good-bye. 'So long. All the best.'

'It's funny,' the barmaid said thoughtfully, 'but I don't remember you ever being in here with Mr. Schenk, for all he's such a pal of yours.'

'As a matter of fact, we never came in together. I used to have a tiddley with him over the road.'

'Then,' the barmaid queries suspiciously, 'how did you know I knew him?'

'Ah! If you could have heard all he said about you!'

The barmaid laughed. 'Oh, go on. Ta-ta. Be good.'

When they were outside David and Tess suppressed their merriment till they reached the corner. There they clung together arm in arm laughing helplessly.

'My dear!' Tess exclaimed. 'To hear you talking all that bunk!'

'Just the stuff to get what I wanted.'

'So I realised. I was mute with admiration. You even used a lovely adenoidy accent. And your melancholy sighs over the unlucky Mr. Schenk! And your comment on the blue check suit that you'd never seen. "Bit hot, that was." I don't know how you thought of such a superbly fitting comment.'

'It's a trick. I suppose one gets it from playing all sorts of parts. One's trained to jumping inside the skin of another man, and making him seem consistent, three-dimensional.'

'It's an art, of course. But doesn't it tend to make you insincere?'

Equally seriously, almost ponderously, David retorted, 'Artists are the only people who are truly sincere. The greater the artist, the greater the sincerity. When art is the thing that matters, compromises with the rest of the world – to gain friends or money or the neat label of respectability – become unnecessary. And being in this philosophic mood, I seize this perfect chance for a quotation – '

Tess chipped in 'Art is long, life is short.'

'I was going to give you Emerson. He said that "Art is a jealous mistress". So jealous, I'm afraid, that the artist often has no time for his wife. And that's something for which I can thank the war. It's made me go in for action instead of acting.'

'Aren't we getting rather deep? And all over the invisible Mr. Schenk. Your dear lamented friend. And how convincingly you lamented him.'

'It's lucky I can talk pub language.'

'You certainly can. What a knack! I haven't got it. Why, if I'd started chatting to that barmaid she'd have thought I was just a new customer being nosey.'

'Which is just what I was.'

'She never guessed. And you got the facts you needed.'

'Just by giving the right cues. At any moment I was ready to retreat, to say I was mixing Schenk up with someone else. But as the details tallied I knew it was all right. Mr. Smith of the garage – who needed electric light bulbs – *is* Mr. Schenk of the Regalia, who got the sore-footed Mr. Crumping to fix his shelves. Smith doesn't exist. Nor does your alleged Shink. I say, darling, have you really got to get back?'

'As fast as wheels can take us, or Sister Allardyce will cancel my free evening tomorrow.'

'Gosh, that's serious.'

They had to search for a taxi, flashing their torches discreetly on the kerb. At last a welcome voice responded. 'Keb, sir? Ry-choo-are, sir,' and off they went.

Their journey went by way of Terrapin Road. Tess said: 'Let's collect those stockings.'

'But it'll make you late.'

'It'll only take a moment.'

'If it dishes tomorrow evening I'll never forgive you.'

David told the driver to wait and ran up the steps. To his surprise, Tess was following. He had not fully appreciated the significance of a pair of stockings to a girl who had used all her current coupons. In his room he produced his gift.

'Oh, darling, lovely!' Tess cried. 'Pure silk and fully fashioned.'

'Don't ask me to get any more. It's not that I'm stingy. I'll buy you anything you like – '

'I wasn't going to ask you,' she interrupted reproachfully. She was inspecting the hose. 'Queer,' she commented. 'There was a manufacturer's mark on them but it's been removed. Look, you can just see scraps of the gilt lettering, where the name was.'

'Very illegitimate stuff,' David remarked. 'But we hardly expected them to have a pedigree.'

'They're heavenly anyway. So long as you don't think they were stolen.'

'No, of course not,' David said, 'The chap I bought them from couldn't do a thing like that.' (As if Pink-eye Bamberger would shrink from theft, when he looked as if robbing widows and cripples was his idea of fun!)

'That's a relief,' Tess said. 'Thanks awfully, Sweetie-pie.'

'Could you spare a kiss? And another? You angel!'

They ran down to the taxi. After Tess had left him David returned, and when he was half-way to his room the front door re-opened. Lipscott was in the hall. He seemed tired and dispirited, so David suggested going out for a drink.

'May as well,' Lipscott said flatly, sticking his cap back on his head.

They were in the dark street. 'Enjoying your bit of leave?' David asked.

'I've been walking around Acton all day.'

'Oh, glory, you're still on that Acton stunt?'

'It's the only place I'm likely to run across her.'

The pixie girl had certainly got a grip on the heart of Terry Lipscott. David said: 'You've been sailing about the world for years, and you must have met scores of wenches, yet you've got to go ga-ga about one you've only seen for an hour or so.'

'Well, that's how it is,' Lipscott said glumly.

They walked on. 'Don't tell me you're going to waste the whole of your leave prowling about Acton on the thinnest chance of finding her.'

'That's not wasting my leave. That's using it.'

The man was obsessed. 'But if she's working in a factory she won't be about in daylight.'

'She was out in daylight this morning, when you met her. Didn't you see how amazing she is?'

David hesitated. 'Well, she's kind of cute,' he temporised. 'It all depends what type you like. She seemed – well, quite determined to be scared by everything. And by nothing at all.'

'That's just it,' Lipscott exclaimed. 'She's scared – and I want to take care of her, so she'll stop being scared.'

David smiled under cover of the darkness. It was no good arguing against that kind of logic. If Lipscott succeeded in destroying the girl's inexplicable fear, he would have destroyed her only definite characteristic. He thought of warning Lipscott that pity is a dangerous emotion, liable to distort a man's reasoning powers, but decided that the warning would be useless.

'Here we are,' he said, 'the good old "Volunteer" – and, by jove, there's Bob Carter. That means we're in for a riot of international goodwill, theories on house decoration, and instruction on how to persuade the unwilling to be willing.'

Lipscott said: 'I don't follow you.'

'You will – if with some difficulty. Hullo, Bob, what's your tipple?'

'Scotch. A double if you don't mind. I've been moving mountains. Hullo, Lipscott, you back? How's the Merchant Navy? Or am I talking careless and letting down Billy Brown? Doing any dog-racing? You ought to be in the pukka Navy on an aircraft carrier, where there'd be lots of room for a dog track. Lordy-lordy, I do believe I'm just a trifle tight.'

'Thanks for letting us know,' David laughed.

'And I don't want quotations from you, because I can manage that sort of stuff for myself. Alas, that man would put an enemy in his mouth to soften his grey matter. Or thereabouts.'

'Very roughly thereabouts,' said David. 'And, anyway, there are five good excuses for drinking.'

'Let's have them.'

'I'm too thirsty to remember a single one.'

TWENTY-FOUR

DAVID WAS ABSENT-MINDED as the three of them stood at the bar. Everyone around them seemed to be gossiping about the murder, it threatened to be an inexhaustible subject, and his own imagination continued to leap with speculations about it.

Suddenly he remembered that Bob Carter probably knew as much about the West End as anyone living. In his job as tittle-tattle writer for the *Social Mirror* he had waded into every society scandal over several years.

So David asked suddenly: 'Did you know the Marquis of Leafe? The old man?'

'Died in his bath in a hot shop in Jermyn Street,' Bob retorted promptly.

'That's correct. He had a flat in Boulters Court.'

'Well, there you are,' said Bob. 'If that wasn't sizzling hot I don't know what is. It's closed now.'

'I never knew the facts about that Leafe case. He popped off on that Sunday in September when Hitler stole the headlines. Accidental death, wasn't it?'

'An open verdict. The old boy had been in his usual roaring health. Suspicious points were that he'd tidied up his affairs and had his pet cat sent to the never-never land. But any old gent might have done that. It came out that he sometimes took a sleeping draught, and the idea was that he'd taken a larger dose than usual, and was still drowsy when he got into the bath. But why all this curiosity over stale news?'

'Just a chance remark I overheard.' David was remembering how Mrs. Meake had taunted Miss Trindle, "It's not the first time you've been mixed up in a scandal". He added: 'One of the dames at Mrs. Meake's was book-keeper at Boulters Court, you know.'

'I didn't know. Who was?'

'Miss Trindle.'

'What, the old sour-puss on the hall floor?'

'She left yesterday. What beats me is how a woman of her type could have done a job in a hectic dump like Boulters Court. Only explanation is that she couldn't have known what a reputation it had.'

'Couldn't have known, my foot! The place fairly hummed. Besides, the finances of that place must have been an eye-opener. The furniture was all to bits and still they charged three guineas a night for what they called a suite. I know, because once when I was flush I went there with a Spanish fancy piece who poured Pommard into the piano. And nobody minded because that was what they were used to. I suppose that's what they charged for.'

'Funny place for his lordship to stay.'

'Still funnier as a place to die,' said Bob. 'But if you want the dope on that, why not ask the Trindle?'

'Because she's decamped, for one thing. For another, she doesn't like me. But it's odd that one death dislodged her from Jermyn Street and another from Terrapin Road.'

'Perhaps she doesn't like death,' was Lipscott's uninspired interpolation.

The topic of Miss Trindle faded out. The clock over the bar indicated that it was twenty to ten, and none of them had had an evening meal. Bob was reverting to his obsession, the plans for opening his club at the end of the week. Lipscott kept dropping back into a kind of reverie – that, so David guessed, circled around a certain dithering and elusive girl.

'I'm going to eat,' David announced.

The other two, it appeared, were still thirsty rather than hungry. David went alone to the "Blue Lantern", where Miss McDrew herself waited upon him, offering him dishes as if he were a fastidious child. Having satisfied his hunger, he walked round to St. Margaret's, just for the joy of passing the walls that sheltered Tess. He would marry her before his week was up, that he swore to the night and the stars. He'd take her by storm, he'd spring at her with a special licence, he'd blow all his savings on a diamond ring. And, of course, a plain gold or platinum one, saving just enough for their hotel bill.

But he'd like to solve this queer murder first. Half automatically, he walked back past Mrs. Meake's and turned again into Cannock

Road, thence into the alley that led to the garage. Only a crescent of moon relieved the black-out, there was a slight ground mist, the neighbourhood was silent at this time of night.

He walked down the alley and stood outside the garage, wondering what secrets it might hide. Schenk, the owner, was in prison. Thelma his employee, was hobnobbing with a man who carried goods from this garage to a black market shop. And that man, so like the victim of Sunday night's crime, had been weeping in the "Mango Grove"...

Idly, David tried the garage door. It did not yield; he had hardly expected that it would.

Retracing his steps, he heard a faint rustle behind him. Like a step on stray leaves. He stopped, a sense of impending danger tingling the roots of his hair. Again silence – an eerie silence – surrounded him. The quietness of open spaces is a natural thing; quietness in the heart of a great city is somehow sinister, like the stillness of some powerful and dangerous beast that may stir suddenly and savagely to life.

He moved on a few paces, wondering whether his tensed nerves were responsible for the renewed suspicion that he was being dogged. Again he stopped. He'd been right, he wasn't alone...

And then something struck him. That was all he could remember as consciousness returned. That something heavy had cracked the side of his head as he turned. He had the very devil of a headache, and as he tried to rise he staggered. His fingers, going automatically to the side of his forehead, touched something warm and gummy. With the back of his hand he wiped the blood that trickled over one eye.

He managed to get to his feet, reeling slightly as he progressed a few steps. The wall was a help, he steered himself by it, and once in Cannock Road he was able to cover the familiar stretch of pavement round the corner to Mrs. Meake's. He felt that all he wanted to do was to lay his head on a cool pillow and sink back into unconsciousness. He was still too dazed to feel anger.

Somehow he unlocked the front door. Closing it, he fumbled for the light switch, and then he had to pause to rally his senses. It was while he was standing there, at the foot of the stairs that the door opened again.

Dimly, he saw the German doctor who had a room on the second floor. Hauptmann...

Hauptmann was at his side in a moment. For some reason that he could not have defined, David gave evasive answers to the questions rapidly fired in guttural broken English.

'I had a few drinks,' he muttered. 'I cracked my head against a wall. No fuss. For heaven's sake, no fuss.'

Hauptmann was guiding him upstairs, uttering solicitous noises. The wound must be sterilised, bandaged. Hauptmann would attend to it. David put up no resistance; he was in Hauptmann's room wincing as the cut on his head was cleansed. Fortunately it was neither extensive nor deep, and being near the roots of his hair would not be too apparent. He did not want to have to answer a lot of questions about it. The pain of the bruise extended further, over the whole of the left of his head.

The attack, David brooded silently, was the direct result of his curiosity about the garage. But to what extent – if at all – could the secrets of the garage throw light upon the murder done within a few yards of where his unseen assailant had slugged him?

It seemed that he had been on the right scent when he tried that garage door.

Hauptmann asked: 'Is better, yes?'

'Fine, thanks. It's decent of you to take all this trouble.'

Hauptmann laughed comfortably. He had a small black pointed beard, and a tuft of hair of almost the same shape on the otherwise bald top of his head. His eyes were nearly black, bright and glinting in his plump but intelligent face. His mouth was fleshy, he had a habit of pouting. He had removed his coat, David noticed how frayed and threadbare his shirt was.

'I'm afraid I'm keeping you up, Doctor.'

'No, please. No trouble. Just my work. Simple for me. Much pain, no?'

'Not too bad,' David said. 'Funny, my ears are singing as if I'd had a shot of quinine.'

'Sleep will make better, yes.'

'What's the time?'

Hauptmann consulted his watch. 'Twelve o'clock, just.'

'Gosh, I must have been out for about an hour.'

'Is good I am here.'

'I'll say it is. I'm very grateful.'

'I haf milk, cocoa. Warm drink to make you sleep, yes?'

'If you've got it to spare.'

'Plenty, plenty.' Hauptmann lit the gas ring, took a saucepan and cups from a cupboard. He moved slowly, as if he felt weary.

'I still think I'm being a darn nuisance,' David apologised.

'But no. I lif – live best at night, most awake at night.'

David watched the plump elderly figure toddling about the room, fussing like an anxious peasant over the cocoa making. Queer, he thought, that my job is killing the fellow countrymen of this kindhearted old boy. He asked: 'How long have you been in England?'

'Four years. Lucky I was, to escape from concentration camp. Lucky to find work here, to find so good woman like Mrs. Meake.' He laughed shortly. 'Lucky – in everything but memory.'

'You mean-your memory of Nazi Germany?'

'Of my poor wife, my dead children, my lost home. My laboratory gone. All that.'

David was silent for a moment or so, before he said awkwardly: 'I'm sorry.'

'When I haf much to do, I forget. You do me a kindness, you bring me a wound to mend.'

David smiled. 'I don't think we need argue about which of us is doing the other a kindness. I've been under the weather, in hospital, for months, and I particularly want to be in working order by the end of this week.'

'You agree that we must all help, one to another?'

'Of course.'

'Then I haf somet'ing to ask of you. There, there is your cocoa, stir it well as it grows cool, it mixes the cream, so.'

'What is it you want?' David asked. He was feeling clearer headed, sufficiently so to be curious, a trifle suspicious.

Hauptmann said quickly: 'Not for myself. For myself I need not'ing. It is this Smedley.'

TWENTY-FIVE

THERE WAS À LONG PAUSE. David repeated: 'Smedley? What's the matter with Smedley?'

'You know him well?'

'Not well. He's a quiet sort of chap. I haven't spent more than a few hours with him, all the time we've both digged here.'

'He is a nervous one.'

David remembered Smedley's limp. 'Maybe a permanent physical disability makes a man nervous.'

'It is possible, on the other hand it may so well make him arrogant. The psychologists explain such contradictions. A man who is afraid of his defect sometimes convinces himself that it is a kind of advantage. A man with a deformed hand, for example, will continually wave that hand, to insist that it shall be seen.'

'That sort of palaver isn't in my line,' David said.

'No, no. Exactly. I understand. But consider this for example. Women are not attracted by Smedley, so he persuades himself that he does not care for women. Indeed, that he detests them.'

'Come to think of it, I've never seen him with a girl.' David pondered for a moment before asking abruptly: 'What are you getting at?'

Hauptmann smiled gently. 'I said, yes I haf somet'ing to ask of you.'

'What's that got to do with Smedley?'

'It is perhaps impossible for you.' The doctor shrugged his shoulders. 'But you haf a good heart. Smedley needs money.'

David asked: 'What for? He's got a steady job, he's had it for years, and he isn't extravagant. So far as I know he doesn't drink or gamble. And as he doesn't go in for fancy ladies – or for that matter, for any kind of ladies, I can't see – '

'He has got into some difficulty. Over a woman. Probably over the only woman who ever has noticed him. Exactly how it is, I do not know. Whether it is her debts, whether it is he has – what is the word? – incurred debts for gifts, I cannot say. However it may be, he is in a difficulty.'

There was a silence. David said encouragingly: 'And he's been confiding in you?'

Hauptmann nodded. 'On Sunday morning – yes, Sunday it was – he asked me to lend him money. One hundred pounds.' Again the doctor shrugged his plump shoulders. 'So willingly I would give it. But I couldn't.'

'So, he wanted a hundred quid? Too bad.' David smiled. 'There's no earthly reason why you or I should provide it for him. I never even thought of borrowing from Smedley, even when I was absolutely stuck, as often I was before the war.'

'It was just a suggestion.'

'Leave it at that. I'm sorry about Smedley. But he's not a kid, and of all people a bank clerk should know how to keep his affairs in order.'

'We will forget it.'

David sipped his drink. 'You certainly know how to make a dish of cocoa.'

'It is good, yes?'

'Excellent. But – where's yours?'

'Tonight I haf no need of it.'

'But I say! I'm pinching your nightcap.'

'Not'ing, not'ing. It is good for you. After such shock, a smooth drink, very hot.'

Hauptmann's benevolence was disconcerting. With almost a sense of guilt, David finished his cupful. He had risen to go to his own room when there was a soft tap on the door.

'Com' in.' Hauptmann had started and seemed apprehensive. Relief spread over his features as Smedley appeared in a dressing gown and bedroom slippers. 'Oh – you,' he muttered, and then apologised aside to David: 'A moment's nervousness, you will understand, in my life I have had bad surprises.'

Smedley looked pale, indeed haggard. His hair was ruffled, as if he had been in bed, his eyes were dark-ringed, his mouth drawn in a thin line. As always, he stood crookedly, with most of his weight on his shorter leg.

'Sorry if I'm butting in,' he said. 'I saw the light under the door.'

As Hauptmann did not speak, David said: 'It's O.K. as far as I'm concerned. I was just taking off.'

Smedley made no comment on the strip of plaster on David's forehead. He seemed to be shaken by nerves, concerned only with himself. 'Didn't want to interrupt. But – ' he broke off before he said explosively: 'I can't sleep. I haven't slept for nights. I'm all in.'

'No. Please – ' Hauptmann spoke soothingly.

'I wondered, Doctor, if you could give me a shot of something? A tablet, some pills, anything.'

David interrupted curtly: 'Why can't you sleep?'

'Because I've got something on my mind,' Smedley almost snarled. 'That's why. It's no business of yours.'

'Sorry.'

There was an awkward silence. As if resenting it as much as he had resented being questioned, Smedley said sullenly: 'It's a girl. She married the wrong man. That's all.'

'Oh,' said David noncommittally. So it was that sort of triangle. Common enough. Smedley was a fool to get involved.

'I thought,' Hauptmann said gently, 'that it was perhaps the matter of the money difficulty.'

'Not now. For heaven's sake, give me something that'll make me sleep. Talking's no good, I'm saying things I'll regret, I'm pretty nearly off my rocker.'

'Steady, steady,' murmured Hauptmann.

'Some drug – you must have something handy, that's what doctors are for. You've got the stuff. I can't lie awake another night.'

Hauptmann said firmly 'I haf not'ing here, I am sorry. Tomorrow, you should see a doctor, some doctor who treats you before.'

'Tomorrow!' Smedley laughed on a harsh note. 'What if there isn't any tomorrow? What if I can't stick it?'

'That's ridiculous,' David cut in firmly. 'Try taking a good wollop of aspirin. I've got some if you haven't. And do as Dr. Hauptmann suggests, see your own medico in the morning.' As he spoke he was reflecting upon Smedley's retort to the comment upon his financial predicament. The money problem wasn't worrying him – 'not now'. What could have relieved the situation? Why, when Smedley had tried to borrow a hundred pounds on Sunday, was he indifferent to the matter on Tuesday? Or rather – for now it was well past midnight – in the early hours of Wednesday?

Suddenly Smedley dropped into a chair and hid his face in his arms. His condition was embarrassing – to David, if not to the more experienced Dr. Hauptmann.

Hauptmann said gently: 'Com', I take you to your room. You get into bed, you put out the light, you will sleep. It is only an idea, a fear that you will not sleep. Believe me, Smedley, it is that simply an idea.'

'I'm sorry. I'm all to pieces.' Smedley made an obvious effort.

David said heartily: 'Come along, old chap. Can't do you any good, sticking around and belly-aching. Good-night Doctor. Thanks a lot for all you've done.'

Hauptmann smiled expansively. 'No trouble. Sleep well, both of you.' He followed them to the door, his fleshy mouth parted in a benign smile.

TWENTY-SIX

DAVID HELD SMEDLEY'S ARM as they left the doctor's room. Outside the door of the back room they paused. 'You'll turn in right away, Smedley?'

'I shan't sleep.'

'Rot. I can see you're dead beat.' David himself felt tired after his unpleasant encounter in the alley. (Who the devil had caught him that crack? And why?) 'Come on now, hop into bye-bye like a sensible fellow.' He thrust open the door to urge Smedley in.

The light was on. They had gone only one step into the room when David stopped dead and Smedley dropped back against the doorpost with a stifled cry.

A man in khaki battledress was standing by the divan bed. A revolver dangled from his right hand. He was of medium build, fair, with steady light-coloured eyes. His face was set, expressionless. He could not have been more than thirty, but the pinched contour of his jaw indicated that he lacked most or all of his teeth.

There was a tense, astonished silence. Then the soldier asked gruffly, 'Which of you two is Smedley?'

Again a silence, till David rapped: 'Who the devil are you, anyway?'

'I'm Delia's husband. That'll have to be good enough.'

David stared blankly. The interloper seemed to sense that his puzzlement was genuine, for he swung towards Smedley. 'You're the swine, are you?'

Smedley was so evidently terrified that David, fearing that he might faint, said quickly: 'Smedley's not too fit. If you've got to have an argument, couldn't it wait?'

'No it couldn't.'

'You can't come waving a gun in a chap's room like this, you know.' David kept his voice on an even, casual note. With Smedley struck dumb and shivering and this queer stranger armed and in a cold, determined fury, anything might happen.

'I'll use it as soon as wave it, if he doesn't let Delia alone.'

David turned to Smedley. 'Let's have your side of it, old man.'

Smedley shook his head helplessly. 'Tell him – tell him to get out.'

'But if there's anything in this suggestion about his wife, you've got to give him some assurance. Well, you can't just dodge a thing like that.'

Smedley said jerkily: 'She needs protection. I'm only out to protect her.'

'That's a husband's job.'

The soldier advanced a step, his expression was ugly with rage. 'She needs protection all right. Protection from herself and her damn play-acting. When I'm about I keep a check on it. I got leave today. Unexpected. And a lucky thing I did, Mr. Blooming Millionaire Smedley.'

The taunt puzzled David. But his attention was on Smedley, who was explosively accusing the other, 'You ill-treat her, you keep her short of necessities. You – you *torture* her.'

A sardonic grin overspread the soldier's features. 'Yes, I know all that. I've heard it before. I torture her, I don't let her have any money. Well, I'll admit I don't give her enough to go running round with the crowd she likes, to posh clubs and smarty bars. Or to stay at West Endy hotels, when she's got a nice little home of her own. I'm cruel, am I? Delia's got a regular five quid a week, and she could earn more if she wasn't a selfish lazy little so-and-so. That's not too bad for a girl whose dad sold cockles from a stall on Southend beach, is it?'

Smedley muttered: 'You're lying. Her father was a Russian aristocrat.'

'Oh lord, the grand-duke! I thought he was a back number. She got him out of a serial in a girl's paper, and she used to put on a French accent, thinking that'd be near enough to make him a relative.' The soldier again became serious and menacing. 'I tell you this much, you'd better keep away from Delia, or you may get hurt.'

David jerked a thumb at the gun, now levelled at Smedley. 'Look out! Keep that down!'

'If it wasn't for men being such mugs, Delia'd be all right. She wouldn't have anyone to listen to her fancy yarns, she wouldn't have anyone to pay for her stunts. So don't say I didn't warn you.' The soldier spoke slowly, impressively. 'If I catch you seeing Delia again, or if I so much as hear you've seen her. I'll let you have one quick taste of this.' The gun was again jerked level.

Smedley neither spoke nor moved. The soldier went on: 'There's too much hanky-panky behind the backs of us chaps. Women left on their own – it's bound to happen. But if it happens in my family, I'm going to provide the answer and damn the consequences. Understand?'

Smedley nodded to indicate that he understood.

'That's all,' said the soldier. He packed his gun away in his haversack.

David asked: 'How did you get into the house?'

He was subjected to a cool contemptuous stare from the light eyes of the visitor, before the answer came: 'Thelma let me in.'

'Thelma! So she's back?' (And how the devil did this fellow know Thelma?).

'I don't know what you mean, "back". She lives here, doesn't she?'

'On and off.'

'She came as far as the door and used her key and told me I'd find what I wanted in the second floor back. Then she beat it. That's all I asked her to do.' The soldier smiled sourly. 'She saved herself a packet of trouble by doing what she was asked, and she knew it.'

David felt that this awkward interview was at an end. 'So that's about all, I take it?'

'Except' – the soldier slid a hand into a pocket, a paper rustled in his fingers – 'except for that. You can take it back, Mr. Blooming Millionaire Smedley. And remember what I said. I meant every word.'

Throwing down the crumpled paper, the man strode out. David stared in amazement, then picked up the paper and smoothed it out.

It was a hundred pound note. 'Yours?' he asked Smedley.

'Yes. It's mine. I – I gave it to Delia. She needed it.'

So that was why the soldier had used that sarcastic form of address, Mr. Blooming-Millionaire Smedley.

Oddly enough, the argument seemed to have steadied Smedley. 'He can't part us,' he muttered stubbornly.

'He's got every right to do so,' David rapped. 'It seems to me you've been making an ass of yourself.' The stock sort of triangle drama was less interesting than the bank note – and the question of how Smedley had acquired it. David added, 'The chap seemed on the level. Not that I hold with gunman stuff in civilian settings. Tell me, how did you meet this Delia?'

'Through Thelma. Last week Thelma told me she'd got a friend who was lonely.'

'So Thelma produces Delia and you produce a hundred quid. Nice arrangement, if it wasn't for the husband element. You must be what he called you, a millionaire.'

'I'm not. My salary just keeps me. I only got this – ' Smedley glanced at the note that was still in his hand – 'a day or so ago.'

It was on Sunday that Smedley had tried, without success, to borrow a hundred from Hauptmann. 'How?' David asked.

'Never mind that.'

And it was on Monday morning that a men had been found murdered, without a wallet, without a single coin upon him... 'How did the Tommy get hold of Thelma to bring him here?'

Smedley growled: 'I don't know. Perhaps Delia talked. She talks a lot. Sometimes it seems as if she can't stop. She's so sensitive, highly strung.'

David suppressed a smile. 'You're well out of that mix-up. You are going to keep out of it, aren't you?'

Smedley paused before he said tensely, emotionally: 'Don't you understand? Don't you? *Can't* you? I – I haven't had a lot to do with girls. I never had a girl in my life, not the way you hear chaps saying they have. I was always afraid they'd laugh at me, with my gammy leg. But Delia never noticed my leg, she loved me, she was crazy about me. You don't know what that meant. You're well set up and decent looking, and you're a hero with decorations and all that – '

'Oh fiddlesticks – ' David tried to interrupt in vain.

'It's easy for you. For me – ' Smedley's self-deprecation was pathetic, 'well, getting a girl to love me, especially when she was so pretty, it made all the difference. It gave me – life.'

This was a moment when it was kind to be cruel, David said: 'Delia's interest was very sudden and it wasn't entirely without profit to herself.'

'It wasn't the money,' Smedley said quickly.

'But she asked you for it?'

'She told me she'd got to have it.' Gradually, the obviousness of her tactics seemed to dawn on Smedley. An expression of bewilderment, then of dismay, tinged his features. 'Well,' he added helplessly 'I just had to get it for her.'

David spoke deliberately. 'You still haven't explained how.'

Smedley averted his eyes, shifting his lame leg as if it hurt him. 'I'd rather not say.'

'Perhaps you'll just say *when* you got it?'

'On – on Monday. It was a private loan.'

'Tell me, Smedley,' David kept his eyes fixed on the uneasy man, 'could you do a murder?'

The reply was startling. 'You've read my thoughts!' Smedley exclaimed.

David waited for him to continue. The next words were an anti-climax, for Smedley went on savagely: 'I was thinking, when that chap was here, that if I could strike him dead, shoot him, poison him anything – Delia would be free.'

'You'd better go to bed,' David advised. 'And one last word if you'll listen to it. Forget Delia. Her husband meant what he said. And no one could blame him. Good night.'

On the stairway David's attention was arrested. Someone was coming down from the top floor. Annie…? Surely not at this time of night. It was after one o'clock. Mrs. Poole? There was no one else up there.

A moment later he saw Mr. Cumberbatch. 'Oh, hullo,' David said awkwardly, feeling self-conscious at having waited merely from curiosity.

'Hullo, Heron. You're up late.'

"What about you?" thought David. He smiled disarmingly. 'I'm not off the lead for long, so I'm burning the candle at both ends.'

Cumberbatch was about sixty, but his snow-white hair was still thick and wavy. His features were colourless, narrow, rather crafty. He was wearng a shapeless old suit and felt slippers. Again David felt the dislike the man had always provoked in him. There was something unnatural about the old fellow, with his wrinkled, watchful eyes, that always seemed to be gazing at something far away.

It seemed that he and Mrs. Poole had made up their differences; they must have enjoyed their coffee party tonight, to prolong it to this hour. Mrs. Poole mightn't be as prim as she appeared. But if she got thick with Cumberbatch it was nobody's business but their own. He was certainly an eccentric fellow, with his passion for preserving his own quarters from intrusion.

Following this line of thought, David remarked: 'I'm shockingly wide awake, and I've got nothing to read. Can you lend me something?'

Cumberbatch stiffened, standing with one hand on the banisters. 'Sorry, I can't.'

'Any sort of a book would do.'

'I don't go in for books. Books do a lot of harm.'

'Oh no, that's hardly fair on the writing johnnies.'

'They throw doubts on eternal truth.'

'I was just thinking of fiction, not of any controversial stuff.'

'There shouldn't *be* any controversy about the transmigration of souls. It's an established fact.'

'Oh – that.' David was at a loss. 'Well, good night.'

Cumberbatch went on to his room as David closed his own door. The man didn't go in for books…What the devil did he go in for, apart from Mrs. Poole's hospitality? He spent a lot of time alone in that barricaded room of his.

As David dropped on the edge of his divan he realised how desperately tired he was, in spite of his boast of being wide awake. It had been a pretty hectic evening, one way and another. His head was aching and his eyes felt like hot marbles.

He shuffled out of his clothes, and nearly choked himself by yawning as he cleaned his teeth. Yet sleep eluded him for some time. His last thought as he drifted towards welcome oblivion was that he would have a quiet day tomorrow.

Tomorrow was today… must be three in the morning by now.

TWENTY-SEVEN

'TESS, WHAT A STROKE OF LUCK!'

David, swinging into Belmont Crescent on Thursday morning with the intention of going to see how Bob Carter's club was progressing, had caught sight of the demure grey uniformed figure in the curve of garden in the Crescent. He skirted the bushes and stepped over the wooden stumps that had replaced iron railings; then he saw that two children were beside Tess on the seat.

'David – but my dear, I'm on duty.'

'So I see.' David grinned at the children, a girl and a boy, hoping to ingratiate them.

'What was the matter with you yesterday? You were awfully evasive over the phone.'

'I can come clean now I'm all right again. Evasion was concussion. I had – an accident of sorts on Tuesday night. I got to sleep in the early hours, but yesterday I conked right out. Meakie was a pet, she plied me with an ice-bag for the heated brow, and held my hand while I drank barley-water. I picked up towards evening, and here I am in my usual health and strength.'

'Concussion! Why didn't you let me know?'

'Because I didn't want you to see me being sick. Not pretty.'

'But how did you get it?'

'Perhaps it was just a whimsy. *Malade imaginaire.*'

'You've got the French accent of an undertrained commando. And as for you being a whimsy invalid, don't be idiotic.'

David grinned guiltily. 'Can't we send the kids to buy toffee or something?'

'Impossible, for a number of reasons. I think you'd better buzz off and I'll see you later for a real heart-to-heart. If Sister Allardyce came along she'd think we'd fixed a meeting.'

David dropped on the seat and lit a cigarette. 'She could think what she liked. She can't stop me taking the air and sunshine, it's the right of every honest citizen. Besides, I'm convalescent, so I've got to

154

keep off my feet.'

'You're an argumentative beast,' said Tess – but her voice was gentle.

'And in that get-up you're a sort of superior imitation of a nursemaid. Everyone knows that nursemaids are entitled to followers. That's what children are for, to give an excuse for any would-be follower to scrape an acquaintance. "Hullo, what a stunning little boy," says the gentleman, and before you can say Jack Robinson he's telling the tale to nursie, and steaming all the starch out of her with his fiery passion.'

'This sounds like the voice of experience.'

'It's the voice of an artist whose genius consists of emotional intensities.'

'Cor! And again – Cor!'

David turned to the children, who were goggling at this interchange of flippancy. 'Hullo, George.'

'My name's Dickie.'

'Well, Dickie, you see that old summer house? That's where the Red Indians lived.'

'Real ones?'

'Of course. Specially savage ones. Some time, if you're very very good, you can go and find out if they left any traces.'

'Traces? A footprint on the sand?'

'There might be lots. I wouldn't know.'

At once the children began to clamour for permission to explore the summer house. Tess gave in. 'But keep where I can see you,' she called after them. 'David, you're worse than insidious, you're plausible. And it was news to me that those kids knew anything about Red Indians.'

'They probably don't. No matter, the phrase was effective. "Words are wise men's counters." Origin of that aphorism can be supplied when my memory functions better than it's doing at this moment.'

'Don't strain it. Words, by the way, are the confidence trickster's stock-in-trade. You've got rings under your eyes. I believe your concussion was a plain, ugly hangover.'

David sighed. 'I was always misunderstood.'

'What did you do after you left me on Tuesday night? I thought you were going straight home.'

'I wandered about under the stars – not that there were any, but it sounds well – dreaming of you. Then I had a drink or so.'

'Your story begins to be convincing.' Tess started as David removed his hat, exposing the strip of plaster on his forehead. 'What's that? Result of a drunken brawl?'

'No lovey. No my sweeter-than-honey. It's the result of being attacked by a desperado who wanted to teach me not to be inquisitive.'

Briefly, David told the story of the attack. 'I haven't the slightest doubt but that it's all linked up with Sunday night's dead foreigner and the sharp dagger. But – ' he added despondently, 'so many links are still missing. Also, just to top off a delightful evening, I was confronted by an angry soldier with a gun. That was at something past midnight.'

'David, you're embroidering.'

'I swear it's true. He waved his gun – well, not *that* far from my ugly face.'

'Handsome face,' corrected Tess.

'Love is blind.'

'Who ever said I loved you? But why the gun, anyway?'

'This is where my story goes to pieces and becomes, frankly, a rotten one. The gunman wasn't out after me, ugly or handsome. He was hunting Smedley.'

'Smedley? Smedley?'

'You've probably forgotten my recital of the personnel at Mrs. Meake's. Smedley is the second floor back. Quiet sort of chap, unobtrusive and usually inoffensive.'

'Then more than ever, why the gun?'

'It was lucky I was there. I think Smedley felt fortified by an ally. I'll explain the gun. This Smedley has never been much of a one for the ladies, but it seems that he fell heavily for a certain Delia – a friend of Thelma Meake's, by the way. And everything might have been fine for everyone, if Delia hadn't been married to a soldier bloke who came on leave unexpectedly two days ago, and found her crooning over a hundred quid note that Smedley had given her.'

'Does he made a habit of distributing hundreds?'

'He doesn't. Smedley was broke on Sunday. And he tells me he got a loan on Monday. On Sunday he was trying to borrow a hundred pounds, without success.' David gazed at the sky as if making a quite casual comment. 'A gentleman was knifed and left penniless in our back garden on Sunday night.'

Tess said quickly, 'No one knows how much money the dead man had before his wallet was taken. That's if he had one.'

'He looked just the sort to carry a fair amount of cash.'

'Who is this Smedley? What's his job? Is he the bank clerk you mentioned?'

'Yes. I always thought he was unbearably respectable. Sort of chap who'd write R.D. very primly on a cheque scribbled in a careless moment by an unprosperous actor.'

Tess smiled. 'What a good thing airmen have no careless moments.'

'I'll let that pass.'

'Charming of you. So Smedley becomes a promising suspect?'

'Smedley provides another problem. It isn't obvious, at a glance, whether it's relevant.'

'You'll have to hurry up. You'll be off on Sunday. It looks as if you'll leave behind a Great Unsolved Mystery.'

'I hope not. And among other hopes – no, it's a certainty, I'm going to marry you, Tess Carmichael, before I go, whether you like it or not.'

'There's just a chance I might like it.'

'Darling, you're adorable. Do you think it would be too outrageous if I kissed you, right here in the bright sunshine?'

'Have a care, good sir. The younger generation have eyes and ears and we don't want them to get complexes.'

'But they're bound to get them if they see me being inhibited.'

The two children had run back complaining that there were no signs of Red Indian occupation of the summer house.

'Then it must be some other summer house,' David said brightly. 'Or perhaps those Indians didn't do their stuff in the matter of traces. Hang it all, it's pretty grim if one can't rely upon one's savages.'

The children nodded in solemn agreement.

'Good-bye,' said Tess. 'We have cocoa and biscuits at eleven thirty.'

She had risen. David, surveying her neat uniform, said: 'You may have been tailored by someone with slick modern efficiency, but you've got what Cleopatra had and Nell Gwynn and Helen of Troy.'

'They probably had halitosis,' said Tess. 'Even their best friends didn't dare tell them. No, not even if they were Anthony and Henry the Eighth. So long, we really must go.'

'But so long for how long?'

'Till tonight. I'll ring you.'

He watched Tess and her charges walking sedately from the Crescent garden. Then rather sadly he continued his way to the embryo club of the twenty-six nations. To himself he mooned platitudinously: 'How sad that life is so short.' And then, as an afterthought; 'Or is it sheer brevity that makes it such fun?'

TWENTY-EIGHT

'YOU'RE A NICE ONE, you are,' Bob Carter said scornfully.

David grinned. 'To tell you the truth, I have my nice moments.'

'You fool! Where the hell did you get to on Tuesday night? And yesterday? The Meake kept saying you weren't in.'

'I was in all yesterday, but in no state for phone chatter.'

'Well I'm hanged. If I'd guessed I'd have come round myself. And what about Tuesday? I was ringing up like a madman and no one knew where you were.'

'But that was the evening I was in "The Volunteer" with you.'

'I mean later. About eleven thirty-ish.'

'By then I was unconscious from a murderous attack upon my person.'

'Are you raving? Or what *is* this?'

'If I never utter again, I was unconscious. If you need evidence – ' David swept his hat dramatically from his head. 'It's not an awfully impressive exhibit, in fact I'd say it was a wonder the skin got broken at all. The weapon was blunt and I seem to remember dodging.'

'What weapon? Were you fighting?'

'Never struck a blow, on my word etcetera.' Briefly, David gave an account of his inquisitive prowl round the garage, and its sequel. 'Yesterday I lived on aspirin and lukewarm milk.'

'Crikey,' Bob said solemnly. He used the word only when his emotions were deeply stirred. He added: 'No wonder the Meake used a voice that suggested you were in a different world. I was on the phone again less than half an hour ago.'

'Ah, that was when I was doing a bit of walking out and courting. But let's have it, why this frenzy to communicate?

'Because I've found the sailor. The chap with the amber beads and daggers and yellow spotted scarf.'

'Holy smoke! Where is he?'

'He'll be back. He's going to join the "Twenty-Six".'

'How did you come across him?'

'It was like this. When I left the pub on Tuesday night I was just tight enough to be getting cautious. I had an idea I'd left a light burning here, and that old half-wit hasn't yet fixed the curtains, so back I came. Ever the man to attend to duty. The sailor was asleep on the steps. Awfully pathetic. Sample of the homeless foreigner for whom the club will cater to perfection. It was too bad there was no light and no photographer. The dagger-dealer is heavily picturesque – or photogenic would be the newer adjective.'

'What's his name? Where does he hang out? When's he coming back?'

'Name, Jules Dupont. Which of course is kind of French for Jack Smith. No fixed residence, he seems to be a rather mobile unit. He'd heard about the sign saying all nations welcome, and thought he could get a drink. It was just lousy having to tell him we hadn't yet got the bottles and barrels in.'

'What is he? French navy?'

'No. Sort of freelance sailor. Before the war he had a fishing smack somewhere near Marseilles. Then he got taken on a Greek ship and found himself at Paramaribo, and he felt kind of miserable and wanted to get back to France – that was just before the capitulation – so he worked his way to Java and got on to a Dutch cargo ship that pitched him into London docks. Anyway, that's his story. Also says that since then he's done four trips across the Atlantic. And to think that he was thirsty and I couldn't give him a mug of beer. They say that Balzac knew something about tragedy. Balzac should have seen our friend Dupont on the front steps here, with nothing but a carpet holdall. Just that, not even a parrot.'

David said impatiently, 'Where is he now?'

'I don't know.'

'But – you fool, you should know. You should have hung on to him, knowing he's the chap that sold the dagger that did the murder.'

'Yes, yes, I realised all that when I woke up yesterday morning. But on Tuesday night I was in the friendly and singing stage, and I forgot all about stabbed victims, the only thing that worried me was not having any liquor. So, of course, when our sailor pal remembered he might find some in a dump off Praed Street, I didn't detain him.'

'You're sure it's the same chap, the one who was hawking stuff in "The Volunteer" on Sunday night?'

'Description tallies. And that yellow spotted scarf is pretty original. Unique, I'd say. It must have been knitted by loving hands for him alone. Besides, he told me about having an argument with the patronne in the pub. To wit, Mrs. Newland.'

'You're a blithering idiot to have let him get away.'

'But he promised to return. I stuck around for a bit, singing *Roses of Picardy*, which always indicates I'm getting sober. Then I rang up your dump.'

'Who answered the phone?'

'A man. Don't know who. Didn't ask him anything but whether you were in. He'd got a soft, mellow voice.'

'It was you who were soft and mellow. In a word, canned.'

'Not completely,' Bob declared. 'I can remember that French chap's name, and all he said. Would I be dreaming about a voice?'

'I suppose Mrs. Meake had a visitor. She's got one or two ancient hangers-on.'

'The fellow tried your extension and said there was no reply.'

'Of course there wasn't, when I was either unconscious in Cannock Alley, or too devilish conscious while Hauptmann cleaned up my forehead.'

'You haven't told me exactly what happened.'

'Someone whom I never saw whacked me on the head with something blunt and heavy, after I'd been inquisitive enough to try the door of the garage in the alley. I got home all right and the German doctor on the second floor gave me the once-over and decided I should survive. When do you think this sailor's likely to return?'

'Tomorrow probably, because that's when we open and I promised him there'd be beer.'

David said disgustedly: 'There he was, the very chap the police are keen to interview, right on this doorstep, and you let him go.'

'I know. I've no excuse. Except that he was rather a decent bloke, and so kind of lost, and disappointed we weren't open. It never came into my head to start talking about daggers.'

'If you'd come along for a bite of food, like a reasonable being, you'd have remembered.'

'I've heard of reasonable beings who have bites of food and then get cracked over the skull.'

'Have you told the police about meeting this Dupont?'

'Not me. They'd probably have taken up hours of my time, when I'm up to my eyes. Come and see our developments. Dot has got something awfully like an office going. Beatrice is decorating the walls of what's going to be the reading room. I rather think the things she's painting are meant to be stags, but I daren't ask in case they're not animals at all.'

'I can't stay. I've got to pop round to a fancy goods shop and do a small black market deal.'

'Funny way of amusing yourself. But if you go chasing murderers, remember – ' Bob broke off.

'What?'

'That they murder, that's all.'

'I'll be here tomorrow. What time is the spectacular opening?'

'Eight o'clock and I'll say it'll be spectacular. I wish Sir Cuthbert Homes-are-Heaven would come in his plus-fours. I saw him once on a golf links and I had to take a cure at St. Moritz. And thus it was that I contracted ingrowing toenails, adenoids, the megrims – '

'And a passion for postwar goodwill,' David chipped in. 'How mysterious are the ways of providence.'

TWENTY-NINE

OPPOSITE THE FANCY GOODS EMPORIUM there was an amusement arcade in which two rows of pin-tables invited visitors to insert their pennies with a view to winning cigarettes, by scoring various high numbers specified on indicators above the machines. Some of the tables were in action as David arrived, round others there were idle loungers. A group of lads were arguing round a weighing machine near the entrance.

The place was a perfect observation post from which to watch the shop opposite. David stood by the pin-table nearest to the street, occasionally putting a penny in the slot and operating the spring handle to make his loitering seem normal. His attention was upon the premises over the road, which he could see by standing obliquely as he played.

There was nothing to distinguish the shop opposite from any other small business doing scant trade, yet David was hoping for some sign of its underground activities, or illicit sources of supply.

For half an hour nothing unusual happened. Only one customer went in and emerged with a packet of cigarettes. Then a large car drew up, and Thelma Meake left the driver's seat. She stood on the pavement for about a minute before the sallow youth – whom David had seen on Tuesday emerging from the back regions of the shop – came out and spoke to her.

Thelma seemed annoyed. The youth handed her a slip of paper which she glanced at before returning to the car and driving off.

Now what, thought David, wouldn't I give to have had long distance ears? The brief conversation would have told him how closely Thelma was connected with the fancy goods dump. He would have learnt whether she was a customer, or a conspirator. But he had felt it would be unwise to approach, betraying his curiosity.

He waited for a short while, before crossing to the shop to study the wilting cartons in the window. Warped boxes of soap that guaranteed an infantile smoothness of skin. Shaving sticks that made the removal of a beard a delicious thrill. So soothing, so healing, so blemish-removing. But all rather dusty.

There were bottles of 'Lemon-teena,' bearing the symbol of a brilliant gilt lemon, under which in the smallest of type was the information *'Contains no lemon juice.'* The whole display reeked of fake and trickery, with only such concessions to truth as were imperative.

David went in, expecting to find Bamberger, the tall bald man with the pink blotch of skin round one eye. To his surprise, the shop was empty. He lingered, glancing round the dimly lit shelves.

A cat walked along the counter, over the sticks of shaving soap and open boxes of assorted toffees. David stroked it as it sat on top of the cash register. If cats would talk, he thought, this one's every Mia'ow would be a mouthful.

He started as he heard a slight cough behind him, and now he realised that a short woman in an imitation fur coat was standing just behind him. She was carrying two large bags. He had caught her eye and some remark seemed necessary, 'Nice cat,' he said.

'Don't like cats, meself.'

There was a silence. The woman went on 'Is Bamberger fetchin' you somethink?'

'No. Shop was empty when I came in.'

'Nice way 'e runs it.'

'Very nice,' was the only reply David could think of.

'Lucky to find it open,' she went on.

'Oh, is it often shut?'

'When 'e's out on business it is. You know about all that, I s'pose?'

David grinned. 'You bet I do.'

'The bacon an' that. Easy enough to kill a pig, but it's gettin' it 'ere that gives pore old Bammie a 'eadache.'

David hazarded a guess. 'There's always the car.'

The woman moved closer. 'Daren't run it, not since that business down Red'ill way. 'E was lucky to give 'em the slip, an' no error.' She scowled impatiently. 'I s'pose 'e'll show up some time or other.'

Bacon and toffee and soap. The shop certainly was versatile in its range. David made another inane remark, so that silence should not antagonise his companion. 'It's terrible the way we've got to wait for everything.'

'Don't know as I'll wait. Might go up the market first an' pop in on me way back.' She moved to the door, but returned to say 'D'you 'appen to know if the what's expected 'as arrived?'

'That's what I'm waiting to find out,' David lied.

'I brought me couple o' carrier bags on the chance. If you see Bammie tell 'im Mrs. Ridge was 'ere, and I don't want no more excuses, I want my share.'

'I'll tell him.' The woman was ready enough to assume that every stray customer was in the secret of the racket, David reflected. Was it true that it was accepted as a matter of course by a large section of the community? Gracewell had declared that the black market was all over the place.

The woman said 'Don't forget. Ta-ta. I can't 'ang about all day.' With that she stalked out.

The door from the back room opened suddenly. The short stout man, whom David had seen leaving the garage in Cannock Alley with a parcel, came through. On close-inspection he was even more repulsive than he had looked when he was crying in the "Mango Grove", blubbering across the table at Thelma. With his dark skin, thick purple lips, and glowering expression, he was hideous, ape-like.

'Eh? Vot you vont?' he inquired.

'Cigarettes,' said David. He wondered if the ape-man, who was now behind the counter, had recognised him, and ventured the inquiry, 'Haven't I seen you before, somewhere?'

'No,' said the man quickly.

David continued: 'I thought maybe I'd seen you in the "Mango Grove".'

'Neffer vos d 'ere.'

'And,' David was determined to provoke some reaction beyond curt negatives, 'I think I've seen you at the garage behind the house where there was a murder on Sunday night.'

This thrust had gone home. The man's sagging face twitched, his hand, now extending a packet of cigarettes, was shaking. 'No,' he said again, huskily.

'As a matter of fact I'm not just guessing. I'm certain.'

'Your cigarettes, if you vont dem.'

'Another thing I'm certain of, too. You're as like the man who was killed as I'd be like my own twin brother, if I had one.'

The man behind the counter jerked back a pace. He had changed colour. A kind of squawk came from his quivering mouth. 'Abie! Abie!'

The door from the back room opened instantly. The bald man, Bamberger, snapped 'Well, what is it?' as he appeared. In response to his beckoning gesture, two other men came through. One of them was the slim sallow youth who had given Thelma a note, the other was a huge black-jowled fellow with a broken nose. He was without a coat, with his immense shoulders heaving beneath his shirt and muscular hands he was a typical old heavyweight bruiser.

'Hey?' queried Bamberger. 'Oh – yeah.' He muttered something over his shoulder. The other two slithered past him and moved to the street door, as if standing on guard.

These hasty manoeuvres were a sure indication that the four in the shop knew themselves confronted by an enemy. Their alertness was an acknowledgment of their fear. David made no move.

Bamberger came forward a few paces. 'You keep out of here,' he said.

'This shop's open to the public, I believe.'

'Cut that. You keep out. Get me?'

David decided to plunge. 'I'll come in just when I want to. And I'll walk down Cannock Alley whenever I like. And you'd better not have me slugged again or you'll be in serious trouble.'

His rounding to the attack evidently startled the man he confronted. The atmosphere was tense now. Bamberger jerked a thumb, motioning the man behind the counter. The latter did not shift. Bamberger snapped, 'Hey, Max – '

The two went into a huddle in a corner. After some muttering Bamberger said more loudly 'Oh quit belly-aching, Max,' and swung round to David. 'Just what is your game? What d'you want? A cut?'

'Cut?' David echoed, for a moment at a loss.

Bamberger said disdainfully, as if explaining the obvious, 'A slice, a rake-off? You can take it from me, we don't fall for the black.'

'I'm not a blackmailer, as it happens. I'm just amusing myself.' David took care to speak casually.

'Funny way of gettin' a laugh. You started on us. You wouldn't think it was so funny if we started on you.' Bamberger's glance went to the two men by the door. 'I got some useful assistants.'

'So I see. Glad to know you all.' David was thinking quickly, in spite of his indifferent tone. Now, he decided, was the moment to make his exit, leaving them guessing. He would watch for any moves they might make after his departure, for it was clear that he had made them jumpy.

He walked to the door. The two guardians of it stood in his way; the big bruiser looked inquiringly towards Bamberger for instructions.

Bamberger said scornfully 'So you'll come in just when you like, hey? And supposin' we let you go just when we like?'

The man called Max, still in the far corner, made some inarticulate remark. Bamberger glared at him, then turned to say almost plaintively to David, 'I'm all right, if only I knew what we're all *doing*.'

There was a silence. At a gesture from Bamberger the two door guards advanced. The big man was smoothing his forearms. A jerk of his thumb commanded David to move: 'In the back room, cocky,' he said. 'The boss wants a word with you.'

David smiled without shifting.

'What do I do, boss?'

Before Bamberger could tell him, David said casually, 'I'm going. If I don't, my friend will arrive. And that might be awkward – but not for me.'

'I don't get you,' Bamberger said.

'Of course I ought to have told you. He's giving me exactly ten minutes, and if I don't rejoin him in the pin-table saloon over the road, he gets a copper and comes to collect me.'

Bamberger's expression was a conflict of uncertainties. He looked incredulous and at the same time defiant. Max again began to splutter. The two men, now within a step of David, remained still, waiting developments. They were so contrasted in height and build that they looked like a pair in a strip cartoon.

'Don't believe you,' Bamberger declared. 'That's an old gag.'

David glanced at his watch.

Max spoke coherently, 'We keep him here, we gain nothing.'

Bamberger uttered a profanity. 'He's been here ten minutes, no one's fetching him.'

A man hesitated on the pavement, just outside the shop, as if undecided about coming in. David threw him a grin, as if of recognition, and called 'Give it another minute, Bill.' The ruse worked, Bamberger barked sharply, 'O.K. boys. Make way.'

The men jumped aside. David walked out. He felt oddly damp under the collar, and marvelled now at his own boldness. The stranger, who obviously had changed his mind about entering, was strolling away, unaware of the part he had played in liberating a prisoner.

'Phew!' David muttered as he strode hastily down the street. If that gang had rushed him he wouldn't have stood any chance. They could have got him in that back room and beaten him up. But the urge to start something had been irresistible; he would have made no progress just snooping round the shop and garage, like a cruiser flirting a battle zone. He'd gone into action – and had come out unscathed.

That was something. He was certain that Bamberger and his lot would not hesitate to use violence – even to the point of disposing of anyone who threatened their safety – if they could do so without being caught at it.

What had he learnt during the last twenty minutes? That Thelma was certainly involved with the shop. That Max knew the man who had been murdered, his face had gone almost green at the mention of his resemblance to the victim, and his yelping for Bamberger had been uttered in sheer terror.

The question now was to decide the next move. David crossed the road and mooched back till he was almost opposite the shop again. He went in the pin-table saloon and lost fourpence in a Roll-em-up machine. He put another penny in the one marked GYPSY ZAZA and received a small card informing him that success would be his if he made full use of his opportunities, but that he must be careful on Thursdays.

This further watch on the emporium yielded no result. He had had more than enough of pin-tables. So he strolled out, still undecided as to tactics, though, having challenged the Bamberger crowd, he wanted to give substance to his challenge.

And then his next move was decided for him – or rather he was offered a chance that he could not resist.

THIRTY

AS A COVERED VAN moved slowly along the kerb, he happened to glance at the driver as it drew abreast of him. For a fraction of time he was puzzled – and then he knew beyond any doubt that the girl at the wheel, wearing a slouch cap and spectacles, with the collar of a raincoat turned up to her chin, was Thelma Meake.

The van moved to the centre of the road, as a preliminary to crossing. David, too, crossed over. He was barely ten yards away when Thelma jumped hurriedly from her driving seat and disappeared into the shop. Instantly, David made for the van, leapt aboard, and was off.

His heart was thudding at his temerity as he craned his neck, looking back to discover if there was any sign of agitation or pursuit. The normal drift of pedestrians was moving on its more or less hurried way, there were no waving arms, no warning shouts.

Whose was the van? It might be Bamberger's. Or one that Thelma had 'borrowed' for Bamberger. He, David, was taking a hell of a risk. But if there were any goods aboard, it was a fair bet that they were stolen. Even now the police might be looking for this vehicle.

David made a quick decision. A few minutes brought him to Belmont Crescent. He went on and into the square round the corner, stopping by a telephone box. The box stood in front of an emergency water supply tank, installed where houses had been destroyed in a raid. The blank brick frontage offered a kind of cover; no observant eyes could peer from windows to question why the van was there. Opposite there were trees in the garden of the square.

Running to the open back of the van, David pulled aside the tarpaulin that covered packing cases. The nearest case was labelled PEACHES. ONE GROSS. Another bore the words PORK SAUSAGE MEAT. PRODUCE OF U.S.A. Others contained sardines, 'packed in pure olive oil'. There was nothing to indicate the correct destination for these tasty goods that had been driven by a disguised girl to a shop full of thugs.

David hurried back round the corner on foot. The door of the 'Twenty-Six' was open and he went straight in. Bob was in the front room, arguing with a man in navy overalls.

'Why David old man, you're the very chap I want.'

'You're the very chap *I* want,' David cut in. 'Badly.'

His glance brought Bob to the door, and they moved down the hall. 'Where can we talk? On the quiet.'

'Gosh, anyone would think you were fleeing from Justice.'

'You've hit precious near the mark. Is this room empty?' David flung open the door and closed it behind them.

'Sorry I've got no secret dungeons.'

'Quit fooling, Bob. This is serious. I've done something that may be very clever – or if it isn't clever it'll just about sink me. I've pinched a motor van – '

'*Pinched?* What?'

'Full of stuff that's almost certainly stolen. Stolen or not, it had got no right to be where it was, standing outside a phoney shop while Thelma Meake, disguised as a young woman of action, nipped inside to report that she'd arrived.'

'Crikey!' said Bob.

'Exactly. Crikey, as you so rightly observe. Now my only wish is to get this van and its contents back to where it belongs, and the police are the chaps for that.'

'Considering giving yourself up?'

'Anything *but*. The last thing I want to do is to be arrested. I'm off again on Sunday, you know. I'm not risking any hitch over that. My job from then is a trifle more important than acting as spotter in the black market racket.'

'But why – what I mean is, *why* have you got to go pinching vans?'

'The van's just one section of an ugly jigsaw.'

'So what? And what do I do?'

'You've been in the club for – say the last half-hour?'

'Sure. Having fun and games with that painter chap for longer than that.'

'Then you couldn't have pinched the van.'

'Who's saying I did?'

'Keep your hair on. No one, naturally. But you're the perfect chap to make the report that it's standing, unattended, in the square round the corner, with a trailing tarpaulin exposing valuable contents. By some extraordinary stroke of luck' – David winked, 'it's just by a phone box, and you can do the phoning.'

'Of all the crazy stunts – '

'The sooner you do it the better,' David said. 'Or someone else may steal the vehicle in real earnest. It's in a most theft-provoking situation, almost secure from observation.'

'But where does all this get us? I thought you were after a murderer, I didn't know you'd gone in for crime detection in a general sort of way.'

'It gets us nowhere. But it might get a rope round someone else's neck. No time to explain, because it's a tangled skein and all that. This is how we work it. We rejoin your painter pal, then you go off saying you've got to post a letter. I stay chatting to the painter. You come back and tell us about the van. If the painter doesn't suggest it, I'll propose that you'd better contact the police.'

'Oh gosh, this is going to take a lot of remembering.'

'It's simple as A.B.C. And by one of those pleasant miracles, I have the phone number, right in my pocket, of a very lively detective inspector. I give it to you, you go and phone Gracewell. That clears both of us.'

'That gets me right into the thick.'

'Boloney. You didn't take the van, you've got an alibi. I certainly didn't, or would I be soft enough to tip you off and give you Gracewell's phone number?'

'For crying out loud. It looks like seven years for both of us,' Bob groaned.

'Speedy action is essential,' David reminded him.

Bob gave a dramatic sigh. 'All right. You're too damn persuasive to be allowed out, but I'll do it.'

They returned to the painter. Bob played his role, remembering that he must despatch a postcard to a firm of hardware manufacturers. To David's surprise he actually brought a stamped addressed postcard from his pocket, and his muttered observation added a convincing touch, 'I usually carry letters about for months, wondering why the accursed people don't answer.'

He went off. David chatted to the painter about enamels, and the surfaces suitable for them. Then they got on to the odd effects of blast from high explosives. They discussed beer, the variable qualities of certain brands.

They were hard at a dispute about Churchill when Bob came in, puffing audibly. 'Such a hell of a lot of things to attend to,' he complained. 'David, old son, there's a van round the corner, no sign of a driver, and the most luscious cases of canned stuff are fairly hanging off the back.'

'So what?' said David in a bored voice.

'Think we might get hold of some of it for the club?'

'You're not suggesting stealing it?'

'Van looks completely deserted.'

The painter volunteered the opinion. 'Vans full of canned stuff don't get deserted unless there's something funny about them.'

'That's true enough,' David concurred heartily.

'Lot of queer customers about,' said the painter. 'It's the war that's to blame.'

Bob hesitated in the most convincing affectation of indecision. 'Think I ought to do something about it?'

'Might be as well to report it,' suggested the painter.

David said carelessly, 'Let's have a stroll round there. If it's still unclaimed we might mention it to a bobby. Or better still, you could phone a man I know in the police. I've got his number somewhere –' digging into several pockets, David finally produced a slip of paper. 'Here, by a lucky chance.'

The two conspirators walked out. In the street David said: 'You did fine. You ought to be on the stage.'

'And you ought to be on Dartmoor.'

Bob used the telephone while David stood in the open door of the booth. Someone in Inspector Gracewell's office was evidently suggesting that the report should be made to another department, for Bob said: 'O.K. If you can put me on to that extension.'

He was repeating his information about the abandoned van, and glancing through the window, gave its number. As he listened an expression of amazement overspread his features. 'Oh! Oh, that's fine. Yes, sure. Yes. My name's Carter. You'll find me at 26 Belmont Crescent, if you want me.'

The receiver crashed down. Bob said exultantly, 'You'll get a medal or something. That van was stolen from a goods yard only thirty-five minutes ago.'

David gave a whistle. 'No medal for me, I don't come into it. It's surprising they didn't change the number plates.'

'I suppose they reckoned to unload it and lose it again in quick time. Come on, we've got to get back. Who'd have thought you were such a dab hand at recovering stolen goods?'

'It's not a habit,' said David. 'For heaven's sake let's stick to the yarn that you acted independently.'

'But I got Gracewell's number from you.'

'Oh yes. That's nothing.' David grinned. 'It's just lucky that I happened to drop in when you needed it. That's all.'

'That won't be all if someone recognised you on the driver's seat.'

'No one did. I was as jumpy as a cat and had eyes all round my head. And hang it all, if the worst comes to the worst, the truth would get me out.'

'I was wrong,' Bob laughed, 'when I told you you should be on Dartmoor. You ought to be stewed in your own jelly. An eel, that's what you are, you slippery old twister. But I suppose your eel-like tricks have stood you in good stead.'

'What do you mean by that?'

'You'd never been a headline in the papers if you'd been just an ordinary fish.'

David quoted solemnly, '"Fame is a fancied life in others' breath". Titbit from Pope.'

They had reached the "Twenty-Six", and David added, 'I think I'll just hop back to Meakie's.'

Bob looked suspicious. 'It strikes me as funny,' he said, 'that you don't want to stay now we know the van was stolen. After all, you'd get nothing worse than a pat on the back.'

'Which I don't want, as I've told you. At moments I'm oppressed by my status as a serving officer.'

'You might hang around, if only to tell the cops about Thelma driving the van.'

'That's my main reason for not hanging around. I don't want her part in the jag to come to light. Not at the moment, anyway.'

'Shielding a criminal, eh?'

David rapped, 'Call it that.'

'But for heaven's sake why? When you hate every brassy hair on the girl's head.'

'Because of her mother, if you've got to know. I'd see Thelma swing and never twitch a whisker. But Meakie's been darn decent to me, all along, and I know what Thelma means to her.' David raked his mind for excuses. 'Maybe Thelma was acting under compulsion. She may have been threatened. I was, by the gang concerned.'

Bob seemed bewildered, as he exclaimed 'An eel – and a sentimental one at that! O.K., old fish, you can wriggle away.'

'If I'm really needed you can phone me. No one takes the rap for me, as a Hollywood thug would say.' A police car swung into the Crescent and David added, 'Blow me, I know something about speed, but this is what I call snappy work. So long, Bob.'

He trotted away, speculating as to whether his departure was arousing any curiosity among the three men in the car that sped by.

THIRTY-ONE

ON THE HALL TABLE there was a letter for him. The envelope was of poor quality mauve paper, of a sort that could be bought in any chain store. David ripped it open and was astonished to see that it was from Miss Trindle.

Dear Flight Lieutenant Heron, it ran, *I am anxious to see you at your convenience, respecting a matter that is of some importance. I shall be in the "Blue Lantern" this evening at 8 o'clock sharp, owing to leaving the office at six and my first aid class takes an hour. Hoping same will be convenient, yours truly, Edith Trindle.*

He read the note through twice, wondering what it might portend. He was surprised at the phrasing, which seemed to be that of an uneducated person trying to be formal. Miss Trindle had always struck him as a competent woman, and she had done secretarial work for years. Perhaps, he concluded, she had felt nervous while writing it.

He would certainly be in the "Blue Lantern" at eight o'clock.

And the thought of the 'Blue Lantern' reminded him that he had had no lunch, though now it was after two. His hunger would provide a perfect excuse for seeing Mrs. Meake.

'Hi, Meakie!' he called down the basement stairs, to warn her of his descent. There was no response. A strange silence pervaded the lower regions as he went down and opened the kitchen door.

Mrs. Meake was sitting in the cane chair by the fire, with some neglected knitting on the small table beside her. Her expression was vague as she glanced up.

David was conscious of shock. He had seen Mrs. Meake overpainted, he had seen her with her flamboyant make-up smudged. But he had never faced her as she was now, without a vestige of artificiality, with her features drawn and the marks of the years cruelly, faithfully apparent. Since this morning, when he had exchanged a few words with her in the hall, she seemed to have aged twenty years.

He realised now, for the first time, that it must have taken a lot of pluck to keep up appearances as she had done. Her life had been a strenuous one, she was no longer young, she had every reason for looking worn and tired. He concealed his surprise, as he greeted her brightly, 'What-cher, Meakie. Everything ticketyboo?'

She regarded him vaguely as she picked up her knitting and dropped it again. David noticed idly that it was some sort of an infant's woollen coat.

Her silence was disconcerting but he maintained his affectation of heartiness. 'I was a bit peckish, and I wondered if you'd got any bits of lunch left over, for me to gnaw on the mat.'

She said, 'Is it lunch time?'

'It's ten past two.'

Mrs. Meake rose. 'Inspector Gracewell's been here again,' she said inconsequently. 'I've answered all his questions so many times.'

'Sorry I wasn't here to take the shooting.'

'It doesn't matter. Nothing matters.'

'Oh come on, that's not my fighting Meakie!' Hoping to rally her spirits, David ran on, 'Everything matters a hell of a lot. Think of the big oceans with rolling breakers, and daisies in the bright green fields, and fish and chips with a dash of Worcester when you're hungry and holding four kings at poker, and being in love with a miraculous girl like my Tess, and having memories like yours of thousands of people clapping and cheering themselves hoarse. It's all terrific, if only you'll give it half a moment's thought.'

'Terrific, terrific,' Mrs. Meake repeated flatly. 'Is terrific anything to do with terror?'

It flashed into David's head that she had been drinking. But she seemed stunned rather than intoxicated. 'Come to think of it I s'pose that's how the word started. Terrific – something so jolly good that it almost frightened you. But we're not compiling a dictionary, you know. We'd want pencils and paper for that.'

'Yes. Pencils and paper.'

(Where was her humour, her usual enjoyment of ridiculous whimsies?) 'If you haven't eaten since breakfast, the obvious move is for us to collaborate on a snack meal. To appease the inner man, don't you know. To tell the truth, my own inner man is devilish hungry.'

'Poor boy.' Mrs. Meake became almost her normal self as she went to her cupboard and produced a tin.

'But I don't want you using up your iron rations,' David protested. 'You may need that tin when we're pitching the Hun into the ditch.'

Mrs. Meake faced him listlessly. 'I can't argue. Please don't force me to. I'm tired.'

He said no more as she turned some kind of ham out of the tin into a saucepan. She chopped fresh parsley and mint, and proceeded to cook a highly savoury dish. In ten minutes or so she set a sizzling hot plate on the table, arranging slices of toast neatly beside it.

'But where's yours?' David asked.

'I'm not hungry.'

He humoured her, starting on his meal without further protest. When he had had a few mouthfuls he pretended to be resentful. 'I can't eat unless you do,' he said. 'Come on, here's your fork. I'll have a bite from my side of the plate for every one you have from yours. Look, I've made a valley down the middle, so you won't get any bits I've meddled with.'

Thus, by a childish trick, he persuaded her to eat. He made more slices of toast, and made a show of sulking when she refused it. 'You're saying I can't even make toast,' he complained.

She ate some, to reassure him.

He feared that she might be steering towards some sort of nervous collapse. She was nothing like her usual buoyant self. And now he was glad indeed that he had not betrayed Thelma's part in the theft of the van. She, by now, had probably resumed her normal appearance and was again synthetically glamorous. She wouldn't sport those tin-rimmed spectacles for longer than necessary.

In the meantime he must try to get Mrs. Meake back to normal. 'That's better,' he said genially as he leaned back. 'Now what about some coffee?'

She made the coffee and produced a bottle of brandy. 'May as well finish it now,' she remarked, as she poured out large tots.

There was only an inch or so of spirit left in the bottle. She must have drunk the rest in the last three days, for Annie had fetched a double tot in a medicine bottle on Monday.

David decided to probe. When a temperate woman like Mrs. Meake flew to brandy there was some poison at work – and poison needed attention. 'What's up, Meakie? You can tell your old David.'

'I'll be all right.'

'I'll say you will. But just now… Is someone in the house being devilish? Because if so I can be devilish too, on your behalf.'

'It's not that.'

'Are you worried about money?'

'Money!' she laughed shortly. 'No, I haven't even tried to let the hall front.'

'Thelma… ?' David hazarded.

There was a long silence. The ticking of the clock on the mantelpiece seemed unusually loud. Mrs. Meake sat quite still, her work-worn hands folded on her clean blue and white apron.

When she spoke her voice was hardly audible. 'Yes. It's Thelma. It upset me, but I had a good cry and now I'm all right again.' Mrs. Meake's smile was bleak and unconvincing.

David moved quickly to her and slipped an arm round her shoulders. 'You poor darling, I wish I'd been here. What a shame.'

'Oh rubbish, I was all right, I don't know why I was so silly. Soft, you could call it.' Mrs. Meake was half sobbing, still trying to laugh. 'I cried so much I got my eyes full of mascara and it smarted something awful. It doesn't matter. I won't be using the stuff anymore. I'm not going to use powder, rouge, nothing. I'm a silly old codger to have bothered with it for so long. Mutton done up as lamb, that's all it makes you. But you get in the way of it, and you're afraid you'll look queer without it.'

'Tut-tut, where's your proper feminine vanity?'

'And now, what's it matter?'

'It matters a whole heap. I'll get you such a smashing make-up outfit you won't be able to resist it. I'll get you Coty and Yardley and Guerlain, all in a lovely big box.'

She sighed absently. 'You can't get them so easily these days.'

'I'll spend quids in taxi-ing round all the shops under heaven.'

'It's no good,' she insisted sadly. 'Not now.'

'What's happened with Thelma? She's played you up often enough, it's time you got used to her goings-on.'

'Oh let's forget it.'

'Come now, it's too late to kid me. Did you see her – let me see – on Tuesday night?'

'Why should I have seen her then?' Mrs. Meake seemed genuinely surprised. So when Thelma had admitted the soldier husband of her friend Delia into the house she must have gone without encountering her mother.

'Or since then?' he asked.

'This morning,' Mrs. Meake admitted. She seemed to be musing as she continued, almost dreamily, 'Sometimes when you're beaten it's hard to admit it. That was my trouble. Thelma had me beaten by the time she was – oh well, let's say nineteen. She ran away do you remember, when she was nineteen?'

'Of course I remember. You cried all over the shoulder of my one and only suit, which never recovered – which isn't surprising as it only cost forty-five bob. And didn't I go hunting round with you, trying to trace her?'

'You were so kind.'

'And that reminds me, she came back on the Sunday war broke out, when we were all on tiptoe making plans, listening to the wireless fiddling about with drawing pins and curtains – and in all that I never had a chance to talk to you. Then I beat it into uniform, and you've never told me where Thelma was for those six months.'

'I don't know even now.'

'Gosh! She just walked in and never explained, even to you?'

'At ten in the morning she got here. The same day as Miss Trindle moved in.'

Miss Trindle... Thelma... Miss Trindle attending the inquest upon the Marquis of Leafe and Thelma slipping back into her old corner in her mother's house. The coincidence of the simultaneous arrival of the two of them in Terrapin Road seemed significant – but of what? He might learn something about that this evening. Miss Trindle had expressed dislike of Thelma on many occasions and venom might make her informative.

For lack of more inspired comment David observed: 'Thelma's led you a pretty dance, one way and another.'

'She's got a stubborn spirit. You might as well try to bend steel. And she never cared how I felt. I didn't want her to care. I've lived my life, and I know what it means to try to struggle and get on. I know what it is to be disappointed, I didn't want to load her with any sore feelings of mine.'

David wondered, not for the first time, who Thelma's father might have been. Mrs. Meake, he had always assumed, was either a widow or a woman who had parted from her husband. He could not question her on the point. But now, as if discerning his speculations she asked abruptly, 'Aren't you wondering why I had sore feelings?'

'I concluded that they were probably the result of the general trials of existence.'

Mrs. Meake shook her head. 'No. I've never got over being taken in by a man from Detroit who was always going to marry me next week or next month. Back home, he had a wife and four kids. His fifth – or fiftieth for all I know – was born just after he sailed with the last of the American forces in the nineteen-fourteen war. And soon after that I had to turn down the only chance I ever got of a star part. So I stayed on in the chorus for as long as I could, saving what I could to buy a pram.'

'You poor darling.'

'It's a long time ago. I never wanted to stand in Thelma's way, without a father she hadn't had a straight deal. She had her own ideas of getting on, and I didn't check her, because I'd found out I wasn't so clever, myself.'

Mrs. Meake paused. 'You're an unselfish poppet,' David murmured.

'But she went too far. She wanted that diamond bracelet and she got it. She wanted a car and she got it. And she wanted a mink coat.'

David laughed mirthlessly. 'Thelma's been talking about mink ever since I can remember.'

'Last week she was wrapped up in seven hundred pounds worth

181

of it. Mr. Schenk, her boss, bought it for her.'

'Oh, yes, I've seen it.' He had been only vaguely aware of what Thelma was wearing when she took him to the "Mango Grove". Some expensive fur, that had been his general impression.

'Seen it? When?' Mrs. Meake snapped.

'I ran into her.'

'You needn't wriggle out of anything. Nothing can hurt me now, not even the truth.'

'Well then, I saw it when I called at the Regalia and took her to a club for a drink.'

'Funny thing to do, seeing that you and Thelma have always scrapped like wild cats.'

'Precious funny thing for me to do,' David agreed. 'But I was worried about her.'

'Why?'

'Because of what you told me on Monday – that she'd left home again. And she seemed to be mixing with a funny pack of outsiders. Schenk for instance. And Schenk's pals.'

Mrs. Meake sighed deeply. 'Yesterday I'd have slapped your face for you, for saying that. Now I don't care. A funny pack is what they are, and I hope she swings with the whole bunch of them.'

'Meakie, you don't mean that?' Had he taken the risk of shielding Thelma in the matter of the stolen van for nothing? Was Thelma acting deliberately, against her mother's advice and not under any coercion?

'I do,' Mrs. Meake said emphatically. 'I hope she swings. She had her chance and she didn't take it. She's just one of those girls you can't do anything about. She's irresponsible, like her father was. Guiding her and loving her, it's all no good. She's heading straight for hell and you may as well save yourself any trouble in trying to stop her.'

'You're not yourself, you're feeling the strain – '

Mrs. Meake ignored the interruption. 'She had her chance on Sunday afternoon and she wouldn't take it.'

David was dismayed. Ever since he had known Mrs. Meake he had admired her gaiety and buoyancy. She worked hard and was unfailingly good-humoured. Her only illogical characteristic had been her absorption with Thelma, her blindness to Thelma's stupidity and selfishness. 'You're not yourself,' he insisted helplessly. 'You ought to lie down, a spot of sleep might put you right.'

Mrs. Meake smiled sadly. 'No, I couldn't rest. You can't be – well, hurt, like I've been and stay the same. Everything's different, and so am I. But I'll get along. And Thelma – '

'Yes?' David prompted, as she fell silent.

'Thelma will get what's coming to her. I'm not a one for talking about the law, but – ' Mrs. Meake's voice rose, 'Thelma won't be coming back here again. I wouldn't have her if she was starving, I'd slam the door if she was sick and dying. I've got no one now, and I don't mind. I've had my life, and lots of it was fun.'

The words echoed in David's mind: 'I've had my life, and lots of it was fun.' It sounded like an epitaph.

The clock ticked noisily on. Neither of them spoke or moved till David said, with a show of brightness, 'Well, we had a nice little blow-out, so I suppose I'd better help wash up.'

'Fine chance you've got,' Mrs. Meake said. 'You buzz off.'

'You've forgotten the end of your line.'

'Eh?'

'It's "You buzz off before I slap your face for you".'

She did not reply, and he rose with the comment: 'Oh, well, it's always the darkest hour before the dawn. So don't be too down-hearted.'

His reassurance failed to convince even himself as he walked out, to stand thinking at the foot of the stairs, feeling that he had been sadly ineffectual. Thelma was deep in an ugly network of black market racketeering – and deep in something even more sinister than dumping stolen goods at the dubious fancy goods emporium kept by Bamberger, Max, and their thugs. The double of Max had died not many yards from where Thelma had been sleeping.

Or not sleeping.

What had Mrs. Meake said? 'She had her chance on Sunday afternoon and she wouldn't take it.'

What chance? Whatever it was, whatever she had rejected, Thelma had had chances enough.

THIRTY-TWO

'CAN I SPEAK TO Miss Carmichael?' David was on the telephone.

'Oh is that you, darling? – I say, I've got to make a slight change in my plans, for this evening. There's a complication.'

'What complication?'

'It's – ' David emphasised his mild jest, 'It's the Other Woman. She's the dangerous kind with capital letters.'

Tess stifled a giggle. 'I've always suspected it.'

'I'll come clean. Twenty minutes or so of her will be enough. The rendezvous is for eight o'clock.'

'Just when, if events were normal, I should be free.'

'Could you be a honey and come along to the "Blue Lantern" at about twenty past? I shall need a rescuer.'

'We're all tangled up getting half a dozen youngsters off to the country in the morning. We're working like beavers, washing, ironing and patching.'

'You can't just abandon me to the Other Woman.'

'I'll come if I can and it'll have to be when I can.'

'I'm relying on you,' David said. 'And in any case we're getting married on Saturday morning. Did you know?'

'Impossible. After tomorrow morning there'll be only four kids left at St. Margaret's and I've got Saturday free.'

'But doesn't that make a wedding exquisitely possible?'

'No, because I'm having a perm at eleven a.m.'

'I'll tell you some stories that'll curl your hair without electricity. I'm expecting you this evening, remember.'

'You'd better be careful, not too many sly glances at the Other Woman, or I shall make a Scene. There's a capital letter to that last word, too, you oaf.'

'Oaf I may be, but you're something in seven letters with a capital.'

'That wouldn't be Hellcat by any chance?'

'No darling. DARLING. Capitals to all of it.'

'I may as well tell you that Miss Allardyce is listening to every syllable. She put your call through. And Smith and Nobby are probably on various extensions.'

'Then they're something in seven letters that isn't darling. And come to think of it hellcat yourself.'

'How I flutter beneath this old-world chivalry. Good-bye, you so-and-so.'

'Au revoir, my desert flower, my grenadilla, my passion fruit – '

But Tess, perhaps wisely, had already rung off. David sat thoughtfully on the edge of his divan, wondering why he had heard nothing from Bob Carter. What had happened about that stolen van? But to Bob everything but the progress of plans for the "Twenty-Six" was unimportant.

Suddenly there was a light tap on his door. He sprang up. 'Come in.'

Inspector Gracewell entered ponderously. 'I'm not intruding at an awkward time, I hope?'

'No. Not at all. Have a chair.' David waited, feeling the tensing of his nerves as he envisaged several defensive, retreating actions he might have to make. He'd brought this on himself by skedaddling with a vehicle that didn't belong to him. He was game enough – but not game for anything that might interfere with his movements beyond Sunday. After Sunday his life was no longer his own; the death of one unpleasant foreigner would dwindle into insignificance beside the prospect of meeting a large number of even more offensive ones, whose early destruction was desirable.

The inspector said: 'The inquest was this morning, you know.'

'Was it? I didn't know.'

'Mrs. Meake was there.'

'She didn't mention it, though she gave me some lunch downstairs. She did just say she'd seen you. And I suppose there's no harm in telling you, by now, she's seen as much of you as she wants to. In her own words you're getting on her nerves.'

'Sorry about that. Part of my unpleasant duty.'

'What was the verdict?'

'Murder by some person or persons unknown.'

'Unsatisfactory, that.'

'Extremely so.'

'And the victim – is he still without a name?'

'That's how it is.' Gracewell puffed out his cheeks. 'I could have sworn that someone would have come forward. It isn't as if the victim was ordinary looking. We published his description – expect you saw it.'

'Yes. It was pretty detailed, too.'

'Not a murmur of reaction.'

'What about the fire-watchers in Cannock Road? They must have been on duty.'

'We questioned them. No result. It's a handicap that Sunday night was so pitch dark. A chap on a roof wouldn't know what was happening in the street right below him.'

'He'd have ears.'

'London's too full of noises, right through the twenty-four hours, for anything to attract attention – unless it's a scream or a revolver shot. We've raked round in quarters where we sometimes get information, and explored scores of false clues. All to no effect. As I expect you know, criminals tend to be conservative in their methods. One chap will use nothing but a length of lead piping to quieten his victim, another trusts to a knuckle duster, another sticks to manual strangulation – or near-strangulation. We ran through the known stabbers. The only one who's ever been seen in this neighbourhood is doing four years in Parkhurst, so he's ruled out.'

'A consistent stabber would have his own weapon and wouldn't have had to buy that dagger,' David observed.

Gracewell grunted. 'It was a neat job that suggests a practised hand. I doubt if the victim had time for a single yelp.'

David said: 'Sorry I haven't a drink to offer you. We might get some tea if Annie's about, I'd rather not ask Mrs. Meake.'

'I don't want anything, thanks.'

There was a short silence before Gracewell said abruptly: 'You've known this house on and off for eight years. That's correct, isn't it?'

'Certainly.'

'So you'll be able to tell me a bit more about Thelma Meake. She's done some film acting, hasn't she?'

'Yes. Just crowd work and small parts. But so far as I know, not very much all told.'

'Most of that would be in the six months prior to the outbreak of war?'

This was news to David. He knew nothing of what Thelma had done in that period, it was when she had been missing and untraceable. 'I haven't a glimmering of what she was doing then. Don't even know where she was.'

'She was living with a mixed bunch on a houseboat at Maidenhead.'

'Was she though!' David remembered Mrs. Newland's comment upon the man who had bought the garage from her. A foreigner... and she had heard that he lived on a houseboat at Maidenhead.

There might be quite a lot in this coincidence, but for the moment he refrained from mentioning it. He wanted to know, first, what Gracewell was getting at. He added: 'No wonder her mother and I drew blanks at hotels and digs houses when we were looking for her. Poor Mrs. Meake was frantic, but she wouldn't advertise. Didn't want a scandal.'

'Well, now you know. The girl was afloat most of the time, when she wasn't playing round film studios. And what I want is information about her companions.'

'Obviously I can't help you there.'

'I've got a list of their names. You might know some of them. Up to now the only one I can contact, of all that jolly nautical party, is Thelma Meake. And she's so bad at facts and descriptions – well it almost suggests she wants to be bad.'

As the inspector produced a typed list David asked, 'Are you concentrating on Thelma in connection with the murder? Or for something else?'

On the inspector's face there was an innocent, bland smile. 'What else would there be?'

'I wouldn't know.' David read the list of names. 'Don't know any of them,' he said. 'They seem to have been a cosmopolitan lot.'

'Yes. A Norwegian couple who went back to Norway before the trip became impossible. They don't interest me. A Frenchwoman, I found out she was killed in a raid in September nineteen-forty. Then there's a George Smith, a Trevor Delaney, and an Otto Klar. And there was a man nicknamed Pinkie.'

'I noticed Pinkie had no initials. Funny nickname for a man, anyway.'

'Apparently he'd got a pink discoloration round one eye.'

David stared. 'A pink blotch of skin? I think we've got something now.' Bamberger of the fancy goods emporium might be Pinkie. And this seemed the ideal opportunity to put Gracewell on to the trail of the racketeers in the High Street, without getting too deeply implicated himself.

Briefly, he described Bamberger and gave the address. Gracewell's expression gave no indication as to whether he already knew of Bamberger's activities. 'Thanks. Now I wonder – I wonder if Thelma Meake knows anything about that fancy goods depot?'

'She might,' David said cautiously. Gracewell would find out plenty if he visited the shop – and more still if he went with a search warrant. Thelma deserved what looked like hitting her quite soon now.

'By the way,' Gracewell still spoke slowly and smoothly, 'I've got to thank you.'

'What for?'

'As I think I mentioned, the black market isn't up my street. But a call came through to my office and was headed straight to the right quarter, which went into action in a matter of seconds. It turned out to be a pretty useful tip-off.'

'Oh, the abandoned van?' David said, hoping that his tone was as guileless as he was trying to make it.

'Exactly.'

'Bob Carter seemed perturbed, so I slipped him your phone number.'

'Excellent. The van had only just been stolen, the report of its loss had just come over the phone, the ink wasn't dry on the notes about it. Then plonk! Along came Carter's information, and the van was retrieved with contents all complete.'

'Good work.' Curiosity impelled David to add: 'Where was it stolen from?'

'The goods yard at a railway terminus.'

'I should have thought goods yards would have been better

guarded.'

'It's like this. Agents of the black market take jobs as clerks and porters at the docks and rail depots. When a van is loaded up it's easy for a phoney porter to distract the attention of the rightful driver. Or a clerk can delay him over filling in some form or other. Of course, when the van's gone, it's the driver who's to blame, if he's already signed the docket for goods received. As to who has jumped on the driver's seat, that's usually a mystery, because any clever gang knows how to provide a spot of confusion that sets everybody telling different stories – often with the best intentions. Meanwhile the phoney driver gets away, unloads the goods, and abandons the empty van any quiet side street. A big job can be tackled and finished well inside an hour.'

David used Bob Carter's favourite expletive. 'Crikey!'

'But the queer thing about this particular van,' Gracewell went on, 'is that it got clean away, only to be left high and dry – and intact – near Belmont Crescent.'

'Remarkable,' said David.

'And you saw it.'

'Oh – yes. Yes, rather. I saw it.'

'I just wondered – ' Inspector Gracewell turned his mildly speculative gaze right into David's eyes, 'if you knew anything more about it, beyond the obvious fact that it was there.'

David hesitated. He said evasively: 'I'm an airman, not a black market snooper. I'm reporting back on Sunday. This is just a week's leave, to get my breath back after hospital.'

Gracewell whistled softly. He had caught the implication of the evasion. 'All right, my lad, if you don't find it convenient. It isn't my pigeon, as I said before, and far be it from me to put, a spoke in your Spitfire.' He broke off, studying his thumbnail. 'I might be a sight more inquisitive with anyone who wasn't on the level himself.'

'I'm on the level,' David declared hastily. 'Keen on anything *pro bono publico* and all that.'

'Of course, you don't have to tell me that.' Gracewell rose. 'I won't say good-bye and good luck, because we'll be meeting again.'

'If we do, it'll be before Sunday.'

'Sure. The quest is just getting lively.'

'You mean – you've got a definite clue about last Sunday night's affair?'

The inspector pursed his lips. 'Call it a sort of inkling. Oh by the way – ' his manner became so offhand that David knew his next remark would be important, 'you'd better know where you can find me at round about nine this evening.'

He scribbled a telephone number on a card.

'Why nine?' David asked.

'Because by then Miss Trindle will probably have spilled what beans she's got to spill.'

'Miss Trindle! Then you suspect – ? But how the devil did you know I'm meeting her?'

'A forcible calligraphy,' said the inspector ponderously, 'leaves an impression on the sheet beneath that which is written upon. Upon pale mauve paper as much as any other, as I found when I called upon Miss Trindle.'

'Where is she?'

'Don't you know? She's gone to live with the sister of the bank clerk who's got the room over this. Smedley.'

'Smedley didn't mention it.'

'Any reason why he should?'

David added: 'But what gave you the idea that Miss Trindle's involved?'

'She left in a precious hurry. That mightn't be either here or there. But there's the matter of a stolen hundred pound bank note that's been changing hands in the last few days. And about that I'm not saying another word now. I must beat it.'

David was so staggered that he almost forgot to pass on his most important item of information. 'Hi – inspector! Just a moment.' Gracewell glanced back from the stairs. 'That seafaring chap who was hawking the fancy dagger has been around. You'd better ask Bob Carter about him, and you'll get what there is at first hand.'

'He gave me the dope on that an hour ago.'

'Sorry to be superfluous.'

'Who said you were? You've told me more than you realise.'

"Have I?" thought David. "And how?" 'Well, here's another titbit that I almost forgot to mention. If you show that list of the houseboat party to Mrs. Newland at "The Volunteer", she might recognise some – or at least one of the names. She owned that garage in the alley and sold it to a gent with a foreign name who lived on a houseboat at Maidenhead.'

'Well, that's something. Why didn't you mention it before?'

'Because Maidenhead is lousy with houseboats, and it's only the chance of your Pinkie being the pink-eyed Bamberger that makes me think it's a trail worth following,' David explained – knowing only too well that his hesitation had been due rather to his hard-to-kill desire to protect Thelma Meake. But not for her own sake.

'Thanks a lot,' the inspector said as he lumbered off downstairs.

THIRTY-THREE

IT WAS MID-AFTERNOON. David's appointment with Miss Trindle was at eight, and after that the day would be gone. He ticked off the rest of his span of freedom on his fingers. Tomorrow – Friday. Saturday. And Sunday was zero hour. Suddenly he laughed, as he hummed 'Tomorrow will be Friday and we've caught no fish to-day.' He had about seventy-two hours left and after that he'd be obeying orders, conforming to routine. If he didn't get the hook into Sunday night's killer, he'd be regretting his failure when he was back on the kite. It was too late to have any qualms about Thelma; the suspense was obviously driving Mrs. Meake mad, and the sooner the crime was cleared up the better chance she would have of recovering from whatever horrible revelations there might be.

Impulsively, David grabbed his hat. He meant to find Thelma, who, as her mother had said, had had her chance and had failed either to deserve, or to benefit, by it.

Mrs. Meake was done with Thelma. David knew her declaration had been made in no fit of temper or impatience. Wavering determination had never been one of Meakie's characteristics.

He took a taxi. The stage doorkeeper at the Regalia said that Miss Meake was not in the theatre and that the office was closed. David, ignoring the rebuff, strode in, flinging over his shoulder a garbled remark to the effect that he must find some gloves he had left behind.

He was aware that the doorkeeper was pursuing him and protesting. He darted through a door marked KEEP CLOSED and faced a network of ropes that dangled from some contraption above and curled in strange shapes on the bare floor. With a sweep of his arm he thrust a dozen ropes aside. There was another door beyond them and he plunged through it.

Now he was in a stone passage that smelt of damp cement and mildew. The doorkeeper seemed to have abandoned the chase. On each side, ahead, were closed doors on which were painted various numbers. At random David opened the first on his right.

Thelma Meake was standing in the small bare room, that had only one straight-backed chair as furniture. There was a bench at dressing table height with a mirror over it. A tap dripped into a toilet basin. An unscreened electric light-bulb glared over the stark scene.

'What the hell do you want?' Thelma rapped.

But David's attention was upon the girl shrinking against the far wall. She had a green knitted hood over her head and a small pointed face...

She was Lipscott's pixie.

He said, across Thelma's shoulder, 'Hullo, fancy meeting you again.'

'Let me out, let me out,' whimpered the girl. 'Please help me to get out.'

'But of course I will. Who's keeping you?'

The girl moved to point a quivering finger at Thelma. 'She is.'

'I'll soon deal with that.' David moved between the two girls.

At that moment the doorkeeper appeared, puffing breathlessly, in the doorway. 'I'm very sorry, Miss Meake. I did my best to stop the – er – gentleman – '

David interposed: 'You hop it, you're not wanted.'

The doorkeeper looked nonplussed. There was a silence till David snapped impatiently: 'Tell him to vamoose, Thelma. Unless you particularly want an extra witness.'

'Witness?'

But the word seemed to scare her, for she said: 'All right, Bert. Mr. Heron's an old friend of mine. He's always obstinate when he's been drinking.' Thelma's glance was venomous.

Bert looking bewildered, disappeared, and David said briskly: 'Now then, what's the idea of holding up my young friend in the green bonnet?'

'Nothing to do with you.' Thelma rapped.

'On the contrary, it's just my cup o' tea.' David moved to the pixie's side and drew her hand through his arm, hoping to reassure her. 'This little green bonnet and I, we stand or fall together.'

Thelma said sulkily: 'The trouble about you is I never know

when you're joking.'

'You ought to read some of my old scripts. I always put "joke" in brackets where you'd got to laugh.'

Again a tense silence, till David said grimly: 'Joke over, Thelma. We're serious now. But you can laugh if you want to when I tell you that I took over the food van you pinched this morning.'

He had to admire the spirit with which she faced the thrust. She tossed her henna'd head and said contemptuously: 'I haven't the slightest idea what you're talking about. Perhaps you're even drunker than I thought you were. Or maybe you're back in your touring melodrama days. Anyway it's clear you ought to have another stretch in hospital.'

'Well played, Thelma. But not good enough.' David kept the pixie's arm firmly linked through his own and muttered to comfort her, 'Stick by me and you'll be all right.'

'What's the game?' Thelma's voice was not quite steady.

'Why don't you come clean? I might be able to help you.' Her expression indicated that he was on the right track and this, he thought, might be the moment to get to the very core of Sunday night's horror. 'I know practically everything, about the houseboat, and Pinkie and your pal Max and the rest of them. But I can't help you unless you're on my side, unless you tell me the name of the chap who was found in the garden with a knife in his back.'

Thelma covered her face with her hands. 'I don't know,' she whimpered. 'I don't know. I swear I don't. I – I was with Dolores.'

A faint tug at David's arm made him glance at the pixie girl. 'Dolores – that's you?'

She nodded.

Her name was oddly surprising. 'So you two were together on Sunday night?'

'Yes,' Thelma said, 'Yes. I swear it's true.'

'Where?'

'In a shelter. She'd got nowhere to go. I took her to a shelter and stayed with her because she was nervous.'

'There wasn't a raid. What time did you go to the shelter?'

'Oh, what can it matter?' Thelma asked desperately.

'Sunday night was rather a special night,' David reminded her drily. 'What time was it?'

'About ten.'

'Before or after ten?'

'Just after,' snapped Thelma.

'That's when I got in. Funny I didn't see you.'

'We didn't hang about. I ran into the kid in the hall and she was stuck over where she could spend the night.'

'And it didn't occur to you to give her a sofa?'

Thelma flushed. 'No, it didn't.'

'You promptly left the house and went to a shelter, though you've sworn I don't know how many times that you'd never go in one, raids or no raids?'

'I can change my mind.'

'Your story's too thin.'

'What's it got to do with you, anyway?' rapped Thelma.

'Just this. That I'm a moderately honest sort of bloke and I don't like thieves – or murderers.'

'I'm neither,' Thelma declared. 'You get out of here or I'll get someone to put you out.'

'Carry on,' David said.

Thelma was silent. He turned to Dolores. 'What's your version of this shelter yarn?'

'There wasn't a shelter.'

'You never met Thelma in the hall?'

'Oh yes, but it was in the middle of the night.'

'How near midnight?'

'I don't know. I was awfully tired. It was late. Or p'raps it was very early next day. It was dark outside, I came out of the room upstairs and thought I'd go to Acton.'

'Oh yes' David encouraged her. 'I've heard about Acton.'

'And I just saw her and she didn't say anything at all.'

'She didn't know who you were and still she said nothing when she saw you roaming the hall at whatever time it was?'

'I wasn't roaming it, I was standing still, I was so frightened.'

David controlled his impatience. 'Did she see you?'

'Oh yes. She stared at me so I thought she wanted to kill me. She'd got a suitcase, a bigger one than mine. I didn't wait, I ran out before she could stop me.'

'Was she trying to stop you?'

'She might have done.'

'Did you shut the door after you?'

'No, because I could see she was going out. I fell down the front steps and cut my knee.'

'You cut your knee?'

'Yes. Look.' Dolores raised her skirt a couple of inches, displaying a neat bandage. 'It hurt. There's a nurse at the factory, this morning she saw I'd got it tied up with a handkerchief and she was ever so cross. I didn't have to pay for the bandage.'

David was hardly listening. The presence of that spot of blood on the steps at Number 15 was explained now. Dolores must have escaped from the house at about the time of the murder – but whether just before or just after it was still uncertain. The stain had been noticed that morning, as soon as police were called to the house. A smudge, that was how Gracewell had described it. It was obvious, now, how Dolores had made it as she picked herself up with a cut knee.

'What did you do then?' he asked.

'I ran and ran all the way to Acton, and policemen were ever so kind and they all told me the right way.'

'That's what policemen are for. But – how the devil did you get here now?'

'I went to look for that nice man in the house where the murder was.'

'But that's quite a distance away.'

'I know. But this lady – ' Dolores glanced apprehensively at Thelma, 'she drove up in a lovely car and she asked me if I'd like a ride.'

David pieced it together. Thelma, encountering Dolores this afternoon, had seized her chance of building up an alibi. She'd seen the girl leaving the house in the small hours of Monday morning; it was merely a matter of persuading Dolores that they had left together at ten o'clock and gone to a shelter and stayed there. If that story worked Thelma couldn't have knifed a man in the garden at approximately three a.m.

As David reflected, Dolores suddenly crumpled up, sagging bonelessly against his side in a dead faint. He carried her to the wash-basin and splashed cold water on the thin childish face that had so intrigued Lipscott. When he glanced round, Thelma had gone.

Dolores stirred and whimpered: 'I wasn't in a shelter, I've never been in a shelter, ever.'

'O.K. kiddo,' David said soothingly. 'Where's your hanky? Or do you mind mine? It's glaringly clean.' He dried her damp features. 'Let's get out of here, we've outstayed our hostess.'

'I didn't want to come,' Dolores lamented. 'I never wanted to be here at all. I only wanted to find that nice man, the sailor who wanted to give me a pound note on the station.'

'Dear dear, that sounds like rather a nasty man, offering little girls quids on stations. But as I happen to know the early chapters it's all right. Come along. And heaven send we don't have to wangle our way through all those ropes. There must be a by-pass, and then we'll find that lovely man of yours.'

'You said you were awful,' Dolores whispered huskily.

'Did I? Astonishing. I must have been having an inferiority bout.'

'But you aren't.'

'I always knew we should be good friends if I persevered. But to be quite frank, pixie girl, you do make demands upon one's perseverance. Come along.'

THIRTY-FOUR

DAVID FELT QUITE AVUNCULAR towards Dolores. Lipscott had been right when he described her as helpless. As she sat in her corner of the taxi her expression was that of a child who is being taken to the dentist's, and doesn't know whether to be afraid of the adventure or thrilled by the promise of a treat to follow.

He asked: 'You're not hungry, by any chance?'

'No thank you.'

'I wondered if you'd like a cup of tea somewhere?'

'Yes please.'

'Oh gosh – Is it very rude to ask how old you are?'

'I'm twenty-one.' She added solemnly. 'That means I'm an adult.'

He resisted the impulse to remark 'Who'd believe it?' Instead he stopped the taxi outside a large cafe near Piccadilly Circus. With the orchestra whining about blue birds over the cliffs of Dover, Dolores and he sought a table. Surprisingly, when confronted by a menu, she declared that she would like some Woolton pie and chips. David, though he wasn't hungry at this time of day, ordered two portions. Dolores ate them both.

'Feel better?' he asked.

'Yes thank you. Oh look, doughnuts!'

She was pointing at a plate on the next table. David ordered cakes and she ate all that were on the plate, making a steady job of it. And she had said she wasn't hungry. He wondered how she would perform when she had an appetite. Conversation was certainly not her long suit. She was monosyllabic between mouthfuls.

He was still wondering how he could fix the time or even the approximate time, when Dolores had seen Thelma in the hall at Terrapin Road. He asked: 'Did you see a clock when you reached the factory, after your long walk? Or rather, your long run?'

'No. I was so hungry.'

Food was going to be a mighty big factor in Lipscott's life, if he hitched up with this young wolf. 'You can still see a clock, even if you're starving.'

'But I was looking at the plates of porridge.'

'Oh, so it was breakfast time?'

'Yes. They gave me some, it was in the canteen.'

'What time do they serve it there?'

'I don't know. We had porridge, and then sausages, and then bread and margarine and marmalade, as many slices as you like.'

David suppressed a snort. 'Well, let's get going again. It's just about time for Terry Lipscott to get back from Acton.'

'I've been to Acton.'

'So I've gathered.'

'What does your friend do there?'

'He walks round and round and round till he's dizzy, looking for you, my girl.'

'So silly, when I'm here.' She laughed. It was the first time that David had seen merriment on her queer little face.

'Now the idea is to stop him walking. And the best way to do that is to get along to where we're likeliest to find him.'

A drizzle of rain was failing and taxis were scarce. At last they found one setting down a fare in Regent Street. When they reached Terrapin Road it looked dreary, deserted, and rather sordid; for the first time number fifteen seemed uninviting, and David wondered moodily what had held him to such a house. It was Mrs. Meake, of course. Her warm heart had glowed like a beacon among the drabness. If anything happened to her, he would never want to see the place again.

They went in and up to Lipscott's room. David held Dolores by the arm, he was not going to chance her escaping from him this time.

There was no answer to a knock, and he opened the door. Lipscott was asleep on the divan. His hair was tufty, his mouth sagged open, he was dressed only in shirt and trousers, and his legs hung at a sprawling angle. He was snoring stertorously. In short, asleep he was about as unprepossessing a specimen of humanity as it was possible to imagine.

Dolores gazed at him. 'Isn't he lovely?' she breathed rapturously.

Lipscott did not stir. He was used to sleeping through all the varied noises of a ship. An opening door and low voices were less to him than the familiar hum of engines. David said: 'There's an old idea that if you wake a man by kissing him, you get a pair of gloves as reward.'

'With two coupons?'

'Of course. There's a penalty for every kind of racket.'

Hesitantly, Dolores crossed the room and stood beside the sleeping man. David gave her a sudden thrust – he felt that he was entitled to one spasm of retaliation after all his manoeuvres. Dolores fell forward. And so Lipscott woke with a start – possibly from dreams of espying a certain green pointed bonnet – to find his pixie in his arms.

'Pixie!' he shouted.

She made a move to retreat but he was too quick and too strong for her. 'Pixie, pixie, my little pixie.'

'The name is Dolores, if you want to know,' David prompted.

Dolores said: 'Take care of me, I wasn't in any shelter, I truly wasn't.'

'What the devil – ?' Lipscott was still grasping the girl, with the sort of gentleness and firmness with which a man might control a wounded kitten. 'What the devil – ? How the devil – ?'

'You can sort it out for yourselves,' David said. 'I've certainly done my stuff in delivering the goods.'

He left them gaping incredulously at each other, and could hardly envy Lipscott, who would naturally ask a lot of questions to which he would get nothing but scatty answers. Still, David mused, every man had his own idea of perfection.

In his own room he stood about irresolutely. He had several hours before the appointment with Miss Trindle. Tess wasn't likely to telephone and she certainly wouldn't be free till later on, in all the fluster of packing for the assortment of children who were leaving St. Margaret's. He rejected the thought of descending to the basement in search of tea and a gossip with Mrs. Meake, as normally he might have done.

How much Mrs. Meake knew of Thelma's coniplicity in the matter of the stolen vanload of goods, and of Sunday night's more serious affair, he still could only speculate. But Meakie certainly knew enough to realise that all her own effort and affection had resulted in one final sad conclusion: that Thelma wasn't worth worrying over.

David pondered upon one or two duty calls that he ought to pay before his week of freedom expired. There was his Aunt Jane, enduring the full horror of having only two servants to wait upon her. There was an uncle, retired from the Indian Army, now clinging like a cobweb to the musty armchairs in his club. There was old Chiddle, who had been a cross between a butler and a handyman in the old home before the final crash came...

One by one David rejected them. He could go and see all of them on his next leave. He could take Tess with him, Tess all aglow with a plain ring on her left hand.

He could hear the hum of the vacuum cleaner in the room overhead, and went up to speak to Annie through the open door. She swung round as if startled.

'Coo, I thought it was Mr. Cumberbatch,' she exclaimed.

'What would he be doing up here?'

''E's always poppin' up. And down too, come to that. Askin' for scuttles of coal, it's awful, time and time again I tell 'im we can't spare that much. I reckon 'e eats the stuff.'

'Perhaps he's got cold feet,' David suggested. 'If I'm wanted I'm round at Belmont Crescent, Number 26. Got that?'

'Cor, that's the "Twenty-Six Club".'

'You've heard about it?'

'Course I 'ave. Mrs. Wicks told me. It's a new idea for all them foreign fifth columns.'

'What the devil do you mean?'

'For foreign fifth columns to give food to parachutists, an' them done up as nuns.'

'So that's the rumour? Holy smoke, don't you realise that the fifth column is an indigenous growth in any country?' David was exasperated. 'But a ninny like you wouldn't know what indigenous means. It's – '

'Oh, don't I just!' Annie interrupted. 'It's what Mr. Middleton talks about on the wireless.'

David groaned. 'Oh well, perhaps you're right. I see you're not under arrest yet.'

'Nor likely to be. I was kind of larkin' when I said I done the murder. It's plain as plain who done it.'

David said sarcastically: 'I suppose that's why no arrest has been made.'

'Mark my words, the name is Trindle.'

'Miss Trindle?' Out of the mouths of babes and sucklings – and sometimes out of the mouths of fools – truth might come. 'What makes you think she's the guilty party?'

'She was mixed up in somethink funny in Jermyn Street, a lady friend of Thelma's told me, a young lady name of Peggy and she went on tour with the Ten Sparklets an' she married a pork butcher in Blackpool an' sent me a postcard.'

'What else did this Peggy say about Miss Trindle?'

'Just kep' sayin' something funny, an' you mark my words it was truth, she was an awful one for drink was Peggy, but if she said it was funny you can take it it was funny.'

'I'd better go,' David said, 'before I strangle you with one of your own dusters.'

'Cor, you aren't 'alf shockin', the awful things you say.'

'Cor, you're shockin' yourself,' retorted David.

He ran downstairs and strolled round to Belmont Crescent. At the club, where he expected to find chaos, a very fair show of good order had been achieved. Bob was chasing from floor to floor issuing instructions, and a score of willing workers toiled like ants to execute them.

'Tomorrow night,' said Bob, 'sees the opening of the most original, the most philanthropic the most universal venture in all history.'

'You ought to be on a tub in the park,' David said. 'Have you seen that sailor fellow again?'

'Not a glimpse: Tomorrow night we fling open these doors to all free men working for a finer and nobler world, aiming at the suppression of tyranny – Did I tell you all this before?'

'All of it.'

'And have you heard my piece about releasing men from the pinioning of the nails of the Nazi jackboot?'

'Yes, I had that too. Isn't there anything I can do apart from listening?'

'Yes. You'll find Dot in the office. You can dictate a tactful letter to the Duchess of Spraight, telling her that we'll be thrilled if she can be here tomorrow night, but we don't think we want her singing "My Ain Folk".'

'I'll construct a poem of a letter.'

'And another ought to go to Wilkins Brothers telling them that the plug on the first floor still doesn't work. Or do you think you could pop out and phone about that?'

'For plumbing you can't beat the phone,' David said. 'I'll attend to it if you'll give me their number.'

'Dot's got it. Dot's got practically everything.'

'And I'll say the poor girl needs it,' said David, as he went off to reinforce the office staff.

THIRTY-FIVE

THE "TWENTY-SIX" was certainly a scene of surging activity. A stream of curious inquirers came to ask for particulars of membership, interrupting the sorting of correspondence – some of it abusive, some commercial, some penned in sympathetic interest.

The matter of dealing with callers was somewhat complicated by Bob Carter's changing decisions. When referred to he would answer any question explosively and impatiently, as if the query had only one possible retort. Five minutes later his angle on any point might be entirely different. At one moment he was for excluding all civilians at another he declared that munition workers could be members.

'That's if they're foreigners,' he added.

'But look here, old chap,' David temporised, 'either you've got to have munition workers of every nationality, or none.'

'I'll have any Czechs who're working in our factories.'

'If you have Czechs you must have British.'

'No one's going to tell me which I have,' Bob retorted. 'I'll have the ones I like the look of, no matter where they hail from.'

'If you're not careful, you'll start several subsidiary wars,' David laughed.

'That's O.K. by me. I'm a natural fighter.'

His decision to have no women members was reversed instantaneously, upon seeing two landgirls who came in to inquire if this was a new kind of rest centre. Their giggles made them slightly incoherent, but a tirade from Bob reduced them to bewildered silence. Rest, he said was a word that should be struck out of every dictionary. The "Twenty-Six" was for recreation and mental and physical improvement, for the encouragement of sympathy between nations, and the provision of beer at the lowest possible price.

The landgirls retreated step by step, with Bob advancing as if the force of his own rhetoric drove him forward. When they reached the front door they fled.

'Nice girls,' said Bob. 'When they come back I'll ask them to advise me about blankets for the sleeping quarters.'

'If they come back,' David amended.

He had had enough of the enthusiastic confusion after about an hour. He reckoned that he had time to go home for a wash-and-brush-up, and perhaps for a quiet twenty minutes with the evening paper, before meeting Miss Trindle.

'I must beat it,' he told Dot. 'I've got a date.'

Dot gave him a coy glance. 'Girl friend?'

'A ravisher.'

'Aha! The blonde.'

Nettled, David asked: 'What do you know about a blonde?'

'Saw you with her this morning, in the gardens opposite.'

'Did you though? Well, she's just one of my string. My honey for this evening is more mouse-coloured.'

'You dirty old Bluebeard,' Dot said. 'What's twelve and threepence, and four and eight, and six and eleven?'

'About the price of a bottle of Scotch if you get hold of an amenable assistant. I'll let you know when I've got a vacancy. I never run more than half a dozen at a time, you might stand a better chance with the Navy.'

'Hog.' Dot hurled a fancy calendar, which struck the mantelpiece bowling over several vases that has been sent by "A Wellwisher".

'Today's good deed,' said David as he made for the door.

It was not yet dark, but already the streets were dim on account of a fog that had thickened as twilight approached. The house, when he reached it, was as quiet as if it had been uninhabited. He stood in the hall, reflecting that the quietness was normal enough, for Miss Trindle and Thelma were no longer on this floor. Cumberbatch, on the floor above, was very rarely visible.

And suddenly he realised that what had struck him was the absence of Annie's clattering and Mrs. Meake's singing. For years, Mrs. Meake had had a habit of humming, almost incessantly, snatches of tunes from old musical shows. Annie couldn't do the simplest job without crashing brushes or dustpans or whatever it might be, against the objects she was attacking. There was not a sound now.

He went up to his room. The blackout curtains were not drawn, and he was standing by the window, wondering whether it wouldn't be better to close it against the murky air that now drifted in, when a faint thud from below arrested his attention.

Cautiously, he peered from the window. Someone was moving in the shallow stone area at the back, to one side of and beneath the iron steps that led to Thelma's room. In the gathering darkness and fog he could not discern any outline, he could not even be sure whether it was a man or a woman moving down there.

He checked himself as he was about to call out. There was another dull thud – almost the sound that would be made if the flat of a spade were smacked against earth. Whoever was down there was working with deliberate secrecy, for it must have been impossible to see in the area, and no torch was flashed.

He made his way silently downstairs. Not knowing whether the curtains were drawn, he had a good excuse for not switching on the light in the basement passage. A sharp draught indicated that the door at the back was ajar. He moved quietly towards it.

The creak of the door betrayed him as he opened it wider. Annie's voice challenged him, 'Someone there?'

'Yes. What on earth are you doing?' He stepped quickly into the area and tripped over something at his feet. A moment later he realised that it was a sandbag, one of those that were usually stacked at one end of the area.

'Doin'? I'm just tidyin' up the sandbags.' Annie was fumbling round his feet, and as she threw the sandbag against the rest it made the sound that he had heard from above. A vague sort of thud.

'At this time of night? In the dark?' David exclaimed.

'It's got to be done some time. They slip and look ever so untidy.'

'What's the odds, if no one ever uses the back door? Except of course – ' David paused to stress his words, 'the police when they're investigating.'

'You keep quiet about the police,' rapped Annie. Even in the gloom, he could feel her fury, could picture her bony features growing sharper with rage.

'Why, are you afraid of them?'

'Not as much as you're likely to be' Annie snapped.

'Where's Mrs. Meake?'

'She's out. I suppose she can go out without askin' your permission?'

'Yes, but not often,' David said flippantly. 'But this sandbag business – Look here, I'm not prepared to believe that you were seized with a sudden fervour for tidiness at this time of the evening, it isn't reasonable.'

'You can believe it or not,' Annie said.

'I'm rather interested in those sandbags.' Deliberately, David adopted an irritating drawl, and switched his torch on to Annie's rearrangement.

In a flash she flew at him. 'You put that light out!'

'It's nicely screened with a fragment of what I believe is called butter muslin. Or ought I, in these days, to call it margarine muslin?' His levity was rudely interrupted. Annie had come close and he felt a stinging blow on his cheek. Her unusual height, and the fact that she rushed to the assault in so unexpected a manner, gave her an advantage. Before David could collect his wits, she had rained several blows upon him – not all of them in regions approved by sporting ethics.

For a second or so he was doubled up. Then he rallied to a full sense of the situation. Annie's attack was savage and uncontrolled; he had no doubt that if she had had any sort of weapon in her hands, she would have used it to full advantage. He swung his left arm, gripped her wrist, and brought his right over as quickly. 'You lay off, my girl. I don't want to hurt you.'

He was holding her so that she could make no movement. Suddenly she began to blubber. 'Whatever it is I do, people pick on me. Just tidyin' up a few sandbags, an' you've got to come dodgin' round and arguin'. It's not as if it's for myself, I got other people to think of.'

'But look here, you started on me. Not that I mind,' David laughed shortly. 'If you really want a scrap, let's fix up a ring and fight fair. But I don't like being jabbed unexpectedly in the dark.'

'An' I don't like you come naggin' in the dark. There's enough to get on a girl's nerves without that.'

'If I let you go, we'll call it quits.'

'O' course,' said Annie.

He loosened his hold on her. Instantly, he felt a sharp kick on his thigh. He staved off a second kick, remarking patiently: 'You ought to study the Queensberry rules. Come indoors, for heaven's sake. Let's switch on a few lights and try to achieve something like sanity.'

Again he gripped her wrist and urged her indoors. There, when the curtains were drawn and the light turned on, he saw with compunction how distraught she looked. She wasn't normal. It occurred to him that the sane man's was worse than the white man's burden. Sane men had to carry the batty ones, to be patient with them and round the rough edges of their battiness.

'Look here,' he began peaceably, 'It's just ridiculous, our scrapping in the back area. There wasn't any need for it. If you'd explained what you were doing, I'd have told you you'd chosen a silly time and the whole thing would have finished at that. Instead, you'd got to take a flying crack at me, and I had to show you I don't stand for that sort of funny stuff. However, it's all over, and there's no ill feeling. Is there?'

He waited for her reply. She had gone a queer colour, a kind of jaundiced white.

'Is there?' he challenged again.

'I'll kill you,' Annie said. 'If I get the chance I'll kill you stone dead and laugh at your funeral.'

'In that case I'm just wasting patience. And civility.' David paused and lit a cigarette to give himself some moments to think.

'What time's Mrs. Meake going to get home?' he asked.

Annie did not reply, but events provided the answer. Mrs. Meake's footstep was audible on the stairs, she was complaining as she came down: 'It's after blackout and the hall blind not drawn – '

She broke off as she reached the kitchen. 'David! You ought to know better than to keep Annie chattering when she ought to be looking after things.'

Mrs. Meake threw down her shopping. It looked innocent enough. A large loaf of bread and two skeins of pale pink wool.

David escaped.

THIRTY-SIX

MISS TRINDLE arrived at the "Blue Lantern" about two minutes after David had made a rather breathless entrance. She was wearing the fur coat that always made her look like a shabby rabbit; her severe brown hat was trimmed most irrationally with a pink rose that bobbed on the front of the brim.

As she advanced through the restaurant David saw that she was sporting green corduroy trousers beneath the fur coat, and gaudy striped sandals. By such atrocities did some women emphasise the fact that clothes were rationed. Miss Trindle's manner was portentous as she greeted him, and she chose her meal with almost religious solemnity, while David chatted pleasantly, inquiring about the progress of her first-aid class, waiting till they had started on their soup before he approached the matter that she had described as of some importance.

He was hoping that Miss Trindle, if of extremely uncertain age and rather vinegary disposition, might at least be precise and coherent.

'There was something you specially wanted to see me about – ' he began.

Miss Trindle consumed a mouthful of soup and delicately nibbled a scrap of bread before replying, with marked lack of directness, 'I have met a number of individuals in my time, some of them respectable and some of them otherwise.'

'Quite,' said David.

'I've had my living to earn.'

'I'm sure you've been very competent.'

The second course, a kind of fricassee, was set before them. Miss Trindle said: 'Might I have a little Burmah sauce? I had a post as secretary to an Egyptologist and he wouldn't eat a thing without Burmah sauce, and you'd be surprised how right he was.'

'I'll see if we can get some.'

But it seemed that Burmah sauce hadn't been heard of by the

wispy waitress. Miss McDrew herself hurried forward with various bottles of relish. Miss Trindle and David exchanged glances, in hers was the commiseration of one connoisseur with another when offered trash.

'Thank you, no.' Miss Trindle shook her head and the pink rose trembled perilously.

'Sorry,' said David. 'But you were telling me – ?'

'Oh yes. About the respectable and the unrespectable. I don't presume to judge any of them, but I do believe in Mr. Churchill, his voice inspires me.'

David, who felt that he was missing the trend of her logic, said enthusiastically: 'So do I, he's great.'

'He's the ideal leader for the prosecution of the war, and freeing the occupied countries.'

'Absolutely,' David agreed.

'So I suddenly saw the light. I saw how I could do my bit.'

David had to control his impatience. Miss Trindle wasn't Bob Carter, who could be told to make it snappy or to shut his trap, as occasion demanded. 'We can all do that.'

'You see,' Miss Trindle leaned across the table, a morsel of fricassee poised on her fork, 'I've met all sorts, but until you came back to Mrs. Meake's I'd never met a human eagle.'

'I beg your pardon?'

'A lord of the air, I might say.'

'Oh, I see.'

'So after some thought, and realising how you were risking your life leaving Lubeck ablaze – '

'I've never been over Lubeck.'

'And Berlin and Havre.'

'Oh yes. If it comes to that. But if you could make your point clearer – '

She interrupted, her voice and manner were intense: 'So I knew I couldn't be wrong if I told *you* the whole truth.' She sighed. 'The truth that will bring suffering to many a sad heart.'

David said jerkily: 'I'd be the last to want sad hearts to suffer but what exactly can you tell me?'

'About the murder on Sunday night.'

He waited, his mind keyed to an almost painful point of attention, till she went on: 'We know that Thelma's got her good points. She must have, because she's human like the rest of us.'

'That's a fact.'

'So you'll realise I don't *want* to send her to the gallows.'

Silence seemed the only possible retort to that one. Miss Trindle asked, with a smile: 'Is there just a wee fraction more of that mashed potato?'

'Lots,' said David, as he ladled it on to Miss Trindle's plate. Murder and mashed potato... In his impatience he could have snatched the rose from her hat, just to give her a jolt.

'I met Thelma,' Miss Trindle went on, 'when I had to go with Mr. Amery – he was the Egyptologist, you know – to a conference about film. It was three years ago or more. He knew about mummies and hieroglyphics.'

'He would.'

'And even British film producers like to get things right.'

'Natural of them, in a way,' drooled David.

'A month later I ran into Thelma, in Swan and Edgar's handbag department it was. Real leather for ten shillings in those days, doesn't it seem impossible? I'd left Mr. Amery and was book-keeper at Boulters Court. Thelma was living on a houseboat at Maidenhead.'

David's attention became even more alert. 'Did you ever go on that houseboat?'

'Never. But Thelma came to Boulters Court. She was – well if you'll excuse the word, nosey about the place, she got the idea it was fashionable and West-endy. Of course really it was terribly dull.'

'Indeed,' David murmured, remembering how many lurid scandals were associated with the place.

'She was talking to me in the office one day, when – No one can hear me, can they?'

'Not a soul.' David was beginning to hope that Tess would be late. 'Yes?'

'The Marquis of Leafe came in. He had a suite on the second floor. We had a little chat, the three of us.'

There was another exasperating silence, and David said encouragingly: 'What about?'

'I really forget. By that time I'd got quite fond of Thelma. She seemed, if you can follow my meaning, so spontaneous.'

David was quite mystified. 'Yes, I think I know what you mean.'

'We spent many happy hours in the Marquis's suite. And then I felt terribly guilty, terribly to blame.'

'Don't tell me the noble gentleman made a pass at our Thelma?'

'No, no not at all. She was more interested, anyway, in her friends on the houseboat. They were very important people. But the Marquis died, quite suddenly one morning, in his bath. Everything would have been all right, if only Thelma had run down and told me.'

'So Thelma and the old gentleman *had* got pretty thick?'

Miss Trindle looked annoyed. 'Not at all. It was all quite innocent. The Marquis had to have baths for his lumbago.'

'Really,' David muttered, his eyes on the salt cellar.

'But Thelma was silly. If she'd come and told me I could have got her out of the way before the doctor came. But she started screaming and the chambermaid went to see what was wrong. I had to give that chambermaid ten pounds and a good reference on the spot.'

'What an expense for you.' David was trying to fathom where all this might be leading.

'Not at all. I was amply repaid. I told Thelma to stay down in the office while I telephoned the doctor next door. He came right away and said the police must be informed. Everything was quite in order. Thelma was never mentioned.'

'Thanks to you,' said David.

'Thanks to me. Lady Amelia Gundry – his lordship's sister – realised that. She gave me a hundred pound note as a token of her gratitude, as soon as the inquest was over, and said she thought I ought to have a holiday abroad. But I never went, because war was declared and I didn't fancy going to America in the middle of a lot of U-boats. It was an open verdict. No one knew if it was suicide or accidental.'

'Which was it?'

'Oh, an accident. The day before, the Marquis had got very tired.

He'd been down at his country place that he'd let to a film director for some country life scenes. The hundred pound note that Lady Amelia found in his wallet was what he was paid for it. Thelma played a small part in the film, and that's how she came to be in Boulters Court that night. She was tired too, and she fell asleep on a sofa, and that's why she was still there when his lordship took his bath.'

'Quite. I mean – yes, all quite logical,' David hoped his comment sounded sincere. 'And then what happened? So far as I remember the Marquis died on the very morning the war started.'

'A good thing in a way, there wasn't so much fuss as there might have been. Then what happened was that I decided I'd had more than enough of Boulters Court – the goings-on were worse than wicked, I can tell you.'

David remembered that not five minutes ago the place had been described as terribly dull. 'I believe you,' he said.

I needed somewhere to go. And – I won't bother you with a lot of details, but Thelma had had a shock. And all she got on that houseboat was shocks. She got hysterical, and was crying and crying about her mother, that she hadn't seen for six months. She was all to pieces and homesick and I was sorry for her. And I'd promised to leave Boulters Court in case newspaper people came asking questions – his lordship's sister made me put that in writing when she gave me the hundred pounds.'

'So your leaving wasn't entirely on the grounds of propriety.'

'No one dictates to me,' Miss Trindle said with asperity. 'But I told Thelma if she'd go home I'd go with her, seeing that her mother kept an apartment house and I wanted a room. And that's how I arrived at Mrs. Meake's just before Mr. Chamberlain declared war on the brutal Germans.'

'So that's how it was. And it wasn't the Marquis who gave you Mrs. Meake's address?'

'Not him. Why should he? He didn't mix up with lodging house keepers.'

David said crisply, 'He raised his hat to her and blew her a kiss at Goodwood, bowing as if she'd been a princess.'

Miss Trindle sniffed incredulously.

THIRTY-SEVEN

TESS, FORTUNATELY, had not arrived when their plates were removed and strange looking ices were set on the table. David said: 'But all that's ancient history. I'm much more interested in the last few days. And nights.'

'I'm coming to that,' Miss Trindle said. 'I'm going to tell you everything. All about my misplaced confidence. You see Thelma got in such a shocking state, crying and sobbing I thought there was some good in her.'

'There might be,' David said dubiously.

'It was hysterics, she'd been swimming in champagne. She's – well, if you'll excuse the word, a wanton. I took her for a simple girl who'd got into bad company. But she's experienced by now. She knows what she's doing. And what she does is wanton, no other word for it.'

'H'm, h'm,' grunted David.

'A strumpet.'

'Before you call her a trollop, let's have the rest of the story.'

Miss Trindle bridled. 'Well, I got her back to her mother's, thinking she'd turn a new leaf and break with that houseboat crowd. I don't think she ever did. Anyway, last Sunday night she was disgracing a respectable house.'

'You mean number fifteen?'

'Yes. A gentleman was in Thelma's room just after nine. I heard his voice, a foreign voice it was, speaking broken English. The people on the houseboat were foreigners, it's one of *them*, I thought to myself. At just after eleven o'clock I went and told Mrs. Meake about him being there. She wouldn't do anything about it, she said this was the twentieth century or something. But at three o' clock, as near as no matter, I – pardon me, I had to go to the – er – er – it's the sort of thing no one likes to mention.'

'I understand. It's next to Thelma's room.'

'And I heard an argument. Thelma and her mother and the man,

214

all talking together. It wasn't ten minutes later that he left, and about time, I said to myself.'

'That was at about three o'clock? Did you see the visitor?'

'No. But I heard him.'

'One footstep is much like another on a carpet,' David said. 'It might have been anyone leaving.'

'But he went right out of the front door. I heard it shutting after him. You're not going to tell me that Mrs. Meake or Thelma would go out at that time?'

Dolores had gone out during the night... 'Thelma was gone by morning,' David said.

'So she was. But the man must have left first... '

'Facts, not probabilities, are what we need.' David was reflecting that if there had been a triangular quarrel, it was true enough that the man had almost certainly left, or been driven out, first. But a man had been stabbed in the garden within a short time of the dispute... 'Haven't you any idea who it was who called on Thelma?'

'Not the foggiest, as the saying goes.'

'Had she mentioned to you that she was expecting someone?'

'We aren't on speaking terms.'

'When you heard someone going out, was it a straightforward exit or was there some delay?'

'It's funny you should ask that, because I heard Thelma's door open and steps along the hall, then there was a minute or so, when someone seemed to be whispering. But there, I couldn't be sure. By that time I was so all a-quiver I might have fancied it.'

Thelma – and Dolores, who had just crept terrified down the stairs...? 'And what about Mrs. Meake? Did you hear her leave Thelma's room?'

'No. It seemed like one creepy step. And then it stopped and there was a sort of pause, and something like whispering, and then the front door closed quietly.'

Thelma and the pixie, leaving Mrs. Meake with the visitor in Thelma's room...? Or had Mrs. Meake crept through the hall, leaving Thelma with the foreigner? It was significant that Thelma had been so anxious to establish an alibi with Dolores.

'I made up my mind then,' Miss Trindle went on, 'to clear out. I knew what could happen with such goings-on, I'd had my lesson at Boulters Court. I started packing at four in the morning. Of course, when I heard there'd been a murder, I was more set on going than ever. And there was poor Mr. Smedley.'

'Smedley? What about him?'

'Wandering about the house by five o'clock. Twice I heard him go out and come in, I know the sound of his limp, so I guessed he'd got something on his mind. The second time he came in I stopped him in the hall and told him I was going. That was before we had all the rumpus about the murder, of course. He said he'd got to get a hundred pounds. It seemed like providence. Because there was me, with my carpet rolled to one side, ready to get my little treasures out from under the floorboard. There was a loose board, and just space to take an old workbox. The hundred pound note was there, as I'd never changed it, along with my little bits of jewellery. I looked on it as a sort of nice little nest-egg.'

'And very useful, too,' David muttered.

'I'd often thought of investing it. And every time anyone spoke on the wireless I made up my mind to put it in National Savings, but I never did. I'm anxious about later on, old age I mean. I wanted that hundred pounds to bring me in a rich reward. And there was my chance! Mr. Smedley's in a bank, he wouldn't do anything shifty, or he'd lose his job. He said we'd have it all in writing, he'd give me ten percent on the money and pay me back within ten years. That's doubling it, isn't it?'

'Seems like it. But I can't see why you should have done him a favour, straight away like that.'

'Oh, it cut both ways. He was very helpful. He's got a sister with a flat in St. John's Wood and the landlords had put the rent up, and she was in a state. She wanted him to go and live with her, to even up expenses, but he wasn't keen. He'd got something on his mind, that was clearer than ever. A woman, I wouldn't wonder, and didn't want his sister to know about it. He said she ought to take a lodger, but not anyone ordinary, it had to be someone refined. Well, Mr. Smedley went out to a call-box, not to wake Mrs. Meake, and telephoned his sister – at that time of the morning, it gave her a shock! But we fixed it all up nicely, and I'm as comfortable as – well, what rude people would call a bug in a rug.'

'That's fine.'

The austerity ices were consumed. David suggested coffee, but Miss Trindle asked for tea. He managed a discreet glance at his watch as he gave the order, reflecting that until now he would not have believed himself capable of being glad that Tess was late. But time was slipping by, and he hadn't learnt much so far. 'What I wish you'd tell me,' he said, 'is something about that houseboat. Who were the people on it?'

'They weren't all British, that's all I know or want, to know.'

'Did you ever hear about a man called Pinkie? He'd got a pinkish blemish over one eye.'

'Never,' Miss Trindle said emphatically.

'Or a man called Otto Klar?'

'Klar? Oh yes, I heard about Klar. There were two brothers, they were Rumanians and they were so rich it would make anyone dizzy. Otto Klar and Max Klar. They were both on that houseboat. Thelma said they were importers or something like that. Rich! Well!'

David had found the answer to the riddle. He knew, almost beyond the possibility of doubt, the name of the victim of Sunday night's crime. Otto Klar. Brother to the squat cringing Max in the fancy goods emporium. There was the likeness of the two men. And Thelma, who had known them both, was running stolen goods for Max.

Miss Trindle had at last said a mouthful that meant something. She was rambling on as she poured out her tea. 'It's my conscience,' she sighed. 'I knew I never ought to have stayed at Boulters Court, when I knew what was going on. I've been lying awake at night, I couldn't think who to trust till I remembered you. Never have so many owed so much to so few – and I saw how I could do you a good turn. You've got to leave Terrapin Road.'

Miss Trindle's logic was persistently confused. 'Why must I leave?' David asked.

'Because it's become a bad house. That's why I left.' Her expression was strangely innocent as she continued, 'It's all I've got, my reputation. Other women have got men to protect them. When I heard that bother in Thelma's room I guessed what would happen. Police all over again, like there were over the Marquis. You can't have looseness without police. I don't want to have police watching me and thinking I'm a loose woman.'

'I'm sure they never would,' David said, with more fervour than was tactful.

'And you've got to get out. It isn't safe.'

David suppressed a smile. 'When you mentioned in your letter, a matter of some importance – '

'That was it. It was important to warn you.'

'That's very nice of you. But I'm off in any case next Sunday.'

'You must never go back, after that. It's a dangerous house.'

'Don't worry over me. The next few days are probably my last there.'

He saw Tess, who would be the cause of his final departure, at the door, and in his enthusiasm started to his feet. She came smiling towards him. She wore no hat and her fair hair swung loosely round her flushed face.

'Sorry I'm late. I hurried all I could,' she apologised.

'It's all right. I've been having a most entertaining time. Oh – sorry, let me introduce you. Miss Carmichael, Miss Trindle. Have you eaten, Tess? Oh – then you'd like some coffee.'

'I'd love some.'

As David ordered it Tess was saying brightly to Miss Trindle. 'So you're the wrecker of my romance? David told me he'd got a thrilling rendezvous.'

'Not at all,' Miss Trindle said primly. She rose suddenly. 'I want to keep out of scandals, I only want to do the right thing, and I thought I was acting for the best.'

Tess was obviously taken aback at the misfiring of her sally. David hastened to assure Miss Trindle, 'Of course. You've been most altruistic.'

'I'm nothing of the sort.'

'I meant of course, you'd acted with the best intentions.'

'That's more like it. I must go.'

Courtesy impelled him to suggest: 'Sure you won't stay a little longer?'

'No thank you.'

'I'll see you to the door. It was more than good of you to tell me so much.'

'Warning you was the important thing. Against danger.'

'Yes. Yes, of course. Danger's a pretty frightful thing.' David felt that he was floundering hopelessly, he was longing to be alone with Tess yet anxious not to slight Miss Trindle. 'Will you be all right? I don't know how you get to St. John's Wood from here, perhaps I can find a taxi.'

Miss Trindle checked his ramblings. 'Don't bother. I shall be far safer in a bus. You never know what sort of man a taxi driver might be.'

'Well, if you feel like that, of course – Good night. And again thanks so much.'

David bowed Miss Trindle out, heaved a sigh of relief at the reflection that probably he'd never see her again, and returned to Tess to say: 'You'll have to excuse me for a minute, darling. I've got to phone.'

'You're behaving very mysteriously.'

'These are the mysteries to end all mystery. Epigram, grade three. Won't be a tick.'

'Give me a cigarette to be going on with.'

He offered his case and she took one. 'Doped, I suppose,' she remarked, as she twiddled it between a finger and thumb.

'Opium and hyoscine laced with morphia. Sorry I hadn't any hashish coupons left.'

He made for the telephone cabinet near the door. Inspector Gracewell answered his call at once without any intermediary. David said briskly: 'Still looking for the murderer?'

'Unceasingly,' said Gracewell. 'Have you seen Miss Trindle?'

'I'm just drying my eyes after her departure.'

'She knows more about Thelma Meake than all the rest of us put together.'

'Sorry if I'm dense, but I thought we were talking about the stabbing.' David could sense Gracewell's impatience, and was in the mood to enjoy a little verbal sparring.

Gracewell, however, was too experienced to be tricked into betraying his anxiety. 'The stabbing and Thelma are more or less up the same street,' he said.

'Really? That's news.'

'There have been developments.'

'Let me have them.'

'If you give me a point or so first,' said Gracewell.

David tried another line of provocation. 'It wouldn't be a bad idea if you got hold of the victim's name,' he hazarded.

'It would be useful,' Gracewell conceded drily.

'If I were given two guesses, both of them would be Otto Klar.'

'Otto – ? He'll be a relative of Max Klar?'

'Oh, so you're on matey terms with the delightful Max?'

'I wouldn't call it matey. I haven't yet had the privilege of meeting him.'

'They're brothers, Otto and Max, as you'd guess in a moment if you saw both of them, alive or dead.'

'I'm seeing Max in a matter of minutes. He's under arrest. And so, by the way, is Thelma Meake.'

'You were right when you said there'd been developments.'

'I'm not in the habit of making false statements. Or even facetious ones that fog the point at issue.'

'I stand reproved.'

Gracewell's laugh was audible. David asked: 'What are the charges?'

'At the moment Max Klar is detained for being in possession of a forged National Registration card. And Thelma Meake is detained over a matter of a van full of canned goods, stolen while in transit from a railway terminus to a provision merchant's.'

David said smoothly: 'I do hope you recovered the van.'

'Indeed yes, thanks to some right-minded person who drove it to a spot from which it was recovered by equally right-minded police officers.'

'How monotonously right-minded of all of them.'

'But Otto Klar, deceased, is bigger stuff. Where can I see you straight away?'

'Have a heart. My girlfriend's only just come within shooting distance.'

'It's an urgent point I want to discuss. And the 'phone isn't always the best medium.'

'Oh well – I'm still in the "Blue Lantern" in Cannock Road.'

'A few doors from "The Volunteer". I'll be in the saloon bar in fifteen minutes.'

David said hastily, 'About Thelma Meake – does her mother know?'

'Yes, and she's pretty broken up about it. I was there half an hour ago. Mrs. Meake was – well, you could only call it stunned. All right for "The Volunteer"?'

'Yes,' said David. He returned to Tess to give her a rapid account of what was happening. 'Keep it under your hat, darling. Or rather under that lovely buttercup hair of yours.'

'Of course. But David –' Tess was stirring her coffee. 'I'm horribly sorry for your Meakie.'

'It's grim, but what can we do?'

'Supposing I went round? I mean, while you and the inspector chew things over in the pub.'

'Would you? Tess, you're certainly an angel. Meakie took to you, she said how sweet you were, and you'll know what to say to her better than any clumsy man would. Bless you, darling. Come along. I've just got time to see you there and nip back to "The Volunteer". And as soon as ever I can I'll side-step him and get back to collect you again. Ready?'

Tess drank her coffee hastily. As they hurried along the dark street and round the corner David enthused again: 'What a grand girl you are, honey. You come along after a tiring day and find your evening all mucked up. And all you do is to suggest being a lovely angel just where a lovely angel is sorely needed.'

'Idiot!' Tess laughed. They reached the house and she added: 'It's all so terribly tragic. I mean for a decent woman to have a daughter like Thelma. But I suppose it could happen to anyone.'

'Not to us, darling. You wait and see.'

THIRTY-EIGHT

INSPECTOR GRACEWELL came into the bar within a minute or so of David's arrival. They took their drinks to a table where they could talk confidentially.

Gracewell said at once: 'There's no doubt at all about those two men being brothers. Apart from the likeness I tackled the one we've got. Max Klar. He was in a cell not twenty yards from me when you phoned. He started blubbering and admitted that the chap found on Monday morning was Otto Klar. Nationality, alleged Rumanian, but I rather think their mother was frightened by a German. Rich as Croesus, the pair of them.'

'So I gathered from Miss Trindle. She didn't know a lot about the party on the houseboat, but she knew that much.'

'That houseboat belonged to Otto Klar. He'd got big interests in the Balkans and imported timber into this country. He owned that garage in Cannock Alley – '

'I thought it belonged to Schenk.'

'Otto Klar bought it from Schenk last week, just before Schenk was run in. Otto also owned a fancy goods emporium that served as a dump and distribution centre for black market merchandise.'

'Must have been quite a busy chap,' David remarked drily.

'He was that all right.'

'I know that shop. What a nerve, running it right in the middle of the High Street.'

'It's a typical stunt. By being brazen enough they reckon to disarm suspicion. The rest of them – Max Klar and Bamberger and Thelma Meake, were just well-paid assistants. There's a big margin of profit in the racket, as I expect you know. Max offered the sergeant who arrested him five hundred pounds to let him go. He'd got the money on him in pound notes.'

David commented: 'A nasty pair of aliens. I can't understand how they got away with it for so long.'

'Bribery, I'm afraid. And they're clever, some of them. They buy identity cards. Max Klar went rather too far by having three on him.'

'What put you on his trail?'

'It wasn't actually my job. But Schenk's arrest started something, and Thelma Meake was shadowed. She led the way to Max Klar and Bamberger, but we couldn't get her under lock and key till we had a definite charge. She was arrested outside the stage door of the Regalia Theatre this afternoon.'

'Must have been soon after I had a lively little chat with her in a dressing room.'

'She's been identified, beyond any doubt, as the girl who drove that lorry off from the goods yard. And a raincoat she'd stolen – to hide her usual fancy get-up, I guess – was rolled up in a bundle in the stage doorkeeper's office. She protested her innocence – for about ten minutes. Then seeing the game was up, she ratted and gave plenty away. Said she'd been influenced, forced against her will to lend a hand, and all that line of talk. We're used to it.'

David smiled grimly. The time for defending Thelma Meake was past. 'I'd like to see the man who could persuade Thelma against her will. She looks like a dizzy ginger-glamour girl, but my! is she tough!'

'So one more black market lot's rounded up,' Gracewell went on. 'My only interest in it is that it's disclosed the name of my victim. Obviously the next move is to discover what special enemies the dead man had.' The inspector laughed shortly. 'I imagine I could spend a year compiling a list of them that would still be dozens short. A man with Otto Klar's record, even the bit of it that we know, might have been killed by A., B. or C. or X.Y.Z. This is where you come in.'

'But how, exactly?'

'Just by telling me why it was Miss Trindle wanted to see you.'

David burst out laughing. 'That's good. Her reason was simply this. To spin me a long rambling tale with a moral on the end of it. The moral was that my virtue and reputation weren't safe at 15 Terrapin Road. I promised to give the matter my attention.'

The inspector looked so disappointed that David relented. 'That, precisely, was all she *meant* to tell me.'

'I wanted the dope about Otto Klar. Didn't Thelma tell Miss

Trindle about him?'

'Very little. Just that he was a Rumanian importer with a side interest in films. However, the awful story that led up to the warning against my dangerous environment contained several titbits about Sunday night's events. But as you've seen her she probably told you as much as she told me.'

'She was obstinately mum about Sunday.'

'So your call was wasted?'

'Not at all. In discussing quite another matter she gave me – quite unwittingly – a good deal of useful information.'

Gracewell's ponderous method of imparting news was at times exasperating. David controlled his impatience. 'Would it be in order to inquire what the other matter was?'

Gracewell shrugged his shoulders, considering the point. 'Can't see why you shouldn't know, as you're in the thick of the inquiry. The facts are these. A certain Mrs. Clarke reported that she'd been robbed of a hundred pound note. Rushed, all hysterical, into her local police station and said that the money had been stolen from its hiding place underneath her stockings. The sergeant on duty took down particulars. There were various odd points about the incident. One was that the police already knew the woman – nothing criminal in her record but she's got a tendency to create scenes in shops and so on. Another point was that her husband's a private in the army, and soldiers' wives don't usually have hundred pound notes strewn about their homes. The third point was that the officer who went to investigate discovered that this Mrs. Clarke knew Smedley. There was a letter addressed to him on her sitting room table. Her manner was so scatty that, adding all the points together, the officer reported the incident to me. He knew, of course, that I was working on the Terrapin Road affair. So off I went and saw the Clarke woman.'

'On the chance that Smedley had picked up that note in our back garden? Was the lady's Christian name Delia?'

Gracewell's eyebrows lifted in surprise. 'Yes. D 'you know her?'

'I think I've heard of her.' David wanted the rest of the story of the episode from Gracewell's angle. 'Carry on,' he said.

'This Delia Clarke is certainly a queer one. At one moment raving over a lot of grievances, the next as smooth as a spirit level. She was all-of-a-jump in case we might think she'd never had the money and was making up the whole thing, and she showed me the back page of her ration book. On it she'd copied the number of the bank note. But she wouldn't say how she'd come by it, and she denied knowing Smedley. That was enough to set us tracing the earlier history of the note.'

'Did you see her husband?'

'He hasn't been about for six months, so she says.'

'If it's the Delia I'm thinking of, he was in London two days ago.'

'In that case there's a chance he took the note.'

'That's exactly what he did. Because I saw him hurling it back at Smedley, who'd given it to the Delia piece.'

'So Smedley did have it?'

'Didn't you discover that, in tracing its history?'

'No. We found that it had been paid out by a bank to the secretary of a film company owned by Otto Klar. The secretary had passed it on to the late Marquis of Leafe, the very day before he died, as a kind of honorarium in return for using his lordship's country house as a film set. Seeing that old Leafe is dead I called on his sister, Lady Amelia Gundry – she was his executor. An amiable and chatty old lady. She told me that she'd taken charge of her brother's wallet.'

'I know this bit,' David chipped in. 'She gave the note to Miss Trindle. Kind of hush money, though how much there was to hush up can only be guessed.'

'And that's as far as I could trace it. Miss Trindle wouldn't say what she'd done with it.'

'Lent it to Smedley, who gave it to Delia Clarke, whose husband found it and bunged it back at Smedley.'

'Are Smedley and the woman having an affair?'

David smiled. 'I don't think Smedley's got much for his hundred. I advised him to keep out of that arena. Whether he'll do so is questionable, he's properly bitten by the woman and he's in an awful state of nerves, poor devil.'

Gracewell drummed the table with his fingers. 'The whole episode doesn't get us much further. Still it's odd that that very note, unconnected with the murder, should have passed through Otto Klar's hands – or at any rate through the hands of one of his employees – and that it should turn up as near as no matter to the scene of his death.'

'Miss Trindle was the link up.'

'I suppose,' Gracewell mused, 'that she's telling us the truth. Part to you and part to me.'

'If she's a liar she's a pretty hot one, getting Lady Amelia Thingummy to back her up. And I can't see that she's got any motive for lying.'

'H'm, h'm,' Gracewell muttered. 'Her behaviour doesn't make sense. If her moral standards are so high that she's got to warn you against endangering your reputation by staying in Terrapin Road, how does she square that with accepting hush money? It isn't reasonable.'

'She's not a reasonable woman. If she were she couldn't wear a rose-trimmed hat with green corduroy trousers, as she did tonight.'

'You've got to remember that clothes are rationed.'

'All right. Rationing equals the green trousers which ought to equal no floral headgear. Let's forget it. I was going to tell you some fancy bits about Sunday night, as garnered from Miss Trindle. Sit back while I get a couple of beers and then I'll start.'

THIRTY-NINE

AS DAVID POCKETED his change and picked up the two tankards he was conscious of some excitement behind him. Voices were exclaiming: 'What, him?'

'Not out of the Grand Union Canal?'

'Oh, how dreadful!'

The name Smedley emerged from the gabbling and David stopped short with the drinks held steadily before him. 'What's that?' he asked Mrs. Wicks, who, true to her gossiping nature, seemed to be the centre of the chatter.

'It's Mr. Smedley, him that lives at Mrs. Meake's, the same as you do. He's been pulled out of the canal, drowned dead, not 'alf an hour ago. They took 'im away in a police 'earse. Mr. Smedley it is, or was I should say, that always walked with a limp, poor dear.'

David was shocked. He asked briefly: 'An accident?'

A man in the group answered gruffly, 'Accident! Not likely. You don't fall in the canal by accident, unless you're a kid fishing for tiddlers.'

David returned to Inspector Gracewell, who had risen to listen to the news from the man on the edge of Mrs. Wicks' group. They dropped back into their seats at the table. Neither spoke for a minute or so, till David said 'Poor chap. I still don't think he's anything to do with the murder. Got unbalanced about this Delia Clarke, that's about the weight of it.'

Gracewell grunted. 'Poor devil. Still – ' he resumed his brisk manner: 'Let's get on to the real stuff. Sunday night.'

David collected his thoughts, but he could not continue without another comment upon Smedley. 'At least he was sincere – and whole-hearted. He fell for this Delia, believed in her. She failed him, and for him that meant that everything failed.'

'You met her?' Gracewell's eyebrows went up.

'I met her husband.'

'Oh, I see.'

Gracewell still looked puzzled. David hurried on to the topic of Sunday night. 'At about nine p.m. on Sunday,' he began, 'Thelma Meake had a visitor at 15 Terrapin Road.'

'She's supposed to have been at the pictures at that time.'

'And at her aunt's for the night,' David said scornfully.

'We exploded the aunt story. But she still stuck to it that she'd been to the pictures, and spent the night with a friend. She wouldn't say where, or who the friend was. We often get that sort of alibi with that type of young woman – and often, sad to say, it's a truthful one. She said she'd invented the visit to the aunt to stop her mother asking questions,'

'She's thought up another alibi since then. That she spent the night in a shelter with a girl I happen to know.'

'I'll go into that later. She was actually in her own room?'

'So Miss Trindle says. That Thelma had a visitor at about nine. Miss Trindle heard their voices, and still hearing them at eleven o'clock she complained to Mrs. Meake – on the grounds of decorum. Mrs. Meake wouldn't intervene.'

'Did Miss Trindle see Thelma that evening?'

'No, but she knows her voice. And as you must have noticed, Thelma's tone is harsh and characteristic.'

'Who was the visitor?'

'Miss Trindle doesn't know. But – ' David added thoughtfully, 'if your doctor's estimate is correct, it was only four hours later that Otto Klar was about the place.'

'And Thelma was his mistress. She's admitted it, in her frenzy to throw all sorts of blame on to anyone but herself.'

'Then it's a fair bet it was Otto Klar in her room. Whoever it was, he had a foreign accent and he was there till three o'clock or thereabouts, when Miss Trindle wandered to the what-have-you and heard a three-cornered quarrel. Thelma and her mother and the visitor. After that there were steps in the hall, some whispering, and the front door opened and shut. Who went out – Miss Trindle doesn't know.' David went on to give an account of how Dolores had met Thelma in the hall, and Thelma's later attempt to base yet another alibi upon the encounter.

'After the hall door shut, Miss Trindle – according to her own account – was so deeply shocked that she started packing straight away. And while she was packing she heard poor Smedley roaming about, that's when she fixed up with him that she should go to his sister's.'

Inspector Gracewell knocked out his pipe. 'A three-cornered quarrel – and one of the three left the house by the front door. If one of the three was Otto Klar, he almost certainly went into the garden by way of the steps from that back room. Did one of the three go with him? Or was a fourth lurking outside?'

David was silent. His thoughts had jumped back to the unfortunate Smedley.

'A lot of arrows,' Gracewell went on, 'seem to point in Thelma's direction. This Otto Klar was in her room half the night. She fixes false alibis. But the only argument that arose was with her mother, so it's hard to see why Thelma should chase her visitor across the garden and stab him. Also, if she did that, the garden gate would still have been bolted on the inside when the policeman tried it in the morning.'

'And,' David put in, 'why did he go by the garden at all, when there was the front door quite handy, and the only person who might have spotted his going was only too anxious to see the back of him? I mean Mrs. Meake, of course.'

'When Thelma left the house – or rather, when she met that other girl in the hall, where was Otto Klar? In her room? Or lying on his tummy in the garden? And why, for heaven's sake, the garden at all?'

'He may have wanted to get to the garage, and that would have been his quickest way, via the rope ladder that he'd left dangling when he came in.'

'Funny he didn't use the gate. He could have got Thelma to unbolt it, in the dark, and to re-bolt it after his departure.' Gracewell scowled meditatively.

'It looks as if Thelma mightn't have been so anxious to see him,' David suggested. 'She'd been getting very thick with Schenk. Schenk gave her a mink coat only last week. If he hadn't been under lock and key he'd have been my first guess as guilty party. Jealousy and all that.'

Gracewell said: 'Someone unbolted the gate, that's certain. But not before the visitor's arrival – note the ladder. There's also the point that his wallet was gone, and he was stripped of everything that might have labelled him with a name. We might still be guessing his name even now – ' Gracewell relaxed and smiled, 'if it hadn't been for some bright philanthropist running off with a goods van today, and for your being thoughtful enough to suggest to Bob Carter that the police should be informed. For thus Thelma Meake was laid by the heels and terror made her talkative.'

David took out his cigarette case as he said casually: 'Isn't it just wonderful how these things work out?'

'Worse than wonderful,' grunted Gracewell. 'We now consider the most important point of all. Who got hold of the dagger when the seafaring chap got rid of it? I've interviewed a dozen women who claim to have turned Jules Dupont from their doors. And incidentally I shouldn't have known his name, if it hadn't been for you.'

'Oh, yes.' David had jotted down Bob Carter's scanty information and passed it on, via the phone, to Gracewell's office. 'He must be a simple sort of bloke, to have thought he could get a drink at the "Twenty-Six" in the middle of the night.'

'I've raked London,' Gracewell said. 'Soho is fairly hopping with men called Dupont: but not one of them fits the description.'

'Our man may be along tomorrow night. He promised to be, for the club opening, when there'll be a terrific waving of flags and blowing of trumpets.'

'Funny he's hanging around, yet I can't lay him by the heels. If he's on the level, you'd think he would have given information as to where he disposed of that dagger. If he's crooked, it's plain nutty to be showing his mug in the neighbourhood.'

'He might not know about the murder.'

'Fiddlesticks! It was in all the papers, you know we published a photograph of the weapon, and everyone's been yapping about the crime.'

'He might not read the papers,' David remarked. 'And it's possible to miss even a hot line in gossip. From what Mrs. Newland said he's of a surly disposition, not the sort of chap to chat to chance acquaintances. At sea he'd lose the habit of reading the news. He may not live near here, and people in other parts won't be so agog about our local affairs.'

'Humph,' was the only comment Gracewell made upon all that. 'We've got to find out who bought the thing. When we know, we shan't have much further to look. It'll be something more substantial than all the conjectures and theories that can be woven around several likely parties.'

'You'd better come to the opening of the "Twenty-Six" tomorrow.'

The inspector was thoughtful. 'If he's there, I wonder how willing he'll be to talk.'

'I gather there's going to be plenty of beer,' David laughed. 'Bob Carter's got a magic touch for contacting the right people, and he's got a big brewer rolling along the barrel. There are so many generous patrons Bob says he'll have to use foolscap paper for his correspondence, to allow enough room to print all their names down one side.'

'Well, the certainty of lots of beer and the possibility of questionable Dupont – it's an invitation I could hardly refuse,' said Gracewell. 'With any luck it's now only a matter of hours before we make an arrest.'

'I wonder if I'm guessing right.'

'I bet you're not,' the inspector grunted. 'Well, I must move.'

They parted outside the pub. David hurried back to see how Tess was comforting Mrs. Meake. The kitchen was in darkness; on the hall floor, by stooping, he could just see a thread of light under Mrs. Meake's door.

He sat on the stairs and waited. It seemed an age before Tess appeared, looking pale and unhappy. 'Well,' she said mournfully, 'that's that. She's gone to bed.'

'I'm afraid she's feeling pretty rotten?'

'She's distraught. Luckily she'd got some bromide and I gave her two tablets. She's exhausted, too. She ought to drowse off.'

'It's absolutely foul for her,' David said explosively. 'Why the hell should a decent soul like Meakie be let in for this sort of jamboree?'

Tess was silent. They went out and made their way cautiously through the dark streets, bidding each other good-night at the door of St. Margaret's. Tonight they could not think of seeking diversion, of being light-hearted.

Walking back alone, David was both angry and depressed. He was nervy too, for each time he heard a step anywhere near, his muscles went taut, on the defensive.

But tonight no unseen assailant trailed him to inflict sudden violence. Reaching the house, he hesitated in the hall. There was no longer a line of light beneath Mrs. Meake's door, and he hoped that she was forgetting her troubles in sleep.

The evening had been a pretty busy one, and until now he had had no time for further speculation as to why Annie should have been rearranging sandbags in the foggy dusk. She was not so observant, or so conscientious, that any slight untidiness would worry her. And suddenly he remembered that the stack of bags had been neat enough on Monday morning, when he'd gone into the garden with Gracewell. He'd noticed them particularly; they were arranged with almost mathematical precision and, being sheltered by the house, had suffered little damage from the weather. Mrs. Meake had explained that they'd been put there by an engineer who'd stayed in the house at the time of the big raids, but luckily there had never been any occasion to use them.

What was the reason behind Annie's sudden activity? David went slowly upstairs, racking his brains for any likely solution. None occurred to him. He went to the floor above his own, and tapped on Lipscott's door.

Lipscott was sitting up in bed reading an evening paper. 'Hullo Heron – I say, I've never had a chance to thank you,' he exclaimed.

'What for? Oh, your pixie.'

Lipscott's genial face creased in a frown 'That's not a very flattering term for a girl,' he said.

'Sorry, can't think how it came into my head.' (Hell! Hadn't Lipscott himself raved about the pixie resemblance?) 'How is the young lady?'

'Fine. I'll show you some snapshots I took. They're not very clear, because the light wasn't what it should have been, and it's the first time I've used the old camera for three years.'

David waited till he had made a show of admiring a sequence of unrecognisable smudges, before he said 'As a matter of fact I came up for advice.'

'An independent cuss like you?' Lipscott grinned, heaving himself out of bed. He went to a cupboard and fished out a bottle of beer. 'You can have my tooth glass, I've got a bakelite cup.'

'Well, not so much advice as inspiration.' David related the incident of the sandbags, adding: 'Now what d 'you make of that?'

'It's certainly a puzzler.'

'Were you here when the engineer chap stuck them there?'

'I was nearer Norway,' Lipscott said.

'There must be a reason for Annie being so deuced active.'

'Seeing it's Annie – ' Lipscott began.

'Well, let's say a balmy reason. And the way she came for me! It wasn't funny. When you're tackled by a man you know what to do, but when a woman comes for you in the dark, kicking right and left, it's a different song altogether. Annie's tall and stringy but she's tough, and her feet are a fair size, the tricky job was to get hold of her without hurting her, or letting her hurt herself. What I want to know is, why was she so wild at being disturbed?'

'Almost sounds as if she were hiding a body,' Lipscott observed.

'It wouldn't be a bad idea to have a look. Get a coat on and come down. Everyone else is doggo by now.'

The two of them went quietly to the basement. The back door opened easily and silently. Lipscott held a shaded torch while David shifted some of the bags. Suddenly, as his hand touched smooth material, he exclaimed: 'Gosh, I believe you're right, after all.'

The hem of a woman's blue skirt was wedged between two bags that were part of the inner layer. David tugged cautiously. The result was pure anti-climax. The skirt emerged, and after it came the rest of a dress. It contained no body. Apparently it had never contained a body, even a living one, for a price ticket still dangled from the back of the collar.

'Well,' David exclaimed. 'this licks creation! What the devil can anyone make of this?'

'Perhaps she bought it and didn't like it,' Lipscott suggested.

'My dear chap, any girl who does that either changes the thing, or sells it to someone, or gives it away. What's the time?'

'About eleven. I haven't got my watch on me.'

'If Annie's not asleep, we'll see if she's ready to supply the answer.'

'We can't go to her room,' Lipscott demurred.

'My dear chap, don't be so mid-Victorian. Come on.'

Upstairs they went. On the second floor Lipscott muttered 'Poor old Smedley's been looking fed up this last day or so.'

'Gosh, you don't know!' David told the melancholy news as briefly as possible.

Lipscott was shaken. 'Lord, there must be a hoodoo on the house,' he exclaimed. 'Two deaths in one week. I wonder who'll be the third?'

David grunted impatiently. Such a speculation, he thought was worthy of some old village crone.

Annie wasn't asleep. Her light glinted under the door and she was humming *Roll out the Barrel* as she clattered about in her room. She could do nothing silently. Even when she'd been shifting those sandbags, she'd slapped them down so that he heard them from two floors higher up.

He tapped on the door. Annie opened it at once. She was still fully dressed. Her eyes fell on the blue dress that David was holding and an expression of terror overspread her features.

'No,' she exclaimed. 'No, no! It's nothink to do with me I never saw it before, I don't want it, anybody can 'ave it, it's not mine.'

'No one said it was yours,' David remarked.

'That's right, it's not.'

'Then why are you in such a stew at seeing it?'

'I'm not.'

'Why did you hide it under the sandbags?'

'I never. I swear I never.'

'But my dear girl, I caught you at it.'

'You're a liar, I'll report you, you come pesterin' a respectable girl, forcin' your way into a girl's bedroom!'

234

David had gone no further than the doorway. At Annie's accusation, he stepped sharply back, nearly knocking Lipscott over. He made a last attempt to gain some enlightenment. 'We don't want to annoy you, either of us. But won't you tell us just why you tried to dispose of the dress? It's obvious it's a new one.'

'I'll scream, I promise you I will.'

David preferred her kicking to any threats of screaming. He tumbled down the stairs, with Lipscott bundling down ahead of him.

'Complete rout,' Lipscott said, as they reached the second floor.

'And I've still got the accursed dress. If it's got something to do with the murder, I ought to give it to Gracewell. If it hasn't, I feel like chucking it out of the window.'

'There's a third alternative. You can put it back where you found it, and no harm will have been done.'

David regarded Lipscott broodingly. 'You aren't what I'd call very constructive in your suggestions. Well, I'll hang on to the thing tonight, and perhaps I'll have a brainwave in the morning. Good night, old chap.'

'Sorry I couldn't help. Truth is, I'm a bit occupied with my own plans. Dolores and I – well, we had a talk over things this evening, we went for a walk round Acton.'

'Still walking round Acton? But there, I suppose it's a habit that's difficult to break, once you start it.'

'I'm serious about Dolores,' Lipscott said huffily.

'I realise that. Let me know whether to get a toast rack or fish knives.'

Lipscott grinned sheepishly and disappeared into his room. Still clutching the mystifying blue dress, David went down to his own.

FORTY

USUALLY HE SLEPT WELL. He could switch off his thoughts and drift into unconsciousness almost as automatically as he could switch off a light. Troubles of the past and threats of the future became as nothing. Darkness meant oblivion except when he set himself against it.

But tonight he was restless, disturbed by a shifting panorama of problems. Above all, there was the disaster that had fallen upon the Meakes. Thelma was a criminal held on a charge of robbery. And heaven alone knew what further charges might follow. She had asked for trouble and had found it in plenty.

Then there was Smedley, the poor devil who hadn't been able to take disillusion with fortitude. It's dangerously easy, thought David, to condemn the sort of weaknesses one doesn't understand. The villain, or rather the villainess of that piece was the nebulous Delia, who doubtless would continue to supply a sequence of tests to such further victims as she could ensnare. Or perhaps Smedley's fate would teach her something.

Uneasily, David heaved himself over beneath the blankets. Did that kind of human vampire ever learn anything? He himself would never know the answer to that one, because Tess with her beauty and gaiety and courage would stand between him and any temptation to experiment in sordid adventures.

The blue dress. Why the heck had Annie stuffed it behind the sandbags? Was she scared, had she bought it illegally, without surrendering coupons? In the dark David could almost feel himself flushing guiltily, remembering a certain pair of silk stockings. His first and last black market deal! He didn't want any more under-the-counter transactions.

His mind switched back to Thelma. That yarn about her having left home at six o'clock on Sunday evening. The still more futile story of having spent the night in a shelter with Lipscott's queer girlfriend. David growled aloud and heaved over in his bed, thinking disconnectedly of Tess and Inspector Gracewell and Mrs. Wicks and his Aunt Jane – whose invitation to Eaton Square still hung over him.

He'd go on Sunday before catching his train. And he'd take Tess... after marrying her on Saturday by special licence.

He must get the licence tomorrow...

At last he slept.

He did not know what time it was when he woke with a kind of horror snatching at his suddenly alert nerves. His door, that had been left ajar, was wide open; that he knew for he could feel the draught blowing freely through the room. The darkness was complete, an utter blackness enveloped him.

And he had a feeling that he was not alone.

Something had moved. He lay still, his limbs tense like those of a man steadying himself to withstand an onslaught.

Was he awake or asleep? Awake and being fanciful, or asleep and enduring a nightmare? As he speculated foggily he put out his hand towards the table lamp. His fingers touched his torch and he realised that it would make a good defensive weapon – if weapon were needed. As he gripped it he thought he heard someone calling out. A man's voice, it seemed to be at some distance.

'Is someone there?' David challenged. And then he stifled a cry. For something had moved across his face, it felt like a series of fingers with hard tips.

He made a grab – and caught at nothing.

Now he could feel the perspiration trickling under his pyjama jacket. The silence was eerie, sinister. Why had the intruder not taken advantage of him as he lay asleep and unaware? Why that exploring of his face – and then retreat?

He moved his hand tentatively towards the light switch, but as he did so something touched him again. This time it was like the stroking of a fur glove, it went across his forehead, across the patch of sticking plaster that still decorated his brow. Forcefully he seized the lamp, found the switch, and turned it.

The room was flooded with light – and it was empty except for himself. The door, as he had guessed, was open. He shuddered, wondering whether his mind was unhinged, for it was but a split second between that last furtive touch and illumination. No one could have left the room in that time.

He assured himself that he was wide awake, the whole thing wasn't a nightmare, he could still feel the tickling of the movement across his forehead. A cat…? No cat could have touched him with hard fingers.

Again the muffled voice called, and now the sound was articulate. A man was calling a name, 'Connie, Connie!'

David dashed to the landing. Above and below him the house was dark. He heard a distant clock striking three. 'Is anyone there?' he asked again, steadying his voice as he switched on the landing light.

No reply. He almost tottered back to his room, and a slight movement drew his gaze to the curtain. On top of the pelmet something scurried – something that made him stare in complete incredulity.

A small brown animal, the like of which he had never seen before, was sitting on a corner of the pelmet board. It might have been a rat, but it was too bushy. There was some resemblance to a squirrel, but the tail wasn't right. And no sort of rabbit could have so pointed a nose. The thing ran down the side of the curtain, along the floor, and clambered up the tumbled bedclothes to perch on the pillow.

'Well I'll be jiggered!' David said aloud. He wondered if the creature had sharp teeth, whether it would bite. Its paws were extraordinary. The wooden fingers…

The little beast seemed tame enough, making no move as he approached, but as he extended a tentative finger he heard a voice and swung round.

Cumberbatch was in the open doorway. His colourless face was even more blanched than usual, his white hair was ruffled. He was wearing a kind of coloured sarong round his hips, his torso was naked. His thin lips were quivering.

David exclaimed: 'Hi, take a look at this!'

'My tree bear,' said Cumberbatch. There was relief in his voice and in his whole attitude.

'Tree bear?'

But Cumberbatch was intent upon the small animal, that now had raced up the side of the wardrobe. He called 'Connie, Connie – '

That's what the distant voice had been calling. Connie... David remembered that Mrs. Poole had referred to the late Mrs. Cumberbatch as Connie. Devilish queer...

'Come here, Connie.' Cumberbatch seemed to despair of catching his pet. 'I'll be back,' he muttered as he went out hastily.

In a minute or so, during which Connie made yet another tour of the room, Cumberbatch returned carrying a peach. He held out the expensive titbit. Connie hesitated before she capitulated and sat on her owner's arm, holding the fruit in her front paws, nibbling juicily.

David said: 'The thing gave me a hell of a scare.'

'She's not dangerous. None of them are.'

'What did you say she was? A tree bear?'

'Picked her up in West Africa, on my way home,' Cumberbatch spoke slowly, as if his thoughts were elsewhere, his eyes had their weird, far away expression. 'They're very friendly little things. They like warmth. Best pet you could have. They get very fond of you.'

'Do they?' David could think of no more inspired comment.

'They're intelligent. This little one, she's got a soul.'

'Really.'

'She doesn't like being called a rock rabbit. A lot of people make that mistake.'

'She's not a rabbit. She's got paws like wood.'

'Hooves. They've all got them. Just like a horse. Here, you have a look at them. Quiet, Connie!' Cumberbatch held up the animal's paws and proved the truth of his statement, then spoke soothingly. 'There, there, my little darling. Oh well, I'll get back to bed. I can't think how Connie got out, my door's always shut.'

Cumberbatch had provoked enough comment upon his closed door. He added: 'I might have left it unlocked. Then of course, if anyone tried it by mistake, Connie would have a chance to get loose.'

'I leave mine ajar. I like plenty of air.'

Cumberbatch stopped on the landing. 'By the way, there's no need to mention Connie to anyone. There's a sort of prejudice against animals, you know.'

'All right, I'll keep mum.' But David was reflecting that far from being prejudiced, the British were apt to be sentimental about anything with four legs. But perhaps not about a pseudo-rabbit with four sets of hooves and a soul...

This time he shut his door. He didn't want any more visits from the soulful namesake of Cumberbatch's murdered wife.

But at least, he thought as he dozed off, that persistently closed room and the endless clamour for coal were now comprehensible. Connie, being a West African lady, would like a tropical atmosphere.

FORTY-ONE

ANNIE TAPPED ON THE DOOR and came in with morning tea. She was unusually pale and her eyes looked as if she had spent an uneasy night. Unprepossessing at the best of times, she was certainly an unattractive spectacle now. David thought it wise to avoid any reference to the previous night's scene, for the present at any rate.

But Annie was not so evasive. 'That blue dress – ' she began.

'Oh yes, If you happen to want it, it's rolled up inside the wardrobe.'

Surprisingly, Annie burst into tears: David leapt up, snatched at his dressing gown, and knotted it hastily round his waist. 'I say, there's no need for this. For the love of Mike; don't make such a row.'

She continued to sob convulsively. She had dropped on to the chair by the table, and now her face was hidden in her hands. 'I'm that miserable,' she gulped. 'I'll never take my Mum out no more.'

'What's this got to do with your mother? Is it her dress?'

'She pinched it. She pinches things every time I take 'er out. Sneaks bits of this an' that off of counters. I don't 'ardly know where to 'ide the stuff. I told you I'd got a guilty secret, an' you wouldn't never listen. You laughed.'

'But hang it all – ' David was nonplussed, feeling sorry for the girl but angry at her muddled logic. 'You told me you'd stabbed the man who was found in the garden. You confessed to the police.'

'I done that to try an' get myself put away, then I wouldn't 'ave to take Mum out.'

'But no one forces you to take her out.'

'Mum frets if I say I won't.'

'You can go and see her at the – wherever she is. The Home. Or if you do take her out, you must stop her stealing. If I've got the hang of it, she's not exactly normal.'

'Normal?' Annie echoed blankly.

'You'd better speak to the matron. Or the Almoner, or whoever it is you see there.'

'I daren't. She frightens me. She's got a blue uniform an' she wears spectacles.'

David drank a cup of tea to gain time for thought. Annie herself was obviously a borderline case. But her instincts were not criminal, or she wouldn't be distressed at being an accomplice in her mother's thefts. He said: 'You see your mother needs someone very strong and firm-minded, if she's allowed out and about.'

'I tell 'er,' Annie said ruefully. 'I tell 'er and she won't never listen.'

'Can't you write to the Home? Explain about the thefts and say you don't think your mother ought to go in shops. You can take the blue dress next time you visit there, and leave them to deal with it. Your mother's their responsibility, you know.'

'I don't know how to spell properly,' Annie said helplessly.

'I'll help you with the spelling. There's a pen and ink and paper right by you. Have you got five minutes?'

'Mrs. Meake's late this morning, nobody won't get no breakfast till after nine.'

'Then write your letter and get it over.'

'It won't get my Mum in prison?'

'Nothing on earth will get your mother in prison,' David said firmly.

He lit a cigarette and drank another cup of tea while Annie laboured over her letter. He was glad she had complied with his suggestion; having tumbled on this secret of persistent shoplifting, he couldn't have ignored it. And already Annie was looking more cheerful at seeing an end to her complicity.

She looked up to ask him how to spell 'Nick.'

'Nick?' David queried.

'I'm saying my Mum nicks bits of this and that.'

'Better put "steals".' He spelt the word. And presently he read the finished letter, a pathetic, oddly phrased missive that, in spite of its faults, still conveyed its meaning.

'That's fine,' he said. 'Now address the envelope and I'll post it for you, then we'll know it's done.'

'It'll be them that stops Mum going out, not me,' Annie said, as if she still needed to justify her action. 'So Mum can't nag at me, can she?'

'Of course not. Now buzz off, I've got to shave. Oh, take that dress, and whatever you do don't forget to take it along next time you go to see your mother. You've mentioned it in your letter. It's not been improved by being stuffed among sandbags, but the people at the Home must do what they think best about it. When they take on anyone like your mother, they've got to smooth out any difficulties that occur through their lack of judgment.'

'I don't know what that means, but serve 'em right,' said Annie. 'You're ever so kind, Mr. Heron.'

'Rubbish. I'll be obliged if you'll hop it.'

'I'd die for you, straight I would.'

David tugged the blue dress from the wardrobe, thrust it into Annie's hands, and propelled her towards the door, which he closed firmly after her. His eyes fell on her letter; he was apt to forget to post his own, but this was one that must not be overlooked. He wondered what sort of symptoms Annie's mother might develop on being baulked of her favourite activity. But that wasn't exactly his pigeon.

He started to shave. Just when his jaw was nicely smothered in lather the telephone rang, and he heard Tess's voice.

243

FORTY-TWO

TESS WAS TRYING to explain that she wouldn't have any free time all day. 'I've got to take this bunch of children down to Sussex by coach,' she said, 'and as I'm getting a completely free day tomorrow I've promised to stay on duty this evening.'

'I'm going to see about a special licence today. We'll use it tomorrow.' As Tess did not answer, David added: 'I'm quite idiotically in love with you and I'm taking it that silence gives consent.'

She said softly, 'Quite right, darling.'

'I can't live without a sight of you till tomorrow. I shall be off for heaven knows how long on Sunday.'

'I know. But you understand how it is.'

'Can I meet you on your return from Sussex?'

'I'm coming back by train that gets to Victoria at six-thirty.'

'That's fine. I'll be under the clock. At least I can drive you back to St. Margaret's, that'll give us a bit of time.'

'All right. I must go – '

'Hi, just a moment. You must tell me all your father's Christian names and what he does for his honest living. Oh yes, I remember, he's a doctor. And your mother's Christian names. And if you'd like any wires sent, so that your contingent can come along, I'll attend to them.'

'I haven't got a contingent, seeing that the old folk are in Canada and Mike's in some far away desert.'

'That makes it all the simpler. Would you like green orchids? Or would they be too sophisticated for a simple girl?'

'Simple girl, my eye. But I prefer scarlet carnations. Oh, and Dad is Henry Alfred James Carmichael, medical practitioner, mother's Evelyn Rose ditto. Doesn't it cost the earth to do something like this in such a tearing hurry?'

'I don't know and I don't care and there's never been anything like this before, in heaven or earth or in the waters under the earth.'

'Idiot!' said Tess.

'Yes, my idiot's delight.'

'Six-thirty at Victoria. And after all I think I like orchids, just to show how quickly I can change my mind.'

'You shall have the rainbows out of the sky – '

But Tess had replaced the receiver. David gulped his tea, hurried over his bath and dressing, and leapt downstairs. He met Annie in the hall with a tray.

'Oh – you're not goin' out without your breakfast?' she exclaimed.

'I'd forgotten all about it.'

'That's through me, bothering you about my Mum.'

'Shove it down there and I'll deal with it.'

'You can't eat your breakfast off of the 'all table.'

'Can't I? I'll show you.' He proceeded to do so, making short work of it, before he headed for the street and found a taxi.

Within half an hour he had learned that it would cost him a mere twenty-six shillings to get married, and that he was expected to provide two witnesses to identify himself and Tess. He was so delighted at discovering no obstacles that he shook hands with the registrar, a clerk and an old woman who was dusting the office.

All the week he had been short of time. Now he had an hour to kill and, early though it was still, he yielded to the prickings of his conscience and went to call upon his Aunt Jane in Eaton Square. She was maintaining her house as a perfect Ivory Tower, forbidding any wartime atmosphere to intrude. She had given up taking a newspaper and had no radio. She, who had the most formal ideas about correct dressing, was full of approval when David appeared in tweed jacket and flannel slacks.

'Far too many men wearing that horrible khaki,' she remarked. 'I expect you get awfully tired of it.'

He realised then that his aunt had never understood to which of the services he belonged. She had addressed-letters with 'Esq.' after his name. She was remoter – far remoter – than the sphinx from current events. They talked about old holidays at Scarborough, and how beautifully roses would grow on clay soil. Together they lamented the modernity that was spoiling the world for reasonable people.

I expect, thought David, that Julius Caesar had to sport the same line of talk in his day with some old aunt of his. But he enjoyed himself and invited his aunt to the wedding. She wanted to know if Tess were a Shropshire Carmichael, and was horrified when David said he hadn't the faintest idea and didn't care anyway, for all he knew Tess's parents were Canadian born, he'd never had time to ask her.

Aunt Jane passed the morning well enough, but the rest of the day, in spite of an hour in a jeweller's choosing a ring, went sluggishly till six-thirty, when David planted himself firmly beneath the clock at Victoria. Tess appeared five minutes later; she was surprised that David had kept a taxi waiting – till she realised that the driver had been given special instructions to go by a remarkably devious route to St. Margaret's.

The ring fitted perfectly, and Tess expressed delight with the three square sapphires set in diamonds. David begged her to wangle a free evening. 'You'd enjoy the opening of the "Twenty-Six",' he told her, 'it's going to be a night to remember.'

'Not a hope. Nobby and Smithy are going to the pictures, they'll be absolutely on the doorstep waiting for me to get back, as they can't decamp till I'm there.'

'And tonight, as likely as not, will provide the solution to the great murder mystery. That lanky *matelot* Jules Dupont is going to turn up, I feel it in my bones.'

But Tess remained firm, and surely enough Nobby and Smithy were waiting impatiently to escape, for they ran out, tugging their coats on, before David was twenty yards from the house.

He returned to Terrapin Road, feeling anxious about Mrs. Meake, for in spite of her declaration of not caring what happened to Thelma, she was certainly feeling the strain of events.

Annie was in the kitchen, with the not very helpful information that Mrs. Meake wouldn't leave her room. 'An' she's off tomorrow,' Annie added.

'What, going away? Where?' He had never known her leave the house, even for a short holiday.

'Don't know. She's finishin' off a kid's vest she's knittin' an' off she's goin' an' that's all I do know.'

David was completely mystified. And uneasy. It wasn't like Meakie to behave erratically, and she wasn't usually impetuous. He had a feeling, as he went off to have an early evening meal, that this was the lull before some unpredictable storm.

If expectations were fulfilled, the guilt for Sunday night's crime would be placed this evening. Half a dozen words from that French sailor, and the murderer would be indicated without much possibility of further doubt. Mrs. Meake's threat of departure suggested that she knew the answer already, and couldn't face staying to endure its repercussions.

Thelma would be brought before a magistrate in the morning on the charge on which she was already detained. And she had little chance, where she was, to construct further alibis for Sunday night.

David reached Belmont Crescent before eight, thinking that he might be of some use. The interior of the house was ablaze with unshaded electric bulbs, and was a scene of astonishing liveliness. Men and girls of various nationalities, some of them in remarkable uniforms, were running about the house, exclaiming at the ingenious amenities that had been devised for their pleasure and comfort. Dot was issuing membership cards that were hardly dry from the printer's. The Duchess of Spraight was already handing out beer, and Beatrice was cutting long slabs of cake.

Rather cynically, David found himself wondering how many laws had been broken to achieve all this. He was in the hall when Inspector Gracewell arrived, shaking a spatter of rain from his felt hat and raincoat.

'You'd better become a member,' David said. 'It'll cost you a shilling. Then we'll go and see about a couple of drinks.'

Gracewell approached Dot, who had a temporary desk in the hall, his shilling extended. 'May I have a card, please?'

Dot said severely, 'You'll have to be passed by the committee. It's the law. If we find out anything against you, you won't be passed, your card number will be cancelled, and you'll forfeit the shilling.'

'This seems to be a highly original sort of club,' Gracewell said.

David winked. 'Unique.'

Gracewell asked Dot: 'What would stop the committee passing me?'

'Oh, if you were an undesirable alien, I expect we'll get a few trying to shove themselves in. Or if you were a crook or anything beastly.'

David said solemnly, 'Stow it, Dot. Mr. Gracewell's a police inspector, he could have us closed down if he just flicked his finger the wrong way. Very powerful gent.'

'Oh fiddle-de-dee,' said Dot. 'If he's stuffed you up with that sort of boloney he must be swelled-headed and you must be soppy and that makes you both undesirable. I wish you'd push off, you're standing right in the way of two lost Australians.'

'I tremble at the prospect of that committee,' Gracewell said.

'That's all right,' David said. 'I'm on it and you're passed. Come along and I'll show you over the premises. They're worth seeing.'

'I'll say they are. Of all the rummy outfits, this beats creation. What an idea! But I doubt if it'll work.'

'It will as long as Bob Carter's enthusiastic. But he's so erratic he might take to gardening or fire-watching and forget the "Twenty-Six" existed. I wonder where he is now. As likely as not he's stoking the kitchen boilers, or redecorating the attic.'

They went to the first floor, glancing in the front room. It was littered with heaps of books. 'Seems to be the library,' David remarked. 'And this back room's the dining room. At the moment the menu seems to be cake and beer. Gosh, what a crowd.'

'Astonishment has given me a shocking thirst. You don't see any sign of our special friend, do you?' Gracewell emphasised the word 'special'.

'Not so far. My arms are longer than yours, I'm grabbing the first two mugs I can reach.' David edged his way forward, and got the drinks, passing a coin over the heads of those in front.

They went to the second floor. In the front room a miniature gymnasium had been devised. Two Chinese were experimenting with tottering parallel bars, the British Navy had taken charge of a rowing machine and were testing its resistance to violence.

The back room was stacked with stretcher beds. 'Seems to be an incipient dormitory,' said David. 'And I believe the top rooms are dormitories too.'

They prowled up. Two men were sitting on the topmost stair. Bob Carter – and a man in a nautical cap, a navy overcoat, and a navy scarf with yellow spots.

Jules Dupont... the dagger-hawking sailor. David nudged Gracewell, who said briskly: 'Hullo Carter. Congratulations on your venture. Hope it'll flourish.'

The sailor still crouched on the stairs, peering uneasily up under bushy brows. His tanned skin was deeply lined, his expression was surly. Bob rose. 'Here's someone who's got something to tell you. He's French, very pro-British de Gaullist French. Monsieur Dupont, Inspector Gracewell.'

The atmosphere was tense. Gracewell made a show of being casual as he spoke. 'Oh yes. How d'you do, Monsieur Dupont? Now what's the news?'

There was a silence. Bob said: 'This gentleman is all right, Dupont. Good friend. *Bon ami, vous pouvez lui parler* – oh hang my French, that's about as far as it'll carry me, seeing that the pen of the gardener won't help.'

'I speak English good,' said Dupont.

'Sure you do, haven't we been chatting with hardly a single misunderstanding? Spill the beans, that means *parlez* all you know.'

Gracewell said: 'You had a dagger?'

'*Pardon?*'

'A knife, a long knife.'

'*Canif*,' Bob interpolated somewhat inaccurately. 'Long *canif*.'

'Yes,' said Dupont. 'I do nothing bad. I only wish – wished to sell.'

'And you sold it on Sunday?' Gracewell asked.

'In the evening, yes. For one pound. It was a curio, very sharp also.'

'Where did you sell it?'

'At a house, near.'

'Which house? In which road?' Gracewell had to insist: 'Tell me the name of the road.'

The sailor shook his head.

'Terrapin Road?'

'That is it. I feared to pronounce Terrapin. On Sunday, I do not see the number. Too dark. Tonight, I go with this gentleman to the exact house. We find the number. It is fifteen.'

'Fifteen!' The word escaped David violently.

Gracewell asked slowly, 'To whom, at number fifteen, did you sell it?'

'A lady.'

'What was she like?' Gracewell paused as there was no reply. 'Her appearance? Was she old? Young?'

David heard the banister rail creak as his hand gripped it. Dupont said: 'She was about – yes, fifty years. She was so *bien gentil*, so kind. Hair bright. *Chatain clair.*'

There was only one woman at number fifteen who could be described as about fifty, *bien gentil*, so kind, with bright auburn hair. David almost wished now that he had taken no part in pursuing this sailor, honest fellow though he obviously was.

'Do you know her name?' Gracewell pursued.

'No. How is it possible? She gave me coffee, a cake.'

'Where? In what sort of room?'

The sailor jerked a thumb downwards. 'It was *la bas*, under the house. I was at the big door, I rang the bell. Another door, under, open and the lady invite me to descend. I descend steps, outside-house steps, into so good a kitchen. Warm, clean, just as my mother have in France. I had coffee, a cake. I sell – sold – the *poignard*.'

David said quickly: 'That proves nothing. It sounds as if Mrs. Meake may have bought the thing, but it doesn't mean she used it. She probably bought it out of kindness, I know how often, with hawkers and beggars she's – '

A gesture from Gracewell silenced him. From below arose an increasing din. A voice shouted: 'Hi, is Carter up there? We want to know what we do about Swedes.' There was something macabre about this life or death interrogation just above the scene of so much excitement and jollity. Gracewell asked the sailor: 'At what time did you sell the dagger?'

Dupont looked blank. '*Sais pas,*' he muttered.

'How soon after you left "The Volunteer"? The public house?'

'Ah, a bad place, that. Ugly patronne, ugly madame.'

'Maybe. But how long after you left there did you have coffee and cake with the woman you describe?'

Another silence.

'Half an hour? An hour?'

'Impossible, I cannot say.'

'Then tell us what you did when you left "The Volunteer".'

'I go to sell the knife. I have also some silk. No good. Furious womans, three, four, five refuse.'

'How many houses did you call at?'

'Ten. More. Fifteen, sixteen, I cannot say.'

'You went straight from house to house till you reached 15 Terrapin Road?'

'I am sorry. I cannot understand.'

'You went direct?' David prompted. 'One house and then the next house, each one?'

'Like that,' said Dupont. 'Yes.'

Gracewell muttered: 'That would make it something before ten when he reached Mrs. Meake's.' To Dupont he said, 'Can you describe the lady who bought the dagger more clearly? Her dress, for instance.'

The man shrugged his shoulders. 'A dark dress. Black perhaps. It is her *tablier* I look at, of blue and white, because it is like one my mother carries, very attractive.'

A blue and white apron. It was Meakie, sure enough...

'You could identify her, of course?'

'Pardon?'

'If you saw her, you would recognise her?'

'But of course. Now, if you please, I am permitted to go?'

'Not just yet. I want your full name and address. You might let me see your identification papers. I am a police officer, you know.'

Rather sulkily Dupont produced his papers. Gracewell made a note or so. He seemed satisfied, for he patted the man's shoulder.

'You'll be all right, I see you're a native of Arles. It'll be a good day for all of us when you can go home.' The inspector laughed. 'Not that we want to lose you, but there's no place like home, is there?'

Dupont stared in a bewildered way.

Again someone shouted from below 'For the love of mike, what do we do about Swedes?'

And another voice: 'Where's Carter? Where the devil is that so-and-so Carter?'

'Here,' Bob called down. 'Shan't be a jiffy.' He said to Gracewell: 'I don't suppose I can be of any more use. I kept this chap here from six-thirty onwards. I feel I deserve a medal or something.'

'Thanks,' Gracewell said. 'No, I needn't keep you. I'll put a call through and then perhaps Monsieur Dupont will come with me on a very necessary errand.'

'I'm sorry,' Bob exclaimed, 'we haven't got the phone in yet. The Post Office seems to be frightfully slow, why, it's nearly a week since I took the house.'

'If you're lucky, you'll get it in six months,' David growled, 'considering the scatty way you send out instructions.'

'Then I'll use the call-box round the corner.' Gracewell faced David deliberately, to point his words. 'You'll stay here with Dupont?'

It was, in effect, a command to stand guard over the sailor. 'Yes. Of course.' David added, to his charge, 'I vote we go and have a beer on the house,' and repeated emphatically, 'Beer.'

Dupont grinned. 'But certainly.'

They all went down to the first floor. David's heart was thudding so violently that he feared he must have got out of condition while in hospital. He felt miserable in the midst of all this ebullient activity. Mrs. Meake had bought that dagger, she hadn't even done so surreptitiously. And now it seemed that nothing could save her from the ordeal of arrest, the horror of trial, the penalty for the most serious possible crime.

All this – unless the dagger had changed hands after she bought it.

FORTY-THREE

THE DINING ROOM BAR was more crowded than ever, indeed the room seemed to be packed so solid with Bob Carter's cosmopolitans that for two or more to attempt to reach the bar seemed a hopeless proposition.

But Dupont, with his long arms, was the very man to overcome such a difficulty. He managed to collect two glasses from the distracted Duchess who was still coping against almost impossible odds with her task as barmaid.

'Let's drink up and get out of this,' David said. 'We'll go down to the hall and be handy for when the inspector returns.' He was in no mood for all the back-slapping and exchange of repartee that surrounded them.

They went down. David went on: 'You won't give me the slip will you?'

'Pardon?' Whenever Dupont was puzzled his eyebrows shot forward over his eyes in a deep frown.

'You will not escape? Word of honour?'

'Why should I wish to escape? I stay with you.'

Feeling in need of air David moved towards the front door. It was open, and over it swung a thick black curtain which was billowing inwards. As, fearing that light might be visible, he put a hand to steady it, he heard a cry: 'Fire! Fire!'

He switched off the nearest light and moved quickly to the steps. Outside it seemed pitch dark after the brilliance within. In the hall Dupont was saying: 'Do I come with you?'

'Fire! Fire!' The cry was repeated away to the left.

And then a man racing invisibly by cried: 'It's St. Margaret's it's the kids' home!'

David did not hesitate. He said to Dupont, who had joined him on the steps, 'Come on, perhaps we can help. Fire... children.'

He raced off with Dupont beside him. The glow of the fire was visible from the corner. He was apprehensive, not only about the children, but about Tess. Then he remembered thankfully that she had said there would be only four of the youngsters left after today's exodus. And the trainees, Nobby and Smithy, had gone to see a film.

A fire engine was already on the scene, and another came clanging round a far corner. A hose was playing on the frontage, but obviously the fire had gained a hold. Flames belched from most of the windows and the crowd that had gathered was silhouetted against the lurid glare.

A gaunt woman in nurse's uniform tumbled down the front steps with two children in her arms, thrusting aside a group of curious watchers as she lurched across the pavement. Someone exclaimed 'It's Sister Allardyce.'

The voice of the matron blended into the general din: 'Out of the way, you fools. Get away, get away – !'

The crowd parted. At that moment David, forcing his way through saw Tess in the blur of smoke and flame. She too was carrying a child as she stumbled from the front door, almost falling as two firemen, dashing in, brushed against her. David had reached the steps, he caught her and her burden in his arms as she shrieked, 'There's one more, there's another, I'm going back.'

A ladder was being run up, extending, extending…

Tess handed the infant she had saved to the ready arms of a woman and turned back wildly towards the house. David held her, 'You can't go back, leave it to the men – ' his voice expired, choked by smoke and fumes. Firemen were mounting the ladder, but flames licking out of the first floor window checked them.

Tess was frantic, sobbing. Her hair was wild and her features streaked with black. 'There's another, on the second floor. And Mrs. Meake's up there.'

'Mrs. Meake! – Look, you won't be wanted.' Another ladder was being run up beyond the fringe of the flames.

'She brought some money – a donation. Gave it to Sister Allardyce. Three hundred pounds,' Tess gasped her explanation.

'Look, there! They'll reach those top windows – ' Even in the excitement of the moment David felt astonishment at Tess's news. But he had enough to do restraining her from trying to return to the house; she was sobbing and choking distractedly as she struggled to break free.

'Stand clear there! Stand clear!'

A gush of ice-cold water emphasised the order. The crowd leapt back. David steadied Tess. And suddenly everyone was looking upwards. Falling back step by step, supporting Tess, David fixed his eyes on what held the attention of them all. At the second floor window, round which smoke swirled and flames danced in long menacing tongues, there was a vague figure.

It was Mrs. Meake. In a moment when the flames leapt high David saw her wild face, her tumbled unnaturally bright hair.

Men were manoeuvring valiantly, but it seemed – in the urgency of the moment – so slowly, on the further ladder some yards beyond the window. The road in front of the house had now been cleared, the mob was crushed against the railings on the opposite side.

'Jump!' screamed someone and the cry was taken up; hoarsely and on shrieking high hysterical notes, 'Jump! Jump!'

Firemen were holding a canvas sheet. Out from the smoky horror of the front door tumbled a fireman, and a moment later several more. One, injured, was being helped by a companion.

At the window Mrs. Meake swayed and swayed, as if she had lost all sense of equilibrium. And now it was possible to see that she was holding an infant in her arms, and was striving desperately to wrap it in a rug or a blanket, most of which trailed over the sill into the smoke from below.

'Jump, for God's sake – '

'The wall's giving. Oh holy Jesus – Save them, save them!' A woman screamed a frantic prayer. Other voices yelled: 'Jump, it's your last chance!'

There was a movement, obscured by fire. And then down from the window came a shapeless bundle that fell safely into the centre of the awaiting canvas.

'That's all of them,' Tess groaned. She slipped unconscious to her knees as the figure at the upper window disappeared completely in a belch of smoke and a radiant eruption of sparks.

David lifted and supported Tess, elbowing away the pressing crowd. Then he saw that Dupont was still at hand, ready to obey an unspoken request to clear a way. The gaunt fellow used his elbows savagely and David plunged after him with Tess in his arms.

As they were rounding the corner, some thirty yards away there was a great crash and a thunderlike rumbling. The walls of St Margaret's had collapsed.

Within ten minutes Tess was on his divan. The house was strangely quiet. Dupont stood, awkwardly silent after having obeyed a succession of small commands. To bring drinking water. To light the gas fire. To get a towel and more water. David loosened the stiff collar that Tess wore, he rubbed her hands, bathed her face and spoke comfortingly as she revived.

'It's all right, darling. You're all safe. Every one of you and the four kids. I saw Sister Allardyce, she was absolutely all right, Nobby and Smithy got back as I brought you away.'

Tess murmured: 'But Mrs. Meake – ?'

'Maybe she's all right too.' David had to control the huskiness that threatened his voice. 'Damn all that smoke, it got in my throat.'

Tess was too healthy, too alert, to be overcome for long. She sat up and was trying to put on her shoes.

David knelt to put them on for her. 'That fire got a hold terribly quickly,' he muttered.

'While I'd gone to the chemist's. It's an old house, there was only Sister Allardyce – and, Mrs. Meake. You say Sister Allardyce is all right, but – ?' Tess's voice faded on a questioning note

'Don't bother, darling. You've been through enough. We'll find out later.'

'I must know.'

David could not restrain her. She went downstairs, he followed, and Dupont lumbered behind them. There was a light in the kitchen.

Inspector Gracewell was there and with him were a police sergeant and a constable. The three of them were standing by an open cupboard. Gracewell was holding a wallet and some loose papers. He said briefly: 'Otto Klar's.'

'You found them – here?'

'Yes. And a letter addressed to you.'

Dupont, standing by the door, was muttering: 'Yes, it was here

– ' Tess had dropped into the cane chair by the fire, where, David remembered with a pang, he had so often seen Mrs. Meake. He read her letter in a silence in which the ticking of the clock was metallically loud, each second a time-beat to mark the end of a tragedy.

Dear David, We were always good friends, thank you a lot for all the good times you gave me and may your future be happy. I am writing this because I am going to St. Margaret's, I want the children to have the money, so Otto Klar's brother doesn't get it. Then I am going to give myself up. On Sunday I told Thelma what I would do if she kept on with that crowd, black market devils, and she laughed. I prayed for guidance and Providence sent me a dagger. When Otto Klar went I followed him across the garden, the way he had come sneaking in. I am so very very sorry to cause unhappiness, forgive me. After I did it I unbolted the garden gate and took the wallet, trying to make it look like a robbery. But now I can't bear the suspense, all the best and do not think too hard of me, and bless you, from Meakie.

David felt his eyes stinging as he finished reading the melancholy confession, that now could damage no one. Instinctively he moved towards Tess. She took his hands and suddenly, overcome, he dropped on his knees beside her. When he regained his self-possession, glancing up shamedly, he saw that the four men had gone. He was alone with Tess, whose arms, soft yet strong, encircled him with infinite comfort.

She did not speak, and he was glad of her silence.

At last he exclaimed violently and miserably: 'If only I'd kept out of the whole accursed affair!'

She said softly. 'It wouldn't have made any difference in the end. In the end the truth would have come out. And sometimes the quickest way is the kindest.'

He pressed his grateful lips against her comforting fingers.

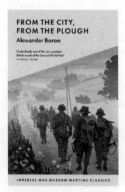

ISBN 9781912423071
£8.99

'Alexander Baron's *From the City, From the Plough* is undoubtedly one of the very greatest British novels of the Second World War and provides the most honest and authentic account of front line life for an infantryman in North West Europe.'

ANTONY BEEVOR

ISBN 9781912423088
£8.99

'A tremendous rediscovery of a brilliant novel. Extremely well-written, its effects are both sophisticated and visceral. Remarkable.'

WILLIAM BOYD

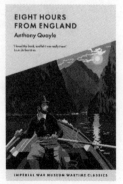

ISBN 9781912423101
£8.99

'Much more than a novel'

RODERICK BAILEY

'I loved this book, and felt I was really there'
LOUIS de BERNIÈRES

'One of the greatest adventure stories of the Second World War'
ANDREW ROBERTS